LEAVE ME
Broken

Ebook ISBN: 978-1-957959-01-6 Print ISBN: 978-1-957959-02-3

Cover Design: Coffin Print Designs

Editing: Dee's Notes: Proofreading and Editing Service

Formatting: KB. Row

Proofreader: Toni

Alphas: Poppy Hopper & Kayleigh Gray

LEAVE ME Broken

KB. Row

To my grandpa, I miss you every single day.

I know it's weird to dedicate a book like this to your grandpa, but he will never see it, so it's fine.

To all the Paysons of the world, it gets better;

You are not alone;

Mental health is important, if you are struggling please reach out to someone.

To the readers

This is a continuation story that must be read in order, starting with *Break For You*

You know the drill by now, Ash Pearson is a toxic Ash-hole.

<u>Leave Me Broken triggers:</u>

Alcohol use

Drug abuse

Self harm

Sexual abuse by parent

Power play

CNC acts between couple

Dub/Non-con between couple

Sexual Violence

Scarification

Blood/Knife play

S/M

Safe Word use/Safe word ignored

MFM sexual acts involving couple

Mention of miscarriage

Mention of Cancer

Death in family

Suicidal thoughts

Suicide/Suicide attempt

Happy Reading,

—KB

1

Ash

As a volleyball player, I never found the appeal of women's uniforms. In fact, I was always annoyed with how much more attention women's volleyball got over men's just because of what they wear. Now I get it. *Fuck.* I wish I didn't get it, but I do. All because of her. Payson Ray Murphy. She changed my life three months ago—even if she thinks it has only been two. From the first moment I saw her highlight reel, I knew we were destined to be together.

It's not normal—my obsession for her. I know this. Luca tells me the same, as do my parents. They are more gracious with their *"she's young, Ashley, give her time to grow."* Luca just tells me I'm smothering her. Payson likes me being around as much as I like being around her, even now when she's pretending to hate me. Her shoulders relax anytime she walks into the gym and sees me there. She hates the relief she feels, but I couldn't be happier about it.

Payson has abandonment issues; it doesn't take a professional to tell me my little Jailbird is fucked up, but I enjoy how her jagged pieces fit my own. As long as she stops cutting her perfect skin, there will be no issues between us.

She will eventually let me explain why I *lied*. I don't believe I lied, just .. . extended the truth, but Luca tells me I did. He is like the voice of reason, knowing why I feel the way I do but also understanding why Payson feels the way she does. It's wildly jarring.

I'm giving her time, but it's excruciating when she looks so fucking pretty all the goddamn time.

Payson's beauty is undeniable, and it makes it hard to believe she's never had a boyfriend before me, or at least dated around. She's lucky she didn't.

Her looks are not what drew me to her all those months back, not the only thing. First, it was her talent in the sport, then it was watching her and the team interact with one another. It was obvious they loved her just as much.

Then there were the photos. I had gone on a deep dive looking for more images of Payson when the reels Amanda sent weren't enough to satisfy what I now know had been an obsession growing inside me. I had stumbled across a few different photos of Payson on the high school sports page; there was one photo in particular that caught my eye. It was during warm-ups before a game and Payson wasn't even the main focus. She was in the background and I was drawn to her. Her attention was directed off camera, a deep frown weighing down her face and not just the resting kind, she was genuinely frowning toward the audience.

There were three more photos where I saw the real Payson. The girl that hides behind the cheers, smiles, and excitement she shares with the people around her. The girl she is when she thinks no one is looking—I love that girl. I love both, but I love Payson at her worst as well as her best.

She hasn't said she loves me back yet, but I don't need to hear the words when I feel it every time we are together, every time her pale green eyes flick my way—even when she's trying to look angry. Every time she lets out a small whimper when we touch; even if it's just a brush of our hands. It's not normal being so in tune with someone else's emotions after this short amount of time.

What Payson and I have isn't normal, but fuck being normal anyway.

"You have that look in your eye, fratello."

Payson dives for a ball, and I'm mesmerized by the way she arches her back. Volleyball is the sexiest sport, and no one can convince me otherwise.

Payson walks back behind the line and shoots a look our way but is quick to advert her attention to Janelle. When Janelle's gaze swings our way and her mouth moves, I know they are talking about us.

Unlike Payson, the only thing hiding in Janelle's eyes is trouble, but she is the Ying to Payson's Yang. She is who keeps Payson grounded. The relief Payson feels for me is much the same for Janelle, based on the fondness in her eyes when she is near her. I'm not sure if I should be able to feel her emotions so clearly, but I can. Her eyes are expressive like nothing I've ever seen before, but it's more than that. It's like we were made from the same stone. Broken apart but still connected in spirit, able to feel everything the other does.

"Do you think she will forgive you soon?"

The murderous glare Payson shoots our way before she runs over for the team huddle tells me no. "Yes." I glance at Luca for the first time. "I'm not going to give her a choice."

He shakes his head with a wide grin on his face and slaps me on the back. "I feel sorry for you."

"Why?"

He backs away, still facing me, and with the flick of his thumb over his shoulder, I find Payson again—on her knees. *Dammit.* I shift my stance, hoping to hide the fact my blood is now rushing south.

Luca laughs loudly, grabbing the attention of various bystanders. "I do not think she is as submissive as she appears." Then he saunters back to join our team with the mischievous smile he's always wearing. Not much different to the one Janelle often has plastered on her face. If she wasn't our player, I might suggest they would make a good couple, but she is and one coach-player situation is enough for one team.

"Be a little more obvious. Maybe you'll start drooling soon."

It takes everything inside me not to growl at that annoying tone. "Why are you not with the team, Ms. Burton?"

Alyssa shifts closer, grabbing my arm. "Aren't we a little past the whole last name bullshit?"

"Get off," I demand. Payson is already struggling to trust me and has it in her mind Alyssa and I are doing the same thing her and I are. I can't say I would behave rationally if Payson had a guy hanging on her all the time, but Alyssa is nothing more than a clingy mistake that won't let go. She wasn't the first but I'll be damned if she's not the last.

"I wanted to talk to you about your little *Jailbird*."

My eyes flick down and I scowl with the use of *my* nickname for her. "Don't fucking call her that."

She rolls her eyes, and unlike when Payson does it, I'm not tempted to take her over my knee. It just really jars me. "Fine. Whatever." Her arm slips from mine. "All I wanted to say was I heard her and Janelle talking in the locker room, saying her grandpa couldn't make it tonight. Thought you should know."

It's parents' night. I planned on him being here because he got out of the hospital a few days ago. The last time we chatted, he was more than excited to be able to walk her.

Panic surges low in my stomach, thinking something else happened, but no, Payson wouldn't be standing here if he was back in. So, what is the reasoning? If he's not here, then who is walking her?

"She has no one else, Ash."

"Coach." I'm quick to remind her.

"Fine. *Coach.* She's going to walk herself because she obviously doesn't have anyone else around. Janelle was going to ask her mom to do it since her dad was meant to be here, but I guess his flight got canceled or whatever, so, yeah, no one."

Is Jason not around anymore? Fuck. I hate not knowing what is happening in her life. I hate it more that I have to hear it from Alyssa, who I have no doubt was only listening to say something senseless to Payson later.

Sure enough, the announcer asks the girls and their parents to line up and Payson stands alone. My heart shatters in my chest. If I could punch someone right now, I'd want it to be her mum, dad—wherever the fuck he is—and the fucking pervert she has as a stepfather, who is very lucky she pulled me away from the hospital that day. I was more than tempted to go into that room and make sure he ended up in a hospital bed with no recovery for all the shit he did to my girl. One day I will. Maybe even throw another punch at her asshole brother too. No one deserves the life she's had to live—but no one deserves it less than my little Jailbird.

"Why did you tell me this?" I drop my gaze to Alyssa when Payson looks away.

Payson is a pro at performing. It comes with years of practice and hiding your true self and emotions. However, I pick up on the telltale signs: the slight shake in her legs and the distant look in her eyes, as well as when her nose scrunches and her fingers work at the skin on her already raw thumb, proving she's not as immune to the pressure as she pretends to be.

Janelle tugs on Payson's plait, grabbing her attention, and Payson jumps. She turns and before her eyes meet Janelle's, they fall on me. Well, me and Alyssa. I narrow in on the small muscle flex in her round cheeks.

"She already calls you daddy, right?" And with that, Alyssa is walking back toward her dad who is too busy on the phone to acknowledge Alyssa's approach. As I look at two lonely girls, one with someone by her side and another with no one—I can't help but wonder how they ended up so drastically different when they share the same loneliness in their souls. I couldn't be happier that they did, though.

Everyone claps after Emika is announced. Her dads each hand her a huge bouquet of purple roses before taking their turns to kiss each cheek. That's when I pass my clipboard to Luca and he grabs it, already knowing my plan. Payson would tell me no if I went over too early but if I get to her right before they say her name, she's most likely not going to deny me the chance to walk her. No one should walk alone. Especially my girl.

"Payson Ray—" My arm slips through hers, I squeeze it tightly against my body so she isn't able to pull away. Judging by her wide eyes, that's what she wants to do right now.

I shoot her a *too-bad* look, using my best "coach" face. She takes as far of a step away as she can but doesn't pull away completely. Even if I'm forcing her to stand by my side—I'll take that as a win.

"Escorted by Coach Pearson."

When she doesn't follow my step forward, I glance down at her face. Her pale face sets an alarm off in my chest. "Jailbird," I whisper. The announcer pauses briefly before continuing his program.

"Payson is the granddaughter of Pastor Paul Murphy. She is a junior and has held first-string Libero all three years of high school . . ."

"Pay," I hiss not able to hide the panic from reaching my voice.

Janelle taps on my shoulder. "She hates this kind of thing. Just pull her, eventually she'll follow."

The announcer is already onto her favorite song, and all that's left is future plans before it will be Janelle's turn and we need to get to our spot on the court. I tug her along. It's not like it's a challenge, she's tiny compared to me.

"Payson's favorite song is 'Mr. Brightside' by The Killers."

My lips tug up into a smile, that's a good song. Her body is pressed against mine and as good as it feels, I get the suspicion she's not doing it out of choice. I don't understand why she's like this. Payson performs best under pressure, so what is different about this? It's simply just walking.

Payson relaxes by my side when the claps are directed toward Janelle and not her. Before she can pull away, I tighten my bicep against her arm to the point she lets out a small whimper. I place my hand over hers just barely threading our fingers so no one can see but us.

"What are you doing?" she hisses in that wanna-be-angry voice she loves to use with me lately. It's gotten better since my car, but still not that convincing.

"Where is your granddad?" I know I should keep my gaze forward because she has a way of swallowing me into her pale eyes, but I can't help it. My eyes fall.

Her long black eyelashes beat the tops of her cheeks with many confused blinks as she looks back up to me. Her eyes are wavering from behind me, to the floor, then back up to me as if she can only handle looking at me for so long. It nearly causes a smirk. I don't let her see that—she's pissed at me enough without blatantly laughing at her. I'm an asshole who takes advantage of the little girl who once crushed on me, but there needs to be a line.

"I don't see how that is your business."

God, what I wouldn't give to bend her over and pinken that ass. I've only gotten the chance once and it's a fucking crime. An ass like Payson Murphy's shouldn't go a fucking day without attention.

"Everything about you is my bloody business. Now, tell me, Jailbird."

Her eyes blaze with fake hatred, making my dick harder. Good thing I am wearing compression shorts or the whole gym would be getting a show.

Payson angry shouldn't be such a turn-on, but it is. Everything about her is a bloody turn-on. "Where is your granddad?"

The crowd erupts in the loudest claps yet before she answers. Neither of us have to look to know who for. Alyssa's dad is the mayor and basically runs the town with his investments in numerous businesses. Something I wish I knew months ago.

"I didn't remind him it was parents' night because I thought it would be overwhelming for him. Happy?"

She's too fucking sweet. I should have called Paul today; I didn't consider he wouldn't remember but of course he wouldn't—he just had a stroke. "I'm far from happy, babygirl."

Payson's chest caves. "Don't call me that." Her voice is breathy.

I lean toward her and drop my lips so I'm nearly touching the side of her face away from the audience. Vanilla and rainwater take over my senses and I'm almost knocked on my ass. Fuck, I miss her. I'm around her everyday but I miss touching her whenever I want, I miss kissing her full lips—I miss *us*. I miss my babygirl that sucked and rode my dick like a pro.

"I have given you your time to act like a spoiled brat without forcing you to listen to my side of things, but I'm at my wits' end, *babygirl*. Whether you want me to call you babygirl or not, does not change the fact that you are, in fact, *my* babygirl. Accept it, or don't. It makes no difference to me because it's still my dick you'll be riding on our wedding night."

Her mouth falls and she shudders. "You're so fucked up."

"That doesn't stop you from dreaming about me. Does it?" I cock an eyebrow.

A deep pink creeps up her beautiful neck; I smile more. "Thought so."

I force my eyes to the audience, because as much as I wish it was just us right now so I could finally force her to listen in the way I want her to, I refuse to end this conversation without my dick in one of her holes and her cum coating some part of my body: hand, face, stomach. If I don't see her head fall back and the dazed look she gets after I make her come, I will strangle someone and obviously, I cannot do that here.

That's when my eyes land on a familiar set of eyes and that smirk I was sporting drops. *What is he doing here?* I kicked his daughter from the team and yet here he sits in the stands of *my* gym like he owns the bloody place. I told him to back off. The last thing Payson needs is another guy creeping on her. I don't know what his deal is, but I'm fucking sick of people being too interested in *my* girl, and *he* is too interested.

No one will ever lay another unwanted hand on her as long as I'm alive. No one but me, although, I know my hand is never truly unwanted.

"Does this mean I get to call you daddy now?"

I whip my gaze back down to a smirking Payson. Gone are the goose bumps I caused. Her nipples are still hard, but I can barely see the little peaks.

She wants to call me . . . *daddy*?

For the first time ever, I can't get a read on her to know if she's being serious or not. She's smirking but it doesn't meet her round and innocent eyes. They are void of any emotion—at all. I narrow mine, not understanding the game she is playing.

"I mean . . . it's parents' night. You walked me across the gym like a parent . . . it makes sense, doesn't it, *Daddy*?"

"Knock it off." My voice is a struggled growl. I don't want her to know what that is doing to me. I was never a daddy guy. I never liked innocent young girls, never understood the daddy kink.

Now I get it. I fucking get it big time. So much I could be the bloody mayor of Daddykinkville. *Why* is it so hot when she calls me daddy while looking up at me with those big green eyes I love so much? I can imagine her so vividly, withering under me, screaming for *Daddy* as she comes around my dick.

"Sorry, Daddy, was your *babygirl* a bad girl?" She pushes her pink bottom lip out in a pout. "Should she be punished?"

"Yes." My dick is fucking throbbing now. *Goddamn her.* "Knock it off, *babygirl*, before *Daddy* makes a mess in his pants that he will force you to clean."

Her smirk dampens slightly. Mine lifts.

"What's wrong? Said you were into *rape play*, right?" Her throat bobs with a deep swallow but she doesn't answer outright. "Maybe tonight is your lucky night."

"You wouldn't," she breathes back.

Aubrey is the last announced and families are dispersing, and I've forgotten all about Mr. Gilbert. Before I let her go, I tug her close again but into a hug this time. I keep my hands in a respectable place but lower my lips to her ear lobe and lick her once. I miss her cool, slightly sweaty skin and how her body molds to mine like a second skin. I crush her against my body willing her to hug me back, but she doesn't.

"Keep pushing me and you'll see what I'm capable of . . . but beware, you might not like it as much as you think, Jailbird."

And with that, I walk off toward Luca and grab my clipboard from him.

"Did you break her?" He flicks his head in her direction.

Payson stands in the spot I left, staring after me with so many emotions swimming in her eyes. So many things left unspoken.

"Not yet."

2

Payson

VOLLEYBALL USED TO BE my favorite part of the day; now it's my least favorite because *he* ruined it with his stupid son. A *son*. He has a freaking child. *Are you a dad? No.* That's what he said. He said *no*. I remember the look in his eyes as he lied right to my face.

The best part about finding out he has a son when he told me he didn't is him kissing my ass at practice. I can do whatever I want and he doesn't yell at me. I tested the theory last week when he told me to go run lines and I flat out said no. His jaw clenched and that vein that pops when he's angry nearly blew but he didn't say a word. The rest of the girls had a lot to say.

Everyone but Alyssa, surprisingly. I don't know what her problem is. You'd think she'd be happy we are . . . over. Or whatever. I mean, I don't even know if we were ever on—or if she even knew there was anything going on between us, but based on the glares I was getting at practice, yeah, she definitely knew. I don't know why she would be pissed . . . and I don't want to know. *Yeah, right.* What do I care if he was fucking around with her *and* me? *I definitely care.* He said they weren't, but he also said he wasn't a dad so obviously he's just one big fucking liar and nothing he says can be trusted.

Music floods my ears before I even walk into Grandpa's house. I want to smile but that pit in my stomach causes me to keep my blank face in place.

Grandpa has been listening to Christian music even more than he used to since being home from the hospital.

Grandpa being home is much less stressful, for many reasons, but not having to see my mother or Fred again is a huge one. They went back to Carolina just before Grandpa was released. I had my aunt text me when they weren't in his room to keep from bumping into them and it worked. I didn't have to see them the entire time. It should upset me that my mother was in the same town as me and never reached out, but it doesn't.

Without the rides from Ash—not for his lack of trying—and my new-found freedom from the ankle monitor, Grandpa has officially passed me the keys to my nana's wagon. The independence is nice. Lonely, but nice.

I spent the time Grandpa was in the hospital at Janelle's because it freaked me out being here alone. The thought of anyone showing up at any time . . . yeah, it didn't sit right with me. We basically spent the whole time together leading the all-men-suck club.

I also stayed the night with her after parents' night because of what Ash said about rape play. Not because I was scared, but because I *wanted* him to sneak into my room. He's my weakness and he knows it. Why I ever told him about that is beyond me. *Maybe because I was stupid enough to believe we would be together forever or some bullshit like that.* Naïve. That's the best word to describe me; well, not anymore. I've learned my lesson . . . *hopefully.*

As soon as my foot lands over the threshold, Grandpa's chili I set up before school has my stomach growling. I've been throwing lunch and dinner in a crockpot before school. Grandpa says he doesn't need me to cook every day, but I don't mind. Plus, him being in the hospital scared me, and I'll do anything to keep that from happening again.

Besides, it's not like I'm going to morning practice anymore. *He* has texted me about them nearly every morning, something along the lines of "I'm at the school if you want to come in." But I don't. After-school practice is torture enough. With how much anger I'm battling with daily, I am killing it at practice, I don't need the morning one. We've not lost a game since. Maybe that's why he's not pushing for us to make up, he's not—not pushing, but he's not doing as much as I know he'd like to. It wouldn't surprise me if *Coach* is holding back until the season is over so we win or some crap like that. *Ash-hole.*

"Grandpa!" I shout over the music. Walking into the kitchen, I scan across the trailer and when I don't see him, I turn the knob on the boom box and shout for him again.

When there is no reply this time, my heart stops altogether.

I hurry back down the hall, because if he's not in his chair, he's either in his room or in the bathroom. Maybe he's sleeping.

Or . . .

I throw his door open without knocking and sigh when Grandpa jumps from his supine position on the bed from my intrusion.

"Dear heavens, Ray-Ray, you are going to give me a heart attack." He slips his green flannel over his white t-shirt. His hands shake more than they used to, and he doesn't even attempt the buttons because he can't do them anymore. At least for now.

The doctor is surprised with how well Grandpa "bounced back" for his age and is confident he should be good as new in no time, but I'm not used to seeing my grandpa so . . . disheveled. We are talking about a man who gets his hair cut every three weeks to the day but had to miss the last one because he was in the hospital, and now his hair lady is on a two-week long vacation. What little hair he does have, is overgrown, and no matter how much he brushes it, it doesn't lay down.

He can't shave on his own, he can get dressed—mostly. He can use the bathroom on his own but someone has to be in the bathroom while he showers, at least for another week. Aunt Vicky usually comes up for that. She said something about how that's a daughter's job and I didn't need to worry about it. I think she thought I would find it weird, and sure, it would be awkward but if my grandpa needs me, I will be there. I don't care how uncomfortable I am. It's just hard seeing him in this state in general.

"You didn't answer me." I pat my chest, hoping to calm my beating heart.

He sighs, turns, and shakes his head slowly before walking over and stopping in front of me. He cups my cheek with his left hand because that's his "strong" arm . . . for now. "I am fine, Payson. You don't need to worry."

My lips twist to the side and I cast my gaze down because I don't want him to see how close I am to crying. I haven't cried since the first day I showed up to Janelle's, and I'm not going to now. I had one moment of weakness. Now I'm fine.

Instinctively, I tuck my arms behind my body in case they show off just how *not fine* I am.

"Now, let's get some of that chili. I've been smelling it all morning and I'm ready to eat."

I'm not a great cook, but I've been looking at Nana's recipes when he isn't looking. I want to surprise him and if he thinks I'm a naturally good cook like my nana, maybe that will make him more proud of me.

I'm washing the dishes from lunch and Grandpa is doing some of his physical therapy behind me at the table. He turns the music back on, as background noise—not like he's trying to throw the first Jesus-loving rave anymore.

"Have you spoke with Jason?"

Hearing his name sends an unwelcomed shot of anger throughout my body, but I don't let Grandpa see that. "No, have you?"

I don't have to look to know he's frowning. And that's why I'm angry. It's not what he said outside the hospital room, not that he abandoned me ten years ago, it's that he up and left while our grandpa was in the hospital recovering from a stroke. He never came back after that night he called me all those names. *Good riddance.* I just wish it didn't hurt Grandpa so much.

"Not since he called the day I got home."

And that's the only reason I'm not worried about him. He didn't say where he was or what happened, but I know he's at least alive. He most likely ran back to the Army like the baby he is. That's a conflicting sentence, but I digress.

"When will Aunt Vicky be here?"

Just then, the door opens but instead of my aunt walking toward me, my Uncle Gary stares back at me with the mischievous smile I love. I squeal only because he's been out of town for training for a little while, and since I'm not going to church, I've hardly seen him.

"Hey, kiddo." No matter how old I get, he's always called me kiddo. I secretly hope he never stops.

"Hey, Uncle Gary. You hungry? I made chili and it's pretty good, if I say so myself."

"Very good," Grandpa chimes in.

Uncle Gary taps his round belly that hangs over his khakis and brown belt. "I've never said no to food this far in life, certainly not going to start now."

I chuckle as I fill his bowl. Uncle Gary is my aunt's third marriage, but they have been married for fifteen years, so he's the only uncle I remember. Based on what I've heard my mother and aunt say about the guy before him, I should be glad. He has no kids of his own, but he took on my two cousins from my aunt's first marriage and honestly, Jason and me like we are his own. I may not have gotten the best dads in my life but I've definitely lucked out in other departments.

"So, where is Aunt Vick today?" I place the bowl in front of him at the table before taking my seat across from Grandpa. I still have ten minutes before lunch is over, but I'm done with classes today. Coach did text me about a meeting in an hour, but I'm not sure I'm interested in a meeting with him. That would require us being alone, and after what he said at parents' night, I'm not sure I want to be alone with him. Being with him in his office alone, where we have shared so many moments, I worry that I'll give in, forgive him, and we will go back to where we were. *He has a son.* We can *never* go back to where we were because he has a son he lied about.

I shake my head and listen to my uncle. I missed where he said my aunt was. Him and Grandpa have moved onto fishing, and I don't feel like asking him to repeat himself, or interrupting, so I sit back and enjoy the company of the two least drama-filled people in my life.

Until my phone goes off. I don't have to look to know who the annoying ding belongs to, I set it as Coach's ringtone on purpose because it's loud and annoying—like him.

Especially when it goes off two more times and Uncle Gary stops talking and glances my way; Grandpa does too.

"Sorry." I flip my phone to silent before dropping it on the table.

"You can answer that, seems like your coach really needs to talk to you." Uncle Gary nods to my phone and that's when I realize it's face up and they can read *Coach Ash-hole* clearly. *Crap.*

Uncle Gary chuckles but continues eating. It's the curious gaze from Grandpa that makes me shift in my seat. When my phone goes off again, I turn it off, because sitting under his stare is uncomfortable, and he saw my name for Coach. I know I shouldn't have set it as that, but I couldn't help it. It was Janelle's peer pressure one of the nights I was with her. He kept texting and calling me, and we thought it was funny. I'm just glad I didn't let her talk me into setting his contact photo as one of the NSFW photos he has sent me. Darn him for knowing my weakness is his body.

"I better get back to school."

Uncle Gary tells me to have a good day and Grandpa reaches up to pull my face close and kiss my cheek.

"I might go hang out with Janelle tonight if that's okay."

Grandpa taps my cheek twice before lowering his shaky hand back to his lap. I wonder if Uncle Gary saw that. Judging by him stuffing his face, I'm guessing not. "Actually, she might—"

"Go," Grandpa interrupts me with a knowing look. "Go enjoy your childhood, Ray-Ray."

I open my mouth to argue but a loud engine pulling into Grandpa's driveway cuts me off, only because I know who that engine belongs to.

You've got to be freaking kidding me.

"Welcome, Ashley." Grandpa greets him at the door like they are old friends.

He smiles at my grandpa before he's pulled in for a *hug*. Grandpa is a hugger but I'm wondering if they are actually old friends with how comfortable they seem. He taps Grandpa's back, but his eyes jerk to me, and the smile he was wearing falls and in its place is a murderous glare that doesn't scare me. It might cause another reaction . . . but I'm ignoring that.

He stops glaring when Grandpa pulls away. Ash's eyes land on my uncle.

Grandpa turns toward us with one arm still around Ash's midsection. He gestures to my uncle with the other. All three sets of eyes drop when Grandpa can barely lift his arm. Grandpa clears his throat. "Gary, this is Ash Pearson, Payson's coach."

Uncle Gary's chuckle is low, and I already know what he is thinking. I drop my head to my hands because I officially hate how everyone knows about my *retired* obsession with the world's biggest dickface.

"Yep, heard a lot aboutchya." He grins my way. Ash does the same with that stupid grin I wish I could punch from his stupidly handsome face. I wish the whole son thing made me despise him enough that I found him ugly now. Unfortunately, that is not the case.

"Yes, I seem to be more famous in this family than anywhere else."

Cocky Ash-hole.

Of course, everyone else takes it like a joke and the room is soon filled with deep laughter. I hate him. I hate that he can charm anyone and anything. *I hate him*!

"Well, our Payson wouldn't stop talkin' aboutchya back in the day. Made it hard not to know who you are."

Kill me.

Before anyone can say anything else I interrupt. "I need to get to school," I announce. Grandpa has returned to his seat and Ash is still standing in the kitchen with his big arms crossed over his equally broad chest.

"Yes, I only stopped by because we were meant to have a meeting that you're late for and thought I would make sure everything was okay since you were not at school." There's a bite in his voice only I can hear because Uncle Gary and Grandpa tell him how thoughtful of a coach he is.

He's thoughtful alright. Thoughtful about how he can worm his way back into my life, and schmoozing my family seems to be his current course of action.

"No, the meeting was at two, it's noon." Not that I was going to go anyway.

"It was at noon. I would not have made it for two, because I have some-thing on my *schedule* at two." What a terrible way to pronounce schedule.

The tension in this room is so high it's suffocating but I'll be damned if I break eye contact first.

"Why don't you have it now? There is still time before two," Grandpa offers like the saint he is.

I want to roll my eyes because if he knew what Ash really had planned for this "meeting," he probably wouldn't be so willing to let me go.

Not wanting to cause anymore of a scene I bite back my annoyance and agree. With a quick goodbye from Grandpa and Uncle Gary and some argument from Ash because I wasn't budging on driving myself, we head for the school. The less time we have alone, the better.

Ash is waiting for me outside the gym doors with his face in his phone. As soon as I'm within five feet, he taps his keys to the device that unlocks the door and pulls it open. He's holding it open for me but hasn't lifted his eyes from his phone, and it's really annoying me. What could possibly be so interesting on his phone that he hasn't looked at me once?

I swear his eyes don't leave me at practice but right now I feel, well, I feel like everyone else. It's not a good feeling. I'm more irritated that I want him to look at me, I want him to slap my ass as I walk by and make crude comments. I want him to do it, but I don't want him to know I want him to.

I must not be moving quick enough for him, because with an exasperated breath, he drops his phone into his navy-blue joggers and regards me like *I'm* the annoying one. "What are you waiting for? I haven't got all day, Payson."

Payson. He called me Payson. *He* is giving *me* attitude. *What the hell?* I don't want him to know his animosity is bothering me, though, so instead of snapping back, I lift my chin and strut right by him.

If he is going to act like I don't affect him, then I will do the same. It's all pretend, because his dick is getting hard in his pants. I might not be as good of a liar as him, but I can sure try.

3

Ash

I LET OUT A silent breath as she walks by. She is killing me. She's angry—rightfully so, but even with all the hostility she holds, she still looks at me the same and it's a mindfuck, to say the least. Payson is young, I know her emotions are all over the place but I'm barely holding it together for us as it is. Feeling her watching me, I know she's waiting for me to look back at her, but I'm giving her space. The thing I have to do today at two is already messing with my mood. I know her meeting Parker will fuck us up even more, but I'm ready for that set back. I'm more ready for her to forgive me.

She's sitting in the chair across from my new desk when I walk in. There's no longer a hole in my wall from when I flipped my old desk over. She makes me fucking crazy and has no clue. The school wasn't happy about having to fix the hole and replace the desk, but I paid for the damages. They don't know how it happened, and I don't plan on telling them.

Payson is on her phone, and I can't help but to look over her shoulder as I head to my chair. She's quick to exit out of what she is on, but I saw it and now my dick isn't fighting to stay hard—it's like a fucking brick in my pants. *Why is she looking at a photo of me?* One of the many I've sent her during my workouts. She never replies. I kind of assumed she just deleted them.

25

I'm biting back a smile when I sit down.

"You got a new chair."

There are papers to my right that are in a mess because I was getting pissed when she hadn't shown up for the meeting. I'm not convinced she would have shown up even if she had the time correct but I needed to meet with her today. I straighten the papers while holding her bright green gaze. "I did. New desk too." She glances at the wooden desk between us, it's similar to the old one but solid oak and heavy as shit. I won't be flipping this one on a whim. A small frown tugs on her lips.

"Oh." Her voice is small.

I wonder if she's thinking about the moments we shared on my last desk. I felt the same way, which is why I didn't get rid of it. The bottom half wouldn't fit out the door without breaking it apart, but I kept the top and plan to make a bench for my room. I won't tell her that, though. Maybe seeing how much this affects her will cause her to come around quicker.

"Yes, with the new desk, it made sense to get a new chair. Besides, the old one was bloody annoying."

"Yeah." She blows out a deep breath and her lips flick up. "Amanda claimed it had character."

I chuckle. From the few conversations I shared with Amanda, that sounds like her.

When our laughs die out, what can be described only as an awkward silence settles between us. The tension in the air at her granddad's is comparable to now as we stare at each other. Payson is the first to break the silence and eye contact. "So, what did you want to meet about?"

Clearing my throat, I lay the papers on my desk and cross my hands over them. "Week of Pink is coming up. I cleared our schedule for that week so—"

"Did you get my email? The car wash shut down, so I'm not able to book it for us. I looked at the other car wash but it's behind a gas station and there isn't a ton of room for us, besides it's not on a busy road and I just didn't think it would be the best option." Smart girl, because I checked it out as well and thought the same. I wasn't very on board for a car wash as it is, so I'm not upset about it. But I am curious what else she has come up with before I tell her my idea. "I talked to Alyssa." I try to not grin at the look of disgust when she says her name, it's cute how jealous she is for no reason. "And she said that her dad is on board with us having it at their place." Of course he is. I have no doubt Mayor Burton would love having a bunch of teenage girls running around his yard in wet swimsuits, covered in soap. I realize the hypocrisy but it's not teenage *girls* I'm interested in. It's just one teenage girl.

"No," I say. Payson stares at me with an open mouth before snapping it shut and rolling her eyes.

"Of course you have to shoot down any idea that isn't yours."

I conflict on whether I want to scold her for the attitude, preferably with my hand, or laugh because I fucking love when she's feisty and the way her small nose wrinkles when annoyed. I do neither and just ignore her; I think she hates that more. "Well, I took the time to come up with something, because you did not keep in touch like you were meant to."

She scoffs. "Surprise, surprise the great Ashley Pearson couldn't even let me do this on my own." I arch an eyebrow. "There's a reason I wasn't talking to you." Her eyes narrow. "Doesn't mean I wasn't doing what you asked of me. Besides, like I said, I did email you."

Fair. "What does me being Ash Pearson have to do with the fact I set up plans for *my* team?"

Instead of answering, she grumbles something. She crosses her arms over her chest, then props her feet up on my desk and shoves her ugly blue crocs in my face.

"Your shoes are ugly." I will throw them away at some point.

"You are seriously the biggest dick I've ever met."

"The biggest you've fucked, you mean." I taunt with a grin.

Her nose twitches and her face deepens in color. "For now."

Payson is truly the most daft person I know if she thinks another dick will ever enter her. "We both know if somehow some other bloke gets past me to fuck you, his cock will be nowhere near as big."

My hands ache to touch her, brush a piece of her dark locks behind her ear, pull her against my body and remind her how good it is with me. She's battling her own feelings with a lost look on her face, so I let her off easy, just this once. "But no, I did not get your email. What was it?"

It takes a minute of Payson attempting to remember where our conversation was, but once she does, she reaches into her kangaroo pocket and pulls out her phone. She scrolls for a second. "Dear Captain of the Bayshore Badgers volleyball team, I am happy to tell you that we will be paying for all the travel and accommodation expenses for the whole team to travel out of state for Week of Pink. I will be in contact with your coach closer to the day to finalize details. Thank you."

My head is spinning trying to figure out who sent her the email because no one has been in touch with me.

"Sincerely, JG Law." Her green eyes lift from the phone and she shrugs like she's not sure what else to say. "I don't know who that is, but that's cool, right? Have they been in touch?"

I shake my head and scratch at my beard. With the other hand out in front of me palm up, I say, "Let me see your phone."

She mutters something about saying please but drops it in my hand anyway. Good girl. The email reads exactly as she just read it. It is from Beatrice Anthony and that name doesn't ring a bell. It's not until I reread the ending remarks and see a familiar signature beneath it that it hits me who this email is from and I'm tempted to smash her phone. JG, as in *Jethro Gilbert*, Olivia's dad.

The only other time I've seen that signature is on Payson's sponsor paperwork. What the fuck is he doing paying for her sponsorship to attend this school let alone paying for seven girls, without Alyssa, and two coaches to travel to California? I glance up at Payson chewing on her thumb. Why is he doing all this for her? Because he feels bad for the girl with no reliable parents? Maybe because her grandfather is a pastor? He's trying to make it to heaven or some shit. No, if that were the case, his sponsorship wouldn't be anonymous and this email wouldn't be sent from who I assume is his secretary. My molars grind together. Or he's a pervert like her bloody stepfather and plans to use this bullshit against her at some point. He will wait till she's eighteen though, law abiding citizen and all that.

I slide her phone across the desk. "Tell them no, word it nicely and say we have it covered."

Her eyes widen as she takes the phone back in her hand. "Are you sure? We don't have long before we have to leave, and we have to buy plane tickets which are going to be really expensive now, not to mention at least five hotel rooms. That's expensive, Ash."

She's right. My idea is good, but I'm not sure it's good enough to raise the kind of money we need in that short amount of time. I could easily afford the trip and accommodations for all of us, but it's the principle. Plus, I am very much looking forward to my idea. "Just send it."

Payson eyes me, and I know she has questions, but I don't have answers. I harden my stare, hoping she will for once listen without argument. She rolls her eyes and pulls her thumb from her mouth and types.

I lean back in my chair and run a hand down my face. The clock behind her tells me it's rounding quarter after one, which means I have only forty-five minutes until I need to be at the airport. Parker sounded indifferent the last time we talked. I know he wants to come live with me, but I didn't get the reason. I'm ecstatic to have my son in my life full-time, despite the issues it causes for Payson and me. I've missed out on sixteen years with Parker. Those couple weeks a year and monthly FaceTime calls are not enough, and I can't miss any more. I know eventually Payson will come around and everything will be great; I'm not giving her a choice.

"Dear JG Law—" She makes sure I'm listening before she continues, "On behalf of Bayshore High School Volleyball I would like to say thank you for the offer. That being said, I have to politely decline because it seems we have reached our goal already"—her thick eyebrows sink a little, probably cursing me in her head—"and we cannot accept the money. Sincerely, Captain Payson Murphy."

"Good, now send it."

"Why are you always so bossy?"

Ignoring her words, it's my turn to prop my legs on the desk. She lowers her phone back to the desk, screen up and stares at me. After a second, she breathes out an annoyed breath. "Well, are you going to tell me what your big plan is?"

"No."

"Of course you're not."

She's so funny when she doesn't even try to be. I break into a smirk that only lifts half my mouth; I know that's one of her favorite looks. She can deny it until she's blue in the face, but the way her pupils dilate and she shifts her thighs, craving some friction, tells me all I need to know about where her head is at. "I really have missed you, Jailbird."

So many looks pass over her beautiful face. Eventually she must not be able to handle it because she stands. I wonder if she's going to leave, but she doesn't. Instead, she paces the small office. I watch her for a while before I push to my feet as well.

"Don't." Her voice is sudden, but she doesn't look at me.

"Why?" I take calculated steps across the small room toward her. One at a time. She's stopped in the corner farthest away from me. *Bad move, Jailbird*. I stop when I can smell the vanilla on her skin, about three feet. If she were to try and slip by me, I could easily box her in. Like my body knows this, it vibrates.

Payson is shaking too. She's wearing gray sweatpants and a matching gray jumper with the school logo, both at least a size too big but I can still see the shudders she's trying to hide. "Because I can't think straight when you're close." She whispers so softly I can hardly hear her over the radiator to our left.

"I like when you can't think straight," I admit, stepping even closer. Payson cowers in the corner, still not facing me. My chest just brushes the back of her head. I love how much bigger I am than her. I fucking love that there is nothing she could do to fight me off. Of course I'm not actually a monster, but the thought is enough to drive me crazy.

"Tell me you've missed me." I take her small hand in mine, palm up, and lift it into the air and kiss her damp palm before leaning down so I can wrap her arm behind my neck. She doesn't let it fall when I move my two fingers back down her body. Even through the thickness of her jumper the pressure causes her to shiver. I lower my lips to her ear and groan, "Tell me."

"I c-can't." There's a tremor in her voice that shoots straight to my dick. I shift closer until she is pressed flat against the wall, and I know she can feel my dick on her back. Her beautiful whimper is not what I wanted to hear, but it will work.

With my free hand, I pull her hair into a makeshift pony and hold it to the side so I have complete access to her neck and throat. My nose skims over her prickled flesh and I drop kisses every few seconds, taking it slow for her. A gentleman, I know.

Payson arches her back, brushing her ass over my groin, and I nearly spill into my pants. I skim her ear with my lips. "Fuck, baby, tell me you haven't missed this—us, I won't believe you."

I push her sweats down and they fall to her ankles with barely any force. Her breath hitches as the cool air hits her bare legs, she doesn't stop me. I smack her partially exposed ass and rub, loving the warmth my hand leaves behind. Her stomach is as soft as I remember when I skate my hand around the side and down the front until I'm teasing the band of her knickers, because I know she loves it. She squirms, grinding her ass against me. I wrap her hair around my fist and tug her against my body while sinking my hand south.

At the same time I let out a relieved breath, she sucks in a quick one. Two fingers skate over the just barely prickling skin until I touch her heat and wetness. I smile against her throat. Payson can tell me whatever lie she comes up with in her pretty head, but her body will always tell me the truth.

"You miss my hands, babygirl?"

She whimpers, "Yes."

Hmm. "What about my cock?" I grind my groin into her ass and nearly pass out when it slips between her beautiful ass cheeks. The euphoric state has me pushing out a grunt of pleasure.

She might regret this as soon as it's done but feeling her hump my hand with so much need, I know it'll be worth whatever she throws at me after she's come.

"Yes! Fuck."

Her pussy squeezes my fingers like a vise. I have to bite down on her throat to stop myself from matching her moans. Someone shouldn't feel this good but fuck, she does. Her cunt was made to take every part of me.

I know something else I'd like to see take me too.

"I knew you'd be wet for me, Princess."

"Kiss . . . my . . . ass."

"If that's what you want, baby, I will gladly obey. Kiss." I press an open-mouth kiss over her ear. "*Eat*." I bite down and tug, she shivers. Her back arches like she likes the sound of that as much as I do. "Tell me, Payson. Tell me you want it and it's yours, babygirl. Tell me you missed me, and I'll give you anything. I'll give you the bloody world if you just admit that you want me as badly as I want you."

There's a battle inside her, right and wrong. Heart or head. Pussy or logic. Thankful for orgasm brain, she throws her head back and cries out as her cunt restricts my fingers. "Yes, I missed you! I missed you so much, Ash. Ah!"

Her tits press against her jumper with each deep breath she takes. God, she's fucking perfect.

I know her orgasm is about to wear off and I'm about to get reamed, so I press a deep kiss into the side of her head. "I know you do. But I'm here. I'm always here." I hope she knows I mean that. Anytime, any place, I am here for her. I'm just a phone call away. Something she's not used to is reliable people, so I'll make it my lifetime goal to always be. "I know I need to earn your trust back, but I'll do it, Payson. When you are ready to talk, you know where to find me.

"It's you and me, babygirl. Always."

There are a lot of things I worried about, knowing Parker is moving in with me. Something I didn't consider is that in a few months, he will turn seventeen and the girl I love and my son will be the same age. They seem lightyears apart when separated but in reality, they're not at all. *Fuck.*

Luca slaps my back, grinning and looking in the same direction I am. "Didn't consider their ages, brother?"

"No," I grit.

Parker flashes her a smile—much like my own—and Payson's eyes fly around the room until they collide with mine. Mortification sinks in when she makes the connection, and my insides fill with unease.

Luca murmurs under his breath before walking away, "probably should introduce them."

4

Payson

I'M COMING DOWN FROM a serve when a guy walks across the court, right in line for—*SMACK*.

Shit.

I rush over to the guy standing in the middle of the court, holding his face where the ball smoked him. Seeing how red it is, I feel a little proud, but mostly mortified. I've been smoked in the face by a volleyball before, it's not fun.

"Shit, are you okay? I'm sorry, I didn't see you crossing the court." *Why was he crossing the court?* I didn't see him, but in my defense, he shouldn't have been there.

Warm brown eyes swing my way. I'm happy to see only half his face is red. "It is not the first time. I was not paying attention. My bad, bellissima."

Holy accent. I've grown accustomed to the English accent, and this is definitely not that. I don't know what that word he said means but I definitely like how it sounds. "Where are you from?" When his deep brown eyebrow inches up his tanned skin, I want to slap myself in the face. That's not how you ask someone that. "I mean. Like where is your accent from?" *Great, now my face is burning and probably as red as his.*

The guy, who I didn't even consider how undeniably attractive he is, grins. A weird feeling twists my stomach, it's not a good feeling, or a bad, just . . . weird. Like, I know him, but I know I don't.

"I am from *Italy*." Wow, I like the way he says Italy. Then he continues to say something in a low almost sexy voice. "Parker." He holds a slim hand out like I'm meant to shake it. So I do.

"What are you doing here? No offense but Bayshore, Michigan isn't exactly a hot spot for travelers. Especially in late September."

His hand is warm, and he holds it for a beat longer than he should but eventually pulls away and uses that same hand to run through his chin-length dark brunette hair, brushing it away from his model-like face. "My Papà lives here. I moved here to live with him."

His Papà? If I remember correctly, Papà means dad in Italian. Or that's what they call their dads anyway. I've never met another Italian in Bayshore . . . oh *duh*. I want to smack my forehead, I almost laugh. "Right. That's amazing, I didn't realize Luca had a son." It makes total sense now. He looks much like Luca. Same hair, same skin tone. Handsome, like his dad. I give him a quick once over. He's also tall like Luca. I don't know if he's my age—younger or older, but he must be close.

"Like what you see, bellissima?" A sexy smirk tugs on his face and my stomach bottoms out. Not because what he said—because the way he is smirking. It's *not* a Luca smirk.

I find Ash immediately. He's standing across the room with Luca. Luca is grinning but Ash looks like what can be described only as a deer in headlights. There's that sinking feeling again.

I take in the boy in front of me. He's moving in with his dad. He's Italian . . . it would make sense for Luca to be his dad, but the look on his face was not inherited from Luca. That's a younger-Ash smirk if I've ever seen one.

"Who is your dad?" I ask breathlessly, my lungs can't seem to suck in the air they need.

Parker's smirk fades and a look of concern replaces it. He reaches out to touch me but I jerk back. In my panic, I hadn't noticed another person walk into our conversation. Ash, not Luca. My lunch turns in my stomach, debating if it should rise or not. I hope not because chili isn't fun to throw up.

Ash says nothing. He flicks his eyes between us. Parker is doing the same between Ash and me, and eventually his face fills with dread like he knows

. . .

Ash clears his throat. "Parker, this is Payson."

Parker's spine steels and his eyebrows sink. He mutters something to Ash after a long minute of staring at me, and Ash gives him one firm nod. So he knows about me. He knows about me and does not look happy about it. He says something else like a question, a really disgusted question and he snarls.

Ash's jaw ticks but he answers in a calm, firm tone. "Diciassette."

Whatever that means makes Parker's eyes open so wide I worry they might fall out of his head. He steps away, like he just learned I'm diseased or something. "Pedofilo."

I don't need to know Italian to understand what that means. It was obviously geared toward Ash, so I'm thinking the conversation was about my age, but I've never been more confused than I am right now. The answer is right in front of me, but I don't want to guess. I want to be told because there's no way what I'm thinking is right. I don't care how many similarities are between the two men in front of me. Luca and Ash look similar too. Parker is Italian so he could still be Luca's. Ash has a son but there's no way he is my age, I mean, right? Sure, his voice was deepish on the phone from what I heard but . . .

Parker turns and strolls away from us with a few backward glances and a new level of disgust tugging on his lips.

Ash is the first to speak because there's no way I can. "You met Parker." It's not a question.

I think I nod but I can't be sure. He doesn't say any more so I force words out of my tight throat. "And Parker is?"

Please don't say it.

"My son."

Fuck.

I've been off my game all night. Thank God this is just a practice.

"What the hell is your problem?" Alyssa snaps.

It's definitely my fault we didn't get the point, it was coming right for me. It's not my fault because Parker came back in the gym from wherever he walked off to and sat in a chair to Ash's left, and I couldn't stop looking back and forth.

"Are you that big of a whore that any guy that comes into sight is fair game?"

"Shut up, Alyssa." She has no clue what she's talking about. Before this year, guys didn't mean shit to me. They still don't, I only care about one—now two, but not for the reason she thinks.

I squeeze my eyes shut, trying to clear my head, but I can feel them looking at me and it's fucking me up. I grind my jaw. Someone shoves my side, I lose my balance and fall to my ass with a thud and a huff.

"Enough! Alyssa, bench. Now," Coach shouts.

She glares at me, and I glare back. It's a bad day, so instead of just letting her walk by, I wait till she's close enough and kick her legs out from under her. Ash tells me not to, like he knew my plan, but I'm not listening to him. This is all his fault.

Alyssa gasps before she falls to her ass right next to me. She doesn't have the extra padding I do; she screams but it must not affect her like she's leading on because she tackles me to my back as I go to stand. She punches my face once, twice before I get my arms out from under her scrawny thighs and shove her off. I know I don't have long before we are broken apart. I pull my fist back and nail her right in the stupid, bitchy face three times. When I'm lifted off, her face is bloody like I can feel mine is.

She spits blood on the floor when Luca pulls her to her feet. "You—"

"Practice is over!" Ash barks in my ear, cutting whatever she was going to say off. He holds me to his body with one arm, and like a toddler, my feet aren't even touching the ground. "I expect everyone here at five a.m. tomorrow morning."

I cringe seeing my teammates' shoulders sink because we weren't meant to practice at all tomorrow, now we have to be here at five in the freaking morning.

Janelle is doing her best to not smile, which makes me smile. I don't hide mine, though. I smile and I smile big to rub it in Alyssa's face that her punches didn't do shit despite the burn in my lips and the sticky blood dripping off my chin.

"She started it because she's a whore!" Alyssa screeches across the gym. Luca is attempting to pull her into the locker room but she's fighting him like a crazy person.

"Look who's talking!" I shout back. "You fuck anything—" Ash's hand clamps over my mouth, not letting me say anything more. He digs his arm into my ribs and shakes me. "Knock it off," he snaps.

I turn my attention to him, feeling angrier than when Alyssa punched me. "Of course you let her talk shit about me but God forbid anyone says anything about your perfect little pet. Does she sit when you tell her to? You give her little treats and tell her how good of a girl she is? And I'll bet she even—"

Ash's voice booms across the gym and in my ears, he doesn't remove his angry glare from me once. "I said practice is done. Go home!"

The girls are quick to scurry away. Ash storms across the gym toward the office and tosses me inside. He slams the door behind him, and I wonder if he will punch the wall with how angry he looks, like Jason used to, but he doesn't. He doesn't turn around. He doesn't do or say anything. His hands are flat against the door and his shoulders are rising and falling at an accelerated pace, so I know he's angry, but if he is going to be angry with anyone—it should be Alyssa.

I grab a few tissues from his desk and shove them in my nose, then I reach down and pull my shirt over my head to stop from staining it any more than it is and prop myself on the edge. "She started it."

The door complains as his hand slams against it before he spins and pins me in place with a look I've never been on the receiving end of. Anger. Sure, I've made him angry, but normally there is lust or amusement under it. Not this time, just straight up anger, and it scares me a little. He doesn't even look at my bare abdomen or cleavage once. "She's right."

His words are like a knife straight to the stomach, *I would know*, and I grip it with the hand not holding my tissues. "Which part?" My voice is weak, exactly how I feel.

"Not about you being a whore, Payson."

Ash walks right by me toward the bathroom and returns with a first aid kit and a bowl of water and rag. He drags the rag over my face in silence, making my anxiety grow. "You do not need stitches and should be fully healed in a week." *Ha, she hits like a bitch. Should have known.*

The water splashes over the side of the bowl onto the floor when he drops the rag into it. He lowers his forehead to mine and closes his eyes.

"She's right because you are easily distracted. Sometimes it works in your favor, like when your mom showed up before the game and you were amazing." I know there's a but, and I already know what it is. "But, like today, you let me"—his eyes flick up open—"and Parker."

I stiffen hearing that name. I don't know why it's affecting me so much. I knew he had a son, maybe because of the way I met him? Maybe because I was completely blindsided? Or maybe because I expected to be meeting a kid when I met Ash's son. Not someone so close to my age. I don't know.

"How old is Parker?"

"Sixteen," he says. "He turns seventeen in a few months."

So, he really is my age. We will be seventeen at the same time for like, half a year. I wonder if that bothers Ash at all? I'm guessing not since his hands are on my thighs and he's tracing small circles with his thumbs.

"You let it affect you and not in a good way. You sucked today, Jailbird." There's a teasing in his voice but he's not wrong.

"I know," I whisper, embarrassed that he noticed. No matter the weirdness between us or how I might feel about him personally. I can't deny Ash Pearson knows his volleyball, and I crave his approval.

I grab the rag from the bowl to clean up since he stopped at my neck, but he grabs it from me and drags the lukewarm rag over my chest where the blood seeped through my shirt. The contrast of the wet and the cool office air causes my skin to prick with goosebumps and my nipples to harden, peaking through my two black sports bras.

I wonder if he notices until his large hand cups my breast over my bra and his dark gray eyes zero in on it. I flatten my hands behind me and arch into his touch. He crowds me, prodding at every exposed part of my body.

"I do not care about protecting her more than you. By the way."

I wish I could roll my eyes harder. "Yes, you do. You let her say vile things to me but the moment I open my mouth, you cut me off, I don't know why. I know you are not doing this with her." *I hope.* "Is it because her dad's the mayor?"

He scoffs against my throat like that's the most absurd thing I've ever said but it's not. It would make sense he kisses her ass because of that. Everyone does. "It's because what you say is accurate. Alyssa says anything that she thinks will hurt someone and it's usually far from the truth. She digs but her words never affect you because you know they are not true. Your words are. She self-projects, where you judge a situation by how it is. Alyssa calling you a whore does not make any sense when I am the only man that has, and will be between your legs."

I take a second to think about that while he pushes me onto my back and positions himself between my legs, kissing from my collarbone up to my ear and across to the other side, just barely brushing over my lips.

I guess he's right. She says the craziest things and hardly do they ever actually bother me. I wouldn't tell lies to hurt someone, but I will tell them the truth, even if it sucks.

My center throbs with his erection between my legs. "Tell me I'm the only one, Ash."

"You and me, babygirl. Always you and me."

I wrap my arms around his neck and open my eyes to find him staring down at me. "One day, you will understand how I feel for you. We will wake up in ten years' time and all of this will mean nothing because it will be you I wake to and vice versa."

I hate and love when he says things like that. The little girl inside cheers at the thought of someone planning to be in my life for so long, but the older part of me, the part burned too many times, has a hard time believing because they are just words. You can say a lot of things. So I pull his mouth to mine and relish in the low moan we both let out when our lips touch.

His tongue slips between my lips, I sigh at the hardness of his piercing. I love it. I love it even more when it's pressing into my—

"We need to talk, Jailbird." But he doesn't pull away. He feels amazing being so close after going without, but it's Ash's smell that makes me lift my hips and thrust my pussy against his erection. He always smells so good but it's right after practice that it's the most intoxicating. When he has a hint of sweat and all man.

"Later," I pant, pulling him closer until I can feel nothing but him.

"Baby," he coo's, halting our kiss and leaving me frustrated. "I can't fully enjoy this unless I know you've forgiven me. I want to kiss, touch, and *fuck* you." *Goosebumps.* "More than fucking anything, but I know you're still not with me one hundred percent."

I drop my arms and he pulls me back to a seated position. Falling into the chair in front of me, he moves closer to keep his arms wrapped around my waist.

"I'm still mad at you," I admit softly.

He holds my gaze, not wavering in the slightest. "I know."

"I don't know if I can get over it."

He swallows but says nothing.

"I never told you about my dad. My bio dad—not Fred," I grit between my teeth. Shaking the thought of him away, I lower my eyes and so does he. To the scar on my stomach, he teases it gently with his thumb. "He left when I was four. Everyone says I shouldn't remember, but I do. I remember everything from that day," I admit.

I get different feelings talking about each piece of shit dad in my life. With Fred, it's anger, nothing but pure hatred. With my bio dad, Hunter, it's a mix of anger, sadness, and a deeper feeling of abandonment. I pick at my finger. "It was a normal day; I woke up and Mom was just getting home from work because she worked nights at the time. The arguments started right away, I don't remember about what, but over the years after he left, I heard he was lazy, never cleaned, an alcoholic, addicted to gambling—whether any of that is true, I don't know, but I assume the argument from that day was one of those things.

"Most of the time their arguments were loud whispering to not wake me or Jason up but I was always up. My mom getting home was always exciting to me because sometimes she would bring me a snack, or a little toy she would get at the gas station on the way home. I sat on the steps, just like every morning, but when my dad saw me and tried to stop the argument, my mom didn't stop. She kept going even knowing I was awake, watching, and hearing everything, her whispers got louder. Jason eventually came down, sat next to me, and tried to cover my ears but it didn't work. I heard my mom tell him to get out."

Ash pulls my hands apart and sucks on my bleeding thumb. When he's done, I thread my hands into his hair. It's longer now, fluffy, curly, and hangs over his forehead. Not long like Luca or even . . . Parker. But longer than the short boyish style he started the season with.

"So"—I shrug—"he did. I stayed with him while he packed since my mom and Jason had disappeared somewhere else in the house. No one seemed to care that he was going away besides me. Jason was always weird with Hunter and was never attached like I was, not that I remember anyway. He finished packing and when I tried, he pulled me into the kitchen, knelt in front of me, and explained that only he was going away. He had never gone away without me before, so it didn't make sense. Then he stood, grabbed the few bags he had, and turned for the door without a look back.

"My mom wrapped her arms around me, not like a hug—like a jail. She wouldn't let me go no matter how much I fought. I begged my dad to stay but he didn't. Mom started to cry like she wasn't the one who told him to get out in the first place. Of course she probably had her reasons, but I was four. I only cared that my dad was leaving and not taking me with him."

Ash drops his forehead to my thigh and kisses several times. I'm tempted to open my legs, because I miss him kissing me *there,* but he's standing, cupping my face, and pressing his lips to my actual lips before I can.

When he pulls away from the too-short kiss, I tilt my head. "What was that for?"

"I just hate everything about your childhood, baby." He pauses and gives me a sloppy smile. "And I spent too long watching you lick your lips without being able to taste them."

My stomach flutters. "It wasn't all bad." I nudge him slightly. "It's what brought me you. You saved me."

He shakes his head and cups my face to make me look at him.

"You saved yourself, babygirl. I'm just the lucky guy that you clung to."

My anger doesn't fade in this instant, but if I'm being honest, I'm tired of pretending like I don't want to go back to where we were. I just don't know if I can. Not fully. "I really have missed you, Ash. But now you know why I can't just get over the fact you have a son. I know it's not right to compare our situations, but I can't help imagining Parker having the same thoughts about you. What kind of person would that make me if I was with you, then?"

"You and Parker's stories are vastly different, my love, and when you are ready, I will tell you, but I promise I am nothing like that. I might not consider myself a dad, but it wasn't by choice. Not completely."

"I want to trust you again," I murmur.

He leans in and nips at my bottom lip. "If I can promise you anything, Jailbird, it's that you will trust me again."

"Okay." I nip at his lip this time and he grins. "Can we go back to where we were now?"

Ash chuckles, places a hand on my chest and pushes but freezes when his door flies open, without a knock, I should add, and slams against the wall behind it. He looks back and goes rigid, his body language telling me it's not Luca like I was hoping it was. Ash could just tell him to get out and I wouldn't need to feel guilty about what we were meant to do. But when Ash turns and does his best to block my body, the guilt comes in tenfold. He's stiff like he got caught doing something he shouldn't, meaning whoever opened that door should not have seen his body pressed into mine.

"What the fuck happened to my daughter?" It only takes a second to realize that's the voice of our mayor, it's basically the male version of Alyssa's. Figures she called her dad. I can't fault her though. If I had someone to call in my defense, I'd do the same. I could ask Grandpa to come down here, but the last thing I want is to stress my grandpa out because I got in a fight.

"Mayor Burton," Ash greets like he's greeting the Grim Reaper. "If you give me a second to clean up, I will be right with you."

"No, you can talk to me right . . ." I stiffen. Especially when Ash's body backs into mine. "You have a lot of explaining to do, Ms. Brighton."

Me? "It's Murphy. And your daughter—"

Ash's head snaps back at me with a look that should scare me, but the anger pumping through my body makes me ignore him because I am not taking the blame for this. I flip my body around and climb off the opposite side of the desk, then walk around and cross my arms over my chest. I'm not embarrassed until Mr. Burton takes in the state of my bare upper body and it's not a look of disgust or blame I see. Something inside me sours but I stiffen my spine. Especially when I see a bloody Alyssa standing behind him.

"Alyssa pushed me first; she also punched me first. It was merely self-defense, Mayor Burton." I wonder if this is how Alyssa feels when she uses her body to her advantage. At least I don't need to worry about him seeing my scars, any of them, because he hasn't lifted his eyes from my chest.

"I understand, dear."

I shoot a helpless look to Ash because I was not made for this. I *hate* this kind of attention. Feeling his grubby eyes take in the curves of my breasts reminds me of someone else, and I don't like it at all.

"Do you have another shirt?" His jaw is so tight his words are hardly understandable.

"Y-yes." The worst part is Mr. Burton is not even attempting to hide his interest in my body. I spare a look to Alyssa but she's not paying any attention either, with her nose stuck in her phone. I wonder what her home life is like and if maybe it's similar to what mine was. I hate that thought so much because it would give us something in common—*besides our taste in men*—and I don't want that.

"Go put it on and go home," Ash snaps a look at me and his jaw tightens even more than when he was watching Mr. Burton. "Now."

He doesn't have to tell me twice. I am moving and basically running by Mr. Burton before either of them can say another word. I glance back and see that Mr. Burton is watching my ass but Ash slams the door behind Alyssa and cuts off his staring.

"Parker." I rush out, hoping to calm my beating heart after running directly into him.

He says nothing and lowers his face back to his phone. I'm in no mood to talk about what I assume he said earlier, so I sneak by him and Luca, with a helpless look before sprinting to the locker room. I expect it to be empty because of how long Ash and I were in his office, but Janelle, Mika, and Monica all sit with impatient and far too interested faces. I laugh under my breath on my way to my locker and my arms pressed to my sides. Gone are the thoughts about Mr. Burton, Alyssa, and Parker.

They bombard me with questions about everything; why I was in the office with our coach for so long, the way he easily held me in one arm—Monica thought it was the most romantic thing ever. I told her I felt like a piñata, but she didn't care. Then came the questions about the new guy, I avoided those like the plague until they asked if the mayor showed up yet. Apparently Alyssa was on the phone with her dad after two seconds of being in the locker room. She refused Luca's help, saying she *wanted her dad to see how bad she was.* Explains the dried blood all over her face. She's pathetic.

I'm still pissed at what she said. She thought I was into Parker, but she couldn't be more wrong. Sure, I was admiring his looks because I knew who he inherited those looks from but that means nothing. I admire Luca's good looks all the time too, I'd never tell Ash that, but Luca is handsome—like a model. Doesn't mean I want to do anything about that. It's normal to just look without acting on it. Not for Ash, he better not be looking at anyone else. The thought alone makes me want to scream. Alyssa, I guess, isn't the look-from-afar type, which doesn't surprise me that every person she's ever found attractive is probably in her bed later that night.

I answer all they want to know, or what I'm willing to share and head for the showers to rinse off the dried blood that Ash was too busy with other things to clean.

"Have you talked anymore?" Janelle is asking Monica when I wander back from the shower. She eyes me, looking for more scars, no doubt, but I turn for my locker to dress while they chat.

"Yeah, we did for a while but it's hard, ya know? Attempting to be just friends when we are far from just friends."

Janelle shoots me a grin and I smile back. "So, when's the last time you had sex?" I ask as I slip into my clean shirt. Alyssa is lucky I always pack extra clothes. Unlucky for me, I didn't pack an extra bra or underwear. You can see my nipples through my shirt because I refuse to wear my dirty bra after I'm clean from a shower. I pull on my sweatpants without underwear until there is little to no skin showing between my cropped shirt and sweatpants. I don't wear crop tops anymore, but I had forgot I cut this shirt last summer before I had an ugly scar I don't like to show.

"A week."

All three of us burst out laughing. Janelle and Monica high-five and I fall onto the bench next to them.

"We aren't together, technically, but we are still hanging out and not fucking anyone else."

"So, you're dating?" Janelle chimes.

Monica glances at me with a weird expression. Then it hits me. "I'm not going to rat you out, Mon. You know that." I'm a little offended that she would think that.

Lucky for me my best friend is a loudmouth. "Yeah, not like he can do much when he's fucking with a player on the regular."

My and Monica's mouths drop open in shock. I stare at Janelle, and Monica stares at me. I snap my mouth shut but it doesn't stop the stupid redness from creeping up my neck and face. "I—" I fall silent. I wasn't prepared for this. Janelle knows it too because she can't stop silently laughing.

"You bitch." I'm really not that upset, Monica is cool, and I know she will get more of a kick out of this than anything. She won't tell anyone.

Monica bombards me with question after question and eventually I have my bag packed and I turn to her. "You guys up for pizza?"

"Oh, hell yes, you are not getting away from me tonight without telling me how big our coach's dick is. I've seen it through his shorts, so you can't lie either."

We are still laughing as we head from the locker room.

"Massive," Janelle tells her eventually. I just roll my eyes. She's right—of course, but I'm not discussing this when we are still in the gym.

We are walking by the coaches' office when the door swings open and Alyssa storms out. She makes us separate so she can storm by. And of course she can't just walk by. She scoffs and mutters something about *leftovers*. There's no time to think about it when her dad walks out. He looks displeased until his eyes land on the three girls frozen in front of him. He eyes each of us individually before his eyes lock with my . . . chest. Monica elbows me and I look down realizing he's looking at my breasts. My nipples are hard. I knew they were, the gym is cold when you aren't running. Doesn't help my hair is still wet either. Mr. Burton isn't even trying to hide the fact he is staring at my chest and . . . licking his lips. *What the hell is wrong with him?* Sure, he's always been creepy but never this obvious about it.

Ash appears from the office, he must know what the holdup is because he walks forward and clamps his hand on Mr. Burton's shoulder. I can tell by the white knuckles and the wince in Mr. Burton's face Ash isn't being gentle. Good, I wish I was Ash's size so I could punch Mr. Burton for being a creep. Eventually he saunters off after his daughter, leaving the three of us staring at our coach, speechless.

Like Mr. Burton, Ash is having a hard time keeping his eyes up and off my tits. But I actually like his attention. So much that when Janelle clears her throat and he peels his eyes away to address her, I frown. Monica lets out a small squeal. I wonder if now that she knows, it's easier to see things between us. We try to be discreet at practice and stuff. It's moments like this, when there are fewer people around that it's a challenge to pretend we wouldn't rather be in his office making out. Or more. My body covers in goosebumps at the thought. It's been a little over a week since I lost my virginity but the memory of how good it felt to have his body all over mine, *in* mine, hasn't gone away. I hope it never does.

"Where are you ladies off to?"

"Pizza," the three of us reply at the same time.

Based on his stiff body language and the annoyance in his face that is not the answer he was looking for, but I guess because we've had a long evening, he's letting it go. "Practice at five a.m. That was not a joke."

We nod and promise to be there. I really don't want to be here at five a.m. It's bullshit we have to suffer because Alyssa is a bitch. It should just be Alyssa running lines until school but then that would require her and Ash being alone, and I don't want that. So I'll be here at five a.m., maybe even a little before.

"Alright." He sighs and my frown returns. He sounds so worn out. I know the fighting bothered him, but I'm not sure how much. I guess having your team—especially one as small as ours—divided can't be easy on a coach. It annoys me I feel bad even though it's really not my fault. Okay, maybe I sucked today but I saw no one else on the team shoving me and calling me names. There are ways to communicate, and Alyssa didn't do it right. Still, I know it's annoying when a teammate isn't pulling their weight. I hate to admit it, but Alyssa and I need to come to a middle ground. Us being bitches to each other benefits no one. Even I can admit that. I hate to do it, but I'll pull her aside sometime tomorrow and attempt to talk to her. If she won't, then at least I tried. I'm the captain, it's up to me to keep the team as a team.

I must have zoned out for a while because when I blink, my friends are walking away. Their fronts are to me and they are calling my name. "We need to get to bed early tonight! Come on!" *Kiss asses.*

I take a step but stop and look at Ash. He is leaning against his door with his arms crossed over his chest, eyeing me.

"What are you thinking about, Jailbird?"

Instead of answering, I walk toward him. He glances to his left at my friends before lowering his confused gaze to me. I stop in front of him, knowing we are inside the door enough to be out of sight of any cameras. He's too tall and I know I won't be able to kiss his lips but I stand on my tippy toes and press my lips to his jaw. "You."

A pleased growl rumbles in his chest and I fall back to flat feet and smile sweetly up to him. "Always you."

5

Payson

We've been at dinner for an hour. I called my grandpa to make sure he would be okay and he promised he would. He also basically threatened me with a grounding if I didn't spend the night with my friends. I know he wouldn't have actually grounded me, but he was smart to do that, because I was already regretting coming out when I know he is home alone. I still worry about him all the time. It swallows me whole when I let myself think on it too hard, so maybe one night with Janelle and Monica will be nice. Plus, I sent a text to my aunt letting her know, and she replied promising me she would call him before bed and after she woke up when I mentioned I have morning practice.

"I need to get laid," Janelle tells us.

"Challenge accepted!" Monica announces while looking around the small pizza joint. It's the same place we came after our game when Janelle was mad at me. It's a decent size dining room but basically empty. It is a Thursday night, after all.

Besides a young family and a table of men who look old enough to be our grandfathers, it's just us, so no such luck. Until two guys who look to be around our age walk in.

Monica and I grin at each other. Janelle straightens in her seat, fluffs her already fluffy hair and pushes her boobs up so they are almost spilling out of her baby blue low-cut top. At her house, before coming here, she changed and used enough dry shampoo to never need to wash her hair again. The blue from her top really brings out the blue in her eyes. Monica's braids are pulled into a ponytail like at practice and she's still wearing her spandex and school sweatshirt, her not-boyfriend-boyfriend's sweatshirt.

Janelle's bras are way too small for me, so I'm still braless but I put on a sweatshirt so you can't see my nipples. I'm over people looking at them today.

The guys notice us as soon as they turn around. They look familiar but I don't stare for too long to figure out why. Janelle and Monica are across from me, pretending to play it cool, but Janelle is nearly bouncing in her seat when they approach.

"You got room for three more?" the brunette asks, eyeing each of us with what I think he wants to be a sexy look. It comes up short—at least in my opinion. Janelle seems happy with it so being the best friend I am, I'll let her have her moment. Maybe one of these guys, or the third they talked about, could break her non-Collin's cherry. I'm still not happy with him but she seems to be over the whole thing. I'm not, and I plan to confront him when he's home for Thanksgiving, but I'm not telling Janelle my plans.

"There's only two of you," Monica acknowledges.

The blond speaks up. "Our third is outside putting out his cigarette."

Ew.

"I'm Kyle, by the way," the blond says.

"Ryan," the brunette tells us next.

Kyle pulls up a chair and sits at the head of the table while Ryan falls into the booth next to Janelle. I'm not the least bit offended no one sat by me. Not like I moved over to give anyone room. I guess I'll have to for the third, but if he's as douchey as these two, I don't think I want to. I'll gladly be a wing woman for Janelle, but I can only entertain douche bags for so long.

It's also in the back of my mind that Ash would lose his mind if he saw us. He would think this was planned. My stomach sinks at the thought. We're not made up yet, but we are okay. I didn't despise being around him today. Especially in his office.

The other four are busy chatting away and since the other guy hasn't walked in yet, I pull out my phone. It's gone off a few times, but I didn't have the chance to look.

An 'xo' text from my aunt. And two texts from Ash on his burner phone he uses to text me. I don't know why he doesn't use his everyday phone because he sends me full-length body photos with his face, but I digress. I press on those.

The first is a mirror picture, and for the first time in a while, I allow myself to click on it and marvel at his beauty. This isn't a workout photo like usual, his hair is wet and hanging down his forehead like he just got out of the shower. He's crouched in front of the same full-length mirror we compared our asses in and holding his phone in one of his hands. His veins are popping on the back of his hand and down that arm. He's shirtless and wearing shorts. They are low and show off that V I love so much. *God, he's so hot.*

Somehow I click off the picture and read his text.

A: I can't stop thinking about my office today.

I glance up to make sure no one is paying attention and am happy when they aren't before I type back.

Me: Please never stop sending those kidn ofpictures. And me either, I did miss you.

It takes a lot for me to admit that. I could have left it as a spur of the moment, orgasm brain or whatever but the truth is I miss him, and I want him to know that.

A second later, my phone lights up with a reply.

A: Fuck. It feels good to read your fucked-up texts again.

Me: LOL maybe I'm just excited ot text you.

Me: Say it back.

A: Say what back?

Me: Don't be an Ash-hole.

A: I don't think I'm a fan of that nickname.

Me: say it!

A: I missed you so much, babygirl. But I've let you call the shots on our relationship for too long. It's time you remember who is in charge between us.

Me: What does thatnmean?

A: You'll see.

A: enjoy your dinner and try and get some sleep tonight, ' babygirl.

Me: I'll try.

A: I love you. Talk tomorrow.

Me: <3

I know my face is on fire and my friends notice, but they won't ask with the guys around, and unfortunately, they are around. I want to talk about how Ash says I love you and how I haven't said it back. I don't know why I haven't, I just . . . can't. Maybe I'm scared as soon as I say it he will somehow disappear like so many others. Or maybe I'm scared because then it's real between us. If I admit my feelings out loud, then . . . that's it. You can't take them back once you've said them. Sure, people try but you can't. Once you say I love you, no matter what you do after, you can never take back the fact that, at one point you, did love them. That's a scary thought, what if Ash does something worse than the stripper or son thing after I admit my feelings out loud? I don't know what could be worse than that, though. Having a secret son is pretty bad. Not worse than a secret wife, though. My stomach twists at the thought.

Me: You're not married right>

A: No.

A: Get out of your head Payson. Enjoy your night. We will talk tomorrow.

I shove my phone in my pocket because, he's right. This is a night to enjoy my friends, even if they are enjoying company that is not mine. It's nice to be able to sit back and relax without thinking too hard on anything.

A tall redhead walks into the dining area. He scans the room, more people have shown up, but it still doesn't take long for him to find us. I guess this is their third. He looks familiar too, maybe more so. They don't go to our school. I think I know everyone in my grade, at least know *of* them—it's not a big school. They must attend Washington High, the other school in our town. The "normal" school, most people call it. That's probably why they look familiar. It's not often but every now and again our schools will go on a field trip or something together to help cut the cost since our school is so small compared to theirs. Wealthier, but smaller.

The guy walks up but doesn't sit right away. He stands next to my bench and stares down at his friends like he's angry. Of course they are too busy gawking at my friends to notice how annoyed their friend looks. I'm happy he's annoyed because he can join the club. His friends are annoying. They are loud and obnoxious. Obviously trying to impress Janelle and Monica and somehow, it's working. Janelle keeps grabbing Ryan's arm anytime he makes her laugh, which is a lot.

"You can sit," I tell the redhead who still hasn't moved. Not that I want to move, but I already did and him standing there is weirding me out.

His brown eyes flick my way and he frowns. *Okay, rude.*

"Or not." I shrug.

The seat under me bounces when he drops onto the bench. We are looking at each other but neither of us look happy about it. He also smells like cigarettes, and I hate the smell of cigarettes.

"I'm Payson."

He lifts his chin in a "sup" way. "Hero."

"Hero? Cool name."

"My mom thought so." I think he's joking, but he doesn't offer even a hint of a smile, so I can't be sure.

Thankfully our food arrives and saves me from this awkward conversation. Our waitress sets my wings in front of me and the pizza we ordered in the middle. The guys ordered a supreme pizza, and we ordered a meat lovers, they made a joke about us loving meat which I promptly ignored.

I'm understanding why I like older men. It's not just the fact Ash can grow beautiful facial hair, or the gray flecks around his ears and temples that make my mouth water when he pushes his hair back, or his mature body—it's his maturity level overall.

I love to joke around and make stupid jokes but I'm also a lover of serious conversations. Talking about the things that have happened to me was tough with Ash, only because it's difficult to talk about, he is a fantastic listener and made opening up as easy as it could be.

Discussing the future of marriage and kids and not see the blood drain from his face. Obviously we are nowhere near that point and won't be for a long time, but I will not waste time with someone I know I hold no future with. I'm not sure why anyone would.

Then I remember that not everyone wants serious. They don't crave the commitment like I do, or the security. I might fear commitment and what's to come but I can't be with someone who feels the same. One of us has to be sure and Ash is definitely sure. His comment on parents' night flashes through my head. *"It's still my dick you'll be riding on our wedding night."* I think he is delusional to be saying that stuff when we're not even together and have only known each other officially for two months. Men aren't scared off as easily as boys. Maybe because they think their time is limited; I don't know, but I appreciate it either way.

Hero's arm brushes mine when he steals a chicken wing from my basket. "Hey!"

He closes his lips around it and cocks a sharp red eyebrow in challenge.

"You shouldn't steal her food. Payson is very particular on her food," Janelle pipes up but Hero ignores her by chugging the rest of my water as well.

"You ass! You can order your own, you know? There's pizza right in front of you."

He's not the least bit bothered by my small freak out. "I didn't want pizza."

"That's not my problem."

Amused, his mouth lifts in a half-smirk but he says nothing.

Another few bites and I'm full. Hero hasn't touched the pizza—he's not regarding the table or anyone at it, really.

"Do you want the rest? I'm full."

He doesn't look away from the wall of posters across the room right away but when he does, he eyes me with that blank stare before he looks to the five chicken wings still in my basket. His cold eyes lighten and it makes my stomach ache. I didn't take into consideration why he didn't order his own food or drink. He didn't eat the pizza but maybe there's a reason. It's obvious he's hungry. He must have thought I seemed like a decent enough person to not call him out for stealing my food.

Great, now I feel like shit.

"Thought you didn't share food." He doesn't sound overly bitter, but enough that I want the bench to swallow me whole.

"I make exceptions, sometimes, and like I said—I'm full. If I'm not going to eat them, figured you might."

I wait anxiously, hoping he doesn't take offense. Not like he knows what is running through my head, but I still feel guilty. I push the basket in front of him hoping to entice him more. It works and he lifts a slim hand. It's not just that his hands are slim, his cheeks are sunk in, and although I can't see his body under his clothes, his sweatshirt is thin—far too thin for middle of fall—and not hiding his protruding collarbone or narrow waist. His skin is nearly translucent, besides the many freckles.

The waitress walks up holding our checks, she passes them out, but I don't grab mine. "Can I get another order of wings, sixteen count, with a full order of fries, to go, please?"

Kyle cracks a joke about how I can eat and one day it'll catch up with me, but I ignore him.

"Thought you weren't hungry?" Hero hits me with a grave look.

I ignore him and look across to Janelle and Monica so I don't have to answer Hero and tell him the food is for him. I don't know how he will take it and don't want to come across like I'm trying to treat him like a charity case or something.

"What do you think practice is going to be like tomorrow?"

"I don't think bad. We have a tournament this weekend, so it's not like he's going to kill us before that," Monica says.

That's true, it's a big tournament too. A three-hour drive, and until today, I planned to drive myself, but I'm hoping Coach might have room for me. Janelle's parents are weekending where we are going, so they won't be coming home, and while they offered for me to stay with them and go up tomorrow night, that's a long time to be away from my grandpa.

"What sport do you play?" Kyle asks.

"Volleyball," we answer in unison.

"Sweet, might have to come check you out sometime," Ryan adds with a wannabe-sexy smirk. Maybe it is sexy because Janelle seems amused by it when she agrees with a smile on her face. Ash really has ruined me for all other guys.

Janelle texts our schedule to Ryan and my food is brought to our table. The three guys get up first with their pizza box. They offer to walk us out but since I haven't paid, I stop at the counter up front. I grab Hero's arm at the last second, stopping him from walking out. I wait till everyone else is outside before I extend my hands with the food in it.

His brow knits. "What?"

"It's for you."

I wait for a pissed comment because I know how this could be taken, but it never comes. He just nods once and turns. I think I hear him mutter a small thanks but then he walks outside to join the others.

I pay, leave a decent tip, and hurry to meet my friends.

"I'm allergic to tomato. That's why I didn't eat the pizza." I jump at Hero's voice, not expecting it.

It's even colder out than it was when the sun was up and I cross my arms over my chest attempting to keep the warmth in.

Letting the door close behind me, I look around for my friends. They are next to Monica's car, still talking to the guys. I let out a shallow breath that fogs up the air in front of me. It's so cold Hero is shivering. I wonder if he is choosing to not wear a jacket like me, or if he doesn't have a jacket at all.

"Oh," I say simply.

We both shift awkwardly until my friends call for me, telling me to hurry my ass because its cold. I turn so my back is to them and I'm facing Hero. "I'll see you around?"

"Sure."

A red car whips around before squealing their tires as they exit the parking lot. Hero curses under his breath and that's when I realize that was his friends. *What assholes!* I don't care how into them Janelle is, she is not fucking any guy that abandons their friend in the cold. Especially when they didn't even consider his allergies. Don't they care their friend looks so skinny the wind could probably blow him away? There's shadows under his eyes that look like no matter the amount of sleep he gets will never go away. What about how his clothes hang from his too-slim body like rags? They were dressed in name brands from head to toe.

"Why do you hang out with them?" I blurt out of nowhere, surprising even myself.

"We grew up together."

Somehow, that's hard to believe. Not just because the obvious; they have money, Hero doesn't but because he seems so . . . kind. Reserved maybe is a better word and they . . . well, they are the opposite. "Really?"

That earns me a weak smirk. "Hard to believe because I'm poor and they're not?"

He's joking—I think, but I don't laugh. "No, they are dicks, and you seem like a decent enough guy."

Hero lets out what I assume is a laugh but it's raspy and now that I remember Kyle, or Ryan, one of them said he was outside smoking. "Decent, eh?"

"How do you afford smokes?" More word vomit.

He reaches into his back pocket and pulls out a single cigarette and a silver flip lighter. Like one of the fancy ones. He flips the lid, cups a hand around it, and lights the cigarette. His hand is bright red, and I wish I had gloves to give him. Once the cigarette is lit, he sucks in a long drag, tips his head back, and blows it back into the sky. "I steal them."

"There are better things you could steal. Smoking is bad for you, you know?" *Payson, shut up, no one cares if it's bad for you.*

He cracks a smile, biting down on the cig but not enough to bite through it. "Is it?"

"You already know that, I assume, but yeah. It is." I take a few steps back and throw my thumb over my shoulder. "Do you need a ride?"

"Nah."

"Okay, well. Don't forget your food." I point to the ground next to his feet. "See ya, Hero."

"Later, Streaks."

Janelle whips around as soon as my ass touches Monica's back seat. "So ... What was that all about?"

I expected it so I just laugh and shrug. "Just being nice."

Janelle and Monica swap faces. "Payson Murphy isn't ever 'just being nice.'"

My gasp is loud and I slap a hand to my chest. "Ow! That's not true. I'm totally nice."

"No, you're nice to girls, adults—relationships that will never turn romantic—but you're not ever 'nice' to boys. I've seen you turn down guy after guy for *years*," Janelle says.

Monica adds, "I've never even seen you look the way of a hot-blooded male besides Coach Pearson."

I'm thinking of something to defend myself, but I can't . . . because they're right. Sure, guys have asked me out, asked for my number, etc., but I've never agreed. I used to make up excuses, then I started saying no and ever since guys learned I will not say yes, they stopped talking to me altogether. Proves that guys only talk to girls if they think they have a chance in their pants, if you ask me, but I digress. All but one guy. "What about Clay? I talk to him every day in class."

I can basically feel them rolling their eyes. "You and Clay are the most platonic thing I've ever laid eyes on. You could strip naked for that boy and he wouldn't even blink an eye." Funny, I said the same to Ash and he didn't believe me.

"Okay, it's the same for Hero, then."

Apparently, something I said is funny because they are laughing like hyenas in the front seat as Monica drives down the street. I drop my chin to my hand and huff. "Whatever. I was just being nice."

Janelle is still laughing when she reaches back and taps my leg, in what is meant to be comforting, I think. "Maybe to you it's the same as Clay because you got a lifelong hard-on for our coach, but if you were to ask Hero to go to the bathroom with you for sexy time—he wouldn't say no, Pay."

I don't know how I feel about what she said, so I push it from my head and change the subject. "Ash told me he loves me, and I haven't said it back."

6

Ash

"Parker, we need to talk about this."

He slams the car door shut and storms toward the house. Luca turns, and without a word, I see the question in his eyes. He wants to know what I'm going to do—or say—to fix the way Parker is thinking about me. He called me a pedophile. I understand why he would think that, Payson isn't even a full year his senior, but I don't know how to explain things between us in a way he would understand. As far as I know, Parker has never been in love. It's difficult to explain that feeling to someone who has never experienced it.

"I don't know," I answer with a tight jaw.

"Tread lightly, fratello. He will come around."

I know I'm lucky that most of my family—brother and parents—and my closest friend is supportive of my relationship, but it has blinded me from the real world. Most wouldn't be—rightfully so. They see a seventeen-year-old girl and her thirty-three-year-old volleyball coach. The power imbalance would show I took advantage, and maybe I didn't give her the option to deny me like I should have . . . but she wouldn't have anyway. The fact I'm her coach, older and bigger, has nothing to do with us being together. Unfortunately, Parker doesn't see that, and I don't expect him to, but his opinion means the most and the fact he thinks his dad is a pedophile has been weighing heavy on me since he said it.

I didn't expect things to be easy when he moved in, but he's only been here a few hours and already we are having our first blowup. It's normal for most families to fight; I definitely beat the shit out of my brother and vice versa when we were kids, but I don't remember fighting with my parents and definitely not about my dad being a pedo. Fuck. I rip a hand through my hair. It's getting long but I can't seem to care enough to get it cut. With Payson being MIA from my life and the stress of bringing my son into it, my mind has been busy. Superficial grooming is far from priority right now.

If I'm being honest, I'm worried Parker is looking for any excuse to go back with his aunt. His dad dating a girl the same age as him is probably a good one—but he can't. He can't go back when I just got him here. Bella has done an amazing job raising him since his mom died but he's my son. He should have been my responsibility when Marzia died, but I didn't know about him then, and once I did, my career was peaking. It would have been no life for him. I thought about quitting, but Luca and his sister told me not to. I still don't know why I listened. I missed out on sixteen years of my son's life. A few weeks in the summer and every holiday I could manage weren't enough. I always dreamed of being a dad, but being a part-time dad was never in the plans.

My dad is the best there is and I wanted to be just like him. Come home to a wife I was obsessed with and a bunch of kids running around. A messy house but full of love. That was always the goal and for the first time ever, it actually seems like a possibility. In the distant future, of course.

I knock on Parker's door. There is no answer, but I can't just stand here and wait for him to come to me. He is sixteen—I'm the adult. I'm his dad, I need to come to him. My breath is lodged as I push open the oak door.

He's lying on his bed tossing a basketball in the air. He doesn't look my way and I wonder if it's because he didn't hear, but when the floor creeks under my heavy step and his jaw ticks in the same way mine does when I'm pissed, I know he must have.

I have to step over his unpacked luggage to get across his room and look away before it can bother me. I won't let him go, if that is what he's thinking; not when I just got him back.

The walls are white like the rest of the house, but I told him we would go pick out paint swatches after the season. I have only weeks left if all goes to plan and I need to be focused on winning. Everything else matches the other spare room Luca resides in, basic wood furniture. I took the chance on buying Parker a blue duvet cover because I assumed blue is the safest color to go with for a teenage boy. I'm hopeful he will eventually settle in and this room will look like your average teenage-boy room in no time.

I fall into the desk chair and let out the breath I had been holding. "We need to talk."

"I don't want to talk about you fucking a child."

I hate the sound of disgust in his voice. "Parker," I scold but keep it light. I want him to know I'm serious but also not a hard ass. "Things are weird, I know. You didn't expect Payson to be closer to your age than mine—"

"The same age, Papà. Not close to my age. She is my age."

"—but trust me. It wasn't planned."

That ticks something inside him. The ball he was tossing drops to the floor. It bounces a few times before rolling to the corner of his room. He sits up and regards me with a look of disgust. "Let me guess, it was not planned, it just kind of happened, sì?"

Fuck. That's so cliché but yes. That's exactly how it is. I nod my head and prepare for his reaction; he simply rolls his eyes.

"I love her, Parker." It's obvious my words catch him off guard. I told him about Payson and things between us but I never let on how serious it actually was. "She loves me too." Despite her never telling me. I don't need to hear it to know. Eventually she will have to tell me with her words, but until then I strive on her eyes speaking what her mouth won't allow to come out.

He scoffs. "She's fucking seventeen, does she even know what love is?"

That's an accurate and fair question. But Payson isn't like most seventeen-year-olds. She's had a very rough road, clung to things she shouldn't, but I'm not a razor blade. I bring more good than harm. "Payson has had a rough road, worse than you can probably imagine, but I will not speak of that. I know it's hard, but I'm hopeful you can eventually come around to us because if I have anything to say about it, Payson isn't going anywhere."

"You want her to be my stepmother?"

"Of course not." I pinch the bridge of my nose and continue, "Technically, when we marry, she will legally be your stepmother—as I am your father, but I wouldn't expect and highly recommend you do not call her mum. Ever."

His lips twitch like I made a joke.

"I'm sorry, Parker. Really. I know it's weird for you, but you'll like her. She really is quite brilliant and I'm not just saying that. Luca thinks so too."

I realize then that maybe he thought she was brilliant when they were talking. I'm obsessive enough to hate that she's closer to his age but smart enough to know Payson enjoys me being older. I don't think Parker could deal with Payson's dark parts either. I wouldn't want him to. I love Payson and accept her for who she is, but Parker is young. The things I deal with regarding Payson are nothing I want him worrying about. Hypocritical as it is, I do not care. I can love Payson and still want different for my son.

"How am I meant to go to school with her knowing she"—he swallows and grips at his long hair—"fucks my Papà?"

I have no fucking clue. "Just don't think about it like that. If you have to talk to her, then talk about something besides me." I would rather Payson only ever talk about me but maybe not with my son, at least for now.

"Well, duh."

Ignoring the annoyance that came with his attitude about it, I stand. "I'm going to work out. We can talk more later; you can ask any questions and I'll try and answer to my full capacity."

He nods slowly and I know that the conversation is over for now. Truthfully, I can't wait to get out of this room and work off some steam in the gym. "You want to join?"

"I am still tired from the time change."

Fair. I pause at the door when I hear him call for me.

"Papà?" I glance back to him. He seems more relaxed now but he's still blushing, and I worry what he might say. I told him I'd answer any questions but I'm not answering anything about Payson that doesn't involve us as a couple. If that's what he wants to know, then he will need to ask her or just wonder. I hope he chooses the latter. I'd like to say there is no part of me that is worried about my son stealing my girl, but that's not the case and it is very fucked up to even need to think about it. "Is Janelly single?"

My face splits into a huge smile. "Her name is Janelle, and yes, I believe so." Which, I'm glad, because that guy around them early in the season irked me. "But she is in her last year of school."

Parker seems happy with my answer and doesn't seem to care about that fact. He falls back to the bed and I swear there's a faint smile on his lips when I walk out.

Jailbird: Got room for one more this weekend? I don't really want ot drive myself and—

I don't need to see the reason she wants a ride. I just want her there.

Me: I always have room for you.

I'll need to tell Luca and Parker. Luca won't care but Parker is . . . a little on the fence about me and Payson. He knew I had a girl—I talk about her constantly, it was impossible to hide from my son—not that I would anyway—but he didn't know that she was my player or that she's seventeen. I hadn't left them out on purpose, not truly, anyway, they are just unimportant compared to everything else about her. I would rather talk about the way her brown hair is always a beautiful mess, or the way her green eyes shine when she's happy. I love the way her nose scrunches and how much she cares for the people closest to her. How no matter what's happened in her life she is the most genuine person I know.

"Payson texted me," I announce at the dinner table.

Luca pauses with a bite of zucchini pasta halfway to his mouth. Parker stiffens but keeps eating.

"She asked if there was room in the car for her on Saturday."

"I don't have a problem with that," Luca says.

Parker shifts when we both regard him, waiting for his answer. "Parker?"

"I guess."

Not a great answer, but not bad. I consider that progress. I will text her after dinner to confirm.

"Payson really is fantastic, nipote. You'll see when you spend Saturday around her."

He rolls his eyes. "Si, I have heard about how *brilliant* Payson is. Can't wait."

Things will be interesting but good. The sooner those two get along, the easier my life will be. As long as they don't get along too well.

The gym is peaceful at five a.m. There is no noise besides the footfalls from Luca and me as we walk around preparing for practice. We're not setting up the net because it will not be that kind of practice. We have a serious issue within the team; I don't expect it to be solved today, but it's time we take a step in the right direction.

Girls will show up soon. Anytime Alyssa and Payson are in a room together—especially when they go at each other, I worry what might slip from their mouths. I'll eventually need to tell Payson everything, but I can tell that she's purposely avoiding outright asking whatever she is thinking inside her head. I wish there was no need to worry—no reason to ask questions. I wish I was smarter and had asked for an ID despite being in a bar. Wish I didn't drink so much that night, or the next time. But Alyssa has said nothing this far, so maybe I'll luck out for once with her and she will let me tell Payson everything. Hearing it from me versus Alyssa might work out in my favor. I know she will hate me again, but in order to move forward, we need everything in the open. I don't plan on telling her anything until after the season. I need her and Alyssa to work together, and if she finds out we fucked this summer—even if it was before we met—I know the odds of them being compatible teammates are slim.

When the door I have propped with a block of wood opens, Luca and I look to see who is the eager beaver that is here thirty minutes before practice. Relief washes over me seeing a sleepy smile stretching her pretty face. She rubs at her eye with a closed fist and yawns.

"Morning, boys."

Yesterday we were at each others' throats and today she's smiling at me. I feel like I won the fucking lottery when her smile is directed at me.

Luca dips his head as she walks by him. "Ciao, Payson."

"Come va?"

"Molto bene."

"Very good?" she asks. I've heard him teach her a few words here and there, but I didn't know she already knew how to say *how are you* in Italian. God, my girl is so bloody brilliant.

"Molto bene, indeed," I mutter when she stops in front of me.

Her teeth sink into her lower lip and I want to bite that lip. She sways as she moves even closer until her front is nearly pressed against mine. Her small hands grip onto my shirt and she tilts her head back. "Can we *talk* in your office? It'll only take a second." My dick bobs in my shorts as her sultry words wrap their way around my body. I know the look in her eyes, and I'll be damned if I let it go to waste.

With one fluent movement, I grab her around the thighs and throw her over my shoulder. She grunts but her small giggle has me wanting to run to my office.

Luca is chuckling to himself when we walk by. "Do not take too long, practice starts soon."

"We won't," Payson promises.

I kick the door shut behind me and she struggles to scramble off my shoulder. When I set her down, her back is against the door and my lips are on hers. Her lips are soft, like the rest of her, and I love how she always kisses me like I'm air and she needs me to breathe. It's intoxicating; I've never had someone need me so bad, and fuck, if it doesn't go right to my head.

"You have a good night?" I ask. Payson moves her lips to my neck, and she hooks my shirt, stopping our kiss long enough for me to throw it off and pull her back into my arms so she can reach my mouth, neck—wherever she wants.

"Mhm." Her breath is hot against my chest. I don't know what has come over her. Usually I'm the one ripping her clothes off, yet here she is in my arms, still clothed in her black spandex top and blue spandex shorts. I can't even get a second to remove anything because her hands are wild over my body.

She squirms out of my arms and drops to her feet. Slowly, painfully slowly, her mouth travels over my abs, down each one until she falls to her knees. My vision is blurry with need, but I still nearly bust when I look down and see her pulling her hair into a ponytail on top of her head. I stroke my aching dick until she finishes and her hands replace my one. The groan that escapes my mouth is unexpected but deepens the hunger swirling in her lust-filled stare.

"I could make you come just doing this, couldn't I?"

"Yes," I hiss.

She smiles and I wonder if that's her plan. Make me have a mess in my shorts all of practice. But her hands leave my dick and her fingers slip into the elastic band. "I'd much rather swallow it."

My head is fucking reeling, especially when her hands wrap around my ass and she forces me into her mouth as her short nails dig into my ass cheeks. The sounds that leave my girl when my dick is shoved deep in her throat are fucking delicious. Yet she still doesn't release my dick. She's the predator this time and my dick is her prey for her to gag and choke on.

This is how every day could be with Payson. When she's not my player and not in high school. I've thought a lot about our future. It would be realistic to wait until she's eighteen, if not graduated, to seriously pursue anything, but that's not what I want and based on the need in her tear-filled eyes, I know it's not what she wants either. Payson needs me like I need to come right now.

I fist the ponytail she put in just for me. Her nails dig deeper, and one finger teases the center of my ass. I scowl down at her but don't make her move her fingers. I shove my hips forward and butt her up against the door. Her green eyes burn so vibrantly. She looks fucking amazing with my dick stretching her mouth as wide as it will go. Her tongue flicks up and down my slit.

Payson removes a hand from my ass to choke my dick and pull the foreskin back. "Good girl." I breathe. "Fuck, babygirl, don't stop and I'm going to come down that tight little throat. Is that what you want? You want my cum, don't you, Jailbird?"

My body jolts when a finger slips between my ass cheeks. I grunt when she teases the tight muscles, and still, I don't stop her. She seems to like that I don't, and I swear I can feel her smile. I take over pistoning my hips and choking her with my dick and she focuses on what she is doing behind me. She doesn't insert her finger but she doesn't stop teasing either. My grunts are loud and unlike anything I have heard before. Her face is beet red and her eyes lost the fight to stay open. I should worry about her getting air but I'm so close.

"So . . . fucking . . . close. Keep going, babygirl."

She penetrates my body in a way I've never had before and I spill my seed deep down her throat at the same time. Her throat squeezes me every time she swallows my cum. I know it was a lot but she swallowed it all like the good girl she is. She drags her tongue up my sensitive shaft when I slip from her mouth. Her hands fall to her lap, and she stares up at me with an excited but dizzy look across her face.

"Learn something new?" I cock an accusing eyebrow. My shorts snap back into place and I move to rest against my desk while she gathers herself. It takes a while for her to stand, shaky legs support her until she is within reach, and I pull her into my body. I fall into the chair with her straddling my lap and she buries her face into the crook of my neck, breathing in the oxygen she lost.

I rub her back and her body melts more. Her raspy voice stops me from thinking she might have fallen asleep. "Did you like that?"

"It was . . . different."

She hums, obviously happy. I always compare Payson to a bunny because of her nose, and she's just so fucking cute but when curled into my body the way she is, I swear she purrs like a cat.

"Monica and Janelle told me to try it," she admits. "I didn't think it would be so hot."

As much as I'm enjoying having her molded to me, I have to see her face, so I bring my hands to her shoulder and push her back. She eyes me with a sloppy smile and sleepy eyes.

"That was hot, for *you*?"

Her head lifts and she nods excitedly. "So hot. I came."

My eyes widen in surprise. "You came . . . from sucking my dick?"

"A little, yeah. And fingering you—"

I kiss her because while I'm not embarrassed and it did feel good, weird, but good, I don't want to hear her say it. "Don't you dare fucking tell them," I mumble against her lips.

She smiles and kisses me back. "Promise. Our *dirty* secret."

I pinch her bottom lip between my teeth and nip hard enough to tease but not enough to draw blood. "Watch it, babygirl. I've been waiting for the same thing." I wave my hand and she places hers in mine. I curl my fingers over hers, nearly hiding her small hand. "And my fingers are much bigger."

7

Ash

"YOU'RE PROBABLY WONDERING WHERE the net is." The girls nod their head. "This practice isn't going to be a practice like you are used to. We have an important day tomorrow and I don't want anyone sore."

"So what are we doing here?" Alyssa snaps.

"Team bonding." Luca steps next to me with the red blindfolds we went out and bought last night. I will not tell anyone that we got them from a sex shop or that I got a few extra items I think Payson will enjoy. I've done my best not to look at her for too long—like every day—so our feelings are not obvious, but fuck, after my office, it's bloody difficult. Second time she's ever sucked dick and she's like a porn star now.

I take half and start on the opposite side as Luca, passing one to each girl. When I get to Payson, I *accidentally* drop hers, knowing she will bend over to pick it up. I bend too and lean in close. "Keep yours when we're done. For later." She pops up and I stretch to my full height without looking down at her. Her eyes go wide and her mouth falls open as she looks to the red blindfold in her hand.

Once all the girls have one, I tell the four girls on the right to put theirs on. That leaves Alyssa, Aubrey, and Erica without a blindfold around their eyes. "Okay, the girls without a blindfold will be paired up and I want you to wrap the blindfold around one of your legs and one of your partner's so you are shoulder to shoulder. Coach Luca will pair you now."

We discussed the pairs, so I stand in my place in the front while Luca moves each girl next to their partner.

"There's three of us," Alyssa announces like I don't fucking have eyes to see that.

"Shannon could not be here this morning. So, both your legs will be tied. One to Payson, one to Emika. Do it now," Luca tells her before joining me in front of the group.

She takes longer than I'd like but I expect Alyssa to fight me on everything. Payson says I favor Alyssa, but she couldn't be further from the truth. It comes out like I am often taking Alyssa's side, even Luca told me last night it came out that way, but that's not how I see it. I expect what happened from Alyssa—I expect her to call Payson names. I didn't expect the punches; I wouldn't have let her punch Payson, but I wasn't that surprised after I thought more about it.

Payson, I hold her to a higher standard. Maybe it's not fair, but it does not matter what is fair. When she stoops to Alyssa's level, I can't just simply keep my mouth shut. Payson respects me as her coach, therefore it's easier to stop her from doing, or saying, things she really shouldn't. Do I disagree with what she was going to say to Alyssa? No. It doesn't mean I want her saying it out loud in front of the whole team.

Payson is captain because she is genuinely a good person. She's a great player and someone anyone could look up to as their role model. I respect Payson the same way she respects me. Probably more. Even if I wasn't in love with her, I would still have chosen her as captain because the team benefits from it. If I allow her to act as Alyssa does, then eventually that's who she will become. I refuse to watch that happen.

Once everyone is tied up, I explain how this will work. Luca and I set up the obstacle and we will time them. The teammate without a blindfold over their eyes is responsible for making sure their team makes it to the end. "Fastest team to finish the obstacle doesn't have to run at the end of practice all next week."

Excited mutters fill the room.

"What about the beginning of practice?" Janelle asks.

"No, the winner will still be required to run in the beginning and participate in all conditioning besides the two miles at the end."

The excitement dies but not completely.

"And the losers?" Payson asks this time. There is a hesitancy in her voice, and I know she is thinking it will be her team. She's already doubting their capabilities and that's the exact reason I paired those three.

"The team to have the highest time will run double what everyone does next week and will be responsible for setting the net up every day."

Her head drops back and she mutters something to Alyssa, who rolls her eyes at whatever was said.

"From this Friday until the end of season, we will meet in the gym at five a.m., just like today, and we will be participating in team bonding drills until the end of season or until I believe my practice will not be turned into an MMA fighting ring. Are we understood?"

Six of the girls nod. "Yes, Coach."

"Good. Aubrey, please lead you and Monica to the blue starting line." They waddle across the floor, and I direct the other girls to head to the sideline so they aren't in the way. The first thing I hear is Alyssa snapping at Mika for being slow.

"If you would direct us on where to go, we wouldn't be slow," Payson bites back. That is exactly why Payson is captain. Instead of letting Emika take full blame, she included herself in the reason they're being slow. That's a team leader. Payson will make a fantastic coach one day.

I wait for them to make it before I head over to meet Luca at the starting line. "We are going to demonstrate how you are meant to do the course to the seeing teammate, so you are required to fully lean on them," Luca tells the girls.

"Pay attention." I bend over and fix my knee brace, making sure it won't give me any issues.

We link arms and move our opposite ankles together. We don't need anything tying us together because we've been doing this same drill for years. We could do it in our sleep. Jumping, shuffling, running, we do it all and we do it perfectly. When we reach the finish line, neither of us are even breaking a sweat. Running through the course three times before anyone showed up probably helped, but we don't need to tell them that.

"Wow, that was amazing." Aubrey and Erica cheer.

"I wanna see!" Janelle complains and Monica agrees.

Luca and I chuckle and he slaps my back. We move to the positions we talked about earlier. I will be at the finish line, and he will be at the bunny-hop part. That's where most injuries happen. Not that I'm planning for injuries, but you never know. Sports are unpredictable. All the preparation in the world can't stop everything.

"It is important to trust your seeing partner. Seeing partner, it is important to have constant communication to avoid any injuries." I eye each seeing girl so she knows I'm serious. Two out of three nod their head in agreement.

"Okay," Luca claps. "Ready, set . . . go!"

Aubrey immediately tells Monica what to do, she's not great at explaining so they keep tripping but laughing while they do it. This drill isn't about perfection despite how Luca and I made it seem. Team bonding isn't about the drills and how perfect you can complete them. It is about the bonding—hence team bonding. The mistakes and laughs that come with those mistakes are expected and that's where the bonding comes into play.

Luca is grinning wide as the girls pass him with their big smiles. I think they have been on the ground more than they have been up, but they are making decent time. By the end, they are laughing so hard they have to crawl past the finish line. I can't help but chuckle myself.

We have been great this season, a "powerhouse" one article last week called us, but you can always be better. We just need that extra oomph and I'm hoping the bonding will be it.

"Nice time, girls. Five minutes and thirty-eight seconds."

Aubrey pulls Monica's blindfold off and busts up laughing when they see each other again. "Try and beat that!" Monica shouts over to Erica and Janelle who are going next.

They must have taken it as a legit dare because they are already halfway through the course at only two minutes. Erica is communicating exactly how she should, and Janelle is listening carefully to everything she says. They are amazing as a team. I hope they notice this. In case they don't, I join in on Luca's praise for them. "Great job, girls. Erica, brilliant communication and Janelle on listening. Good job, girls, over halfway now."

Instead of discouraging them, Monica and Aubrey are right next to Luca and myself cheering them on, exactly how a team should. I'm very proud of each of the girls; it causes a tightness in my throat. I can't believe I didn't do this before.

All those feelings leave when the last group can't even get to the line without arguing. Alyssa snaps at Mika, Payson snaps at Alyssa. There is no way this will go well.

Payson

If I hear Alyssa bitch at me, or worse, Mika, one more time, I'm going to punch her again. I wish Coach could see my eyes, he would know how close I was and maybe, just maybe, he would stop this bullshit. I get team bonding, but he could have paired me with anyone else. It's like he wants to torture me. Knowing Ash, he probably does.

We've tripped and fallen more times than I can count. Unlike the laughs I heard from Monica and Aubrey, there is an argument anytime we do. Alyssa blames Mika, and I snap at Alyssa for passing the blame to Mika when she's not giving any directions.

I don't even know how far we've made it in the course when we fall, again. I'm going to be covered in bruises. Someone, I assume Alyssa, is leaning on my back pushing my boobs into the floor. I grunt and try to get her off, but she doesn't move. "Get off," I tell her for the third time.

"I'm trying just hang on a second," she snaps.

My boobs ache and it affects my breathing, in a rage, I shimmy her off.

"I said give me a fucking second!" Alyssa screeches.

"Unlike you I have boobs and them being crushed into the ground fucking hurts, Alyssa." That was a low blow, but I've had enough of her today and it's not even six a.m.

"Well, unlike you, I didn't have to buy a bigger size in spandex just to cover my fat ass this year."

"Wow. A fat-ass joke. How original," I mutter like I'm bored, because I am. I'm not fat. I might be curvier than her but I'm in amazing shape. I'm just bigger than I was last year.

"Guys," Mika warns. Mika and I can see nothing, but I'm shocked our coaches haven't broken us apart yet.

"You steal that from your bitchy sister? Where is she now? Jail?"

"I don't know, why don't you call up your buddies down at the station and ask?"

I roll my eyes even though she can't see. "Ha!" I bark out a fake laugh. "Are you going to make fun of the fact my dad left next? How about the fact I live with my grandpa because my mom doesn't want me? Go on, brag about how perfect your life is in that big house on the hill." Someone says my name, but I keep going. "How about how your daddy comes to your rescue whenever you give off the fucking bat signal? In fact, should I be waiting for him to pull me out of class and yell at me for this too, because somehow in that thick head of yours you'll twist that this is somehow my fault as well?"

My breathing is the only thing I hear when I'm done. The room is eerily quiet and guilt twists in my stomach. Not from what I said—that's all true, but because I'm a captain. A captain is meant to be better than this. Alyssa is an annoying, skanky bitch, but my problems with her outside of volleyball shouldn't happen during volleyball.

Biting back any more mean things that want to come out, I sigh. "Look, we obviously don't get along, but we are a team, we only have weeks left of dealing with each other, then we never have to look at the other again. Can we please just move on for the sake of winning? I'm sorry for what I said—not that it's not true, but it's not appropriate as your captain."

"You're only captain because you suck our coach's dick when no one is around." She hisses just loud enough for me and Mika to hear.

What a bitch. "Jealousy isn't a cute color on you," I snap back.

There's a beat of silence before Alyssa opens her big mouth again. "You want to know where my sister is?" Her voice is still hushed. "Why don't you ask your little boyfriend? I bet he knows. In fact, I think he has a good *hard* idea where she is."

I want to tell her a good hard idea doesn't make sense. I get what she's hinting at, but I will not let her use Ash, or Maggie to get to me. "Stand up," I tell them and ignore Alyssa altogether. We need to get to the end of the course, then we can all suffer together next week because there's no way we haven't gotten the worse time.

The girls are cheering for us as soon as we stand. I just want to finish the course, so I ignore every bitchy remark from Alyssa she makes along the way. Mika must too because somehow, we make it to the end.

"Time," Coach announces, then he sighs and it's full of disappointment. "Nine minutes and fifty-five seconds. At least half was spent arguing."

I hate that he's disappointed in me. I hate letting Alyssa drag me down to her level, again. I need to ignore her, but I don't know why that's so hard for me. It's always been difficult but it's worse now. When Olivia was around, she was the bitchy one and Alyssa kind of let her lead the bitchy train. She'd never been nice but Olivia was the main bully. Now it's like she's taken over the spot and is making up for lost time.

She is holding something over my head. Dangling so it's just out of reach. Maybe it's what Maggie said in the restaurant that day about Mr. Gilbert and Mr. Burton talking about me. Maybe it's something else, but I'm over it. I just need to move—

"My sister works at Cherries, right, Ash?"

My teammates' cheering stops. Everything stops. My fucking heart stops. No one says a word and I rip my blindfold off. My eyes take a second to adjust but when they do, I glare at Alyssa. She's not paying me any attention, instead looking over my shoulder, looking at Ash.

I shoot Luca a look, but his eyes are too busy bouncing from me and over my head to Ash. A silent Ash. A *not-denying* Ash.

Please. Please tell me the stripper that got off on his lap wasn't Maggie Burton. Please. *Please.*

Everything moves in slow motion when I turn and see a pale Ash staring right at me. His eyes waver for a second, flicker with what I would assume is regret, disappointment, hurt, or maybe that's me reflecting my feelings on him.

No. I shake my head delicately. My teammates stand next to and behind him but all I see is him. All I ever see is him.

When he told me about the fucking stripper, when I saw the video, the girl was brunette. I know she was because Janelle said something snotty about . . . I swallow thickly, her *wig* slipping off. I clutch my stomach, begging myself not to throw up in the gym.

"She wanted me to tell you thank you, by the way, said that was her best night of work yet."

"Alyssa," Luca scolds with more anger dripping from his voice than I've ever heard. "I will not listen to anymore inappropriate words come from you."

Alyssa stiffens and I wonder why we are still tied together. Mika is right there with us. Wide eyes and everything. Every girl has shocked eyes like they are waiting to see what happens next. I level my stare with Janelle. She knows what I'm thinking, and I guess by the absolute horror etching her features, she must have made the connection too.

I whimper.

Ash snaps out of whatever state he was in and steps toward us. He winces when I snap my glare to him—warning him to not come any closer. I don't know if I have a right to be angry with him about something I thought I got over. Hearing the stripper was *Maggie,* my childhood bully—*everyone's* childhood bully. The girl who said vile things to me a few weeks ago. The girl that landed me in Ash's bed for the first time because *he couldn't let me go without knowing I was okay.* He must of saw her that day, right? Meaning he knew what she looked like and still let her get off by riding him. Clothes or not, it doesn't matter, Maggie fucking Burton got off on *my* boyfriend's dick. And he *let* her.

"Why not? You were there too, right, Coach Luca?" Alyssa is grinning like she's officially lost her mind. "Did you see my big sister or did Ash keep her all for himself?"

"Enough." It's Ash this time that says something. "Everyone go shower."

It takes a blow of Luca's whistle for girls to snap out of their shocked state. Everyone heads for the shower but the three of us still tied together. I can't move. It feels like cement has replaced everything in my body and I'm rooted to the floor.

"What's the big deal? You're red-blooded males. There's nothing to be embarrassed about going to a strip club and getting off on a hot girl. Daddy spent good money on Maggie's tits, it would make her happy to know they were appreciated."

I'm mortified hearing her words. I can't tell who she is trying to hurt anymore. I thought me, but her words seem to cut Ash more. My anger dwindles a hair because worry takes over. Something isn't right in Alyssa's dead eyes. She lacks all morals, obviously, but she's genuinely getting off on this. Embarrassment doesn't begin to describe what I see in Ash and Luca's faces. She's totally disrespected them in front of the whole team.

She opens her mouth again and I interrupt, "Enough, Alyssa. Stop."

I wait for her to throw another punch that I'll be able to dodge. Thankfully, Mika has since removed herself from us and is joining the rest of the team in the locker room.

"Enough," I repeat. My voice is calm, hoping something will break whatever spell she's in. Alyssa is a bitch, but she's not coldhearted. I would argue the opposite, saying she feels everything tenfold but instead of handling those big emotions with crying like Janelle does, she lashes out. Today, however. She's snapped.

"Why? Don't like hearing your pussy isn't enough to keep our coach satisfied."

I slap a hand to my mouth. As do most of the girls behind us, I guess they stopped to watch the show too. Sure, three out of the five know about me and Ash, but it's not something we openly talk about. Certainly not at practice.

I'm not even offended at her words, mostly. The stripper bullshit is past. I'm just disgusted she ruined team bonding by being a cunt.

When she leans toward me, my spine steels. "Don't worry, neither was mine."

Her words are soft but I know our coaches can hear. Luca's eyes fly open in horror. I gasp and once again cover my mouth, hoping to stop me from saying anything I'll regret. Ash does nothing. He stands, eyes on me, completely frozen and not giving anything away.

Well, not—not anything because if it wasn't true, Luca wouldn't look so guilty, meaning he knew. If it wasn't true, Ash would be up in arms throwing her out of the gym or off the team altogether, but he's not. He might as well be a fucking statue.

Disgust rips through me like a knife. It's serrated and leaves my broken pieces in shambles. I wonder if they can be put back together or if this is it. If there is one thing about Ash Pearson, when he cuts me, he cuts deep.

8

Payson

Lies. Always more lies. I wonder if anyone ever tells the truth.

Yeah, kids, Santa is real.

Leave your tooth under your pillow and the tooth fairy will bring you money.

No, Mom, I didn't sneak out last night.

Yeah, this is my first time too.

No, Officer, I was wearing my seatbelt the whole time.

I'll always be here for you, P.

No, I'm not doing the same thing with Alyssa as I am you.

I love you so fucking much, Jailbird.

Lies. Bullshit fucking lies.

Pain is temporary.

I laugh because I'm just as bad as everyone else. Cutting my arm hurts but it's just enough pain to distract from the ache in my heart.

Pain is not temporary. It makes you think it is but it's always there, living in the shadows, waiting to strike when you are at your best. Always there, reminding you that everything is a fucking lie.

9

Ash

HURT. ANGER. HORROR. JEALOUSY. Distrust. Loss of respect.

That's everything I saw in Payson's eyes when Alyssa dropped the bomb. I knew it was coming. I knew what Alyssa was working up to and yet, I let it happen. I told myself I wanted to be the one to tell her so I could beg her to hear me out, but I just stood there like a bloody waste of space and watched the girl I love be ripped apart by past mistakes. Maybe deep down I wanted Alyssa to tell her because I knew I couldn't. Opening wounds we just patched pulls us backward, and all I want to do is move forward.

The girls have long gone to class, and I've dropped Parker off for his first day, wishing him a good one and hoping he believed my fake smile.

I'm pissed. Pissed at Alyssa and pissed at Jason for taking me to a fucking strip club in the first place. Pissed at the bartender and waitresses who kept bringing me alcohol and pissed at myself for allowing everything to happen.

It's my fault Alyssa is out for Payson. She's still pissed about this summer. I thought we moved on after the last time. I thought it was over, sure she made comments and hung on me but I knew it was petty and her attempt to tease Payson. Alyssa has known since the beginning it was never her and never going to be her.

It's my fault I didn't say no to Jason. I wanted him to like me for some fucking reason I can't remember now that my fist connected with his jaw for offending my girl the very next night. It's my fault I kept ordering drinks. I thought it would help ease my mind. I was so nervous about slipping up and spilling everything to her brother that I drowned myself, hoping it would stop the bad choices.

It didn't and I made an even worse one. It was stupid to ever think a bloody stripper could make me forget my Jailbird when nothing else has. Of course that stripper had to be Alyssa's sister. Talk about adding a cherry to this fucked-up cake.

My phone ringing cuts the music in my ears. I think of ignoring it but it's my mum, and I know she is calling to check in on Parker. I push everything aside in hopes I can have a normal conversation with my mum.

My mum is like a bloodhound when it comes to her kids being upset, and an hour later, she's nearly got me in tears. I'm not a bitch, but I'm fucking lucky to have the mum I do. I've seen shitty mums in my lifetime. Payson's is a perfect example.

"You have to forgive yourself in order for anyone else to forgive you, son."

"I can't, Mum. You should have seen the look on Payson's face when Alyssa told her we had been together."

Most kids would find it awkward discussing this with a parent—it's not exactly comfortable, but my family has always had open communication. The way families are meant to be.

"It was a surprise, not a great one either. She's going to be hurt, but if you are hurting because she is hurting, who is meant to help her get better?"

"I don't know."

"You do, and it's you."

"She doesn't want to talk to me. I do not need to read minds to know that." For the first time since meeting Payson, I did not want to read her mind. I'm always curious what runs through her pretty head but not this morning.

"Maybe, maybe not, but you need to. You need to tell her everything, Ashley. You hid being a dad. You hid the situation with Alyssa. She keeps finding out your worse qualities by surprise. If you would show her them before that, it wouldn't be so catastrophic. Lay it all on the table, Ashley. You want a future with this girl, then invest in her like there's a future. Protecting her from your mistakes is doing no one any favors, son. Payson has had an image of you in her head since she was young, you sit on a pedestal for her and that is fine, but you need to show her you are human and despite all the mistakes and wrongdoings, it is her you choose."

I run a hand down my face and scratch at my beard, thinking. I know she's right. I guess I've wanted to protect Payson from the bad parts about me to live up to the unrealistic standard she set for me, but by doing that, I made things way worse because now she thinks I was hiding things for more sinister reasons. Lying about Alyssa makes it seem like there was bloody feelings involved. I want to punch myself.

"You need a haircut," Mum tells me a minute later.

I grumble an agreement.

Luca walks into the kitchen rubbing his eyes and scratching his groin. I'm thankful he's in underwear. He went to lie down after we got back but I couldn't. I had to bring Parker to school, but I stayed outside the school until the first bell rang, hoping I would see Payson and could pull her aside. I didn't. I saw her nana's car, but she must have already been in the school. I drove home, worked out, and have been cleaning ever since. That was three hours ago.

Luca walks past me to the sink, grabs a glass I just washed, and eyes my phone. His smile is huge when he sees who I'm talking to.

Luca became instant family the moment I brought him home during break from volleyball. Especially after we found out I knocked up his sister. He didn't know Parker was mine right away, he didn't know I had fucked his sister either and was not happy when he found out, but he came around.

I take my earbuds out and disconnect them so he can see and hear my mum squealing.

While he is chatting with Mum, I put dishes away, jumping into the conversation where I feel necessary. After another hour, Mum hangs up because Dad got home and they were going out.

I check my texts hoping to have one from her, but I find one from Parker instead.

Parker: American girls are obsessed with accents, why did you not tell me before? I would have been here ages ago.

Me: Please ace in something other than manipulating girls with your accent.

I chuckle and slide my phone across the counter to Luca. He reads it and laughs loudly. "Like father like son."

I grip the back of my neck. Those comments make me feel a way I can't describe. Like it's impossible for me to believe Parker is like me at all when he didn't grow up around me.

"He asked if Janelle was single."

Luca cocks an eyebrow. "I worry Janelle may be too much for my nephew."

I turn to grab an apple from the counter and snort. "I warned him the *second* time he brought her up. Seems his mind is made up, though."

"God speed be with him, then."

Me: Talk to me, babygirl.

Me: Payson.

Me: spend the night with me tonight.

It's been an hour since I sent the last text and I've lost hope that she will reply. Payson is a lot of things, and stubborn is one of them. It's a quality I love and hate about her. I love when it's not directed at me, not in this way anyway. I want her to want me, I want her to need me. I know she does, I just want her to admit it.

I've been angry all day, expected a call or visit from the mayor but nothing came. Yet. Something will and I will be ready. Alyssa is a good player but she's not worth ruining my team over. I got rid of her best friend because I saw the same qualities on day one.

My phone dings but I don't let myself get excited because that basic ringtone is not the one I have set for Payson. I pull it to my body anyway. Maybe it'll be a distraction.

It's a distraction alright, but not one I want.

Alyssa Burton: Can we talk?

Me: There is nothing to discuss. If you need to discuss anything with me, you can wait until practice on Monday.

Alyssa Burton: Ash, please. Talk to me and I won't bother you anymore.

I know her and I know how manipulative she can be, but the thought of her never bothering me about this summer, never trying to get between me and Payson again sounds pretty irresistible. I shoot her a quick call-me text, hoping this doesn't come to bite me in the ass.

A second later, my phone rings with a video call.

Leave it to Alyssa to not be happy with a regular phone call. I roll my eyes but answer anyway. Maybe if she sees how irritated I am, she will be less annoying.

Then I remember who I'm talking to and know that's impossible. I'll never forgive myself for this summer. If I wouldn't have been drinking so much that first night, this would have never happened. That was the start of my downfall.

The screen opens with Alyssa sitting against her fuzzy headboard. Her hair is wet and brushed back like she just got out of the shower. Her fake eyelashes make it look like she's wearing makeup all the time. I ignore the fact she's only in a robe and trying so hard to get me to see her cleavage by angling her phone down.

"Hey." Her voice is breathy.

"What did you want to talk about, Alyssa?"

"You're already being crabby with me," she pouts and my anger spikes.

"I'm waiting on a text. Please continue."

"Text from Payson?" It's not a dig at me or Payson, but a genuine question.

"Yes."

She shifts, noticeably uncomfortable with my honesty. Her voice sways as she sits up higher and raises the phone so her breasts aren't the main focus. Instead, it's her downturned face. I don't particularly enjoy seeing her eyes flood with tears but there is nothing I can do. She is hurting her own feelings, because I've told her since I woke in her room not knowing who she was that I was not interested in her. Sure, the other two times sleeping together might not have been great to tack on after, but I still made it very clear I was not interested in anything serious with her. If she decided in her own head there was a chance, that is not on me.

"Why her?"

"Excuse me?"

"Why Payson? Why not me? I'm legal. There would be no issue of us dating after the season is over."

This wasn't a question I expected—not from Alyssa, especially because it was never her. Even from the first night we were together it was never her. I called her Payson for bloody sake. I don't understand how she can ask that.

"Really want to know?" I'm giving her a last second to bow out. I'm not dancing around the question anymore. Not with someone who can't affect my or Payson's careers in a serious way. Alyssa is a lot, but I would like to think she has enough humility to not blackmail us. At least I hope.

"Yes, I need to understand because I can't on my own."

"Easy, I love her."

10

Payson

Alyssa's gasp is loud over Ash's phone, and I can't stop myself from smiling like a schoolgirl. I wasn't about coming over but if I'm being honest, I can't leave things like that between Ash and me. I can't walk away with all these questions. I need answers so I can have a clean break.

That was the plan when I came over. That was the plan when I heard Ash say Alyssa's name. I assumed the worst when I heard her voice over his phone. My anger roared to a boil, and I'll need to apologize to Luca because he came upstairs to check on me and I snapped at him, because I couldn't hear what was being said in the room. The anger isn't gone now, not completely but it's back to a simmer.

The door is cold against my ear, attempting to hear what else will be said. He already told her he loves me, so I definitely want to hear what is said next.

"It was never you or her, because it was never you. I don't understand why you are even asking the question in the first place when I made it clear that there never was or would be anything between us. And Payson's age is not of concern for me."

I love what I'm hearing but I want to see him, I push the door open with snail speed, glad it wasn't completely shut in the first place, not to disturb him.

I'm not the first woman to see Ash Pearson shirtless, but I'm so glad he's not right now. Alyssa has seen enough of his body for, well, ever.

His phone screen isn't clear from this far away but clear enough to see that Alyssa is wiping her eyes. I kind of thought things between them were superficial, but if Alyssa is crying, maybe it's possible she developed feelings during their time together, however long that might have been. I hate the thought, but I also can't blame her; Ash Pearson is amazing when he wants to be.

"I just thought that you would get over her. You would realize the age is a big deal."

I freeze halfway across his room and wait for him to answer her. He's standing at the foot of his bed, back to me—rigid and uncomfortable and not at all how he is when I'm around. I smile.

"Love is not just something you get over. Everything about her calls for me, her voice, her eyes, her smell. Her soul is an extension of mine. I love every single thing about her, and when she's around, I can think of nothing more. Practice is excruciating because all I want to do is grab her, hold her, and never let her go. You convinced yourself my feelings might change but they have been sure since the beginning. Payson is a drug and I'm a user, I can't let her go and I don't want to."

"So she's bad for you." It's not a question.

Ash sighs and runs a hand down his face like he does often. "Alyssa." He pauses and I take that time to walk in front of him and wrap my arms around his stomach. He tenses but a second later, he's sinking into me and pulling me closer.

"Hi, babygirl."

I tip my head back to see his phone but he crushes me back into him. "I muted it. Please tell me you're staying, because I need to talk to you."

I came in here expecting to officially end things, I mean that would make the most sense. He lied about having a son, he lied about whatever happened with him and Alyssa. I don't know if I can trust him but how can I leave when he said all those things about me? Maybe he knew I was here, maybe it was staged. Maybe Luca texted him telling him I was here and this whole thing was planned. Or maybe he means it. The way his body relaxed when I touched him makes me want to believe the latter.

I can't believe anything without talking and I can't talk while he's still on the phone with her. "Hang up, we need to talk."

Roughly five seconds later Ash is tossing his phone onto the chair behind him. He faces me from across the room, debating his next move and I give no hint on what to do. If I'm being honest, I like the uncertainty in his eyes. I even like the bit of fear he is holding in his stormy gaze. That means he is afraid of losing me like I am him. I'm still so pissed at him, pissed that he lied. Pissed that Maggie was the stripper. Pissed that both Burton sisters have got off on *my* boyfriend's dick.

Will this be something we can move on from or will it always be in the back of my mind? Right now, I don't know. It's still so fresh.

What about his whole ass son that is somewhere in this house? What about his baby mama? Is she in the picture is that yet another woman I have to compete with?

I don't want to compete.

"You're thinking too hard." His voice is like a bucket of cold water. Refreshing but also a reminder of everything.

"I'm trying to decide if the anger is something that will ever go away."

He deflates with my words. "I understand."

"Do you?" Tension settles between us. "Really. Do you? How could you? You're the only man I've been with. You're the only man I've ever wanted. For years I *obsessed* over you. I prayed to you. Like you were a god,

Ashley Pearson. I *worshipped* you. How could you ever relate to that when I'm no more than a notch on your bedpost?" My eyes fleet to the right, eyeing said bedpost and wincing.

"No one has been in this bed, this room, or this house. Only you, Jailbird," he mutters. He walks toward me. With each thump of his feet, anxiety creeps up my body, causing a cold sweat to coat my skin. He doesn't stop in front of me, but behind me, and his chest brushes the back of my head. His touch is electrifying. His fingers graze my thigh, outer hip, stomach, and up. "You think you are just a notch," he spits the words. "But you could not be more wrong, my sweet girl. You've had years of this *obsession*. I've only had months; but I promise, babygirl, in those months *my* obsession has grown at a rapid speed and our feelings are a mirror of the other."

My neck tingles when he kisses me there. "You're not the only woman I've been with." I can't stop the low snarl from leaving my body. He chuckles and his teeth skim my sensitive skin. "But you are the only one I've wanted this badly. I've had my fair share—"

"If this is meant to make me less mad at you, it's not working," I snap. "I don't want to hear about the sluts you've been with before me."

"Sluts?" He chuckles.

I pull away, and spin to pin him with my glare.

"How do you know they were sluts?"

I know I'm slut shaming these women for simply sleeping with him, but he is making me crazy. Logic is nonexistent in my head. "Because they aren't me."

He settles a heavy hand on my neck and strokes my cheek with his calloused thumb. "No, they weren't." He studies every inch of my face instead of settling in one place. "None of them matter. All that matters is we are here now, together.

"And I'm going to worship *you* until you forget about any anger you hold against me."

Ash picks me up around the waist and tosses me onto his bed. He climbs on next. His big body makes me feel even smaller. The closer he gets, the more I want to sink into his soft pillows. He must see it on my face because he stops, hovering over me, instead of diving into my mouth. "What are you thinking about, Jailbird?"

There was a time that nickname bothered me, but not anymore. It feels special, something between just Ash and me. He could call any girl babygirl, and while I still love hearing it, Jailbird is something only I will ever get.

"I'm debating if I want to push you away and leave or pull you closer." I twist my hands together, playing with his shirt when I do. "I'm still so mad at you."

I whimper when he slowly presses his lips to mine. He kisses me passionately and I eat up every bit of it. This could be the last time we kiss. It doesn't feel like goodbye, especially when my arms move of their own accord and pull him down on top of me. He still supports his upper body on his angled arms, but his lower body is pressed into mine, unmoving.

I sink my hands into his shaggy hair and fist it. He grunts when I pull but it only makes his kisses deepen. Every part of my body lights up.

Kissing Ash is like swimming in the ocean—in the dark. You're weightless, floating, but deep down you know there is danger.

Also, both make you incredibly wet.

"I know you're mad, Princess." He nips at my throat. "Take it out on me. Fuck me like you hate me and I'll make you come so hard you'll remember just how much you love me."

11

Ash

I EXPECT PAYSON TO take a second to agree with what I offered, think over my words, but she doesn't. Her kisses turn rushed, like if she doesn't kiss me, she will back out of whatever is on her mind. She attacks me like an insatiable lioness.

"Bloody hell."

The soft skin of her palm is like velvet wrapped around my hard dick. I haven't been this hard, well, since the first time we had sex, and if I'm not careful, I know I'll come prematurely, again.

Payson flips us over—with my help—so she is straddling me. She grips the bottom of her shirt and pulls it over her head and tosses it to the floor. I place a hand on her chest, stopping her from falling. As she heaves, her breasts press into my hand, but my eyes are pulled to her arms and the bright pink cuts.

Payson stutters over an excuse, but my hand wrapping around her throat cuts off anything she might come up with.

"What have I said about doing this to yourself?"

Nothing.

"Answer me, Payson. What did I say?"

Her lip disappears between her teeth. I tighten my hand on her throat. Even if she wanted to reply, she wouldn't be able to. "You bleed, I bleed. Remember?"

Her throat flares, attempting to swallow beneath my grip and failing. "Yes," she croaks.

I pull her face close to mine, loosen my hand on her throat, loving the way she sounds when she's gasping for air. I drop my voice. "If you want to hurt yourself, come to me. Let me do it because I can't watch you destroy your body anymore."

"O-okay." She rubs at her throat that looks so pretty with the outline of my hand. "But what will you do to make the urges go away?"

That's a good question. I actually am not sure. I suppose I could talk to Luca and ask what helped subdue his urges, or . . . "Lie down."

She blinks several times, watching me with bright eyes. "Why?"

"I'm going to fuck you how I should have fucked you the first time."

I don't know if this will help, but little by little, I will help fix my broken girl. I may have contributed to the cracks on her heart but I will never leave her broken. I will always heal whatever she needs healed.

"I might be the reason you bleed, but I'll be damned if I leave you broken."

Payson

Ash crawls up my body, kissing a trail the whole way, and spending extra time on each nipple. The way he mewls as he latches onto my hardened nipple leaves my clit throbbing for the same attention.

"The whole house is going to hear you scream for your *daddy*."

I shudder at his words, or the use of *that* word, and grip his hair to pull him to my throat. He twirls his tongue in the exact spot I want him to—because he knows me and what I like.

His breath is hot on my damp skin when he says, "You know I've never had anyone call me daddy before?"

My stomach flutters knowing I get at least one first of his. Sure, maybe a daddy kink wasn't what I had in mind—but it makes sense. Ash Pearson is definitely daddy material. "You're the first person I've called daddy in thirteen years."

He pauses making out with my neck. I bite back a smile when he pushes up to see my face. "It is not the time for your childhood trauma, Payson."

He cuts off my giggle with a hard kiss to my lips. "I've been dying to be in your pussy since the first time. You have no idea what it was like falling asleep knowing your tight cunt was just up the road waiting to be filled with my cum."

"I masturbated to you a few times." I promised myself I would never admit that out loud. I felt disgusted, well, no, it felt good in the moment but after, I hated myself for thinking about Ash in a sexy way when I was mad at him.

"It makes me want to choke you out for putting us both through that shit."

I scowl at him but he's too busy making out with my tit to notice. "You're the one that lied. You could have had this pussy everyday if you just didn't lie."

Ash opens his eyes and shoots me a stormy glare. He releases my nipple. "I lied for a good reason, Payson." Then he shakes his head impatiently. "Now, shut up and let me enjoy your body."

Ash-hole. Even when making me feel so good, he's still an Ash-hole.

Ash slips his hand between my legs, I part them, craving him inside. My body must not have gotten the memo, because when he enters two fingers, I seize up and a painful whine slips past my lips.

"It wouldn't hurt if you didn't make us take a break. This is your body punishing you. Now let me in, because my fingers are nowhere near the size of my dick, baby, and I promise sex tonight will make your first time seem like a walk in the bloody park."

"My body is punishing *me* for something *you* did?" I seethe. He twists his fingers inside me, stretching me. It's painful but better with each pass.

"Your body is on my side, Jailbird. When are you going to realize this? Your body calls to me. Like a baby bird to it's mum; your pussy is the waiting bird and my dick is the worm it's waiting for."

Did he . . . did he just compare our baby-making body parts to a baby bird and worm? "Are you drunk?"

He huffs and pushes onto his knees. "No, I'm fucking horny. Open your legs."

They are technically already open but I spread them farther on the deep blue silk sheets.

Ash tugs his shirt off and slips from his pants, and I'm happy to see he is going commando. There's something so naughty about it and I'm a big fan.

He settles between my thighs and with no warning, presses the head of his cock into my aching pussy. I gasp and must clench because he slaps a hand against the wall over the headboard and groans *loudly*, but it isn't a pleasure-filled moan, not completely. There is some pain mixed in. *Good.*

"Bloody fucking hell. Did you get tighter?"

"I don't think that's possible. Maybe you got bigger."

Ash keeps his hand on the wall but drops his head to look at me. "Maybe. That means you need to open even wider. Can you do that? Take all of me like a good little girl?"

My nipples prick with his words, my body shivers, and he slips in another inch. Ash smirks. "Still my dirty little girl." Another inch. "You're so fucking filthy, babygirl."

His hips rest against mine and he exhales a relieved breath. I suck one in.

"Your cunt is fucking *intoxicating*." He pulls out and slams back in.

I scream out, not expecting the sudden pain from his thrust. It's so much worse this time.

"Does it hurt?" He thrusts again, even harder.

I don't actually want Parker and Luca to hear me scream, but I don't know how I can keep quiet when it feels as if he is literally ripping my body in half. "Yes," I hiss when he thrusts three more times.

Ash's eyes darken, and he grins. "Good."

I look down, wanting to see just how my body stretches in order to take him. His stomach flexes with each harsh thrust. His dick battles with my body to enter but knowing it's my pussy that's making him make those sounds lessens the battle.

"You like watching your greedy cunt take all of me, babygirl?"

I nod my head vigorously. "Yes, *Daddy*."

He thrusts another time, the hardest yet, before settling deep into my pussy and staying there. My cervix is even taking a beating for him. "Too bad."

He pulls out and I whine at the lack of dick inside me. "What are you doing?"

Ash drops off the bed, stands, and stares down at me. Hunger still burns in his stormy eyes but there is a bit of indifference, and my stomach turns. "What are—"

"On your hands and knees, face the wall and stick your ass in the air."

I debate listening, but I'm desperate for his dick I will *not listen* some other time.

Ash settles behind me once I am the way he wants. He grabs my wrists and my face drops into his pillow. He folds them behind my back and holds them with one hand while spanking me with the other.

I shift my hips, waiting for another, but he drops onto my back instead, pushing my face into the pillow and his mouth by my ear. "I'm going to take your cunt as hard as I want, then you can ride me as hard as you want until all the anger between us is gone, do you understand?"

My mouth is covered but I nod my head and he proceeds. With a last kiss to my spine, Ash sits up and does exactly what he said.

He fucks me way harder than he did the first time. I didn't think he had held back but since my ass cheeks are sore from his hips slamming into them and my pussy aches for him to stop, I know he did.

I cry out but he continues. It's only when he grabs me by the hair and pulls me flush with his front that he acknowledges me.

"How's my pussy feel?"

"Hurts," I whimper. His thrusts aren't as hard with this angle.

"Are you learning your lesson?" He sinks his teeth into the curve of my neck. "Is you're angry gone yet?"

"Y-yes,"

"Yes, what?" he growls around my throat.

"Yes, Daddy!"

Ash slaps a hand down on my pussy before pushing me back down. He slaps me again. "Your cunt is so fucking nice, babygirl. I'm pissed you made me miss out on this for so long."

"It wasn't—" He smacks my ass again. I shoot up the bed at the sting.

"Say it was my fault. I fucking dare you," he growls.

I turn my head to glare at him. "It was."

"You really shouldn't have said that."

The slapping of skin on skin is mind numbing as Ash assaults my body. His balls slap against my clit but it's not enough to ease the ache between my legs.

"You had a son you didn't tell me about," I ground out. "It was your fault for our 'break.'" It wasn't even a break—we still saw each other every day. We just didn't fool around; he's being dramatic.

He pulls out and has me on my back and my ankles on his shoulders before I can even breathe. This angle is new, and I swear he's even deeper.

"Fuuck. I'm so fucking deep in your bloody cunt."

He is. So, so deep. It's so painful and I love it. Ash looks so hot using my body as he pleases. His hard body thrusting into mine, giving me everything. He's never looked better than he does right now.

My back arches when his thumb drops to my clit, swirling it. "Y-you're too deep. It's t-too much."

"Take me anyway. Take me like the dirty girl I know you are. I know your cunt loves it."

I do, I close my eyes and arch into his thrusts. I can focus on his thumb and the stimulation there verses how raw my pussy will be when we are done.

My orgasm builds in my entire body, starting at my toes and creeping up. The need to come doubles when he slaps me across the face and wraps that same hand around my throat. "Harder."

Ash roars, pounding into me. He slaps my face again and the burn is welcomed. Matches my ass and my pussy. My legs slip to his waist, and he drops forward. I dig my nails into his back and drag. He hisses.

"Do you love me yet?" he grinds out. His dick is throbbing inside me, I know he's close. His thrusts have turned to long, slow, deep ones. I settle into the bed, cling onto him, and rock my hips, meeting his thrusts.

"Make me come and we'll talk."

Ash grins against the side of my face. "I fucking love you, Jailbird. You and your smart mouth."

That pushes me over the edge, that, his dick, and his skilled fingers on my clit. Goosebumps coat my entire body and his dick throbs inside me, shooting his hot cum deep into my pussy and I cry out for him. For my *daddy*; over and over that word slips from my lips like it never has before.

Ash cleans us up with a washcloth from his bathroom before slipping into bed and pulling me against his chest, cuddling me like he's been waiting his entire life for this moment. "Are you feeling okay? That was a tad rough."

A tad is an understatement, but I liked it. "I feel good."

He kisses my head and I turn to kiss his chin after.

"I really did miss you, babygirl. You are not allowed to keep me away ever again."

"And miss out on moments like that?" I taunt. "Never."

His chuckle is deep and comforting, and that's how I drift to sleep. I came over to talk, but we can always talk tomorrow.

12

Ash

PAYSON IS STILL FAST asleep when I sneak from the bed. I had to roll her off for the first time all night, my girl loves to cuddle. Anytime I tried to roll her to her side instead of right on top of me so I could spoon her, she whined for me to roll on top of her. I worry I will crush her but she loves it, and if I'm being honest, I do too. I love feeling her pinned under me, even in my sleep. I love feeling her chest rise with each breath and knowing she is close.

I'm surprised at the two faces peering back at me when I walk into the kitchen after my workout. It wasn't an overly long workout because of the tournament today but it was enough to work up a sweat and pump my muscles. I slap the towel I was using to clear sweat from my forehead to my shoulder and head for the fridge, ignoring them until I get my protein made.

"What?" I snap because they haven't stopped staring at me since I walked into the kitchen.

Parker and Luca exchange looks, Parker is the first to look away—back to his plate of eggs, Luca is hiding a smirk behind his protein shake. Guess I know why there was a sweaty ass print on my bench now.

"Sleep well?" Luca asks.

I catch the hint of teasing in his voice, meaning he heard what Payson and I got up to last night, but I'm not embarrassed. It worries me that maybe the house isn't as soundproof as I thought. I don't care about Luca hearing Payson, but Parker shouldn't. That must be awkward for him. He's still not okay with us, and I know it will take time. Hearing her orgasm maybe isn't the way to bring him around to us as an actual couple. Doesn't help she was calling me daddy.

"Yes." I narrow my eyes and shake my head from those thoughts. I'll need to address things with Parker but not this early. "Did you?"

Luca snorts, but he nods. "Si, very well . . . after *she* fell asleep, that is."

Blood rushes past my ears, drowning out Luca's chuckles. Parker has a small smile on his face when he stands with an empty plate. He taps my back on the way to the sink like he's giving me congratulations. Does this mean he is over yesterday? *Did hearing Payson somehow convince him?* This is so fucked.

"Why wouldn't either of you let us know you could hear us?"

They exchange faces that look far too similar and it irks me. I've always thought Parker was more like Luca than myself, but Luca assures me Parker is a spitting image of how I used to be but more difficult to see given my size. Still, it causes a dull ache deep in my chest because their connection is stronger than Parker's and mine. I'm glad they are close; they are nephew and uncle, after all—but I'm his *dad*. I should be laughing with him about this, not Luca.

"And interrupt? No, fratello—not a chance."

To distract myself, I grab the pan Parker must have used and the eggs from the pantry to make my breakfast. I'll make breakfast for me and Payson since she will need the fuel for today and everyone else has seemingly eaten. We weren't up late or anything but fuck, it felt like we were having sex for hours. In the best way. If I'm sore today, I have no doubts she is too. Fuck, I should have thought about the tournament today, the last time we fucked she had a limp and last night I was rougher than the first time. "We need to leave in forty-five minutes so make sure you both are ready."

"Whatever you say, daddio." That was Luca.

"Go get showered, you're irritating me and it's too early for it," I grumble eyeing the clock on the stove in front of me. I'll need to wake Payson soon, make sure she doesn't need pain killers or anything, but with these two dickheads, I don't want her walking into a sausage fest first thing in the morning. Especially when they heard her come. Maybe I should have told her to be quiet but how can you tell the most perfect girl in the world to be quiet when she's coming on your dick? Short answer—you can't.

"You're meant to be a great mood after sex," Luca says. "But you're still acting like you have a stick up your arse."

"How would you know what you're meant to feel after sex?" I volley back, grinning to myself as I reach for the beans to plate our food. "Been a while since you had pussy, you probably don't remember what it feels like."

Luca argues something in Italian but I'm too busy to pay attention.

"Zio Luca is right, Papà. Nothing makes you happier than pussy."

I whip my head to the side to eye Parker with a cocked eyebrow. "Excuse me?"

He only rolls his eyes and pushes from the counter. "I'm sixteen, Papà. Not a little boy."

He might be sixteen but he's *only* sixteen. There I go again, being a hypocrite. How can I be upset over Parker having sex at sixteen when a freshly seventeen-year-old girl lies in my bed full of my cum? I just don't want the same fate for Parker, not mine with Payson but mine with his mum. "Are you safe when you have sex?"

Luca and Parker cringe and I can't help but blow out a laugh. "I know that sounded like a dad, but I don't want you to end up a father before you're ready, Parker."

"Like you?" he challenges.

My face drops to a stern frown. He doesn't look genuinely upset but Parker isn't the easiest person to read either. He's more sarcastic than . . . well, than Payson.

"Yes," I tell him honestly. I've been honest with Parker since the beginning. His mom might have wanted to keep him from me and told him crazy lies about his dad like he lives in a submarine and only came up every ten years, but I won't do that. After we met, Bella and I were honest with him about the situation. "I don't regret my decisions that caused me to father you, but I want you to think about it before you end up in the same situation as me. Do you want to be a Papà at the age of seventeen?"

"I wrap it, bene?"

I shrug and run a hand down my face. This is too much for five a.m. "Brilliant. Nothing to worry about, then."

"Rubbers aren't a hundred percent effective."

Now it's our turn to shoot Luca a look. He holds up his hands like a truce and the three of us go back to focusing on whatever we were doing before this conversation. Awkwardness has settled heavy over us like a blanket so I let out a sigh of relief when soft footsteps sound on the stairs.

The air shifts again when an eye-rubbing Payson steps into the room in nothing more than a t-shirt she must have grabbed from my closet. I want to take in everything about her, how cute she looks just waking up, the beautiful smile on her even prettier face—specifically for me. The awkward way she shifts, waiting for me to open my arms, and the fact my shirt has never looked better than it does on her. But I can't appreciate any of that because I catch Parker out of the corner of my eye and the look of absolute horror on his face feels like a punch to the gut. He obviously was not aware the girl he'd heard last night was Payson.

I've never introduced him to anyone, and this is awkward. Especially when Payson pads across the room with a limp and nudges into my arms. I, of course wrap her in a hug because I can't deny her, ever.

She pushes to her toes to kiss my jaw. Everything inside me calls to throw her on the counter and devour her bruised neck—but I don't. I stand there with a steeled spine, hugging her, one arm around her waist and the other hand resting on her ass to make sure my shirt doesn't lift too high.

"I'm sore." Her voice is extra raspy in the morning. My body lights up when her lips brush my ear. "And you left me."

She forces my eyes to hers without even touching me as she sinks back to flat feet. Her bottom lip is puffed out in a pout and my will power is crashing with every passing second.

I clear my throat and spin her in my arms. "You need to eat."

Payson is probably wondering why I pushed her away without actually pushing when she steps to my side with her brows furrowed. *Fuck.* This is hard trying not to offend my son and keep my girlfriend happy at the same time.

"What's for breakfast, chef?" Her voice is light. I'm thankful she has let it go, for now at least. Parker's eyes are burning into my back, and I can't focus on anything but that.

"Uh, toast and eggs."

Payson smiles but it falls when she looks to the two plates sitting in front of us. "What the hell is on my toast?"

Luca chokes on a laugh behind us. Payson jumps, realizing we aren't alone. Her eyes drop down her body, right to her exposed arms. I didn't think much on it since Luca has seen her scars, but Parker hasn't.

"Morning," she squeaks over her shoulder. She looks at Luca first, then her eyes drift to Parker and once again she stiffens. Parker's eyes drift down her body, his jaw clenched so tight his molars must be crying out for him to let up. I know mine are at watching them. Payson shuffles as she pulls her shirt down, but I see the longing on Parker's face as he looks over her round ass, he's a teenage boy. I can't fault him for looking but it doesn't mean I want to see it. "Hey," she breathes out and it sounds weird even to my ears.

Thankfully Luca picks up on it as well and drags her attention to him. "Good morning, coniglietta. How did you sleep?"

Payson tries to get the information on the nickname, but Luca holds firm. I finish with our plates before sliding them across to the two empty stools.

"Why don't you go get ready, son?"

He doesn't move right away but he doesn't argue. One more look down Payson's stiff body and he shoves from the counter and stomps upstairs toward the hall bath and slams the door behind him.

Luca smiles at Payson, she flashes a quick and very forced grimace before she slips onto the stool next to me. I could have my toast gone if my stomach wasn't twisting so bloody much.

"Seriously, what is on my toast, Ashley?"

"Beans. Very popular breakfast in England. Eat."

Her nose scrunches up. Luca is grinning ear to ear at her looking at the plate. "I'm not eating beans and toast. That . . . that doesn't even make sense. It's two carbs."

"Beans are a starch, now eat."

"Whateverrrr. I'm not eating that." She pushes the plate away and turns to me. "No offense to your country, but no. Gross."

"Payson," I scold. "Just eat it, it's good, I promise."

Her eyes flare and she bites her lip, so I know whatever crosses her mind is not something she wants to say out loud. I lift an eyebrow and point. "Eat."

"Ash, I'm not eating that. Seriously."

"It's not like the beans you are thinking of," Luca tries to help but she still refuses. She even goes as far as comparing it to a meal her granddad would eat when he was a kid—during the Great Depression. I ate mine, hoping her seeing me eat it would help, but she still refuses to even try it.

"Fine, at least eat the egg. Please," I beg, with the last bit of rationality I'm holding onto this morning.

She eyes it for a long time and eventually picks up her fork. I praise God when she takes three bites. It takes longer than I would have liked but eventually the egg is gone, the beans and toast are pushed nearly off the plate, not to touch anything, and her milk is gone. Luca tosses her an apple and she happily eats that as well.

"Come on, we need to get ready." I offer a hand. She slips her small hand into my large one. I kiss her knuckles and turn for the stairs, planning on heading to my bathroom so we can shower and get dressed. And so I can wash off all the emotions from this morning.

13

Payson

If I thought it was awkward in Ash's kitchen this morning with Parker, it's nothing compared to the car ride. We are sitting in the back of Ash's car, he wasn't happy about it, but it obviously makes more sense for Luca to sit in front with him. The back seat is an okay size, I mean, Ash and I have fooled around back here but right now, it feels the size of a shoe box. Who knew being in a small space with someone who hates you could be so suffocating?

"Are you ready for today?" Ash has been trying to keep conversation going the whole two hours we've been on the road, and it works when his questions are directed at Luca, but I can't manage more than a word or two. Better than Parker blatantly ignoring him.

"Yes," I tell him. He catches my eyes in the mirror, his eyebrows are bunched with stress. Things with Parker are bothering him, he didn't talk much during our shower, but I can tell anytime Parker ignores him and his shoulders deflate.

"What are you going to do about Alyssa?" *Why not move from one miserable conversation to the next?*

"I don't know."

"She punched me."

Parker pipes up for the first time all morning and of course it's annoying. "You punched her back?"

Annoyance hits me hard. Seems to be a Pearson thing, or whatever Parker's last name is, to defend the princess of Bayshore. "Yeah, because she's a bitch."

Luca's deep rumble hits my ears a lot better than Ash's grunt of irritation. I said I had to be a team player, I'm not around my team right now and even if I was, Alyssa is a bitch. At least Luca is on my side.

"Well, whatever, it's not like I thought you were going to do anything, anyway." Instead of arguing, his hands turn white from choking the steering wheel.

Ash-hole.

"Alright, ladies, yesterday didn't end how we wanted but it's a new day." All eyes look between me and Alyssa on complete opposite sides of the circle. "A fresh start, and I want everything from yesterday behind you. I want your only focus to be going on that court and doing your best. We can take home gold today and I expect it."

"Yes, Coach."

"Good. Now go warm up with Coach Luca."

Janelle and I pair off to start our warm-ups.

After peppering, we move onto spiking drills. Luca tosses the ball and I bump it for Shannon to set to the rest of the girls. It's going great until Alyssa's turn. She spikes it just fine but as she's circling back to the line, she "trips" and slams into the side of me just like Thursday at practice. Only this time, I feel a popping followed by excruciating pain when we land on the floor, her on top of my knee.

"Oops, sorry." Alyssa leaps to her feet, not affected at all. She flips her blonde ponytail over her shoulder and prances back in line behind the rest of the girls.

I catch Janelle's wide eyes while I try and not freak out about the pain radiating from my knee. She steps toward me, but I shake my head, subtly telling her to stay put. My leg is bent the wrong way but it's not bad enough to worry me too much. The pain is mind-blowing, but I can't let my coaches see. If they think I hurt my knee, I won't be able to play today and I have to play today. Especially Ash, he is wildly strict about caring for your joints.

I sit up on my ass, trying not to look at my leg but it's impossible. The shooting-pain is still there and it's already swelling. *Dammit.* I shoot a murderous glare at Alyssa and for once, she doesn't return it. Worry is just barely marring her face but it's there. That pisses me off enough I clumsily climb to my feet, trying not to use my left leg but also keep it subtle.

A warm hand engulfs my arm, lifting slightly so it relieves weight from my left side. I don't meet his eyes.

"How bad is it?"

My leg isn't the only thing burning now, my eyes flood but I don't let him see that either.

"Payson," he demands. "Can you put weight on it? Did you tear your ACL?"

His questions aren't helping me forget about the injury. Seeing my leg swell so much so soon makes me want to throw up. If I tore my ACL—that's it. That's the season. I refuse to lose my season because of Alyssa fucking Burton.

I roll my shoulders and step on my leg, giving it my full weight. It hurts, holy fuck, it hurts but it's bearable. The question is, can I play on it? If I tore my ACL, I know I won't be able to shuffle side to side, dive, or crouch. I'm a Libero and all those things are very important.

The gym has gone silent; all eyes on me.

"Talk to me, Pay."

"I can play, I just . . ."

Coach removes his hand. I lied when I thought my complete weight was resting on my leg; without him holding me, my complete body weight settles and I wobble, a lot, but I don't fall. I *don't* fall. Okay, that's good.

"Take a step, Payson." His voice is hard, but also full of worry. I wish it wasn't. If he's worried, it means . . . I take a step and my knee buckles, and I drop. I'm not able to stop the scream erupting from my lips this time. It only lasts a quick second, but it is enough for Coach to grab me under my shoulders and lift me. Janelle is on my other side and between her and Coach, they don't allow me to place any pressure on either leg. He is holding my leg so carefully I want to scream and tell him to stop treating me like a baby. They help me off the court and carry me to the medic waiting patiently on the sidelines.

For the first time in a long time, I close my eyes and pray.

14

Ash

"IT'S NOT TORN, YET," The doctor says while eyeing Payson, then me.

I let out a relieved breath. The last thing I want for Payson is to be stuck wearing a knee brace for the rest of her life whenever she wants to move more than walking. If we both have fucked-up knees, who is meant to crawl on the floor with our kids? I shake the thought away and look to Payson to see how she is taking the news.

Ever since I pulled her from the tournament, she has held the same emotionless expression. She refused to come to the doctors until after the tournament, as much as the medic at the tournament said she should. She wasn't about to leave her team. I made her captain for a reason but the boyfriend in me hated that she struggled to get anywhere all day; especially when she refused anyone's help—when she refused *my* help. The tears that never fell but stayed hanging in plain sight when she wasn't able to join her team on the court was like a bloody arrow through my chest.

Hearing her ask when she can play again and the sinking of her shoulders when the doctor looks to me instead of answering might be worse.

"Pay—"

"Doctor," she urges. "When can I play?"

I bite the inside of my lip and fist my hands.

"I would suggest this season be ove—"

"That's not an option," Payson snaps. "So, what *is* my option? *How* can I play?"

He flips between the x-rays and MRI they did. I'm not sure what he is looking for but he spends an eternity looking. He purses his thin lips. "I suppose if you wear a knee brace it should hold your leg stable enough—"

"How do I get one?" She looks at me for the first time.

I clear my throat. "Mine was custom made. It took weeks to get."

"I need to play now."

I sigh and look to the doctor, hoping he can give my girl some good news. I don't know how smart it is playing on a strained ACL, but I can't fucking stand the look of disappointment in her eyes. If I have to watch her from the bench like I did today for the rest of the season, I will lose my fucking mind.

"We can send you home with a stock size today until your custom comes in. I will have it sent to your local hospital and the orthopedic surgeon will make sure the fit is correct."

Finally, Payson smiles. It's not big and it doesn't meet her eyes but it's better than nothing.

He measures Payson's legs, the good and bad to see how bad the swelling is. He frowned, so I'm thinking it's not great, but Payson is happier now, so I'm *happier*.

I'm not happy. Far from happy, and Alyssa and her dad will receive a visit from me as soon as I have Payson settled at home, but for now, my main focus is Payson. The way I like it.

"You didn't have to do that," Payson murmurs as we walk away from the desk in the doctor's office. "Pay for the visit. I'm technically covered under my mom's insurance." Her eyebrows furrow. "I think."

Now that we are in the hallway and no one knows who we are, I thread my fingers between hers and cup her cheek with the other hand. I stroke her soft cheek and stare into her big green eyes. "You will share my name one day, Jailbird. It does not matter if it's five years from now"—*it wont be that long*—"or tomorrow. What's mine is yours."

She sinks into my hand and flutters her thick eyelashes. "I secretly like when you talk like that."

I chuckle as I lean in and kiss her forehead. "I know you do, babygirl."

"What are we going to do about Alyssa?" Luca mutters.

I glance in my mirror at the sleeping girl in my back seat. She passed out right after we ate. She insisted on going through McDonald's and used her injury as leverage, so after she polished off her cheeseburger and gave her extra fries to Parker, they fell asleep. I'm doing my best to ignore how close they are. Her head is on her pillow in the middle and his is still on the seat but one bump away from falling next to hers. I don't know how they are comfortable since they are still buckled but fuck, if she doesn't look so cute. Her leg is stretched out between my seat and my door. Her foot is swollen but I'll get her my ice machine and hopefully that will work. The doctor said ice for fifteen minutes every hour but my machine will do better than an ice pack. Even if it's not torn, we will do our best to keep it that way. If that requires a little over the top protection than so be it.

I sigh and bring myself back to present time. Luca eyes me from his side but waits patiently for me to get out of my head. He's used to it when Payson is around. It's hard to focus on anything but her. "I do not know."

"We have to do something, Ashley. She purposely hurt her teammate. *Again.*"

I clench my jaw. "You think I don't know that? That *teammate* is my *girlfriend*."

"La tua ragazza? Is it finally official?"

"Official enough." I eye Payson again with the need to touch her. She's talked about how she worries I might not be real, but she has no clue I feel the same way about her.

I've waited thirty-three years to feel a love like this. Grew up watching the best love story between my parents. My sister found love in grade ten and they are still together. My grandparents were married until death. Everyone around me has been in love, and I've watched and waited for my moment, sure it would never come. Then a short brunette with eyes so green and mesmerizing walked into my life, and I felt it instantly. I wrap a hand over her bare foot and squeeze gently, wiggling her light blue painted toenails. As long as Payson is in my life, I know everything will work out.

I hate leaving Payson; I want to be there to wait on her hand and foot, but I know her granddad will do a brilliant job caring for her while I deal with the Burtons. I called Chuck after the short talk with Luca, telling him we needed to meet. He tried to tell me he was busy, but I wasn't buying that shit and told him to clear his schedule because I was coming over and speaking with him—schedule full or not. Alyssa has gone too far. Payson could press charges, and I almost wish she would. I'm sure the gym has cameras. I'm not sure how clear it would be, but Luca said it was obvious Alyssa's "trip" was on purpose. She was in major pain when we finally got home and that was the only reason I didn't mention pressing charges. I'll tell her it's an option she has and I will support her no matter what. I don't want to see Alyssa get in trouble per se, because I know how her dad will act, but I won't sit back and watch her hurt the people around her. Especially when Payson is one of those people. Alyssa needs a reality check, and I'm going to give it to her if no one else will.

I park next to the black Range Rover and cut my engine. I should have changed from my team windbreaker before coming here but I just wanted to get it over with. Luca wanted to come too but I asked him to stay home with Parker. He doesn't need a babysitter but he's in a new house in a new country. I don't like leaving him alone if I don't have to, and I can handle this meeting without Luca.

I only have to knock two times before the door flies open and a short, round woman stands behind it not making eye contact.

Normally I might greet her but not today. I'm feeling extra combative, and it wouldn't be fair for me to blow up at her.

"Mr. Burton and Mr. Gilbert are waiting in the den for you, Mr. Pearson," the woman tells me softly.

Chuck *and* Jethro? I want to roll my eyes. Somehow Jethro is always fucking involved with shit. His nose is always where it shouldn't be. Ever since that first day with Payson and the way he was looking at her, I haven't liked him. It wasn't like Chuck, and I can't put my finger on the look in his eyes when he was watching Payson, but it wasn't normal, and I am not a fan.

My trainers squeak with every step across the original wood floors. The walls are a matching wood, and it makes the big room look even bigger. The ceilings are also wood but so tall it doesn't shrink the room either. Their entry looks more like a ballroom than an entry. Chuck throws enough parties that I have actually seen it used as a ballroom once. A beautiful house with a wretched family living inside of it. There are not photographs anywhere, only adding to the coldness of Chuck's heart.

I hate him.

I drum my knuckles against the large door at the end of the first hallway on the right. I've been in here one other time to "toast to me being the coach." It was really a way for him to butter me up in a lame way to get his daughter on my team. I made it clear that my team could not be bought and whoever made my team would need to earn it. He laughed but it wasn't a nice laugh. Alyssa only made my team because she was good, unfortunately, and had nothing to do with her father's attempt at bribery.

It takes longer than the front door but eventually the wooden door in front of me opens. It's not Chuck who opens the door, instead is a young redheaded female. Definitely not his wife. I've met her—once, it wasn't a great experience, considering she threw herself at me. This girl looks the opposite of her right now. Terrified and *young*. Not illegal young, but early twenties, at most. Chuck is not younger than fifty and age gaps shouldn't disgust me but anything involving Chuck is fucking gross.

"Ahh, Ashley." I hate when he calls me that. It's my name and my family uses it. Even Payson when she's annoyed with me but I'm okay with that. Chuck, I'm not okay with. I introduced myself as Ash and I know he uses it as a weak attempt to manipulate me. Like *I know you hate it but I'm going to do it anyway just to show I'm a dick*. I grew up with money, nothing like this but enough to have grown up around people like the Burtons. They act as if money makes them invincible but eventually money stops saving you, and I can't wait for their downfall. He's a mayor. He's a mayor who owns a few businesses in Bayshore. You can't convince me he isn't sitting pretty on dirty money, and eventually dirty laundry must be aired.

"Chuck." I dip my head and step through the door.

His eyes crinkle because he hates that name, probably more than I hate him calling me Ashley.

His name is Charles Brian Burton and he goes by Brian or Mr. Burton in public. I just don't care.

My eyes dart to the other two females in the back of the room sitting on a couch looking just as terrified and young—lacking decent clothing like the redhead scurrying across the room to join her friends.

"Like what you see, Ashley?" Chuck drawls.

I shake my head in disgust. I'd like to know why he has three girls, in less clothing than appropriate, hanging out in an office with two, now three old fucks waiting on them hand and foot.

Which leads me to "Jethro," I greet him with the same animosity as Chuck.

He doesn't even bother opening his mouth. I receive a single nod and that is all. His face is like a mirror of Payson's from earlier. Stoic and obviously unhappy but hiding it with *nothing*.

"Please sit, Ashley. We were having a meeting, but it can wait since this was so important."

Chuck walks behind his desk. Another power move, one I also use on Payson, but not because I'm a wanker with a small dick and trying to make up for it in my ego. I just like to see her eyes dilate the way they do when I'm in power.

I take a seat in the empty chair next to Jethro.

"Sasha," Chuck barks, eyeing something over my shoulder. I glance and find the eyes of one of the girls, this one blonde, a few years older than the redhead but still young. *What the fuck is this?* "Get our new guest a drink please, sweetheart."

I drag my eyes back to Chuck because seeing the fear in the girl's eyes is enough to send a chill up my spine, and I don't want him knowing that. I land on Jethro instead. He's staring at me, anger seeping from every pore on his body. I wonder if he's pissed I interrupted whatever the fuck their weird "meeting" is or if it's something else. I'm not utterly repulsed by Jethro, I can't place my finger on it but he doesn't give off the same vile vibe as Chuck. But he is constantly hanging around Chuck, so maybe he is as bad and is just better at hiding it.

The blonde he ordered stops by my side, and with a shaky hand, she passes me a crystal glass with an amber liquid in it. I take it from her with a quick "Thanks" before I set the glass on Chuck's desk.

His weak jaw ticks but he brushes it off with a fake smile. "What was so urgent you needed to see me on a weekend, Ashley?"

"An incident happened at the tournament today involving your daughter."

"Yes, I recall her mumbling something about her tripping. I had Louise check her over and she is fine. I appreciate you checking in on her, but a call would have been just fine."

I have no fucking clue who Louise is and I don't care. "Alyssa isn't the injured one."

His cold blue eyes tell me nothing about what is crossing his mind. "Then who was?"

"Payson Murphy."

Jethro shifts next to me as soon as the words leave my mouth. His phone comes out of nowhere and he rapid texts on it, still oozing that same anger. Chuck looks the opposite of angry. He looks . . . proud almost. No wonder Alyssa is a royal bitch. Her dad is king bitch himself. Who the fuck is happy when someone else gets hurt? Even if he doesn't care about Payson, he should be worried why I had to drag my arse over here.

"And Payson's injury has to do with my daughter how?"

I straighten my back. "We have good reason to believe Alyssa purposely *tripped* which resulted in Payson straining her MCL and ACL. A very serious injury," I clarify in case he's as stupid as I think and doesn't understand.

He still doesn't lose his stupid fucking smirk and I want to bloody punch it off of him. "Why would Alyssa hurt someone if there was a chance she could get hurt as well? That doesn't sound very smart."

Yeah, no shit. "Precisely."

Finally, his smile fades. "You come into my home, accuse my daughter of purposely hurting her teammate, and now you're insinuating she is not smart? Some nerve they teach you in Britain, *init*?" He attempts to mock my accent but I do not say *init*—ever. I lean back in my chair and give him back that same smug smile.

"I said no such thing. You thought I said it which tells me all I need to know on how *you* think of *your* daughter."

I might not care for Alyssa but fuck, having a dad like the piece of shit in front of me would be enough to send me over the edge.

"I will not have you tell me what *I* think about *my* daughter," he snaps.

Jethro stiffens next to me, lifting his eyes from his phone for the first time since I said Payson's name. I wonder if he's going to pull the lawyer card. Make sure no charges could be pressed or some shit. Fuck, I didn't even think about that. Truthfully, the girls in the back threw me off and that's probably what Chuck wanted. Fucking bastard but a grade-A manipulator. That is something Alyssa and him share.

I push to my feet, he does the same, but he could have stayed seated with the height difference between us. I'm mid six foot and I would doubt he's even six feet. "I came to warn you about the repercussions from this because there are some. Alyssa is not invited to attend Week of Pink with the team, and she will sit the bench in team apparel, not uniform, and take book until I believe she has become a team player." Which will probably be never. Luca and I want to kick her off the team, but we are already so low on numbers, and with Payson's future unsure, I can't afford to lose a player. Even a cunt like her. It will kill her sitting the bench, so hopefully it will be the wake-up call she needs.

The more seconds that pass, the more his ugly mug turns a deeper shade of crimson. "You will not bench my daughter."

"Luca and I agreed. Our minds are made up."

Chuck's large nose flares and I bet if this was a cartoon, smoke would shoot from his red ears. What an unpleasant sight he is when angry. "I am the mayor of this town. My daughter will continue to play and that is final. I will make her apologize to poor Payson but removing Alyssa from her last year is not an option."

Poor Payson? Fuck no. "Do not pity my player because of a choice *your* daughter made." I roll my knuckles and lean across the desk so he has to bend his neck to look at me. "You may be the mayor and you can run this town from your iron throne but within those four walls, *I'm* in charge. I call the shots and I say Alyssa's season is over. Actions have consequences and since you refuse to teach her that, I will"—I drop my voice—"and *that* is final."

Chuck is shaking with anger when I turn for the door. The redhead from before jumps up and sprints over in front of me and pulls the door open.

I walk out without looking back.

No one has stood up for Payson. No one has been around or cared enough to advocate for her, so I will. I can't punish everyone that has ever hurt her as much as I would like to, so Alyssa sitting the bench is the least I can do. It's not like she doesn't deserve it. Any other team, she would be kicked off. If this was professional, she would be in jail. I know if any legal stuff came up, Chuck would make sure nothing happened to Alyssa, so I will not convince Payson to press charges as much as I would like to. With Payson's past, it might be better to keep her out of anything dealing with the law.

I want to smile thinking about the meek girl doing her best to hide her ankle monitor and failing miserably from the beginning of this season. If only I knew what was in store for us back then.

I pull the door open to find two people making out on the porch. The girl is blonde in a black silk robe and the guy looks like he rolled out of bed and threw on half an ill-fitted suit.

They don't hear me and if they do, they don't care or stop making out. I step around them, but as I do, a feminine hand snaps out and grabs my arm.

I look down almost expecting Alyssa but find an older version of her instead.

A semi-familiar face.

I swallow hard and fist my hands.

"You're Ash, right?"

That voice. I step back and scowl, making her hand fall from my arm. The guy still has his hand possessively around the girl's waist like he's worried I will steal her away. *Trust me, kid, I'm not interested.* What he doesn't realize is by tugging on the robe, he has loosened the tie around her midsection and the robe hangs open about two inches. I keep my eyes to her face because I have no interest in seeing her body. Again.

"You are. I remember you." She laughs carelessly.

I cringe and turn for my car.

"You can come back anytime, you know! Just request Mercedes."

"I won't, thanks."

Soft footfalls hurry after me, and all but running to my car doesn't get me away quick enough before she is throwing her body at me and pressing herself to my front. "It's not fair my sister got the real thing and I didn't," she pouts.

I push her off and throw my door open as a barrier, shielding her mostly exposed body. "I am not interested," I snap. *What the fuck is with the Burton girls not taking no as an answer?*

"You're kind of rude." Maggie, I think Payson said her name was, twists her swollen lips from making out with the poor guy awkwardly standing on the steps. "There's no way Payson Murphy's pussy is as good as mine. I can promise that, *Coach*."

It's been a long day. That's the only explanation as to why I snap a hand out, wrap it around her throat, and lift her so we are eye level. She's on the taller side so her toes just barely leave the ground. "You and your sister keep talking about *my* girl in a negative way and you'll find out how *rude* I can actually be." I let her drop not caring if she falls or not. "Stay the fuck away from me *and* Payson."

I fall into my seat and slam my door. Anger simmers deep inside me because this is yet another thing I've caused because of my stupidity. Alyssa causes enough problems without her sister doing the same. I know nothing about Maggie, but Payson seems to hate her even more than Alyssa, so I'm assuming she's not the logical sister.

I slam a hand into my steering wheel. I keep causing drama for Payson. She has enough without me, yet I keep putting a fucking target on her back. I wish I was a better man to leave her and let her live a happy life without me—but I'm not.

My passenger door flies open and I'm ready to punch someone, I don't care who it is. Until Jethro's face is the one I see. I don't particularly care for him but he hasn't pissed me off, today. Besides, punching a lawyer probably wouldn't work in my favor.

"What?" I snap so he knows I'm not in the mood.

"We need to talk." He sounds equally angry but I think that's just him. I have no clue what he wants to talk about, or what could have made him so pissed.

"I'm not discussing Alyssa and the season anymore. I've made up my mind and I don't often change that."

"It's not about that."

I narrow my eyes. "What is it about, then?"

Could he be thinking this is a way to get his daughter back on my team? Because I just said my word is final, like it was when I kicked Olivia from my team. I haven't regretted it once, and I would never take her back. She was even worse to Payson and way more unstable than Alyssa. I can't risk anything more happening to my girl. I refuse to keep putting her in harm's way.

"If it's about Olivia, I don't—"

"It's not."

Not about Alyssa, not about Olivia. What the hell else could he need to talk to me about? I catch sight of the two people still on the steps, making out once again. "If this is about Maggie, I have no control over that. Speak to her father if she's breaking a law by dressing like that outside of the house." He falls into my seat and slams the door behind him.

"I don't give a fuck about the Burtons. And Olivia is happy where she is. Drive."

Jethro Gilbert might even be a bigger asshole than me. Probably the same height and size. He's covered in tattoos that just barely peak out from his all-black suit. His brunette hair is always gelled back, and his face gives off a don't-fuck-with-me look. Payson says I'm moody—and I am when it comes to her, but Jethro is on a whole other level. Like if he smiled, hell would freeze over and birds would fall from the sky.

"Stop fucking staring at me and drive."

I throw my car in drive, not because he told me to but because I don't want to be here anymore than he obviously does. "What about your car?"

He waves me off, typing on his phone. "I'll have someone pick it up for me."

"I have plans, so what do you want? I'm not replacing Alyssa with Olivia if that is what you want." I eye him from the side as I pull up to the gate. Jethro rolls his window down and without a word, the guard opens the gate. I'd love to know what this dick's deal is. He seems to have ins everywhere.

"I'm not bringing Olivia back to this hellhole," he deadpans.

Okay, then what the fuck is he doing in my car?

Jethro slides his phone into his jacket pocket and sighs while scrubbing a hand down his sharp jaw. "You seem to care for Payson Murphy."

I pull my lips into a firm line. "She is on my team, yes."

His green eyes burn into the side of my face. "More than a coach *should*."

It's not hot in my car but I'm fucking sweating. Most people I would probably tell them exactly how much I care for Payson, but it doesn't seem smart to admit to a lawyer about my inappropriate relationship with a player.

He continues, not waiting for my answer. "I'm going to give you the benefit of the doubt and say you are not a pervert who is preying on a younger girl." He pauses dramatically and I stay perfectly still, only focusing on my driving. I don't know where I'm heading because I was heading to Payson's granddad's but I'm not bringing Jethro Gilbert with me.

Figuring I need to say something, "Payson has had a hard life. I think she requires more guidance than the rest of my team, yes."

"I agree. Which is why I'm in your car."

What does he mean he agrees? What does he know about Payson? "What is it you want to talk about, then?"

"I want to talk about Payson."

15

Payson

Having a strained MCL and ACL sucks. I can't imagine them being torn. Ash is being such a baby and hardly letting me practice. I agreed to sit out the games this week, and since we don't have any games this weekend, I have plenty of healing time before Week of Pink. Unfortunately, that leaves me riding the pine with Alyssa, but surprisingly it hasn't been that bad. She hasn't really talked. That's been the best part of this whole thing. Alyssa genuinely acts like she feels bad. Not that I care, I want her to feel bad. I want her to feel more than bad, terrible actually.

I use the handrail on the bus steps to help me up. A small hand grabs my arm as if they are attempting to help me too, but failing. I know it's not Ash, so I assume it's Janelle, but when I look back, I see blonde hair, just not my best friend's golden blonde.

"Don't fucking touch me."

Alyssa rolls her eyes. "I'm just trying to help, Murphy."

"You want to help?" I snap. "How about you go back to Saturday and not *tackle* me and cause this." I point to my stupid leg. I'm wearing sweatpants so you can just barely see the stupid brace under it, but I know she knows it's there because she winces like I hit her. "Why don't you just leave me alone and stop trying to ruin every single part of my life? Your entire family has spent so much time doing your best to hurt me. When will it be enough?"

A single tear tracks down her face but she's quick to push it away. Her back steels but she says nothing.

What is there to say? It's true. Our whole childhood her sister bullied me, and when she got sent away, Alyssa took over like it was a position that needed filled. Their bullying hardly affected me because of what was happening at home, but they sure tried. When they weren't coming after me, they were going after my best friend. Never Ronni, always Janelle.

Now they know what is important to me: volleyball and Ash, and they are going after both. "Just leave. Me. Alone. If we ever talk again, it'll be too soon."

I drop my eyes to my team behind her waiting to get on the bus, meeting a sharp gray set of eyes last. He dips his head as if approving of my words. I don't need his approval but it's nice he finally seems to see how big of an issue Alyssa is. I was shocked when he announced that she would sit the bench the rest of season or "until she proved to be a team player." Well, she never has before, I don't see it happening now. *"Actions have consequences and no one on my team is exempt from them."* Alyssa's head was bowed the whole time, so it was obvious her suspension wasn't news to her. I thought Janelle's jaw was going to drop to the floor though.

I fall into my seat in the back of the bus. We are such a small team, we each get a seat to ourselves. We have to stop and eat but then I plan on curling up with the blanket I packed and napping. My sleep has been shit without volleyball wearing me out.

I've thought about texting Ash to come over so he could lie on top of me and I could actually get some sleep, but I can't do that for many reasons.

"I'm proud of you," Ash mutters from his seat behind me.

I wish I could tell him how those words make me feel. How my throat grows tight and my skin prickles. I can't put that into words, so I just say a basic "Thank you" instead.

The driver pulls away from the curb once everyone is seated. I didn't think about the fact he probably saw and heard everything with Alyssa—shit, I hope he doesn't tell my grandpa I was cussing, I know he goes to his church.

"Listen up," Ash announces in his coaching voice. I jump in my seat, not expecting to hear his voice so loud. On the way here, he spoke softly in my ear. "Week of Pink is soon, and as you know, it is in California." The bus fills with cheers. "Yes, very exciting." He doesn't look or sound excited at all. "But it requires money. The tickets have already been purchased, thanks to an anonymous sponsor—but we need hotel fee, food, and we need to pay for the bus that will shuttle us to and from the gym. Meaning, we need a fundraiser." Ash places a heavy hand on my shoulder. "Your captain was responsible for coming up with an idea, but I did not like her ideas.

"No offense," he adds after my team stops laughing at me. "I have come up with an idea and have already made the preparations so, even if you are not a fan of my idea, I do not care."

"What is it?" Janelle blurts.

Ash thins his lips like he always does when it comes to Janelle. Like a worn-out parent. "Well, with the help of Janelle's mum, Mrs. Wick"—when I look at Janelle, she shrugs obviously having no idea about this—"and her being good friends with the owner of an up-and-coming clothing boutique downtown, she asked if my girls would be interested in a fashion show. All eight of you will be participating because it was too late to tell her I only have seven girls flying to California."

Excited murmurs fill the bus and Ash explains that we will model her clothing and the audience will be bidding on the outfits. We will get half of whatever the outfits sell for. Apparently, the up-and-coming boutique is known for having expensive clothing so we should make good money. The issue is—it's a fucking fashion show. I play volleyball and wear sweatpants as much as I can. My body is not meant for expensive clothing. I'm not like Janelle, Ronni, or Alyssa—or actually anyone else on my team. They are all tall and thin and I'm . . . not.

"What the hell were you thinking when you agreed to that?"

Ash looks down at me as we walk off the bus to head to Pizza Hut. His eyebrows furrow like he doesn't know what I'm talking about, but he's fully aware what I'm talking about, he's just being his usual Ash-hole self.

"Ashley," I hiss. "You shot down my ideas for a-a freaking fashion show?"

"Yes."

"Well, I'm not doing it." I cross my arms over my chest.

Ash spins and pins me against the side of the bus. A hand on my hip and the other gripping my hair. He smashes his mouth into mine, and my head slams against his hand and into the bus. He licks and nips at my lips, not letting me breathe until my head is spinning.

"You do not get a choice. You are a part of my team, and my team is walking." His tongue is hot against my lips, making the cold air even colder when he pulls back. "Understand?"

I'm still catching my breath but grab each side of his windbreaker and pull his warm body back against me. "If I say no, do I get more of that, *Coach*?"

My center throbs when he pushes his hips against my stomach and the rigid length of his cock presses into me.

"If you walk in the show, you can get whatever you want, babygirl."

I sink my hands into his soft hair and pull his face back down to mine. "Anything?"

He lets out a groan-moan mixture when I drag my tongue across his bottom lip.

"Anything." His voice is strained. I love that I affect Ash as much as he affects me. It makes me feel so powerful that I have this giant of a man wrapped around my finger. If I asked him to get on his knees and lick my pussy right here . . . I bet he would. I'm so tempted when his tongue swipes across his bottom lip and the sparkle of the silver ball in his mouth grabs my attention.

"I want you to eat my pussy."

His gray eyes blaze with need. "Now?" He removes his eyes only for a second to look around. We are on the opposite side of the bus so we are hidden from the eyes of the restaurant, and behind Ash is a thick line of trees. He probably could eat me out right here, but I shake my head. "After the show. Like an award. I walk the show and you eat me out after." It's so cold you can see our heavy breaths but neither of us are in a rush. I trail my finger down his neck and over the patch with the team logo on his pec reading the word **COACH** under it. "Maybe I can tell my grandpa I'm staying at Janelle's but go home with you, and I can spend all night returning the favor." My hand drifts south over the belt on his black slacks and down the length of him. He's so hard. "What do you say, *Coach*?"

He blows out a hard breath. "I say you are in for a long bloody night with everything I have planned for you."

I whimper against his mouth and hot liquid pools between my legs. I'm not wearing underwear and it slides down my thigh. "Maybe I can just come over tonight?" It's a school night but I'm so desperate, I'd rather go to school on no sleep than have to wait. I grab his hand and lead him into my pants.

"Fucking hell, Jailbird. You're dripping down your leg." Dragging a hand up my thigh, he cups me. He doesn't move but the roughness of his palm feels good enough—especially when I move my hips.

"I'm so horny." And pathetic, but he's the one that makes me pathetic.

He groans the sexiest sound. "You and Parker have school and I don't want to keep either of you up all night."

I tilt my head. "Why would Parker be kept up?"

His lips curl back over his bright teeth and he chuckles. My stomach twists waiting to hear what he will say, because he's smiling like the freaking Grinch when he was planning on ruining Christmas. "You kept Luca and Parker up last time."

Horror fills every part of me. "I what?!"

His fingers curl and invade my body, he does a swipe, then pulls his hand out and brings it to his mouth and sucks. "You're loud, babygirl." I'm so embarrassed . . . mortified really. My boyfriend's friend and his son have heard me come. Well, no wonder Parker hates me. He heard me calling his *dad*, daddy.

Reading my mind, Ash pins me against the bus again. His head drops and his lips brush my ear. I shiver despite still feeling embarrassed. "I like that you're loud. Makes me so fucking hard hearing you scream for *me*."

"I'm so embarrassed."

"Don't be, we're all guys. Hearing a girl moan with pleasure is never a bad thing." He tenses and I know he regrets the words as soon as they leave his mouth. "Hearing *you* moan is never a bad thing."

"Too late, Ash-hole. Let's go before someone comes looking."

We get to the front of the bus and Ash drops his hand from my back. I miss his warmth right away. "What are you doing?"

"Payson, I have a raging boner I can't walk in there with this." I smile, seeing the large bulge in his pants.

"Stop smiling."

"What are you going to do?"

He shrugs and shoves a hand through his hair. "Think about my nan or some shit, I don't know, just go because it won't go away with you here."

His grandma? Weird but okay. I walk back over to him. His eyes are hard, much like his dick when I brush my fingers over it.

He hisses. "Stop."

But I don't. I drag my hand up and down the length of his dick. I love the sounds he's letting out. I love that his head falls back against the bus and he doesn't push me away.

His pants are so soft I'm able to feel where his shaft starts and his tip ends. I use it to my advantage and cup my hand around it and jack him over his pants.

"Payson." His throat bobs and his voice cracks. "Stop, fuck, stop." But he doesn't stop me. Ash could easily push me away, grab my wrist and force me to stop but he doesn't, and I keep going.

"Are you going to come?" I whisper, hoping he says yes.

He doesn't say it.

He fucking *whimpers* it. "Yes. Fuck. Make me come, baby." God, hearing him whimper for me the same way I do for him makes me stroke him harder, faster. I want so bad to take him in my mouth and make him whimper again, but I really want to make him come in his pants.

His breaths grow shallow. He's moaning my name and other vulgar words with it. He's never looked hotter and it's all because of me. Ash has shoved his hand in my pants and made me come against my will so many times, it's only fair I return the favor.

"Come for me, *Coach*. Come because your player is stroking your big cock where anyone could walk up and see us."

The bus rattles when his fist slams into the door. "Don't, stop. Don't fucking stop, Jailbird."

With that nickname, something inside me bubbles. I shift closer, craving more closeness from him but keep pumping my hand. My arm wants to cramp but I am not stopping until he spills in his pants. I open my mouth but nothing comes out. It's on the tip of my tongue, but I'm scared. I don't want to ruin the moment. His moans are louder now, so loud that if someone came outside, they would probably hear him. I still don't stop and that bubbling in my throat boils over.

"I'm not, *Daddy*."

It catches us both off guard when that word comes out. The other night was a fluke, I thought. Something that slipped in the middle of an orgasm. My hand trips up but Ash is quick to throw his hand over mine and keep it going.

"Make your daddy come, baby."

Ash isn't the only one whimpering now. Not even three pumps later, he grunts. His eyes pop open and he glowers at me down his nose. A familiar look etches his face that's so. Fucking. Hot. He thrusts his hips and I know he's coming. My hand stays on his dick until his hand falls away.

Ash grunts when I touch the tip of his penis. I can't see it with the badly lit parking lot but there is a definite wet spot. I guess it's a good thing his pants are black.

"Happy with yourself?"

I nod encouragingly. "Very. Did I do good?"

Lust flares but his dick softens under my touch. It's not often I get to feel it soft and want to leave it that way.

With a lazy hand, he pulls my forehead to his lips and murmurs, "So fucking good." I burrow into his body—without the distraction of Ash coming, the cold air is biting through my clothes. Now that I think about it, my knee is hurting too. "But you're definitely going to pay for making me bust in my bloody trousers." He grips my hair and tilts my head back. A wicked smile on his face. "Remember what I said the last time you almost made me bust in my pants?"

I swallow.

"You made *Daddy* make a mess in his pants. On your knees, babygirl."

I back away because I know we've already been gone a long time. Way longer than explainable but also because the predator look in his eyes is frightening in the best way. That excitement that bloomed in my stomach forever ago, the first time I sucked him off, is back and double what I felt before. Except I forget I can't walk backward. I stumble but Ash is quick to catch me with an arm around my waist.

He doesn't pick me up, instead drops his forehead to my collarbone. He sucks in a deep breath. "You're so fucking lucky your knee is protecting you from what I want to do."

I chew on my lip and giggle. "Yeah, what's that?"

It's not Ash that answers. Someone clears their throat and when I look the way it came from, I see we aren't hiding behind the bus anymore. People inside wouldn't be able to see us but someone standing in front of the bus can.

Mr. Burton is watching us with a nasty smirk. Everything in my body goes cold and not because Ash is quick to stand us up and let go of me completely. He steps in front of me, but it doesn't stop the shiver that racks my body from the look on Mr. Burton's face. Like a stray dog looking at a steak and not in a good way.

"Payson, go inside," Ash demands.

There's no room for argument in his voice, not that I want to. I hurry as fast as I can, making sure I take the long way around the back of the bus because I don't want to walk past Mr. Burton. I don't look back and throw the door open. The smell of garlic and tomato sauce makes my stomach growl.

Janelle is walking by from the bathrooms. She eyes me with a wild look in her eyes. After a quick glance to the dining room and seeing no one noticed my entry, she pulls me the way of the bathroom. I have to tell her to slow down, which she does.

She locks the door behind us and spins to me. "Are you guys crazy? You've been out there like fifteen minutes. The food has already been delivered."

Fifteen minutes? That's all? It felt like way longer, if I'm being honest. "I know." I breathe out an exasperated breath. "Trust me, it wasn't planned."

"Well, spill the details because I covered for you."

"Jay," I scold.

She scoffs. "Come on, Pay. I've gone so long without sex I'm pretty sure my hymen has grown back and I'm once again a virgin."

I burst out laughing. I love how Janelle can always make me forget whatever is on my mind—like Mr. Burton. "I just kind of gave him a handy."

Excitement dances in her eyes. "Uh-huh and?"

"That's it. I mean he came in his pants bu—"

She gasps and even bounces in place. "Oh my God! Like his black pants? Is he going to walk in here with a wet spot? We have to go see!" She spins and flicks the lock so fast I go dizzy but I'm able to grab her arm and stop her from leaving. "I don't know because Mr. Burton walked up on us. Not like during anything but he was, uh, nuzzled into my chest. Obviously not like a coach would be."

Janelle's eyes drop. "I don't blame him." I shove her and she laughs. "But that's scary as fuck. What did he say? Is he going to report Ash?"

Oh, my word, I didn't even think about that. Things are so easy with Ash I forget our relations aren't meant to happen for a reason. "I don't know."

Janelle's smile sinks into a frown. "Mr. Burton is the grossest piece of shit out there. No way he can report Ash for *hugging* you."

I want to tell her it was more than a hug and I'm not sure how long he was actually there watching us, or how much he saw—or heard, but I need to make sure Ash is okay.

We exit the bathroom, and to my surprise, Ash is sitting in a booth with Luca and Parker, laughing about something. No trace of anything bad like the possibility of him being arrested. Also, he's wearing a pair of gray school sweats now. I let out a deep breath.

Janelle claps my back. "One of these days, you guys' luck is going to run out. You need to be more careful, Pay."

"I know," I tell her. I do know, he just makes it so hard. When we are together, I don't remember our ages, or the repercussions of what could come if our relationship became public anytime soon, but I need to remember because it's a very real thing. I don't know what happened with Mr. Burton, he's no where in sight but Ash is happy, so I'm hoping everything is okay. I have a sinking feeling in the back of my mind that it's not.

"Bummer I don't get to see the evidence of what you did, though."

We are laughing when we walk up to the table with my teammates.

"Where the hell have you been?" Monica asks, announcing my entrance to the whole dining room. It's our team and a few families. Ash glances my way and winks.

I let out yet another sigh. Maybe it really is okay.

"Found her stuck on the shitter," Janelle tells everyone.

I shoot her a glare and elbow her stomach. "I was on the bus icing my knee. Coach waited for me."

Alyssa rolls her eyes but I ignore her. Everyone else, those that don't know the truth, seems to believe me, so I take my seat next to Mika and ignore how easy it has become to lie to everyone's face.

16

Payson

THE BOUTIQUE IS NICER than I expected. I'm not sure what most high-end boutiques look like but I didn't expect white marble floors, matching white marble walls, gold accents, and crystal chandeliers. At least not in Bayshore. I look down at my clothes. I knew we would be given clothes to wear but I look like I'm lost with my black yoga pants and a gray school sweatshirt.

People walk around setting up but not a single person I recognize. Bayshore isn't a huge town, so it's weird not to recognize at least one person when you go somewhere, and the ten or so people walking around in full black outfits don't look the least bit familiar.

"Yes, can I help you?"

I do a double take at the woman walking toward me in the highest heels I've ever seen and maybe the tightest off-white dress as well. It hugs her body like it was sewn just for her and her thin figure. Then I realize it probably was. She gives off an expensive aura; I'm sure all the clothes she wears are tailored specifically for her. A mix of Heidi Klum with Serena van der Woodsen's hair.

"Miss?" Her voice is less friendly since I haven't answered and have just been staring at her like a freak.

"Uh, yeah, I'm here for the—" *Why does saying fashion show sound so ridiculous?*

"Yes, the fashion show. Everyone else is in the back." Her lips twist and she hasn't lifted her eyes from my body and the unimpressed pinch of her face leaves behind an ugly feeling of self-awareness. Because I'm fully aware I wouldn't look like she does in anything I put my body into.

"You can join them . . ." It sounds like a but is coming and I brace for it. Thankful the door behind me opens, someone steps inside but because I'm so close, their body brushes against mine. I yelp and do my best to jump away only to meet Ash's stormy eyes when I do.

He stares at me for a second longer before lifting his eyes to the woman next to me. I want to shove her away to bring his eyes back to me.

"I'm Ash Pearson. I'm assuming you must be the owner, based on Mrs. Wick's description." *What the hell does that mean? What did Janelle's mom say?* He extends a big hand. "We emailed a few times."

Great, she has his email. *No one emails anymore, Payson. Stop it.*

Ash might not be affected by her but she's definitely not immune to him.

"Yes!" *Where was that excitement with me?* "Chanel." She slips her dainty hand in his. Of course her name is fucking Chanel. "I had no idea *Ashley* Pearson was a man. An extremely handsome one at that."

Oh for fuck's sake.

Ash grimaces when she says his name. They are still holding hands and I want to take the pen from her hand and stab his eyes out. "Ash, please." He drops his hand.

Chanel giggles like she's twelve and no joke, flips her hair over her shoulder. "Of course, forgive me, I'm just so blown away by how handsome you are."

Two times she's called him handsome in the span of one freaking minute.

Once again, he ignores her. Instead turning his attention to the room. Looking at the catwalk and the fifty or so white chairs that surround it. Nerves settle in low. The walkway isn't long, but the longest I've ever walked on. Which is none.

"Place looks great. All my girls arrive?"

As if she forgot what we were here for, a slight frown pulls on her bright red lips. "Yes, I've sent them to the back." Her eyes fall to me.

"You can join them." More like *get out so I can continue to seduce your coach*; I think not.

"Thanks, but I'm waiting on my friend. She had to grab something from her car." I give her my best fake smile and even tilt my head, really leaning into the sweetness.

Right on cue, the door opens, the annoying bell above it dings, announcing Janelle's entrance. Right behind her, Parker and Luca saunter in. I worry Parker's eyes might pop out of his head when he sees *Chanel*. Luca, on the other hand, strides forward and shakes her hand confidently.

"Payson."

Ash stares at me with a frown nearly mimicking my own. "Let me help you to the back. I notice you're limping."

I'm not and he hasn't seen me walk but I don't disagree. The longer he's with me, the less time he will be with *Chanel*. Janelle stays back to wait for her mom, leaving me and Ash to find our way.

"Excuse me?" I stop one of the workers buzzing around to ask where we go since Chanel wasn't specific. What is with everyone in this stupid place looking like they stepped right out of a *Vogue* magazine. "Where is the back?"

A smile teases his full lips. "Through there," he says, pointing at one of the two double doors on the farthest wall. "If you hit an exit for outside you've gone too far."

"Thanks."

"Sure thing, beautiful."

Did he just call me beautiful? I stumble over my feet and hiss at the pain. Ash grips my arm and tugs me forward while lifting weight off my left leg. "*Beautiful.*" He scoffs in what I think is meant to be an American accent.

Should have known he wouldn't let it go. Fine, two can play that game. "*Wow, you're like, so handsome,*" I mock in my best valley-girl voice. She didn't sound valley but it makes me feel better.

We reach the door and Ash cocks an eyebrow. "She did not sound like that."

"You would know."

Ash chuckles softly. He glances around before lifting a hand and pushing a piece of hair behind my ear while tilting my chin to look at him. "I wish you wouldn't get jealous, but I must admit I love how cute you are when you do."

"How can I not?" I grumble. "Look at her." My eyes dart across the room back to Chanel, Mrs. Wick, and Janelle. All three look like they belong here, like they are all cut from the same cloth.

"Look at you," Ash tells me pulling my eyes back to his. He lowers his hand because it's not appropriate, but his hard eyes keep me locked on him. "You do not see how effortlessly beautiful you are to me."

I want to believe him, but how can I when he looks like . . . holy shit, he looks amazing. I was too busy in my jealous rage to even appreciate Ash right now. Of course Chanel was all over him. I've seen Ash in gym clothes, no clothes, semi-dress clothes but Ash in a full-on suit . . . *damn.*

His pants are tailored perfectly for his thick thighs and cut off just above his sleek black shoes. He's wearing a blacked-out dress shirt, black necktie, and a black suit jacket. He looks like he works for the Mafia, and I couldn't be more turned on.

"Like what you see, Jailbird?" His voice is a raspy whisper.

I nod my head, knowing no words could come out, even it I wanted them to. He looks like a million bucks and I . . . I look back at Chanel again. I bet if they stood side by side, she would be the perfect height for him in those heels. He wouldn't look like a dad picking up his kid from school whenever they are together. She's closer to his age and *hello, beautiful*. I know I'm not ugly but there are multiple kinds of pretty and her and Ash are the same kind of pretty.

"It's you who will be taking it off me tonight, babygirl." His lips brush my ear. He straightens and adjusts his tie. His pupils are dilated, and I bet if I looked down, he would have a tent in his pants that wasn't there before.

"Put that away before someone gets the idea it's for them."

He chuckles, angles his body away, and does that. "I'm wearing compression shorts because I knew it would be hard to hide seeing you, I guess it did not work."

I have to smile. I have no doubts he's actually wearing compression shorts. If there is one thing I can count on, it's that Ash will always have a boner for me.

Janelle pops out of nowhere, startling Ash and me. "Ready to model?" she squeals. Ash covers his ear closest to her.

"Not even a little bit."

She grabs my arm and tugs me close to her, then she eyes Ash. "She's mine for the next couple hours. Hands off."

He scowls. "Payson is mine at any and all times of the day."

My stomach flutters. As if he can hear it, he winks. "Have fun. I love you."

A cloud of hair spray lingers well after everyone's hair is complete. I'm not sure why so much hair spray is required for basic ponytails—I'm convinced mine will forever be slicked back on my head and never be the same. At least there will be seven other girls with the same issue.

Now we are waiting to be assigned our outfits. Everyone will be given two outfits to wear and try and sell. Chanel and another girl have us standing in a row and are going down the line, deciding who will wear what. The girl with her is less intimidating because she is a few inches shorter but just as beautiful. Shoulder-length brunette hair styled with loose, beachy waves. Her eyes look to be brown and as cold as Chanel's blue ones. Same thin body and style of clothing but with deep skin. Chanel has changed into what I assume is her show outfit, one long sleeve and the other side is sleeveless. It's jet black and complements her pale skin and bright hair amazingly. Tight in the bust and waist but a little flowy on the bottom with a slit down one side that starts well before her hip bone, making it very obvious she's not wearing anything underneath. *I hate it.* Not really, she looks stupidly stunning and I'm jealous. Her friend is in a red silk gown that looks like melted wax over her mocha skin, hugging every single small curve on her body. Spaghetti straps and a straight neckline that still shows off a bit of cleavage.

By the time they reach me, I'm feeling sick to my stomach thinking about walking in front of people who will see that everyone else pulls off these expensive outfits better than me. If I sell even one outfit, I'll be shocked.

"Payson," Chanel reads off her board in a monotone voice. Much less enthusiastic than she was with the rest of my teammates. I know why I don't like her, but I don't understand why the feeling is mutual.

"That's me."

Her beady eyes narrow. She lowers her clipboard to the side and tilts her head as she looks over my body. I'm trying not to be self-conscious but I'm in a bandeau bra and a thong like the rest of the girls and she's fully clothed, high heels and all. I keep my arms glued to my side.

"You'll need to wear heels. Probably five-inch to even make you close to the rest of your squad."

"Team," I correct her. Squad sounds stupid.

"Whatever." She looks to the brunette next to her and orders her to go get some kind of heel. The girl leaves without a single word, and Chanel spends the entire time she's gone staring at my body like I disgust her.

"I don't wear heels. I'll never make it down the catwalk."

She puffs her bottom lip out in a condescending way. "Then I guess you won't be walking."

She's far too happy about that.

The brunette pops up with the shoes in question.

Hell no. How is anyone meant to walk in them but especially someone who has never once worn heels? Not to mention my knee.

Frick. I forgot about my knee. One thing the doctor said was to not wear any shoes that could cause me to tweak my knee. If any shoes will do that, it would be these. I didn't bring my brace because it would just be walking in a straight line. Not like I could wear it even if I had it. Chanel has an issue with my height—something I can't control—a huge black mechanical thing on my knee wouldn't make the cut. If I refuse, then I don't walk. The green monster inside me hates that thought. I don't want to walk but I want Ash to see me in pretty clothes I will never actually wear again.

I rip them from her grip. Somehow the brunette knew my size, while the shoes are ridiculously uncomfortable, they at least fit. It took longer than I wanted but somehow, I get the shoes on by the grace of God himself and maybe a little stubbornness. When it comes to straightening my back, that's a whole other thing. But I do it and don't let it show even for a second how uncomfortable or excruciating painful it is on my knee. My knee wasn't swollen today because I spent the morning with it up and iced—Ash's request—but I have a feeling after tonight I'll need a whole ice bath to calm the swelling.

Chanel gives me a tight smile. "Perfect." She could create diamonds with how much pressure she is putting on her jaw right now. "Lilly." I guess that is the brunette's name—perks up. "What do you think for Payson? Make sure to notice how far her hips stick out and how her breasts sag."

Fucking bitch.

Lilly takes in my body with the same unimpressed expression as Chanel. "I think a two piece would benefit her. Balance out her curves but it can't be pants because of her height, so a skirt. I might suggest our *Alexa* skirt."

Chanel taps her thin lips with a single finger. I can't tell if she agrees or not, she's not giving anything away. She walks around my body like she hasn't been staring at me for the past five minutes, and stops right behind me. "You should tell your boyfriend it's not classy to leave behind bite marks."

Ash knew about the fashion show so he knew there was a chance they would be visible. I almost smirk thinking about him biting me so everyone knew I belonged to someone. I quite enjoy Ash's possessive side.

Eventually she makes her way back in front of me and orders Lilly to grab some things which she returns with in record time. Thank God, I'm ready to have Chanel's attention off me. They hold up a few different outfits and eventually decide on a black snakeskin skirt and matching black cropped sweater. My second outfit is a short green crushed velvet dress. I already love the looks of the dress but I'm nervous to try it on. It looks small, and even though the material is soft, I'm not sure it will stretch enough for my hips.

Chanel leaves to greet the audience, with some bullshit, I'm sure, leaving the rest of us to get ready. Apparently all the first outfits are black and the second are a range of styles and colors of dresses. Janelle's first outfit is a pant suit and I'm extremely jealous. She's already dressed by the time I can even get my shoes off so I can actually move to get dressed.

The pants wide leg make her legs go on for days while the top is completely lace with a small triangle bra over her boobs. With the dark smoky eyes and nude lips we are all wearing, she looks ready for fashion week. "I can't believe how good you look."

Obviously feeling good, she strikes a pose, then another. "Get dressed so I can say the same. Not that your bra and panties aren't doing it for me, because they are." She pumps her eyebrows twice and crudely gestures with her hands like she's squeezing my chest. I swat her away with a laugh.

I'm reaching for the skirt when someone throws down a pair of black tights and a bra. "Put these on first, then your skirt and top. Tuck just the very front of the sweater in your bra to show this." Lilly holds two fingers about two inches a part and then places them on my stomach. Her fingers are freezing and my stomach flexes when she touches me. Her eyes flick to mine. Something in them makes me feel weird, so I look down to see what she's looking at but realize I don't have to look. It occurs to me she is staring at my scar. I forgot that was there. I'm more surprised Chanel didn't mention it since she had no problems mentioning my weight in front of everyone. Or the ones on my arms. I did my best to keep my arms glued to my side so no one would see but it's still possible she could have.

"Just make sure the scar isn't visible." Her words are soft but her eyes are still ice cold. I don't get the same bad feeling about her as I do Chanel. I wonder if her bitchiness is a front. Not that she's overly bitchy per say, just straightforward, I guess? "All of them."

Swallowing hard, I instinctively cross my arms behind my back. With a tight voice I say, "Okay."

She nods and backs away to help Mika with her outfit. Chanel was the most excited about Mika's body and took the second longest amount of time deciding what she would wear. I took the longest but not because she thought everything would look good on me.

I'm pulling up my skirt when someone bumps into my back. "Sorry," Alyssa mutters.

The skirt is tight, like no way I could sit down in this, but I don't look like stuffed sausage so it's fine. Actually, I feel kind of sexy. That's not a feeling I feel . . . well, ever.

I reach for the sweater, but someone passes it to me instead. I don't tell her thank you, I just stare at her while she stares at my outreached arm. I rip my arm back after a second and scowl. "Mind your business, Alyssa."

"I wasn't going to say anything." I hate how soft her voice is. I hate not hearing her snap or be a bitch. This version of Alyssa, the quiet one who hands me my clothes and doesn't steal them away, is confusing and more uncomfortable than her seeing my arms.

"What is your issue?"

The muttering from the other girls stops. Alyssa nervously looks at them, then drops her eyes to the ground. "Nothing."

"Bullshit. You've been quiet and not bitchy. It's uncomfortable."

She gives me what I think is meant to be a smile, but fails. "You want me to be a bitch?"

"No, I just don't want you to act like this. It's annoying because I'm the one hurt and you are the one pouting."

Anytime I mention my injury, Alyssa flinches—this time is no different. "I didn't mean for that to happen."

"Yeah? Well, it did."

"Will you get to play the rest of the season?"

"Yes."

Alyssa chews on her bottom lip, obviously wanting to say something.

"Spit it out, Burton."

"I'm not ready for my playing career to be over." Her voice is vulnerable, more than I've ever heard.

"What can I do about that?"

She huffs, it's killing her having to be nice. Having to ask me for a favor. "I was hoping you could talk to As—Coach."

I want to claw her, hearing her slip up on his name. "And you think I can convince him to let you play again?"

Her eyes sag. *There's the old Alyssa.* "Yeah, I think *you* can."

She's right, of course. I probably could. "I don't know if I want to. How can I trust you won't hurt me again when I get back to playing? Or someone else on the team when they are having an off day?"

"I guess you just have to trust me."

I laugh, I don't mean to—but I do. More of the old Alyssa comes back and she crosses her arms over her chest. "I will never trust anything that comes out of your mouth, Alyssa." Her anger fades again and my heart squeezes. I don't know if I would say I hate Alyssa, I don't like her and if it wasn't for volleyball, I wouldn't be talking to her, but the truth is—she is one of the best players on the team. If we want to go far this season, we need her. Especially with my knee. I bite my lip, then blurt as she's about to walk away. "Fine."

She pauses. "I'll *talk* to him but I can't promise anything. Coach Pearson might be the most stubborn person I know."

Her lips quirk. "I know. Thanks."

She has to throw it in that she knows. Ugh. I'm already regretting this.

"There's a couple things before I fully agree."

Alyssa mutters something under her breath but faces me and shrugs. "What?"

I take a minute to think over what I want to say. I'm on a power kick lately, first with Ash in the parking lot and now holding Alyssa's destiny over her head. I kind of like it. I like it a lot.

"You'll be a team player, I mean, really. No more bitching at us, no more condescending remarks to anyone on the team over anything."

"Fine."

"You will not hurt another person on our team no matter how bitchy you are feeling. I won't have an injury on my conscious because you can't control your emotions."

Alyssa levels my stare with a silent acknowledgment and my power kick continues.

"Apologize."

"What?"

"Get on your knees and apologize to me." Adrenaline courses through my entire body. I don't know what it feels like to be high, but I imagine it's a lot like watching a defiant Alyssa Burton drop to her knees in front of you, ready to apologize. "I'm waiting."

"I'm sorry," she snarls through clenched teeth.

The rest of our team stands behind her with wide eyes and gaping mouths, watching the scene go down in front of them. I feel bad so I grab her arm and pull her up. I even help her dust off her knees. Like me, she's wearing a skirt and top but her skirt and top wrap around her body with peekaboo pieces showing through on her slim stomach.

"I just wanted to see if you would do it." I snort when she's done fixing herself.

"I still hate you."

I smile a genuine smile, and I'm pretty sure I see her lips twitch too. "Me too."

Lilly rushes through the curtains, telling us five minutes before disappearing again.

"Better get those heels on, Murphy."

I roll my eyes but she's right. I really, really don't want to but I don't have another choice. "You dress like a hooker most of the time, right?" I'm joking but she takes it in stride anyway with an easy agreement. "Teach me how to walk in heels."

"In five minutes?"

"Yes."

Alyssa sighs. "Okay, but you can't be a smartass."

As if.

17

Ash

HAVE WOMEN ALWAYS BEEN this desperate and I've been blind to it? Or is Chanel just extra? I'm thinking a little of both, but she's relentless. I don't know how I can make it more obvious that I am not interested. I was ready to fake sickness and leave but I can't do that because I have to see Payson.

That's why I agreed to do all this in the first place. That, and this will be a good confidence boost for my girls. I don't care who you are, all teenage girls need a confidence boost every now and then, and what's better for that than getting dressed in nice clothes and walking on a catwalk at the center of attention? I don't actually know if it's good for that, but Mrs. Wick said it would be, and Payson trusts her, so I will do the same.

It's been announced the show will be starting soon, so I make my way from the bar to my seat. I was hiding at the bar from Chanel because it is farthest from the back where she keeps having to disappear to.

Luca catches up with me halfway across the room with a knowing grin. "Enjoying your fan club?"

"Fuck no. Jarring as fuck."

He muffles his chuckle with the back of his hand when we get to our seats and read our names; I want to bash my face in seeing the name next to mine. How did she do this so quickly? We met an hour ago and she's been busy with the girls for more than half of it. Parker is already sitting in his seat on the other side of me playing on his phone, so I tell him to switch me. He looks at the name next to mine and he jumps from his seat excitedly.

I glance at Luca and can't help but matching his smile. "Eager, are we?" I ask and take my new seat.

"Have you seen how hot she is?"

There's no denying Chanel's beauty, and Ash Pearson a few months ago would appreciate her eagerness and maybe even give some back. I'm not him anymore. She's nothing compared to Payson, and seeing Payson so easily dismiss herself earlier is exactly why we are here. She doesn't see herself the way I do. Probably never will, but if she can even see an eighth of what I do, maybe she won't be so quick to assume I have a wandering eye.

Chanel is older, she's had years—of most likely getting any guy she's wanted—of compliments. Luca mentioned her being a retired model, so she's had years in the spotlight with all eyes on her. Payson has had none of that. I'm in her life now and will tell her daily how beautiful and bloody brilliant she is until she believes it herself, then I will tell her just because she deserves to hear it.

"She is alright."

Parker mutters something about being blind but I ignore him. He doesn't understand and I'm okay with that.

Chanel saunters onto the stage yapping about the turnout and since the audience is beneficial to me as well, I'm actually happy about that. She goes on talking about mundane things like how she came across fashion; an excuse to talk about her modeling career. Which she does for ten fucking minutes. I am zoning out when Luca nudges my arm. Chanel takes her seat next to Parker with a disappointed look on her face, I ignore it.

One by one, my girls walk down the catwalk. They look beautiful in the clothes picked out for them. I'm happy they kept it classy and not at all how Chanel dresses; they are teenagers, after all. The most surprising part was how natural Emika walked. It was like she was a trained model herself. She really came to life up there, and for a second, it felt like I had made the best decision doing this. Until Payson stepped from behind the curtain.

I'm not even sure what she did could be called a step, more like a stumble. One that left her wobbling; I was tempted to go save her but she eventually found her footing. She still doesn't move, though. Payson stares out at the audience with a face of mortification mixed with . . . pain. My eyes drop down her body noticing the swelling in her leg from here. *Who the fuck put her in those shoes?* I don't even have to ask because I know. Chanel must have been able to tell my feelings for Payson because she was a bitch to her from the beginning. Somehow, I keep making enemies for Payson without even trying.

Another minute goes by and the murmurs pick up because Payson still hasn't moved. She's shaking like a leaf and her fucking knee is twice the size of the other one. At least she looks amazing. Amazing is almost an insult for her right now.

Breathtaking, stunning, gorgeous. Every good word is how she looks standing on that stage. The skirt hugs her round hips like it was bloody made for her and the cropped sweater is the perfect touch of Payson. She doesn't wear makeup a lot and I love it, but I can't help but appreciate the subtle smoky eye that makes her large eyes look even bigger. Also makes her look older. Like it's almost a glimpse into what the future will look with a mid-to-late twenty-year-old Payson. Beautiful. The thought of watching her become this version. I can't wait to watch every version without rushing to them. While I don't particularly love that she's jailbait for me, I love her, so I love everything about her. I can admit things will be much easier after her next birthday, though.

I am too busy picturing my future with Payson, I don't even see right away who saved Payson from her misery and walks with her. None other than Alyssa Burton. They are halfway down the walk. Payson is leaning into Alyssa's body, obviously giving her most of her weight so she doesn't have to put much on her left side. When they reach the end, Alyssa steps back and lets Payson pose. She's right in front of me but she doesn't look at me, her knees shake and she's tearing at her thumb, not enough to make it bleed. She's nervous and probably trying not to fall in those heels, so I don't take it personal. The moment she turns, Alyssa is back on her side and throwing Payson's arm over her shoulder.

Luca and I look at each other in utter shock. Then our smiles grow. People clap right before they disappear backstage, but Luca and I give them a standing ovation. No one else joins in because they don't understand how big of a moment this is. It's huge—a turning point, hopefully. It needs to be because I refuse to see Payson hurt again, and if Alyssa knows what is good for her, she will do whatever she can to keep peace.

Chanel takes the stage once again, calling the girls back out but to stand in a line.

"We will be having an auction for the second set of outfits. If you would like to purchase any of the current outfits, please feel free to meet with me after the show."

I hold Payson's gaze until Chanel says my name and Payson looks away.

"I'd like to say a special thank you to Ash Pearson for volunteering the Bayshore volleyball team to model my clothes tonight. Don't they look stunning?" She gestures behind her to all the girls, each of their smiles wide.

My heart warms seeing my girls look happy up there. Even Payson's grimace is almost believable. I'm not sure if it's because of the attention or her knee.

"The money raised tonight will be going toward their . . ." She trips up on her words, obviously forgetting what it's for.

Luca jumps up before I can and strides onto the stage and politely grabs the microphone from her. He explains what the money is for and what Week of Pink is about. At the end of his speech, I'm even wanting to pull my wallet out. Luca has always been the better public speaker, and this proves it. He always said I was too aggressive with my face.

"Thank you, Luca." Her words are tight, probably embarrassed she needed saving. "Let us get on with our show!"

Payson's ass is something to drool over. Especially in that tight little skirt. I would buy it just to see her wear it all the time, but I know my girl, and there is no way she's putting that back on her body after tonight.

Luca leans toward me. "Thought you should know, the mayor and his shadow are in the audience."

Looking around the room for the first time, I find Chuck and Jethro in the back row. My fists tighten. It's bad enough the rest of the audience gets to see my girl in tight clothes showing off her assets, but arguably, most of the audience is female.

Chuck seeing Payson, hell, Chuck seeing any of these girls in these outfits has me on edge. The wanker is a pervert. I mentioned the whole situation in his office to Luca and he was as weirded out as I was, so at least I know it wasn't just my feelings for Chuck making me think a certain way. Luca is not a fan either, but he hasn't been around him as much as I have to fully understand the nature of Chuck. If there is anything I've learned about politicians, of any level, they are master manipulators.

Him catching Payson and me at the bus is probably the worst thing to happen. Payson has a level of vulnerability about her when she is with me. She lets herself go and feels everything to the highest degree. Chuck even witnessing several seconds of that is too much. The thought of him going home and imagining himself in my place makes me want to walk across this room and blind him from seeing anyone ever again.

Bright green eyes lock onto me as her gorgeous legs carry her my way. Everything else fades but her and that fucking dress. It's dark green but in the shadows looks black and in the bright light it shimmers, and the closer she gets, the easier it is to see the soft material of velvet hugging her body. I bet it would feel like butter under my hands as I drag them up and down, feeling every curve and crevice she has to offer. I can imagine the whimpers she would let out because she loves my hands on her as much as I love them being on her so bloody clearly. It's long sleeve, and the neck dips enough to show off her beautiful chest. Payson is short but with the dress hitting just higher than mid-thigh, her legs look a mile long. She's able to walk by herself with the lack of heels and I wonder if that was her decision or Chanel's. Either way, it's more Payson, she's not in pain and I love the flats even more. I didn't plan on spending money on any outfits tonight but if I'm not able to rip that dress off her body, I will be in a terrible fucking mood.

Hearing a string of Italian curses from Luca, I know it's worse than I thought. Payson is catching the eyes of everyone, including my best friend.

"Watch it."

"You know I am just looking, brother. I would never overstep that line; I quite enjoy my women to be legal." *Wanker.* "Besides, Payson is too infatuated with you to notice how sexy I am." He winks.

Parker elbows me and leans my way to mutter something about *"he gets it now."* He has the eyes to enforce his feelings too.

Everyone is fucking jarring tonight. Payson turns and I swear the room lets out a bloody sigh. Maybe it's in my head but I know what I'm taking my anger out on as soon as she's off that fucking stage. I need to be careful with her knee, but I'll make do with what I can.

Everyone in the room must know who Alyssa is and who her dad is because her applause is by far the loudest. Alyssa has been better than I imagined sitting the bench. I haven't heard one crude remark or a complaint since. She's not even looked at me once. She's merely accepted her punishment for what she did. It's the bottom of the barrel, yes, but more than what I expected from her. Plus assisting Payson on the first walk. I do believe if this was a few weeks ago, Alyssa would not have done the same. Her good mood might have to do with guilt more than anything, but anything that levels her out is fine.

"You're going to buy it for Payson, aren't you?" Luca asks when the girls walk back onto the stage.

"Yes. I can't let anyone else take the dress." I shoot him a look.

"It will make it quite obvious of your feelings, fratello."

I hadn't been thinking about that. It is easy to forget we can not be seen as a couple to the public eye when things are so real between us. "Then I will bid on someone else as well."

"You realize you agreed to let Jethro pay for the trip in full after your talk, sì? We don't actually need any of the money from tonight."

This is also true. Jethro insisted and I was angry enough with him to agree. But money can always be used somewhere in sports. "We can buy warm-up apparel for next season."

His eyes narrow. "You plan on being here next season?"

"I plan on being here as long as Payson is here. She has another year left in school, so, yes. Besides, Parker likes it here too."

"We will see after his first *soccer* season this spring."

I grin knowing he is right. Not that it will be much different than what he is used to but Bayshore is a sport-focused school, their standards are higher. Parker is a brilliant player though and will absolutely make the team. Once volleyball season is over, I will bring him to the gym to run through drills. I played some football—*soccer* as American's call it, when I was younger because it's the biggest sport in England, but it never stuck like volleyball did.

The bidding starts and to my delighted surprise, there are numerous bids on all the girls' outfits. Shannon's dress went for twenty-five-hundred dollars to a woman in the audience after I had bid a grand as a front. We've easily raised over five thousand.

And with Payson, we'll double it.

"Payson Murphy is wearing an emerald-green crushed velvet dress. Can we start the bid at two hundred."

Chanel started every other girls' at five hundred. She even started Emika's at seven fifty. So, why Payson at two hundred? It doesn't make sense when she looks the most radiant. Maybe I'm bias, but she looks gorgeous.

Payson shrinks at hearing her start her bid lower but when the first person who bids raises the price to one thousand, surprise takes over disappointment.

Unfortunately, hearing who it is that bid that much leaves nothing, including surprise, inside my chest. I shoot a look across the room. Chuck lifts a flute of champagne in my direction.

Chanel stumbles over the bid, obviously not expecting it. A battle roars inside my chest, half wanting to bloom with pride and the other half urging me to shove that flute down Chuck's slimy throat.

"Will there be a twelve hundred?"

"Fifteen." My voice cuts through the silent room like a hot knife.

"F-fifteen."

"Two thousand."

A growl rumbles deep in my chest. "Three."

"Four."

We may get more than warm-ups next season. "Six thousand."

"Six thousand?" Chanel says, more like a question than an announcement.

Chuck swipes his tongue over his thin lip. It feels more like bidding for the girl than for the dress. I'll be damned if I let him walk home with the dress Payson is wearing. He will have one of those poor girls I saw in his office put it on, and I refuse to let him fantasize about my girl.

"Do we hear sixty-five hundred?"

Chuck lifts his glass. "Seven thousand."

This bloody—Luca nudges me and I glance down, it must be important if he is bothering me now. He nods toward the stage, and my eyes lock with a worried green set. I clench my jaw knowing who is making her feel this way. She doesn't want Chuck to get it either. Payson is not stupid, in fact, I wish she was more ignorant with this subject, but unfortunately, she's not. She knows exactly why he wants the dress, and I'll be damned if I let him have it.

"Ten thousand."

Payson's jaw drops, followed by various gasps and a louder one right into the microphone. "Ten thousand?" She doesn't bother hiding her surprise this time. She asks me in a way that sounds like she's asking *why?* at the same time.

There's a long moment of silence. I smirk at Payson when Chanel closes the bid.

I fall back into my seat and let out a long breath.

"You are getting lucky tonight, fratello." Luca chuckles to my right. I join in because he's right, but I was getting lucky before I bought my girl a ten-thousand-dollar dress.

The auction ends with Alyssa's going for six thousand, thanks to her dad. He was willing to bid seven on Payson but not his daughter. Most people have cleared out and I stand toward the back after turning my check in for Payson's dress, waiting for her to appear, hopefully still wearing it. I was going to ask Chanel to tell her but thought better of it. Bad enough I spent ten grand on my player's dress. I bid a little on each girl, but no where near ten thousand. I'm sure that will earn me a few questions, but I'm hopeful most people here tonight are not the same people attending our games and being where I am.

"Hefty number for a volleyball coach."

Chuck stops next to me and pins me with a knowing scowl.

"You forget I've been to the Olympics. Three times, and I brought home gold each time."

He narrows his eyes. "Of course." He pauses. "It's great that your team is going to have so much money for whatever volleyball teams spend money on."

He's trying to get a rise from me. Knowing this, I flatten my lips. "There is plenty we can do with the money."

He waves his hand and a wicked grin stretches his leathery skin. "Of course, of course. Spending ten thousand on a dress because you need new balls or something. Nothing to do with the tight little pussy wearing it, right?"

I'm going to fucking kill this pervert. Red clouds my vision and I whip around, grab him by the collar, and shove him against the nearest wall. He is smaller than me and easy enough to manhandle like the sack of shit he is. "You bloody say another word involving Payson and—"

"Everything okay here?" Jethro's harsh voice hisses lowly.

Chuck's suit wrinkles as my hands curl tighter. "Fine." I let him go and step away, giving me space so I don't kill him in front of all these people.

Jethro's eyes are burning into the side of my face but I don't look his way. Chuck straightens his suit and tie, pretending nothing happened.

"Just fine, thank you."

The doors open and a few girls walk out, one of them being Payson, still in their outfits. She smiles when she sees me but it slips at seeing my company. God, she's so fucking pretty, but I wish I could shield that pretty from Chuck's beady stare.

She's called for photos with the rest of the girls as are the coaches. "Jethro." I dip my chin once, ignoring his intense green eyes.

Several photos are taken for the newspaper and Chanel's blog or something she said before joining into the photos. Thankfully, next to Luca, on the opposite side of me.

"I can't believe you," Payson whispers. "But thank you."

I brush my fingers over hers. "There was no way I was going to risk not being able to take it off you."

Her giggle is soft and so bloody sweet, but it shoots right to my dick that is struggling to stay flaccid with her so close. The vanilla scent on her skin permeates the air between us.

Luca wanders our way with wide eyes and Chanel trailing behind him like he's a gazelle and she's a lion stalking its prey.

"She has a question for us," he mutters when he's close enough so she won't hear but I will.

Payson lifts a brow in question.

Luca twists his face up. "Something you are not going to want to hear, coniglietta."

I'm trying to work out what it could be when Chanel stands in front of us and tugs the neckline of her dress even lower. I don't take the bait. Payson stiffens by my side, and I stroke the back of her hand.

"I hope you enjoyed yourselves." Her voice is far too sexual when she says that in front of my team. I guess most have scattered, but still.

I have to force the words out from a tight jaw. "Yes. I hope my girls got what I wanted them to from this."

Her eyes tighten. "We had a fantastic turnout. All purchased items will be drycleaned, delivered to their respective purchasers, and then the money will be deposited to you early next week."

"Thank you."

Her eyes fall to Payson by my side and all the excitement and sultriness she was wearing for me and Luca is replaced with annoyance. "Including yours. You are released to go change now."

"Actually . . ." I cut off anyone who might have spoken next. "She can keep it on. I purchased it for her."

Chanel gapes, shooting a look between us for several seconds. "Are you two related?"

Payson blurts out an obnoxious laugh, mine and Luca's is more of a subtle chuckle. "No, not related. Just her coach." *And her boyfriend, the guy that took her virginity, and the man who, one day, she will share a name with.*

Chanel's face fills with disbelief. "Mhm. Well, I wanted to ask you *two*"—she points her manicured finger between Luca and me—"something, but it's not kid appropriate."

Please, this *kid* has seen more in her life than most twice her age. And she takes my dick better than anyone.

"Go ahead. I'm not a kid and my *coach* is *my ride*." I pick up on the way she emphasizes coach and ride like there are multiple meanings to both.

"Very well." She steps closer to Luca but reaches out and brushes my arm. "I was wondering what you were doing after." She flutters her eyes. "Both of you."

18

Payson

I HATE HER. OH, I hate her so much. Who on earth asks two people in the middle of a fashion show they met less than a few hours ago if they want to have a freaking threesome? Okay, maybe the show is over and technically she warned me, but still! Neither of them gave off the impression they would be interested in that—at least I didn't see it. There's that green monster threatening to ruin my thoughts once again.

Is it possible they made her believe they wanted a three-way with her? He didn't seem the slightest bit interested when I was around but how can he not be? She's perfect for him.

She obviously doesn't know how big Ash is because there's no way you are taking a whole other dick with what's in his pants; I suspect that Luca isn't lacking either. I cannot imagine trying to take both of these men. I don't hate the idea, though. I really can't even blame her for trying—but I still hate her.

"I beg your pardon?" Ash asks.

"I think you heard me. It's not my first rodeo and I'm sure you two have tried it before. I promise to make it worth your while."

She runs her slim hand down Ash's arm. I let out a breath of relief when he pulls away almost instantly and glances at me with a frown. I can't read what he's thinking but it feels like disappointment. I'm not sure about what though.

"No, thank you," Ash tells her firmly, in the tone I know leaves no room for argument. Of course she doesn't know that so she does her best to persuade him. If I wasn't so lost in my own thoughts, I would probably laugh at her pathetic attempt to seduce my boyfriend after seeing how uninterested he obviously is.

"Come on," Chanel singsongs in a whiny voice. "You boys have done three-ways before, I assume?"

That's something I never thought about. Sure, I've pictured it a time or two, but I never actually considered the possibility of it being a reality.

Luca butts in, saving Ash from the spotlight of Chanel's begging. "Back in the day. When we were young." He laughs easily. "Not so much these days."

My mouth drops open.

"Too bad," Chanel purrs raking her greedy eyes down both their bodies. They just *have* to look like irresistible Mafia men tonight. "What about just one of you, then?"

She is insufferable. Persistent too, I have to give her that much. Luca takes her up on the offer, slapping Ash's shoulder and winking to us like he's doing us a favor.

Chanel does one of those wannabe-cute giggles. Before she turns, she looks over my outfit again. "Enjoy your dress. Will look cute for home-coming, I'm sure."

I hate that she is talking to me like I'm dirt on her shoe.

Ash wraps a hand around my waist. I jolt and quickly look around for anyone that might see us but the rest of the room seems distracted. Still, he shouldn't—

"She won't be wearing it to homecoming because it's probably not going to last the night."

Oh, my word.

"W-what?" She gasps. Luca drags a hand down his face.

"The excitement that comes from unwrapping your own present makes the present even more exciting." Ash eyes me hungrily. "Rips are inevitable. Don't you think, Chanel?"

"The fashion show was only meant for players," Chanel bites out bitterly.

Ahh . . . she thinks I'm not Ash's player. This is even better. Ash opens his mouth to speak but I cut him off. "Oh, *Coach*?"

"Yes, Murphy?"

"Chanel wanted me to tell you it's not classy to leave behind bitemarks." I puff out my bottom lip.

His eyes blow wide and he can't hide his smile now. He clears his throat and with a serious voice says, "I'll keep that in mind. Thank you, Chanel."

He grabs my hand. "You two have fun." He slaps Luca's back and tugs me out the front door without waiting for her shocked reply.

We laugh like teenagers when we exit through the front door; I don't even notice the rain right away. Ash grabs me by the waist, pulls me to his body and presses my back against the white brick wall. There is a small overhang protecting us from most of the rain but Ash's shoulders are getting wet because of his size. It's not pouring yet but we need to get in a car or his outfit will be ruined and that would be a shame.

"That was so hot," he mutters into my neck.

I giggle softly and tilt my head—exposing my neck more. "That was so much fun! Can we make every skanky bitch look like that when they come on to you?"

"Gladly." Ash nips at my throat. "I need to grab Parker, then we can go. Here." He pulls his keys from his pocket and places them in my hand. "Do you have a bag I need to grab?"

"My duffle bag, ask one of the girls and they can grab it for you."

He takes a second to look around and makes sure we are alone before leaning down and placing a needy kiss to my lips. "I'll meet you at the car."

I grab his arm before he can pull away, and he eyes me curiously. "Don't get hung up on anymore needy blondes, please."

Another kiss to my lips; he tells me I have nothing to worry about before jogging back inside as I head for the car.

Thankfully he wasn't that far from the door so I'm hardly wet when I fall into the passenger seat. I crank the heat and pull my hair from the ponytail, doing my best to brush it out with my fingers. I look like an untamed lion but I leave it because there's nothing I can do without a shower. A shower I'm hoping Ash will be in with me.

I'm needy, seeing the way he watched me all night has me wound up, and I'm glad I told my grandpa I won't be home tonight. Then Chanel and, for a second, I worried about how beautiful Alyssa looked and what Ash would think, but I quickly pushed that from my head because I can only be jealous of one girl at a time. Eventually I'll have to deal with whatever happened between them, but not tonight. Tonight, I'm going to fuck my boyfriend all night long; he won't even remember he's been inside any other pussies besides mine.

Unfortunately, I'll have to be quiet because I can't face Parker in the morning knowing he's heard me come, *again*. It's bad enough I know he will be in the same house as us.

I'm surprised at how quick I've come around to Ash being a dad, if I'm being honest with myself, because it really doesn't bother me. I want to know where Parker's mom is but neither of them have mentioned her, and

I'm worried what might come out when he tells me. But Parker is cool, I like him as a person, even when he is moody toward me. I can't even blame him because if my mom was dating someone the same age as me . . . well, honestly, I'd be happy it was anyone but Fred, but still, I get it. It's weird.

I jump when Ash's door flies open and he drops into his seat. He slams the door behind him, tosses my bag into the back seat, and eyes me like a rabid dog. "Parker is going to a movie with some of the girls."

"So that means . . ."

A dark chuckle rumbles from him as he backs out of his spot. "Yes, babygirl. Just you and me for a few hours."

The storm picks up and Ash is forced to slow his speed, much to our dismays.

It's been only ten minutes of driving but I'm squirming in my seat with need. He was holding my thigh but because the rain is making it harder to see in front of us, he grumbled about needing to use both hands.

Now I'm left empty and needy.

The veins on the back of his hands protrude and his jaw is sharp and tight. Everything the number on the dash goes up that small muscle in his jaw flexes.

My clit is swollen and throbbing for attention. I need friction *now* and if he can't do it, I will. I clip the button for my seat belt.

"What are you—"

I kiss Ash's cheek on my way to the back seat where I'm able to lie down. I lift my bad leg and prop it on the door and the other I let fall off the seat, exposing my bare pussy to the warm air in the car when my dress rides up.

"Payson—" he breathes. "Fuck. You need to buckle up."

"I c-can't." My voice shakes when I place my fingers over my clit. I don't even rub, just feeling some pressure has my nipples tightening and my back arching. "I have to come, Ash."

"Go-shdammit, Payson." The car whips as he turns down a road we don't need to go down. I have no idea where we are or where he is taking us, but I don't care because when I move my fingers, I lose the will to care about anything but coming.

I've masturbated a few times lately and have felt empty each time because I know what it's like to come with Ash, coming without him is lack luster.

But, coming while he watches me—unable to do anything but look? Mind-blowing.

"I swear to God if you come, Jailbird, I'm going to fucking *ruin* your pussy."

His words send a shiver over my body. I don't stop. I rub my fingers exactly the way I like. Unable to stop it, my eyes drift close and I moan, louder than necessary, but I love him watching me.

I love it so much I get lost in knowing he's watching me put on a show for him. I'm so close. My pussy is throbbing for something to fill it while the need to come radiates in every single cell of my body.

"Payson," Ash growls. "Don't."

A moment later, when I'm yelling out for him as my orgasm crashes over my body, the back door opens at my feet, and that's when I notice we stopped.

Ash stands in the now-open door at my feet, his burning eyes jumping from my fingers still moving against my clit and my face. "Bad fucking move, babygirl." He leans into the car, grabbing me around the waist and tugging me from the warm interior into the cold wet air outside. His big hand wraps around my hair and pins my ass to the wet car with his hips. He tilts my head back so the rain is pounding against my face.

"I told you not to come." He slams the car door shut.

I whimper. My body still tingling from my climax. The rain is cold and heavy, and heightens my shivering even more. Ash still doesn't let me go, obviously not caring about the rain soaking and most likely ruining our clothes.

"And you did, didn't you?"

I say nothing.

He leans in and licks from my cleavage up to my chin. "Tell me you came on your pretty little fingers, Jailbird. Tell me how you disobeyed."

"You know I did. You know how I sound when I come, Coach."

"No. Tonight I'm not your coach. I'm your fucking *daddy* and you're going to learn what happens when you disobey your daddy."

My stomach flips with excitement. I bite my bottom lip and enjoy him sucking on my flesh.

Lightning strikes in the far distance and a minute later, thunder booms. Ash pays no attention to the storm raging around us as he marks my skin.

I grip his wet hair but he's quick to grab my hands with the hand not in my hair. He crosses my wrists and holds them above my head.

Ash pulls back and glares down at me. His hair is soaked and showing just how long it has gotten. His curls make it seem shorter, but it nearly hangs to his nose. Showing enough of his eyes to make him seem dangerous. Excited nerves bloom low in my belly.

Lightning lights his already heated gaze—piercing right though my soul.

"What are you going to do to me?" I whisper, not knowing if he can hear me over the rain pelting his car. It's louder now that he has moved us to the hood.

A wicked smile grows across his gorgeous face, his white teeth cutting through the darkness that surrounds us. "I was thinking I might fuck you and not allow you to come." His eyes sharpen. "But your cunt is greedy and I know you would come faster knowing I didn't want you to."

He's right. I'm already gearing up for another orgasm just thinking about it.

"The old Ash might call up an old fling and make you watch me fuck her instead of you."

I bare my teeth but images of that rush through my head.

Ash wraps his fist around my hair for a second time, tugging on it just outside my pain threshold. "But I'm so pussy-whipped by you I'm not sure I can get hard for another pussy anymore."

"Better keep it that way," I warn.

"So, I think it's only fair you have to watch me come without your help."

That doesn't seem like much of a punishment. Seeing Ash jack off is hot, and I've only gotten a small taste of it, so seeing the full thing? Yes, please.

Ash digs around in the trunk, only returning to the hood when he finds whatever it is he was looking for. He slaps something down on the roof. Eyeing the . . . jumper cables, I flick a look to him.

He doesn't let me ask before he's reaching into his pocket and shoving something rubber into my mouth, making it impossible to speak. I drag my tongue around the inside and eye him. There are holes so I can breathe but can't talk. He secures it behind my head.

"It's a gag ball," he tells me. My eyes pop open.

What the hell is he doing with a gag ball in his car?

"Remember these?" He holds up a red piece of fabric. "We bought these at a sex shop. I bought a few extra things for you and me to try out as well. I was—"

Ash lays it down next to me. He cups my face. "Fuck, you look so goddamn hot." I scowl because he knows I hate when he says that.

He smirks. "Does it bother you that you can't scold me?"

He nods my head for me.

"Too bad."

My skin pricks with goosebumps when his fingers drift down my throat to the scoop of my dress. I long for his heavy hands all over my body but he continues tracing the neck of my dress with soft fingers.

"It's a shame. I really liked this dress, babygirl." I tilt my head. His grin widens and I get a sinking feeling in my stomach. "You just had to go and be a bad girl, didn't you?"

In the next minute, Ash is gripping my dress and gone are the gentle touches when he freaking tears the top part of my dress. His eyes darken with hunger when my breasts break free. I mean to gasp but with the gag, it's more like a weird moan. I really liked this dress and he ripped it like it was nothing. Plus, he spent ten thousand freaking dollars on it!

I can't believe he did that.

Thunder booms and he tears the rest. Fabric hangs off my naked body, only staying up because of the sleeves.

I look around where he brought us to. I don't recognize it right away until I see an old swing set across the field of nothingness. When I was a kid, there used to be two baseball fields here. This is where I played t-ball, but the school got a huge grant several years ago and built a softball and baseball field across town. Closer to the school. They tore everything out of here and it's sat empty since. People use it as a makeshift dog park now, so it's not like anyone will be here this time of night, especially during a storm. The lightning is still in the distance and seems to be going around us, but the rain is still coming down and anytime it thunders, my heart rate picks up.

"Good girls get pretty dresses." He pulls the sleeves off my arms one at a time, and I let him because what good are sleeves with no dress? "Bad girls get to stand in the rain naked."

He brings my arm up and eyes it with a furrowed brow before kissing each noticeable cut, and breathing harder every time. "My girl's so broken." His voice is soft and for a moment, I forget I have a gag in my mouth and this is punishment, because he places a longing kiss on my forehead. "One day you won't be. One day your scars will be old, and we will look back on moments when they were fresh as a lesson."

I push my forehead into his lips again as if I'm agreeing. I don't want to cut forever but stopping is proving to be more difficult than I expected. I don't have a problem—there's a lot going on, and honestly, a lot of the reason is staring me in the eyes right now. I regret nothing, though. He really helped the other night, so maybe rough sex is the answer.

"Until then, I will bring you the pain you require."

He picks me up and sets me on the hood of the car. The metal is freezing under my ass. It was a warmer day but the sun has set and the rain is cold. I can't imagine it's much warmer than forty-five. I shiver.

"Good girls get fucked in a warm bed."

My usual pout doesn't work when there is a ball in my mouth, but I still attempt it, hoping my eyes say enough, he always says my eyes are expressive—I hope he's right.

"Bad girls get fucked on the hood of a car like a cheap whore.

"You are getting neither of those things tonight."

Ash picks up the blindfold, I shoot a look at it, then him. He said I would get to watch but if I'm wearing a blindfold, how will I get to see him?

"I saw these in the back and thought this would be a better punishment. You looked far too happy about seeing me masturbate. So I'm going to blindfold you and you can *listen* to me come."

This really is torture.

Ash ties the blindfold around my eyes and my hearing picks up. The rain is louder even though it doesn't feel like it got heavier. The thought that Ash isn't standing in front of me anymore worries me; I lift my hands and grab his shirt. He steps closer.

"I'm right here, babygirl. This is punishment, a test to find your limits. But I'm not going to leave you. Okay?"

I nod slowly. I believe him but the little girl in me is crying for him to stay right here where I can touch him.

"Take my shirt off, Payson," he demands in a harsher voice than before. My body is shaking and my fingers trip over each button several times, but he doesn't rush me. It's molded to his body; I have to peel it from his shoulders just so it will fall to the ground. I bet Ash looks so sexy shirtless in the rain.

He doesn't step away and I take advantage of it—running my hands everywhere. I love the ridges on his hard body. The way his arms feel like they were carved from granite and I can't wrap my hands around his bicep even when I use two hands. The hair that covers his chest in the sexiest way and trails down the hard plains of his stomach. He flexes under my fingers and releases a shuttering breath when I trail over the deep v.

"The way you touch me is fucking irresistible. It's like you're nervous but also can't get enough. You tremble and the way I know your eyes have lost focus, even though you cannot see me. Hmm. You have no idea what that does to me, Jailbird.

"I hate to compare you to a child when I'm holding nipple clamps in my hand." My nipples are already painfully hard from the cold but hearing he is holding nipple clamps hardens them even more—I'm sure I could etch glass. "But your love is so childlike. You are an astonishing woman, but you cling to me like a child clings to their favorite toy."

A small chain jingles, then his fingers graze my mouth. He must connect something because when he pulls away cold metal hangs down my chin. "The innocence your eyes hold." He tsks. "It's like a fucking drug, Payson. And when you call me daddy." My scream is muffled by the ball but the pain isn't as something hard snaps onto my left nipple. The burning continues when he doesn't pull it off. "I want to bend you over my knee and tan your arse for making me like it so bloody much."

He fixes the other clamp to the ball gag and wastes no time clamping that one to my right until both of my nipples are burning. The burning in the left nipple has gone down but anytime I shift or breathe too hard, the sensation starts all over again.

"You've turned me into this, Payson."

I've stopped rubbing his body all together because any movements tug on my nipples. The rubber clamps are connected by metal chains and I worry about the lightning for a quick minute only to realize I haven't heard thunder in the last few minutes. That could be because my blood is rushing like a river through my ears, or because the storm has moved. The rain feels lighter too.

Ash clears his throat. "Arms behind your back."

He ties my wrists together with the harsh cables until I can't pull them apart anymore. My chest works overtime, attempting to calm my beating heart. I hate this. I can't touch him, I can't see him, I can't even talk to him if I need to.

Ash can pretty much read my mind, he grabs the sides of my face. "Calm down, Jailbird. I told you I'm not leaving. You are sitting on the car. Remember? I can't leave without my car."

He can't leave without the car.

"You need to remind yourself of what is going on. The rain and cold should remind you where you are. The nipple clamps will keep you in the present and my voice will remind you who you are with. Okay? You and me, babygirl."

Me and you.

"I'm going to take five steps away, okay?"

I whimper through the ball gag.

Ash kisses my forehead. "Maybe next time you'll listen when I tell you not to come."

Panic surges through my body when his warm hand disappears from my hips and I'm left wet, naked, and cold. My ass slips against the wet metal.

"Listen to my footsteps, Payson."

The ground is wet and each step squishes under his weight. Like he said, five steps later, the footsteps stop, and his voice is farther away but not far enough to upset my abandonment issues. Yet.

"Good. Remember everything I just told you. You and me. Always you and me, Pay."

Me and you. He can't leave without the car. I'm at the ballpark with Ash.

My ears perk up at his zipper being pulled down. I shift and my ass slips a little more.

"Don't fucking move." Ash's voice is tight and I can't see why. Is he touching himself already? No matter how wide or narrow my eyes are, I can't see through the red fabric. Everything is black.

Me and you. He can't leave without the car. I'm at the ballpark.

"You looked gorgeous tonight, but you look bloody brilliant right now, babygirl."

He has to be touching himself now. And I can't see it.

What if someone else can? Someone else can see the most perfect man stroking his most perfect dick and I can't.

He said the old him would fuck someone else and make me watch. Maybe he called one of them and this was his plan, but which one? Alyssa? Chanel's not an ex but she was sure interested enough. What about Maggie? They are all in town, close enough he could have told them to be here. I don't hear anyone else, but I can't hear much past my accelerated breathing. Drool pools in my mouth and Ash moans loudly. Like when he's being sucked off.

I strain to hear gagging, but it's no use. I have gotten myself so worked up; my thoughts are louder than anything.

Me and you. Can't leave without the car. At the ballpark.

It doesn't work this time. More drool pools and I have to tip my head forward to let it flow from the holes provided. Is it possible to choke from one of these?

"I made sure you couldn't say your safe word," Ash growls. "Would you say it if you could? Nod your head."

If I nod, will he stop? Do I want him to? I don't know. My head is clouded. So many images flash through it. Him and Alyssa. Him and Chanel. Him and Maggie. Alone and all three together. Maybe Luca too and they are all making fun of me because I'm tied, gagged, and silenced. My legs dangle free but I don't think I could hold myself up if I even wanted to.

I thought listening to him would be hot. Maybe it would be if I was sure we were alone. We are in the open and anyone else could be the one making him moan.

It should be me.

"Fuck, baby."

Baby. Not babygirl. Not Jailbird. Not Payson or Pay.

Baby.

"You never answered me, Payson." His voice is tight. "Would you use your safe wor—ah, fuck, yes."

I nod vigorously. I hope he stops. I can't handle it anymore. Tears burn my eyes, drool drips from my chin yet my throat is dry. I tug on the jumper cables, willing them to loosen.

I call out his name but the ball stops any actual words from forming.

"Your mind is playing tricks on you, isn't it, babygirl?" Why does he sound so hollow?

I nod again. *Please stop.*

Me and you. Car. Ballpark.

But what if there's someone else? I tug on my wrists.

Ash groans loudly and I tug again.

It all happens at once. One wrist comes free and I slip off the car, landing on my side in the drowned grass. One nipple clamp rips off in the fall and I scream.

I rip my other wrist from the cables and toss them to the side, then remove the second clamp. I'm exhausted and slow moving, and my injury keeps me from climbing to my knees like I want to.

"Don't stop, baby. Keep going," he urges whoever is sucking his dick. I think I even hear someone gag but that could just be me.

Fat tears fall from my eyes. How could he do this? Punishment is one thing but letting another girl suck him off isn't punishment. It's cheating.

I don't even attempt to figure out the ball gag, I just rip the blindfold from the back of my head.

Everything is darker than before. Rain pitter patters on my back and water drips from every part of my body.

Then I see him. Ash, just Ash in all his glory. Shirtless. Pants undone but . . . he's not stroking himself. His dick isn't even out of his pants, and I swear he's soft.

No, that doesn't make sense. He was moaning.

I rip the gag off and nearly throw up from all the saliva in my mouth. I lean over and spit it into the grass. Tears still stream from my eyes. The heavy makeup I was wearing must look tragic after the rain and tears.

Ash doesn't move from his place exactly five Ash-sized steps away. More like four now that I'm on the ground and not on the car.

"You got lost in your head. Hearing things that weren't happening. Didn't you?"

My throat is still so dry, and I'm not sure I like the harshness in his voice. I quickly glance around, then back to him, and we are, in fact, alone. I nod.

"What was it? Fred, or me with other women? Those are the only two things I can imagine would leave you screaming and crying."

A sharp breath rushes by my lips. "You a-and—"

"Who?" he demands.

I don't like how disappointed he looks, but I hate even more that I let my insecurities get in the way, again. And the only reason I answer him is because he doesn't look like he's in the mood for me to ignore him, and the last thing I want to do is disappoint him more. I dip my head, look to the dark green grass and sigh. "All of them. Alyssa, Chanel—" I attempt to swallow the bitterness but it doesn't leave. "Maggie."

Ash mutters something I can't hear.

"What?" I whimper.

"I said goddamn your past! I would call out one person in particular but there's not a single fucker to blame. It's all of them, isn't it? Every bloody person in your life has either caused an issue or not done anything to fix them." I've never heard him shout before. "First, your bio dad for leaving in the first place. No—not even leaving, but leaving and not giving you the fucking time of day to keep in touch.

"Then you have the biggest wanker of them all, Fred. That cock-sucking pervert, who is probably the main reason we are together, fucked your little head up so much you get off on calling me daddy and being held against your will." Ouch. *Ouch*. "Your brother couldn't even stick it out. Your friends looked past your cutting because there's zero possibilities they couldn't tell when I could within fucking days of knowing you!" He bends forward and rips at his hair.

"Your nana died and your mom checked out. Not that she was ever there for you in the first place." He scoffs, or laughs. A bit of both. "Your granddad does his very best, but *no one* has helped you, not really. No. One."

I don't look up as I continue to sob. My cries are loud and my stomach churns. Is this part of his punishment? Because I don't understand why he is calling me out like this. I know everything he said. I know it all and yet he threw it in my face like I didn't.

"It's your fault too, Payson," he adds. "You let everything get in your head. You come up with these crazy ideas and you run with them. You had a full-on panic attack because, somehow, you convinced yourself I was fucking someone else." He throws his arms out to the side and spins in a circle. "We're fucking alone! You knew we were and *still* you let your mind take you there."

"You told me you would fuck someone in front of me," I say, defensively.

"I said the old Ash!" His voice is the loudest yet. "Since the day we met I've done nothing but prove my love to you and it's still not enough."

I push onto my knees, ignoring the shooting pain, and drag my hand under my snotty nose. "If you don't recall, you've also given me reasons not to trust you, *Coach*."

Ash glowers at me. Three steps later he is in front of me, his hand around my throat lifting me from the ground so we are eye level. I gasp for air but he doesn't move. "Those *reasons* are past mistakes that came out in the wrong way."

My head tingles with the lack of oxygen and I slap at his hands, "Strippers."

Ash tosses me backward. I land on the hood with a loud pop as the metal bows under me and pops back out. He grabs my ankles despite my kicking and drags me toward his body until he's settled between my naked thighs. He slams a hand onto the hood next to my head. "We weren't fucking together and nothing. Happened."

"Letting a naked girl grind on your lap isn't something? So if I strip naked and grind on some other—"

He grips my cheeks and squishes my face together and drops his forehead to mine, our hot heavy breathing mixing. "If you finish that sentence, I'll kill you." He closes his eyes. "Don't make me kill you, Payson."

If anyone should kill anyone it should be me killing him.

He flutters his eyes back open, still frowning. "What can I do to make you trust me?"

I never stopped crying but the burning is back as warm tears pour down the side of my face mixing with the cold from the rain dripping off Ash's hair. I brush it back with a shaky hand. "I don't know."

19

Ash

IF SHE DOESN'T KNOW, then I will have to figure it out, but right now, I'm going to fuck her because I'm so fucking mad, and if I'm not balls deep inside her in the next ten fucking seconds, I will strangle her.

She pushes against me, doing her best to get away. I grab her wrists, slamming them to the hood with one hand while I work my trousers with the other. The second my dick is free, I spit on her cunt and shove inside in one thrust. We gasp at the intrusion and I take a minute to make sure she's not about to circumcise me, then I thrust, hard.

"I'm not sorry for what I said. It's true."

I let go of her wrists and not to my surprise, she slaps me across my cheek. I bare my teeth and slam into her, praying I rip her pussy as punishment for her being so bloody insecure.

I love Payson. Everything about her—even her flaws—but it didn't even take five minutes for her to panic. I had just unzipped when I noticed something wasn't right, and I knew there could be only two options. So instead of assuring her, I wanted to see how far I could push it before she either snapped or pulled herself back to reality. Payson knew there was no one but us here and she still let my stupid words and her thoughts run wild.

What I said wasn't the smartest, but it's true. I forced an old fling—one that stuck around longer than a weekend—to watch me fuck someone else because I caught her slipping some drunk her number at a club.

I would never do that to Payson. If I caught her doing the same . . . my hands clamp onto her hips to the point she whines. I don't know what I would do but my dick will never touch another pussy. She never has to worry about that, and yet she does. She can blame the strippers, or finding out about Alyssa but it's more. It's the fact she's never experienced unconditional love. Of course there were her grandparents, and even Janelle's family, but it's not the same. She should have learned about this from her parents but she didn't, and look where we are.

A naked seventeen-year-old being fucked by a man twice her age on the hood of a car in the rain.

All that shit brought her to me and I'll never regret that, but I'll forever regret not coming into her life sooner. Not to fuck her even younger, but to guide her. Had I met Payson younger, maybe I could have helped her heal sooner. Maybe she would heal to the point she wouldn't want an older man.

My head flashes with images of me and Payson but not like we are now, angry fucking like animals, a normal coach-player relationship. One where she would come to practice and do her best. She would lead the team to states, nationals, and so on. The most we would ever do is hug. That's what a good coach would do.

I've accepted I'm not a good coach to Payson. Overall, yes. But not specifically to her. The first day of practice I saw her bright eyes and instant love, and I took advantage of that. If I could go back, I'd like to say I would keep my distance but I'm not the guy in my head. I'm the coach who is fucking his player and loving the way she is pretending to hate it.

"I h-hate you," she cries. She even looks pretty when she's crying.

"Yeah?" I ask pistoning my hips even harder until she's crying out for me to stop. She knows the word to use if she wants me to. "Because I love you."

Her green eyes fly open and she locks with mine. "No you don't."

God, this girl will be the death of me. I wrap a hand around her throat and squeeze just enough to see anger change to panic. "If I didn't love you, I would have fucked you the first day and never looked back."

We're soaked and she's shivering. This might be the least sexy sex I've ever had but I don't think I've ever been harder. Maybe it's the adrenaline from arguing with her, or the fact I never actually got to come.

"I wish you would have."

I squeeze her throat harder, loving how her lips go from purple to blue from the cold and lack of oxygen. "Sometimes I do too," I growl.

She bursts into tears again—slapping at my arm, chest, and face and screaming at me to get off. But I don't.

I spill deep inside her and collapse on her body. I let go of her throat. Payson shivers in my arms cocooning her as I kiss her shoulder tenderly. "I love you, Payson Murphy. Even with your fucked-up little head. And one day, we are going to heal together." I drop a kiss to her chattering lips. "It just won't be today."

She's still sobbing but her arms engulf my neck and squeeze. "Me t-too." Another beat passes and everything has calmed down, so I pull back enough to see her face. Makeup that was cried off and washed away by the rain streaks down the entirety of her face. Her lips are raw from the ball gag, eyes swollen and nose running from crying, and her hair is soaked, sticking to the side of her face and neck and still she's never looked more beautiful. "Can we go home n-now?"

Home. I like the way that sounds.

20

Payson

"I s-swear to God H-Himself if you don't hurry with-h the s-s-shower I w-will punch y-you in the f-face."

"It's for your own good, ba—"

"Do n-n-not call m-me babygirl r-right now."

"I forget your age a lot of the time, but moments like this remind me how annoying teenagers are." He runs a hand down his face while simultaneously shaking his head.

"Not annoying enough t-to not f-fuck," I mutter. I didn't mean for him to hear but he did. He turns from where he is feeling the water for the shower and pulls me against his cold body. I almost cry but I'm all cried out. We didn't talk about what happened once we got in the car and it's fine by me. It was . . . weird. And hot, and eye-opening. Really a lot of things but right now all I can focus on is how long his water is taking to get warm. It's been like five minutes.

"No, not annoying enough to not fuck you." He spanks my freezing cold ass and I yelp.

Ash didn't want to stay in the shower as long as I did, so when I get out, I find him leaning against his headboard with the bedside lamp creating a warm glow over the equally warm room. I'm so happy the room is warm. The shower felt amazing but not shivering when I stepped out was even better.

"Come to bed, babygirl." He sets down the book he was reading and pulls open the covers on his side. I tiptoe over and nearly jump into his arms.

I bury my face in the crook of his neck and he tightens his arms around me so all I can smell is him. "I wish it could be like this every night."

His beard tickles against the side of my face. "Me too, babygirl. One day."

I lie across his chest as he picks the book up and reads some more. I can't see the cover and I can't get my eyes to focus enough to read the words. I'd rather stay buried in his chest. "What are you reading?"

Ash finishes the paragraph he was reading before lowering his book and kissing my head. "It's about mental health."

"What about it?" I ask timidly.

"How to help people that struggle."

I pull back to see his face and he turns the book at the same time so I can read the title: *Loving Someone With Mental Struggles*. It's all right there in the title. *Loving someone*. It's moments like this that I don't know how I can ever question his feelings for me. He's reading a book to understand me better. He spent ten thousand dollars on a dress just because he liked the way it looked on me, probably had to do with the other bidder too, but I digress. Everything Ash does is for me.

"You really do love me, don't you?"

His eyes soften. "Yeah, Payson. I really do."

Me too.

He sets the book down and wraps his large arms around my body. My cheek is against his chest—I like how his soft chest hair feels against my face.

Guilt burns deep inside me. Guilt for making Ash lose his temper. Guilt for making him tell me over and over how much he cares, when he's right, he's proved it since the beginning. Sure, we've had bumps but everyone does. Guilt because I can't say it back.

"I know, babygirl. It's okay. We will get there together."

Together.

I've been playing with his chest hair and didn't realize he had fallen sleep. As much as I love cuddling with Ash, especially a naked Ash, I've been resting more than I ever have because of my knee and it's boring me. I'm tired after the breakdown, but I'm not ready for bed yet.

Ash weighs like a million pounds when sleeping and slipping from his huge arms is nearly impossible. I'm not sure if the cold from being soaked in the rain for so long acted as an ice pack and numbed my knee but it's not tight like it usually is when I stand. I make sure Ash is all tucked in before I grab his shirt and quietly duck out of his room. My stomach is growling and there is no way I can go to bed on an empty stomach.

I pad down Ash's short hallway for the steps. Eyeing the door I know is for Parker's room, I see the light is off so he must not be home yet. I should text Janelle and make sure everything is going okay. It's nice they invited him out. They invited me too, but I knew I needed to take advantage of my time with Ash. Across from Parker's room is another bedroom and straight ahead is the shared bathroom. Luca's room is on the main floor and is the original master bedroom that Ash was keeping as a spare for when his family came to stay so his nana wouldn't have to walk upstairs. Since no one has visited and Luca moved in, he took it over. Ash's house is huge including a basement with another room, bathroom, family room, and the laundry. It's the only part of the house that hasn't been updated yet, and the only part I haven't seen.

The rest of the house is wide plank floors stained dark with white walls and various accent colors throughout. Typical farmhouse style with added industrial touches like the black pipe hardware in the kitchen and bathrooms. My favorite room in the house is Ash's room. Might be because compared to the rest of the house it's the most basic. Especially now that Luca and Parker live here, there is life everywhere that wasn't here the first time I stayed with him. Luca's books fill a few of the built-in shelves in the living room that surround the shiplap fireplace. Parker's bookbag is by the front door next to various men's shoes. I was never big on decorating my room, maybe that's why I appreciate the simpleness of Ash's.

The stairs open to the wide entryway with the living room arch to the right and the kitchen to the left. I turn left for the kitchen and find the light already on. Luca leans against the counter with a glass of red wine in one hand and a slice of . . . cheese in the other.

"You're home."

Luca is slow to lift his lazy eyes from the ground in front of him over to me. He smiles and that is also lazy. *Is this how Luca looks after sex?* His long hair is pulled into a better messy bun than mine on my head, he's shirtless and his yellow basketball shorts are hung low on his narrow hips. Luca is beautiful. He was amazing at volleyball but man, he could have easily done modeling. "Si. I expected to come home to the sound of animal planet but heard nothing. I assumed you and Ashley would still be on the side of the road somewhere." His smile is friendly, but it doesn't stop hot embarrassment from staining my cheeks.

I duck my head and wander over to the fridge. "Something like that," I mutter not wanting to get into it.

"How was your night?" I can't help the bitterness in my voice from spilling out.

Luca doesn't seem to mind and chuckles. "Good."

Good? Sex with Chanel was good. What the hell does that mean?

"I had to fuck her mouth just so she would shut up about the little show you two pulled." He cocks an eyebrow as he takes a sip of wine.

"Was that the good part or was there more?"

Luca pops the cheese in his mouth and once again sips his wine, not stopping until the glass is completely drained. His Adam's apple bobs with a swallow. "We did not have sex. I fucked her mouth and she rode mine, then I made an excuse to leave." He snorts. "I was not feeling it tonight."

"Oh." *Oh?* "I'm surprised, she was pretty." Yeah. *Pretty.* Like a Victoria Secret model—she was perfect.

"Yes, she was."

"Do you think she will gossip about what Ash and I said?" Or worse, go to the school or police.

Luca sighs. "No, I think I handled it. Do not worry your pretty head, but you both need to be more responsible if you are going to do this. I will not be able to cover you guys forever."

I know he's right, but it's so hard watching girls flock to Ash like he's single, because he's not.

Ash's fridge is disappointing when all you want is cold pizza—or pudding. It's stocked to the max with pre-made high protein meals, and raw fruits and veggies are not what I'm craving.

"I am making pasta if you are willing to wait. Judging by the noise I heard come from your stomach, I am not sure you are." Luca chuckles from the stove. I didn't even notice he was cooking but now that I smell the garlic, my stomach growls, again.

I glance at the clock on the stove seeing it's ten p.m. Pasta at ten p.m. is odd, but I'm not going to argue with it. Shutting the fridge, I walk over and take a seat at the barstool across from Luca.

"Pasta sounds amazing. Real pasta, though, right? None of that fake cauliflower or zucchini noodle crap that Ash loves so much?"

Luca scoffs and curses something in Italian. "No, coniglietta, none of that bullshit. My nonna would roll over in her grave."

I smile. "Good. So, what's on the menu, chef?"

Thirty-five minutes later, Luca and I are sitting at the kitchen counter with two huge bowls full of an Italian pasta dish I'm not sure how to pronounce but it's probably the best food I've ever eaten. While Luca cooked, he told me about how he grew up not eating food like this. His parents were poor and could barely afford any food to feed a family of five. When he grew up, his first job was at a restaurant and that's where he learned to cook. He fell in love with it immediately and never looked back. The only reason he didn't attend culinary school was because his volleyball career kicked off instead.

He polishes off his bowl and his fourth glass of wine. I'm still working on my first bowl but I'm already getting full, so I ask him to put it in the fridge so I can have it as leftovers later.

"Leftovers were not a thing in my household. Too many mouths."

"I grew up on leftovers," I say, "Well, leftovers and *Hot Pockets*."

"What is a *Hot Pocket*?"

I explain what it is, trying my best not to laugh at his pure mortification.

"You would cook it from frozen? In the microwave?"

I nod my head.

A string of Italian curses and a head shake later he sighs. "That is disgusting and you should be glad I am in your life now to cook for you."

"I'm glad." I grin.

Despite it being so late, Luca grabs all the dishes and begins to wash. When I offered to do it, since he cooked, he cursed me out again. It was in Italian so it could have been something else but it felt like cussing.

It must be the late hour, or the fact I've been thinking about it since Luca talked about it, but I can't stop my curiosity from slipping past my lips. "How can you have sex with no attachments?"

He was already watching me, and his eyes turn thoughtful, then he shrugs. "Women are beautiful. Each in their own way, but fucking one to the next is like riding a bike versus driving a car. Sure, they are different but both get you where you want to go. You understand?"

"But . . . I don't get how you don't get wrapped up in it. Ash and I—"

"Ah, that is where you are confused. I am not having sex with *my* Ashley."

I scrunch my nose and he laughs. "You really do resemble a baby bunny sometimes, coniglietta." Ash has told me the same thing. "What I mean is I do not fall for any of the girls I fuck because I have already been in love. Fucking for me is not like what you experience with Ash. I fuck to get off. You two fuck because you are in love. It is just another way for you two to tell each other without words." He purses his lips. "Or for him to tell you in multiple ways and you in one."

"He told you about that." I cringe. "Great."

"There are no secrets between Ashley and me. We have been through too much."

Oh, even better. I sigh and run a hand through my hair, moving on from thinking about Ash sharing everything with him. "What do you mean you *were* in love, though? With who, and where is she now?"

Luca doesn't answer me right away and judging by his serious face, I'm not sure he wants to. My eyes catch his bare arms in front of me and the many healed scars. I reach a hand across the counter, eyeing him as I do so he can pull away if he wants to. He doesn't and I glide a single finger over his arm. It's not rough like mine because his cuts are healed, but it's not smooth like Ash's skin either. "Why did you used to . . .?"

Luca frowns while looking at my bare arms next to his before skimming his finger over my scars. I cringe when he hits the fresh cuts.

"Ashley mentioned you were chatty." He chuckles. "Are you sure this is the conversation you want to talk about? It is not a nice one."

I can't believe Ash says I'm chatty. *Does he think I talk too much?* I shake my head, focusing on Luca, I can bother Ash about that later. "Yes. I'm . . . struggling lately and"—I shrug—"I don't know, maybe hearing your reason will make mine seem dumb."

Luca tsks. "Everyone has their reasons for doing what they do. But I will tell you because it will answer both your questions." Both? The love and cutting are connected, then. I pull away and lean back into my chair, giving him my full attention.

"My family was poor but that was not why I cut. In fact, I never understood how poor we were until I got a job and saw how other people lived. As a kid, I did not pay attention to what my friends had and what I did not because I had my family—my siblings. I was happy with just them. My parents were worried about money, but I never would have guessed that. They were happy, always smiling.

"I cannot count how many times I woke in the middle of the night to soft music and found my parents dancing in the kitchen together. It was magical. Seeing two people so in love. I grew up and always wondered what it would be like to love someone so much you do not let the stress of outside issues affect what is inside. That is true love. Instead of fighting the outside battles and then fighting made-up battles at home, you fight them all together. Much how I see you and Ashley and the struggle with your mental health."

That book Ash was reading pops into my head.

"You two have battles—ones you have not even fought yet and still, when you are side by side, it is like nothing else matters. You two easily get lost in the other and it is magnificent to watch. When you are in a room together, you can almost feel the pull between you. The one you are having to fight, but it will not be like that forever, coniglietta. You are young, I do not want to scare you but the love I grew up seeing with my parents is how I imagine you and Ashley—several years down the road—kids will be sneaking out of bed to catch you dancing in your kitchen."

Emotion thickens in my throat, making it impossible to reply, or swallow.

He continues, probably seeing my struggle. "A love like that is rare, maybe even once in a lifetime." He pauses and with a heavy tone he adds, "I had love like that once."

21

Ash

AN EMPTY BED is not what I wanted to wake up to. I didn't even want to fall asleep but bloody hell, it's hard when you're lying next to the person that can make anywhere feel like home. Especially when she oozes so much love it steals your breath. Especially when she sucks all the emotion from your body in one evening.

I was hopeful when we got home we would have a hot shower and end the night with her so full of my cum there's no way a baby wouldn't be born in nine months.

I don't think I actually want to get her pregnant—not while she's in school anyway—but Payson with a round belly carrying my child makes me think that's a great idea. Maybe then she would believe I'm not going anywhere. But I'm not sure how Parker would react to Payson pregnant, so it's probably best to hold off.

The night is still young, so if I can leave her full of my cum, I will, baby or no baby. If I can find my girl, that is. She's not in the bathroom, or anywhere in my room.

I'm surprised to hear Luca's voice when I hit the top step. I assume he's talking to Parker, but it's not Parker I hear.

"I'm struggling . . ." Ahh. There's my girl. I step onto the ground level but hesitate outside the kitchen. It sounds like they are having a serious conversation, and I'm curious what they could be talking about.

"My family was poor but that was not why I cut." Not exactly the conversation I was hoping to overhear because it's not one I like thinking about my best friend going through, but I don't interrupt. I find a seat on the bottom step and just listen.

"She worked at the restaurant with me. She was the head chef—the one who taught me to cook, she was his daughter."

Payson's little gasp makes me smile.

"Giana was her name; we were fifteen when we met."

"Was?" Payson whispers.

I can imagine Luca's grim but thoughtful nod. "We hit it off right away. A week after meeting, we were dating. My family could not be happier because, like I mentioned before, my family was built on true love. They could all see how in love we were. Her family on the other hand . . . they were not as accepting. My great relationship with the head chef was burned, as was my relationship with the rest of the restaurant because they all took his side. That we were too young to know what love is and we were wasting our time. She was wasting her time being with me." He doesn't sound bitter, and he will still tell you how amazing of a chef that man was, but I'll never understand how he can talk so highly about a man who allowed his own daughter to die.

"Why would he think that? You're amazing."

"I was poor, coniglietta. They were not. Profile was a big deal to them. They saw their daughter marrying in the same class and they thought I got in the way, even at such a young age. I was good enough to be a worker just not a boyfriend for their beautiful daughter.

"Giana and I would hardly speak at work, and after, we would reconnect in bed. Like I said, we were young and most of our relationship was spent in the bedroom. What was spent outside was great—until it was not. The stress of everyone at our work whispering terrible things about us—her for only being with me to rebel and about me for only being with her for the money, it became too much, and we started taking it out on each other."

"That's so sad," Payson mutters.

Luca agrees. "The thing with deep, true love like that is if you do not choose to fight your battles together, you will end up fighting each other alongside those battles, and there are no winners in war."

My heart picks up speed. I think we found that out tonight. I'm just glad we came back together in the end.

"We would make love, then go back to arguing. It was a routine daily for a year until she found out she was pregnant."

"P-pregnant? How old were you?"

I can hear the weak smile in his voice. "We had dated for a year before anyone found out and this was a year after, so we were seventeen."

"That's so young," Payson replies. She must not have done the math for Parker and myself.

"Sì. Which is why her dad lost his mind the day we told him. We took both our parents out to dinner because we hoped my family being there and being so happy would help them see past their anger. It did not and it caused the biggest fight yet. I'm not like Ashley, I'm not intimidating, and I definitely wasn't at seventeen. I did not enjoy the fighting and because I was young and still trying to process how a father could speak to his daughter the way he did, I missed the blood that started falling down Giana's leg."

I peek around the corner after hearing Luca's thick voice. Payson is cupping her mouth.

"The stress from the argument had caused Giana to miscarry. It took three weeks for her to pass the baby—our baby—and by that time, she was only a shell of who she once was. We both were. When we were not crying over our loss—we were arguing. It was a very dark time in my life. I was so heartbroken over losing what could have been and angry at Giana's dad for causing it—I missed all the signs. I missed how she stopped arguing with me and would just sit there and stare when I would. I pushed her away when she wanted any affection because I was so worried about hurting her. I was a terrible lover and I abandoned her in her most crucial time of need."

"Luca," Payson whispers, emotion thick on her voice too.

Luca hangs his head and his shoulders shake. "She killed herself. I left for work, and I did not even tell her I loved her. I did not kiss her; I walked out not knowing my beautiful Giana was planning on taking her life the moment I left. When I came home, I found her on our bed curled into a ball . . . I will spare you the details but there was a note."

Payson pushes from the counter and walks around to Luca. She slips between the counter and him and wraps her slim arms around his waist. He's hesitant and suddenly he is looking right at me. His eyes are rimmed red, causing my eyes to burn. I nod because I know that's what he is waiting for. He drops his head and wraps his long slim arms around Payson, and he cries.

It's an out of body experience seeing your best friend cry into your everything's arms. Part of me, a small part but a part, hates seeing her in any man's arms besides mine. The better and bigger part wants to bloody cry seeing them together. It's like two of the most important pieces of my life are falling together. I just need Parker and my family here and I would be the world's happiest man.

Luca normally doesn't cry telling this story anymore, though. Sure, it's been a while since I have heard it, but I am surprised to see how much it affected him telling Payson.

"I'm so sorry, Luca." Payson's voice is hushed into his body.

"You remind me of her, you know."

I freeze in place because he never told me this before. His eyes open and he looks at me.

"I do?"

He nods a few times. "You love so viciously, Payson. You feel everything so deep, and so did she. She could not understand the issues everyone had with us, they meant very little too her because she loved me that much."

Payson pulls back but keeps her arms on his waist. "You know people call me a robot, right? I don't have feelings, Luca."

She has no clue what I—apparently *we*, see in her.

Luca smiles because he must think the same thing. He lowers a hand and wraps it around her wrist, raising it into the air.

Luca presses a deep kiss to the freshest one. It's not romantic, at least it doesn't feel romantic to me. He's Italian, everything they do is romantic. A kiss is like a handshake over there. Reminding me I don't want to take Payson to Italy for a vacation.

"You feel. Just differently."

Luca lets go of her arm and she stares down at them, looking at her scars with a furrowed brow. "Why do we let other people affect us so much we scar our body because of them?"

Luca and I trade looks because neither of us know how to answer that.

"I do not know," he tells her gently. "That is a good question that hopefully we can find the answer to."

Payson sighs and her shoulders sag as she lowers her arms back to her sides.

"And one day, your arms won't be your expression of emotion. One day you will be able to use this." When his thumb brushes over her bottom lip my eyebrows nosedive. Now I feel like punching him.

Luca is grinning when he moves across the room to sit in a stool, leaving me glaring at him, and Payson staring at nothing with shock written all over her face.

My eyes fall to her pointed nipples. "Those better be because of the draft and not because my best friend just touched your lips."

Payson jumps at my words. She looks at me and follows my eyes down, scoffs and throws her arms over her chest but it's too late. Luca is laughing from his seat, and I can't help but smirk at how embarrassed Payson is.

Until she flips the script. "You guys used to have three-ways."

I can't tell if it's meant to be a question or an accusation but it pisses me off anyway. I am not sharing Payson. I refuse, even with Luca who I love like a brother. Maybe even more than my idiot brother, but I'm not sharing her.

"Yes."

"Of course you did," she grumbles.

I step in behind her and wrap my arms around her curvy body. "Jealous?" I growl into her ear.

Her breathing quickens but she doesn't answer.

"You want us to share you?" I taunt. "You want Luca to watch as I fuck you?"

Luca loses his smile and lifts an eyebrow in question.

"Or maybe you want him to join."

Payson whimpers. I grip her breast in my hand and squeeze. "You think you can handle two dicks, babygirl?"

Luca's hazel eyes are focused on my hand massaging her breast, and he licks his lips.

"Ash," Payson gasps. Her back arches and she pushes her ass into me. I have to use every ounce of self-control to keep from getting an erection.

"What is it?"

Luca pushes from his stool. Payson's heart rate doubles under my hand as he saunters around the island, heading our way. I also notice the growing tent in his pants and the look on his face. A look I haven't seen in a long time. It's probably been over ten years since we have shared a girl.

Payson tenses when Luca stops on her side. He's not touching her, but she is shaking with anticipation. I growl just at the thought.

"I-I don't..." Her eyes fly to mine, wild, but also worried. "I don't think..."

"Good," I say. She *shouldn't* think anything about this.

"*She is shaking*," Luca mutters in Italian. I'm glad he is in on this with me because if he really thought I was going to let him anywhere near Payson—in that way—he's dead wrong.

His hand moves toward her hip but pauses when a growl rumbles from my chest. Payson is flush to my front as much as she can be. When he connects with her body, she tenses even more than she was. Her arm hooks around my waist and she whimpers. Not a sexual whimper but as if she really is afraid.

Good. She *shouldn't* want my best friend. The fact he is touching her at all has me wanting to grab his wrist and break it in half.

Luca walks away chuckling. "If you think I am stupid enough to cross that line, Payson. You do not know me at all."

"I'm home," Parker announces from the front door.

Luca returns to his seat across from us and I turn for the fridge, needing to rid my half-erect boner from having Payson's ass pressed to my front.

"Me too!" another voice says. Feminine voice. I shoot a look at Luca, but Payson is the one I find smiling.

Parker and Janelle wander into the room. Parker kisses me, then Luca on the cheek and awkwardly smiles at Payson. She does the same back.

"Well, I see you've already had a *big* night," Janelle says, looking over Payson's attire. It's a good thing I'm so much bigger than her and that I happened to be wearing one of my bigger shirts before she threw it on, my shirt hits mid thigh, nowhere near showing anything that shouldn't.

"I'm not discussing it," Payson deadpans.

Janelle must see something on Payson's face I can't. "Ohhh."

Awkward silence falls on the room, that is until the girls laugh like hyenas. Janelle throws an arm over Payson's shoulder and drags her from the room. "She's giving me a tour!" she shouts already halfway up the stairs.

I shake my head and grab the orange juice before closing the door and offering some to Luca and Parker.

"How was the movie?"

"Uh, good." Parker's tanned skin deepens to a dark pink. I cock an eyebrow to Luca. Luca claps a hand on his shoulder and Parker jumps. Guilty.

"What did you see, nipote?"

More pausing. "The new marvel movie."

Luca's eyes flick to me, we smirk. "Ah, yes the one with the raccoon?"

He nods vigorously. "Mhm, yes, that one."

"Funny." I tuck my tongue in the corner of my mouth and cross my arms. Doing my best not to laugh at my son's embarrassment. "I didn't think that came out for another six months."

"Uh, well, it, uh . . ."

Luca barks out a laugh first. "We are kidding, Parker. That movie is out, I went to see it last week. It was good, you should *actually* go watch it sometime."

"What were you really up to?"

Just then the girls' laughs echo throughout the entire house. Parker's eyes dilate hearing it, a look much like Payson's when she looks at me.

"Ah . . . I don't think it is *what* was he up to . . . but *who*."

"Shh." Parker shushes his uncle. "Okay, yes, we . . . made out but I promised I would not say anything so *silenzioso*."

"Why does she want you to keep it a secret?" I ask.

He shrugs. "She says she is too old for me."

Again, Luca and I swap looks and a humorous laugh breaks out between us. "She knows you are nearly seventeen, yes?"

Luca snorts. "Yes, notice how your dad is graying and Payson is young and beautiful." He flicks a heated look at me but it's gone just as quick.

"I am not fucking graying, stop saying that," I snap. Luca is a few years younger than me but thinks it's hilarious I sometimes find a few gray hairs. More so in my beard and since I haven't shaved, they stand out a bit more.

Payson and Janelle stroll into the room. Janelle walks across the room and sits in the seat farthest from Parker. He frowns, and I glance to Luca who is smiling at them. I adjust my eyes on Payson when she walks my way. She changed while upstairs into tiny blue shorts. I bloody love the way her thighs jiggle with each step. Makes me want to drop to my knees and sink my teeth into the soft flesh.

She stops in front of me, lifts her hand and strokes down my beard and knifes through my hair near my ear. "I like the gray."

I pull her tight to my body, gripping her ass with one hand and holding her lower back with the other. "And I really like that I can see your little nipples through your shirt," I whisper only for her to hear. My eyes drop to the tight white top hugging her body, her deep pink nipples just barely visible.

"I really like how I can feel your dick getting hard," she whispers back.

All the blood rushes from my ears to my hardened dick. "I really like how you thought I was going to let Luca anywhere near your pussy."

She shivers, whimpers and her hands tighten in my hair.

"I'm not about to watch you two fuck. Bad enough I have to hear it," Parker grumbles.

Payson pushes away from me and gasps at the same time. "Stop talking about it!" she screeches. "It's worse that you keep bringing it up!'"

"It was worse hearing it!" he shouts back.

Janelle watches them like she should have a bowl of popcorn in her hand, but I couldn't be more concerned. I thought they were getting along but it's almost like they are arguing like . . . *siblings.*

"Tell me about Parker's mom, please."

Payson and I are lying in my bed, she's between my legs and staring up at me, playing with my chest hair like she always does when it's exposed. To think there was a time I used to wax it bare would blow her mind. I'm doing my best to ignore how my dick is resting between her perfect tits.

We played a few games on the Wii much to Payson's and Parker's dismay. I could not let everyone go to bed after their argument in the kitchen. They seemed better by the end of the night, I think Janelle helped that, but I still don't enjoy hearing them argue.

Even Janelle stuck around and is sleeping in the spare across from Parker's room. I pulled Parker aside and told him to be smart. I know I can't stop him from doing what he's going to, but if I can help prevent anything we don't want, like a child, I will. That's why I gave him a box of condoms from my closet. Not like I'm ever using them again.

"You sure you want to know?"

"Yeah. I think it's time I stop avoiding things just because I don't want to think about them. Hearing about a girl that far in your past seems like the easiest. That is, unless you're about to tell me a story about your one true love like Luca." Her lip puffs out.

I brush a piece of hair back from her face and around her small ear. "My only true love is you, babygirl."

"Really?" I don't miss the excitement in her voice. It warms my heart.

"Mhm."

She settles her head on my stomach, her fingers still tangled in my chest hair, and smiles. "Go on, then."

She's so fucking pretty. I do not understand how Payson could think my eyes would wander even for a second when the way she looks at me makes me want to buy a diamond ring and slap it on her finger right now. If she knew how obsessed I am with every single thing about her, she wouldn't let those insecurities from her childhood affect her so much. But they do, and even if I have to spend my whole life assuring her we are forever, I will do that.

"When I was sixteen, I went to Italy for a few weeks in the summer. I had just finished school and was leaving for America in fall, so my parents decided to take all of us on a family vacation as a goodbye since they were not able to move with me."

"That's so young to leave your family." She frowns.

"Yes, it is."

"I'm excited to meet them next month." Payson does this often, changes the subject in the middle of our conversations—I just roll with it.

"Me too." Everyone I love being in the same house will leave me with so many things to be thankful for. I know my family will love Payson as much as I do. My mom asks about her every phone call and has even requested to call when we are together sometime, but we haven't had time.

"My aunt always does Thanksgiving at her house on Thursday. I would invite you but . . ." She bites her bottom lip.

"I understand." I push a hand through her hair and watch her eyes flutter as I massage. "One day we will attend all holidays together but until then, you are more than welcome at mine."

She closes her eyes. "You talk about our future a lot."

"I mean every word I say."

The room falls silent, and I give her time to think. Her body is still tense, so I know she's not fallen asleep. After a few minutes, Payson's small voice breaks through the silence. "Thinking about our future scares me," she admits.

"I know."

"I'm young, but I won't be forever. Are you still going to l-love me when I'm not?" It doesn't surprise me that she stutters on the word love. Eventually I'd like to discuss professional help. She opens up around me, she's able to tell and show me her feelings, but I see the mask she slips on in front of everyone else. Not as much as it used to be, but she's still hiding a piece of herself. A professional could help lessen the weight on her shoulders; maybe get rid of it completely.

Tipping her head, she blinks open her eyes and I stare into them for a long while. "It's you and me, Jailbird. Always."

Her throat bobs with a deep swallow. "Forever."

"I will love you when you are forty and I am fifty-six." She pushes onto her hands and knees, keeping her bum knee straight out behind her. My hands sink into the soft skin on her abdomen as I pull her up my body and roll us so she's on her back. "Sixty-six and eighty-two." She knifes her hand into my hair and pulls my lips to hers. Before I kiss her, I brush my lips back and forth. "I will love you at all ages just as much, if not more than I love you now."

"I promise the same," she whispers.

Payson hasn't said the words but that's the first time she's hinted at them. The obsession I've done my best to keep at bay is nearing the surface, threatening to burst and show itself to her. She's not ready for everything, but there is something I'm curious about. "If I asked you to marry me, would you?"

Her green eyes shine and she gawks at me, not believing what came from my mouth. "L-like now?"

I dip my chin. "Yes."

"B-but I'm seventeen. I'm in high school. You're my *coach*. We met less than three months ago, Ashley! W-what do you mean, *'yes'*? That's *illegal*; you would be *arrested*!"

"Shh." I stroke a hand down her sweet face hoping to calm her. "It's not illegal if you get a parent or parental figure to sign off."

That doesn't calm her at all. Bloody hell this really has her worked up. I haven't seen Payson this distraught, well, probably since she found out I had a son. "Ashley James Pearson." I smirk at her use of my full name. She pushes on my chest and sits up. The lamp behind me gives off a warm yellow light that brings out her tan and the gold flecks in her eyes.

She's obviously bothered but I can't stop thinking about how beautiful she is. How beautiful she will be walking down an isle to me in a white dress. Knowing Payson, she won't want a wedding but it's not something I'm willing to compromise on. We will have a wedding and she will get a dress and I'll be in a suit, and we will confess our love in front of everyone that loves us. One day. Maybe not as soon as I'd like, but one day it will happen.

Payson's stressed voice pulls me from my head and back to the present. "Are you listening to me!?"

"Yes."

She scoffs, shoves me off of her and throws her arms over her face. "I can't believe you just asked me to marry you."

"I didn't. I asked if you *would*. I'm getting the feeling the answer is no."

Another girlish scoff and she props up on her elbows and looks up at me. "Same thing, Ashley. I can't believe you. You know we're not even dating?"

"Then date me." I move onto my knees needing the leverage over her.

"You're my coach."

Payson whimpers when I shift so I'm on all fours over her lower half, waiting to pounce.

"Date me in private until I'm not, then. Commit fully to me, Payson, and I will do the same."

Her eyes track down my body, pausing on my arms for a moment until she finds my face again. "No more strip clubs."

I'll never forgive myself for that. Especially after finding out who the stripper was. The Burton girls are trouble but it's my fault I let them be the trouble in my life. "Of course."

She nods thoughtfully. "No more secrets."

I'm level with her face now. "Parker and—" I sigh, hating that I have to mention her when we are having a good night. "Alyssa. That is all." The only other thing I know that she doesn't isn't my place to tell her. I wish Jethro would have kept me out of it altogether.

"I want to know everything about you and Alyssa, one day, not today. You exhausted me in the ballpark."

"I'll answer anything you ask." I don't remember much from the time I spent with Alyssa, but I will tell Payson everything I can remember if it means she will officially be mine. Titles don't mean a lot, but it's a step in the right direction.

She twists her lips and her gaze falls from mine. "Okay, one question about Alyssa, then I want to hear the rest of the story you were telling me before you stopped to ask if I would *marry* you." She nearly spits out marry, and it would make me smile if we weren't talking about Alyssa.

"I believe *you* interrupted *me*, but go on."

"Did you know she was eighteen? Like is the age gap something you're into?"

This is a valid concern for her and shows just how mature she is. Why would she want to be involved with a man who got off on young girls? "No. I was at a bar, she was there. I was . . . very drunk. I was not aware she was eighteen. Young, maybe midtwenties in my drunken state, but I'm not into you because of your age, Payson. I have never wanted anyone that much younger than me. Obviously, having been with Alyssa and now you it seems I am lying but please believe me when I tell you I had no idea on her age."

"I believe you," she mutters, and it's the best thing she's ever said to me. "You're only a pedophile for me. Got it."

She giggles like that is the funniest thing she's ever said. I take her moment of vulnerability and dive down, crushing her body under my weight. She gasps but continues to laugh. Her laugh is contagious but I'm not letting her get away with calling me a bloody pedophile. She cries out when I tickle her sides, but I don't let up until my fingers cramp and fat tears pour from her eyes.

She sucks in a deep breath from not being able to while I tickled her. "You're a pedophile *and* use your strength to overpower me."

My eyes flare and my dick hardens more than it was from having her body thrust against mine while trying to get me off. *Damn right I do.*

"I like when you fight me." I kiss the base of her ear. "And I like that I can take anything I want from you." I snake an arm under her, teasing her ass before slipping a finger deeper. She gasps and squirms and it's fucking beautiful. "I'll show you a fucking pedophile, little girl."

I grip her hips and flip her over on her stomach, not as rough as I'd like to be because of her knee. I even take my time to angle her in a way I know I won't hurt her when I fall on top. Then I do. Not giving her all my weight but enough so she can't move. Her ass recoils when I spank it and she moans into her pillow. I spank her again, loving how my palm burns and her flesh turns pink. Her shorts are so short I don't have to pull them down to see her ass cheek because they have ridden up, but I do it anyway. Much to my pleasant surprise, she's not wearing anything underneath, and when I toss them to the floor, she pulls her good leg up and arches her back so her ass is in the air. I spank her again.

"You want to repeat those words to Daddy again?" I spank her right over my reddened handprint, knowing this will probably bruise her, and I love it.

"N-no."

The beast she woke on parents' night bangs against my chest, begging to come out. I growl. "No, what?"

She turns her head, and wild but innocent eyes meet mine. "No, *Daddy.*"

I groan loudly and palm her bruised ass in my hand, massaging the sore spot. On the edge of her ass are the bite marks Chanel must have been talking about. It's not even that noticeable so she must have really been looking. The thought makes me angry. She was looking for a flaw so hard and all she found was my imprint on her ass.

"Bite me, Daddy. Leave more marks on my body," she begs softly. "Please."

I hold her eyes until my mouth is hovering over the spot with my mark already. I find the faded divots of my teeth on her otherwise smooth ass, and bite. The sweet scent of Payson permeates the air, and my eyes roll back. I don't break the skin but I must come close because Payson shifts her ass like she's in pain.

I pull back and she begs me to do it again. This is how I know our souls are one.

I sink my teeth into her beautiful skin five more times until she has my love bites on her ass, hip, waist, and throat. She complained about that one saying it would be hard to cover, but I didn't do that deep like I did the others, so she will be fine. And if not, well at least people know she belongs to someone.

Now we are back to lying side by side, breathing hard, and I'm left with a raging boner tenting my pajama pants. Payson keeps rubbing her thighs together, and I imagine she's as needy as I am. I almost thought she was going to come when I bit her hip, but she didn't.

"Can you finish the story so we can have sex?"

A weak laugh bubbles out of my mouth. "Story?"

"About you and Parker's mom."

"Okay, but as soon as I've answered all your questions, I'm going to be balls deep in that tight cunt."

"Deal. What is her name?"

Her name used to send a ping throughout my chest. Not because she was my first love or anything like that, but because we shared so much, a son. Now it does nothing. I will always think fondly of Marzia; as the mother of my first child, she gave me the most precious gift.

"Marzia."

"Pretty name," she grumbles.

I love my jealous little girl. I really should have this conversation when we are not lying in bed. Any serious conversations we have should be said where we can't fuck, which I haven't found many places I can't take her on, but the bed is the worst. It's meant for fucking her tight cunt.

"Like I said, I was sixteen and my family took us on a vacation. Dad, my brother, brother-in-law, and I were playing volleyball on the beach court when a kid a few years younger than me wondered over and asked if he could play." I smile at the memory and look at Payson wondering if she caught on, but she is staring intently at my chest, so I keep going. "Said his name was Luca and he liked volleyball."

She jolts. "Luca? Like, Luca downstairs?"

I nod and chuckle. "Mhm. A string bean at the time but damn good at volleyball. I was glad he chose to be on my side."

"That's when you became friends?"

"No, just when we met. I saw him one more time before leaving the island, but we weren't friends until he showed up in America claiming to be the best Libero around."

Her body shakes with a soft laugh. "He's not wrong."

No, he's not. "But we played volleyball and then his family showed up and he joined them, and my family left for dinner. A few mornings later, I was out for a jog just after sunrise—"

"Ugh." Payson slaps her hand to her face. "Is this going to be some romantic meet cute how you ran into a girl while jogging and it was love at first sight or something?"

I have to bite back my laugh because she's not far off and I know laughing wouldn't make her happy or this story easier to hear. "Young Ash was not the confident sexy man you are lying next to today." Her scowl is murderous. "He was awkward, so don't romanticize it."

"So what's different now?"

I narrow my eyes. "If you want to hear the rest, you will shut up."

She rolls her eyes and makes a motion like she's zipping her lips. "Thank you. Anyway, yes, we bumped into each other while jogging and she explained how she saw me playing volleyball with her brother and she thought I was good."

"Wait. Her brother?" She shoots up in bed. "Parker's mom is Luca's sister?"

I thought I mentioned that. If not, she must have heard Parker call Luca uncle. "You were not aware of this?"

"No." Frustration tugs on her face, pulling it into a frown. "Well, isn't that fantastic. Your baby mama is your best friend's little sister. How fucking cliché."

"You shouldn't be jealous, Payson. There was nothing between us back then and there definitely isn't today . . . since she died thirteen years ago."

Her mouth falls open and her face shifts with guilt. "I'm sorry. I didn't know."

"I wouldn't expect you to. Besides, I told you we weren't close. I wasn't aware of her death until a year after she died."

"I don't understand."

"Marzia and I slept together twice. On the beach that morning we met and once the night before I left to head back home. That second time I saw Luca?" She nods. "That was when I was doing the walk of shame from his sister's room. We greeted each other but his English wasn't so well back then so it was mostly just staring. Anyway, Marzia found out she was pregnant after I was gone and since we didn't keep in contact, she had no way of telling me." I pause. "She *could* have, she *chose* not to."

"What do you mean?"

"I told her where I was going to school, if she wanted to tell me—she could have. We weren't serious and she knew my plans for volleyball and thought it would have *inconvenienced* my life to tell me I had a child walking around this earth with no father. As if children are some kind of inconvenience." My blood boils any time I think about that. Most of the time, I don't, I just remember how blessed I am to have Parker now and have a relationship with him for the past twelve years. But I'll never be able to get those years back and that will haunt me for the rest of my life.

"I get it," Payson mutters, her voice like a blanket right off the line in summer. "She didn't give you the option to say if having a son would inconvenience you or not."

"It wouldn't have."

"I know." I thread our fingers together and stare at how much smaller hers are than mine. It's a good thing she's not a Hitter because her hands are tiny. "I see how you are with him, Ash. You love him. I think that's why I got over you having a son quicker than I expected. It was a big deal, especially since you lied"—her eyes flick to mine—"but I could tell how our situations differed. Parker loves you just as much, even missing those first years."

My parents have said the same but coming from someone like Payson with every reason to be spiteful toward the situation but still be able to see it so clearly, causes a lump to form in my throat.

"I want to clarify this before I continue. At the time you asked, I did not consider myself a dad. I know you probably will not understand because while, yes, I fathered a son, I did not raise him. I don't consider that a dad. I might be now, but that's a big might because Parker is almost seventeen. He hardly needs raising. I would not consider your father a dad, and I won't consider myself one.

"I know it feels like I lied, I guess technically I did but I was ashamed. It's an excuse, I'm aware, but I grew up with a brilliant father. He was at every game, he taught me to ride my bike, to shave. I have always considered my dad a best friend and when I was around Parker, despite loving him more than life—it was awkward. Not best friends, hardly friends at all. He didn't know me and I didn't know him, but I tried so hard to be my dad with someone who didn't know how to accept it because I wasn't around enough for him to accept my role as his dad."

Payson stretches forward, cups my face and kisses the cheek closest to her. My skin warms under her full lips. "You might not feel like a dad. But being there as much as you could is more than a lot of *real* dads can say. You are a dad, baby." *Baby*. I fucking love when she calls me baby.

I close my eyes and sigh, having her lips brushing over my skin feels bloody good. "She was never going to tell me. I only found out because Luca was FaceTiming his other sister, Bella, one day and I caught a glimpse of a little boy who looked exactly like me as a child minus the gray eyes. Bella didn't deny it, but she wasn't aware I didn't know he existed. Marzia had told her I didn't *want* to be involved. Luca was completely unaware Parker was mine at all, but he saw how upset I was at the news. I'm fairly sure that's the only reason he didn't punch me for sleeping with his sister.

"I lost my virginity and conceived a child on the same day."

22

Payson

WHEN I FOUND OUT Ash lied about having a son—I figured it was for selfish reasons. He knew about my issues with the "dads" in my life and didn't want me discovering he was just like them. Or he just didn't want me to know he had a son because he didn't consider us serious.

Now I'm lying here minutes after he asked me to *marry* him—I'll come back to that one—listening to him talk about how the woman who fell pregnant with his baby after his first time having sex kept his child a secret from him and then died. Obviously dying isn't her fault, I'm not completely insensitive.

"How did she die?"

"She battled cancer as a kid. It came back when Parker was three and she died a year later."

"That's so sad." My heart aches for Parker. Even Ash. He never got his closure. I know he says there was nothing between them, and even if that's true, she is the mom of his son. He gave his virginity to her. There is a bond there. He obviously has hard feelings toward her for keeping Parker a secret, he's never gotten to deal with those and still blames himself for not being in Parker's life.

"Parker was so young he hardly remembers her, but Luca and the rest of his mom's family do their best to tell him stories." His eyes are closed, and he looks peaceful despite the hard story.

I'm always needy for Ash Pearson but right now, when he's being vulnerable for once, has me itching to crawl into his body. Not on top—but inside. I want to burrow into his body and never leave so he knows I'm always there. That's impossible, obviously, so I just crawl on top, with my hands in his hair and my head resting on the pillow next to his so I'm able to still kiss him when I want. He wraps his arms around my naked lower half and squeezes my ass. The thing about Ash is no matter the conversation, he's going to always let me know sex is on his mind. "Thank you for telling me."

"Thank you for listening. I know finding out the way you did about Parker was a shock. That's not how I planned to tell you."

"You were planning on telling me?"

His throat makes a little noise in my ear, almost like a scoff. "I plan to spend my life with you, Payson. I think you would have found out I have a son at some point. He wasn't meant to move to town until after the season, I thought I had time to drop the bomb, but he decided to move early."

I mutter something about him being a smart ass and he spanks me. I do my best not to focus on the dampness between my legs, but I can't help if spanking makes me wet. He knows it does, so it must be what he wants.

"But, yes, I planned on making you a nice dinner and end the night having dessert in my room." He pumps his bushy eyebrows twice.

"You were planning on breaking the news of you having a son while you took my virginity?"

"I made him losing mine, so." He shrugs and I burst out laughing.

"I don't want to hear about you losing your virginity."

His stomach shakes when he chuckles. "Does it help if I tell you she didn't come?"

Does it? I think it over for a few minutes. "No. In fact it makes it worse because that means you couldn't last, meaning her pussy was good."

"I was sixteen, Payson. Her pussy could have been rubbish and I wouldn't have known." He rolls us to the side, flips me so he is spooning me. "The fact I couldn't last with you is much more impressive."

Hmm . . . I suppose that is correct, yes. I smile to myself and back up against his hard body. "You're too charming."

Ash presses himself tightly behind me and wraps an arm around my stomach, laying his hand over it, he gently runs a thumb over my scar. A peaceful silence settles over the room.

Until I can't stand it being quiet because like Luca said, "*I'm chatty.*" Might as well prove that to be true. "Can I ask you something?"

"Anything."

"I know we're dating now but . . . what about the public stuff? We can't kiss, hold hands, or even touch. Aren't you going to get tired of having to hide all the time?" I have no experience with relationships so not holding hands in public isn't a huge deal for me. By the sounds of it, Ash has *lots* of experience.

He rolls me onto my back and cups my face with one hand. The room is just barely lit by an outside light so I can only see the outline of his features.

"I can't kiss you when we're out—" He leans down and brushes his lips over mine and down my chin, until he reaches my collarbone. "But I'll bite you in private." His tongue is hot, licking over my love bite from earlier. "I can't hold your hand in public—" His fingers slip down my stomach into my folds, he curls them until two fingers are seated tightly inside me. "But I'll hold your pussy when we're alone."

I push him onto his back. Slipping his fingers from my body to straddle him.

"I can't show the world how much you mean to me, but you will never go a day wondering my feelings for you.

"I'll fuck you so brilliantly you'll never forget how much I love you. Because I do, babygirl. Through all the obstacles we have—or will face during our time together—I promise to never stop loving you, Payson Ray Murphy."

My heart thunders, he must feel it against his chest, he doesn't acknowledge if he does. I can hardly see his eyes but I know what they look like, and I stare into the beautiful eyes of my coach, boyfriend, and man promising me his future. "That's a big promise, Ashley."

"I've never meant anything more, babygirl. It's you and me."

Oddly enough . . . I believe him. I have no reason to believe him. So many people, including him, have shown me how easy it is to abandon me. I should build my walls higher, push him away and go back to looking out for myself before I get hurt. But I'm tired of being alone. For years I prayed for Ash Pearson and now he's here, like I always wanted. Anytime I get with him is better than no time.

"Always and forever."

He pokes my nose and rolls us back to our sides and we curl up for the night, not knowing what the future holds for us.

"Do not forget it."

Never.

Clay is already in his seat when I get to calculus. I fall into my seat behind him. The teacher announces our work for today and Clay turns his seat around like always.

"How are you today, Payson?"

"Actually, Clay, I'm doing really well. How are you?"

He ponders my question, then offers a firm nod. "I am fine."

"What are you doing now that cross country is over?"

Clay tells me about the camera he found at the resale shop in town. Apparently it's a collectors camera and he got it for the cheap price of two hundred and fifty dollars. To someone like Clay, I suppose that is cheap, not so much to me but I don't focus on the price and just enjoy seeing how excited he is about it. Most people wouldn't recognize he's excited, but his eyes expand more than normal, his hands move more rapidly with his words and his body relaxes, which doesn't happen often.

"That's super cool. What are you going to photograph?"

"I am not sure yet, Payson. Whatever catches my eye, I suppose."

I can't fathom what might catch Clay's eye, but I know him and when he puts his mind to something, he puts in 150 percent.

I take my seat next to Janelle at lunch, but she doesn't pull her eyes from wherever she is looking across the room. Upon some investigation, I come up empty-handed. All I see is Parker and some freshman girls hanging around him. Even with his age, he's still a sophomore so to see him with freshman girls is not stare worthy, at least to me.

"Earth to Janelle." She blinks when I wave my hand in front of her face.

The frown tugging on her lips lifts and she sighs. "Hey."

"You okay?"

Her eyes flick in the direction she was staring in, she shrugs. "Totally. Now, tell me about the vampire you got into a fight with."

My skin burns with her acknowledgment. "Are they really that notice-able?"

She laughs, but it sounds fake. "You look like Edward Cullen invited you over for a sleepover and Jasper was home."

Great.

Our phones vibrate at the same time, saving me from this embarrass-ment.

Coach Pearson: I have forwarded the information for flights and hotel stay. Please review and pass along to anyone that will be joining our week in California.

Janelle and I look at each other, sharing the same kind of face. The face that knows we are going to the same state as our third best friend but no clue if we will really see her because she's not opened our messages in a month. We've each received two letters since the first one, but they were generic. A little about her modeling and nothing about any letters we have sent her. It doesn't make any sense, and one of the nights I stayed with Janelle, we tried reaching out to her mom but her number changed. They are both MIA on Facebook. The whole situation is weird, which is why we aren't sure if we should be excited about seeing her when we aren't even sure we will. For all we know she could be in Milan, Paris, or some other place models hang out.

As if she knows we are wondering about her our phones ding with a message. Our eyes grow wide and we click on the chat at the same time.

Ronni: Can't wait to see you both!

That's it? She's not texted us in a month, not called, not communicated in any kind of normal way and that's the message we get?

"What the fuck is this shit?"

Well, at least I'm not alone with my thoughts. "I don't know."
Janelle's fingers fly feverishly over the keyboard on her phone.

Jay: That's all we get? Where the fuck have you been?

Me: we miss you, Ron. This is weird.

Ronni: See you guys soon!

I pinch my eyebrows; Janelle slams her phone on the table and the rest
of our team eyes us, waiting for answers we won't give them because we
don't know either. Whatever is going on with Ronni will be figured out at
Week of Pink. I'm not leaving California without knowing what the hell
is happening with my best friend.

23

Ash

I KNOCK ON THE wooden door, noticing the hinges probably need some care.

It takes a minute but Payson's granddad pulls open the door with a surprised look on his face. He's wearing a blue plaid flannel and slacks like most days I see him. Which is quite often. This is another secret I haven't told Payson but there's no way she could get hurt from me visiting with her granddad during the day. It started as a way to be around someone connected to Payson, a way to hear more stories and put pieces of my girlfriend together. I still love saying that—but now it's more so him. Paul Murphy is a brilliant man, and I couldn't be more thrilled Payson was blessed with at least one good and consistent person in her life.

"Coach, you're late. I didn't think you would be coming today."

He steps aside and I duck as I walk into the small double-wide. The ceiling is maybe an inch or two taller than me but the doorways are five inches shorter. Perfect for the small man in front of me.

"I apologize, sir. Had a few things to handle this morning that took longer than expected."

He waves me off and shuts the door before heading over to the coffee machine like every other time I'm here. I take my seat at the table where we will have a terrible but warm cup of tea before moving to the living room where we will chat and watch whatever gameshow is on TV. I don't come every day, but I try at least once sometimes twice a week.

My eyes catch on how much his arm is shaking as he pours the hot water from the kettle into two cups. His shaking has gotten worse since I was here last week. I wonder if anyone is keeping an eye on that. His daughter comes up here daily, as does her husband so I'm hopeful they have noticed. His cheeks seem more translucent and sunk in than rounded like they once were. I know elderly skin can become like that over time, but I've only known Paul for a few months, I wouldn't notice that if it was gradual. Which tells me its more drastic than it should be.

I'll chalk it up to the stroke and how much that wore his body down, for now. I wonder if Payson has noticed this stuff. Now that we are better and together, I could ask her, but I'm worried how she will handle talking about the health of her granddad in a negative way. My guess is not well.

She's doing so good right now I don't want to go back on the progress she's made.

A small drop of tea splashes over the edge when he sets the cup in front of me and the same for his cup in front of his seat. Paul grumbles as he grabs napkins from the center of the table out of a John Deere napkin holder that matches other John Deere décor around the trailer.

"Are you feeling okay, sir?"

The fist he crumbled the napkin in shakes more than the other one. Seeing me eyeing it, he lowers both hands to his lap. "Nothing to worry about, son. Just a little gift the stroke left me. The doctor is confident the shaking will get better. Says I need to stay active."

"Smart advice. The only way to keep muscles healthy is to keep them active."

He nods in agreement. "Yes, very true. Very true."

"Luca went to school for physical therapy for a while. Didn't get the degree, but he's knowledgeable in the subject. If you want, I could—"

"I have cancer."

And for a moment, the world stops. I stare into the kind blue eyes of Payson's granddad, turning over what came out of his mouth.

His untrimmed eyebrows furrow and he lowers his eyes to the table. "I found out at my last checkup. They found cancer on my lungs and it's spreading. Rapidly."

"I don't know what to say." I surprise myself, hearing the vulnerability in my voice. All I can think about in this moment is Payson. I should be thinking—worrying about the man sitting in front of me who's losing his battle with cancer. He doesn't have to say it, I know that's what he means by rapidly. But my mind pulls to the girl who is already so lost in life. She doesn't find serenity in many things but her granddad is a big one. I notice the tension leaving her body whenever she steps foot in this trailer. Like it's her safe place. So, I know there is no way Payson knows, she would not be acting how she has been.

She's been lively lately, lively for Payson, anyway. Things most people do on the daily: laughing, joking, enjoying life. None of those things will happen when she finds out. My heart and head battle with what to do. It's not my place to tell her but if she finds out I knew and didn't tell her, she will hate me. Paul isn't aware of that, he knows Payson and I are close but he assumes it's a normal coach-player relationship, so he's probably not worried about me outing his secret. Sometimes I wish that's all we were. Not because I regret anything but because it makes things complicated. Knowing when to step in as her boyfriend or leave things be as her coach. I guess that's the thing, neither is the right answer because I am both.

Paul explains what they are predicting and how without treatment his lifespan isn't looking more than a year. Then he tells me how he's not doing treatment.

I don't cry but there is a burn behind my eyes. "Sir, with all do respect..." My words fail. How can I ask him to go through with the hardest treatment in the world for selfish reasons? What would be better for Payson? Seeing her granddad alive but worn to the bone from the harsh treatments, or him passing before it gets to that point. Truthfully, I'm not sure. I can read Payson but sometimes she surprises me, and a moment like this is new territory.

Paul lays a fragile hand on top of mine. It's like I'm chatting with one of my grandparents. Moving from England at such a young age was hard but I did live with my dad's parents every summer for a while and those were the best summers. Paul reminds me of that.

"I have lived a wonderful life. Raised four kids to adulthood. Have more grandchildren than I ever thought and have seen most of them grow up. Of course I would love to be around for their whole lives but that's not how it works." He lets out a shaky breath and holds my eyes. "My only concern is Payson and Jason." Mine too. Not so much Jason, I'm not thrilled with him and what he said to Payson, plus, he skipped town after. "The rest of my grandchildren have guidance, someone looking out for them, and while Payson and Jason have their mother..." He frowns. "Well, it's complicated." *Don't I know it.*

"Have you heard from Jason?"

The heaviness in the room lifts a small amount. He pulls his hand back and cups his steaming mug. "Actually, yes. He is in Oklahoma with Amanda."

"With Amanda?"

His lips part with a gentle smile. "He called me yesterday, in fact, and filled me in on everything in his life. Apparently Jason never re-upped his time in the Army and has been out for nearly six months. In that time, him and Amanda started talking and now they are living in Oklahoma together. I think he held off telling me because they aren't married and living together." He chuckles.

"My grandchildren have this idea in their head I was not young before. I might be a pastor now, but I have lived a life in my eighty-seven years. You know what the biggest misconception is about Christians, Ashley?"

I shake my head. I have no clue; I wasn't raised in church like Payson. Sure, my parents tried but eventually they stopped fighting me and my brother to go.

"Christians are seen as these judgmental people who look down on anyone that doesn't live according to the Bible. I preach the Bible, I've read the Bible more than I can count and next to all the things people turn their nose at, you know what else it says? It says to love. Love everyone and not to judge. I live truly by that. It is not my place to judge the way other people live, I'm not condoning anyone to Hell for the choices they make, that's not my place. I'm not even turning my nose at it. I love my grandchildren just like I love anyone else, well, maybe a little more." We swap smiles. "There is nothing they could do to lose my love and respect. No matter how they choose to live their life."

"Do you love Fred?" The question falls out before I can stop it. Judging by the deep lines that form in Paul's face when he frowns, I think it's fair to say I might have overstepped.

"As difficult as it is, yes. Not how you might imagine." He lets out a sigh that sounds as if he's been holding that single breath his entire life. "Alfred is one of my main focuses when I pray because I hold hatred in my heart for what he has done to my family." *Yeah, you and me both.* "I'm guessing you know everything."

I dip my chin, hoping I'm doing my best to hide the angry buzzing in my body. "Payson told me everything during her trial time. Said I needed to know the full story."

Paul leans back in his chair and folds his hands together, a puzzled expression on his face. "She's not even told me everything."

I wasn't aware of that.

"Again, my grandchildren trying to protect me." Hearing the disappointment in his voice is oddly comforting. "But I know enough to know Payson doesn't want to live in a house with him. I know Jason moved as soon as he could because of him. I might not know why, but I know those two don't act on impulse, meaning there is a reason. One I might not like hearing." He eyes me like he is trying to find the answer, but I keep my face empty.

There is no point worrying his already worried mind. I can handle that side of things. The next time I see Fred, he's a dead man. I can honestly say I've never killed someone, but I would for Payson. I meant what I said in the hallway at school, if I see her with another guy, I'll kill him. That wasn't a bluff. Payson makes me crazy and knowing there is a man on this earth that hurt my girl? Well, that thought brings out my most primal instincts.

"I can only hope my daughter will wake up one day and realize her mistake and that Payson will once again be able to open her fragile heart for her mother. There is meant to be no other love like a mother's."

There's not. It breaks my heart that Payson doesn't know what true, unconditional parental love is. There are many reasons I want to marry Payson, that wasn't a spur of the moment question, well, it was, but I did mean it. One of the many reasons is to legally give her a family she deserves. My mom already loves her, and they haven't even met, but I talk enough about her. Dad is also a fan and while we don't need to be married for her to be considered family, I want to be. I'm thirty-three. I'm not getting any younger.

"Anyway, enough heavy. I want to discuss something with you."

My heart rate jumpstarts in my chest. I've been told I have a rather good poker face, I hope that holds true, because Paul is studying me so intently. "What is it, sir?"

"More on my grandchildren attempting to protect me . . . I suspect that Payson is courting someone."

Forget my heart beating hard it nearly fucking stops dead in my chest. "You do?"

He nods slowly. "She's happier. I'd love to say volleyball and the fact she's back into the world and not stuck in the trailer, but it's a happiness only love can bring. I remember it fondly."

Not only does he think Payson has a secret boyfriend, but he thinks she's in love with the boyfriend. She is, of course, Payson loves me very much. I've known this but knowing he can see it in her too has my hand itching to wrap around her throat and kiss her until she passes out.

"What I'm wondering is if she has mentioned anything. Or have you seen her with anyone? I know you're her coach, but the two of you seem close."

Oh, we're close alright. I hate having to lie to Paul, he's a good guy and I respect him a lot. But if anyone is going to tell Paul about Payson's relationship status, it should be Payson. I can't rip the rug out from under her again.

"Payson was quite fond of you as a child, I think she looks up to you and oddly enough trusts you more than the people who have been a part of her life for a long time. Sometimes it's easier to spill the truth to the people you've known the least amount of time, yes?" I gather he is meaning the conversation we just had. I nod.

"It can be, yes. I hope you know I will not repeat what you have told me."

He waves the thought away. "My daughter and son-in-law know, that's why they are bothering me so much," he grumbles. "I did inform Jason but asked him not to tell his sister. Not that I have to worry about that since they don't speak." It's obvious that bothers him but he continues without pausing, "The truth must come out eventually. If I can wait till after the holidays for my Payson to find out, that would be greatly appreciated, though."

"I was going to be selfish and ask the same for after the season." I offer a meek smile.

He laughs loud and raspy, and I can't help but to join until our laughs fill the small trailer.

"I will keep an eye out on Payson and any boyfriend, but that is against team policy so I highly doubt it."

Paul smirks. "Payson has been known to push the rules, Coach."

Don't I know it. My little Jailbird didn't earn that nickname for no reason.

"Now that you mention it. I did see her and Parker talking at practice." That's going to come back to bite me in the ass.

"Parker, your son?" Paul grins. "Well wouldn't that be something. Crush on the dad as a child and dating the son as an adult."

Wouldn't that be something indeed.

"My grandpa thinks I have a boyfriend?" Payson gasps and not because I'm balls deep inside her either.

I move my eyes from the bruises I left on her rounded hips, up her clothed body to her shocked face and thrust again. Her eyes roll back and she grips the edge of my desk so she doesn't fly off. "Yes. I told him it's against team policy and he told me you've been known to break the rules." I lift an accusing eyebrow and thrust my hips again. "Is that true, Ms. Murphy?"

She bites her swollen lip and nods. "Yes, Mr. Pearson."

"What do we do to little girls who break the rules?" My back tingles and my balls draw up. The remnants of me making Payson come drips down my shaft, so I grip her thighs and push them up exposing her whole pussy and giving me the perfect angle to fuck her as deep as her body will allow. My dick pulsates and I spill inside of her. Spent, I fall on top of her little body with my forehead pressed to her collarbone.

"We get punished."

Goddamn this girl, her mouth, and her high sex drive. I guess that's where our age difference comes into play. I'll be damned if I don't try and keep up as much as my body will allow, though.

My dick slips easily out of her tight pussy with the lubrication of my cum. It was easier slipping into her today as well. I didn't feel like she was about to circumcise me, but it could have to do with the two orgasms I gave her beforehand.

I lower to my knees, ignoring the pulling in my weaker knee. Keeping her legs pushed up, I wait for her to sit up enough to watch me before I lean in and lick up the bit of cum dripping from her pussy and shove my tongue inside putting it back where it belongs.

She fucking purrs when I shove my fingers inside and suck on her clit simultaneously.

"This doesn't feel like punishment, Mr. Pearson. This feels so fucking good." She drops back onto the desk. I'm so tempted to make her scream for me, but she's right—that wouldn't be punishment.

I pull off, already hating not tasting us mixed together but if punishment is what she wants, then that is what I'll give her. I slap her cunt with the hand that was just buried inside.

Payson gasps and her back arches.

I slap her again, loving how it sounds and feels. Almost as good as slapping her thick ass.

My knee locks up as I stand but I don't let it stop me from pulling Payson up, spinning her, and pushing her face down on my desk. I flip her skirt over her perfect ass, nearly salivating at the sight of Payson in her school uniform with my cum dripping down her thighs.

I flatten my hand against the warmth of her ass. My flaccid dick twitches in my pants but doesn't harden just yet. "You remember our safe word, Jailbird?"

"Y-yes." Her voice shakes as if she's really afraid but if I know Payson, excitement is the only thing she's feeling inside her little fucked-up head.

"I'm not stopping until you say it. Understood?"

"Yes, Mr. Pearson." I didn't even have to tell her to role play the teacher kink, she just did it, and bloody hell if I don't love it. Coach-player is my favorite because it's not even role playing, but Payson in a short plaid skirt and blazer is so fucking hot. I didn't have sex in secondary school like a lot of my friends. I never got to flip up girls' skirts and fuck them, but I get to now and it's so much better than it would have been back in the day.

I pull my hand back a good distance, knowing the first spank will sting. My hand connects with her ass. "I specifically put a no-dating rule out, and you disobeyed."

"I'm sorry, sir."

I spank her two more times. Each time harder than the first and each time her moans are louder. "You're only sorry because you got caught."

Another spank. The tanned skin on her ass is a beautiful pink color now. "Harder," Payson mutters.

My jaw clenches with her request. "You can't handle harder."

She angles her head to look back at me. Lust burns bright in her pale green eyes. "Try me."

She really shouldn't have said that.

I keep spanking her and she keeps moaning. After fifteen, I expect to hear the word slip from her pouty lips, but it doesn't. My hand is stinging so I know her ass must be too, but neither of us stop.

Not even when her ass has what I think will be a permanent handprint. I look down at my burning palm and back to Payson, seeing both cheeks littered with blue and purple bruises and popped blood vessels. I'm hard as a bloody rock but still my brows furrow. I've spanked her well over twenty times—she never once said the word. I know Payson likes pain, but this has to be excruciating. She won't be able to sit properly for days, maybe even a week.

I lay my hand across her burning skin, feeling the warmth I didn't feel while I was spanking her. Her thigh muscles tense, and still, she's silent.

I pull my hand back for the last time, giving her the chance to say, "grapefruit." When she doesn't, I crack my hand the hardest yet and leave it there massaging the sore area.

The only noise in the room is the equally hard breathing between me and Payson. It's not that she's in so much pain she can't speak. She was muttering dirty words almost after every spank, so I know she could have said the word, but she didn't. She didn't say it, meaning she wanted me to keep going, and I did. I spanked her flesh raw. I'm convinced my palm might even bruise and yet she stays bent over my desk like she is waiting for more.

Confliction bounces around inside me. The part that craves pain and loves seeing her perfect skin bruised and marked, knowing I did it, urges me to keep going, but the part that cares deeply for Payson and worries about her constantly is fighting an internal battle that has me wondering if Payson is as okay as she seems. Lately, things have been decent but the conversation with her granddad earlier has me wondering if she's a ticking time bomb and using me as a temporary diffuser.

The thing about bad habits—most people don't know how to break them before it's too late.

"I am not pretending to date her."

Payson scoffs. "I don't want to pretend to date you either, but you don't have to be so rude about it."

"I have heard you call my Papà—daddy. You are lucky I am even sitting in the same car as you."

I thought these two were getting along yet they continue to fight. It's only because they are close in age. Which doesn't help my argument since I'm the one dating a girl six months older than my son.

Even if I asked them to pretend to date—I'm not—it would never be believable because they can't pretend to like each other let alone be in love like Paul said.

"Both of you, shut up. I am not asking you to pretend. I am just giving you a heads-up for what Paul thinks." I don't mention it was me who gave him the idea because that's not important. All that is important is he doesn't think it's me dating Payson. I wish he did; not only think but actually knew it for sure, but that can wait until Payson is ready.

"Well, make him unthink it."

Payson shoots me a look from the passenger seat like *would you deal with him*? I reach over and thread our fingers before placing a kiss on her knuckles. "It's fine," I tell her.

"Oh, me next," Parker chimes sarcastically.

Payson rolls her eyes and turns for the window. I meet Luca's eyes in the mirror but he's no help because he is loving this, sporting a big smile.

We pull up outside Payson's granddad's. Payson and Parker are still ignoring each other, making the silent car even more awkward.

I angle my body toward Payson so I can see Parker and her both staring out their windows. "He probably won't even ask and if he does, tell him he was misled. It's not an issue, okay?"

They grumble agreements.

Payson reaches for the handle but stops and furrows her eyebrow. "Whose car is that?"

Looking past her into the dark yard, I frown. And even more when I recognize the vehicle. I glance back at Luca but I never told him about my chat with Jethro, so he's as confused as Payson. I unbuckle my seatbelt. "Luca, take Parker home. I'll call when I need a ride."

Payson's worried expression deepens when I push my door open, walk around, and pull hers. I grab her bag at her feet. "Ash, what's going on?"

I sigh and take her hand. "I don't know but we will find out together."

24

Payson

THE LAST THING I expect to see inside my grandpa's trailer is Mr. Gilbert sitting in my nana's chair with my grandpa in his, crying.

My heart beats painfully hard in my chest because this makes little sense. Grandpa cries, but usually at church during prayer. Not in his living room with—Olivia's *dad*.

"Grandpa?" I ask timidly, stopping in the kitchen and bouncing my eyes from my sad grandpa to a very stern Mr. Gilbert. At least *he* looks like his normal self. I can't look at my grandpa, if I do, *I* might cry. Or, even worse, I won't and that will feel somehow worse.

"Sit down, Payson." Mr. Gilbert gestures for the chair he was sitting in. He narrows his eyes to Ash.

I walk across the room slowly, looking at Mr. Gilbert the whole time. Until I go to sit down and remember how my ass looked in the mirror after Ash was done with me, then I veer to the right and stop next to him, facing the room. "I'd rather stand."

Ash isn't smirking like I almost expect and my already tight stomach sinks. The tension in the air is even more than the car with Parker. But worse because the room is also filled with my grandpa quietly sobbing.

"What is going on?"

Mr. Gilbert pulls his lips into a firm line. Grandpa dabs at his eyes with his handkerchief before he lifts his head to look at me. I suck in a breath and prepare for whatever is about to come out of his mouth.

"Mr. Gilbert stopped by to deliver some news." He sniffles. "I think you'll want to sit down for this, Ray-Ray."

"Why are you delivering news? You're a lawyer. I don't understand."

For a second, his forest green eyes soften but then he's back to looking like his normal butthole self. He flicks a look to Grandpa while I glance between the two men who couldn't be more different from the other, wondering what the hell is going on. Grandpa is the best man I know, he's kind and generous and would do anything for anyone. Mr. Gilbert looks like he steals candy from babies and spits on puppies.

"I'm your uncle," he blurts so suddenly I almost don't understand him.

But I do. I heard and understood his deep voice perfectly.

He said *he's* my *uncle*.

Someone could drop a pin in the back of the trailer and I would hear it with how silent all three men are right now.

"You're . . . my uncle," I repeat. It doesn't make sense for him to be my uncle. My grandpa has never mentioned it. *No one* has even mentioned him, ever. I wasn't sure my family even knew he existed. If he was my uncle, my grandpa would have definitely mentioned something. I know he would have.

But he didn't.

And, he's not saying anything now.

"Grandpa?" I pull my attention from Mr. Gilbert's demanding stare to take refuge in the comforting face of my grandpa. Even if his old eyes are still swollen from him . . . *crying*.

Then it hits me. He's crying because he didn't know Mr. Gilbert was his son. That would for sure make Grandpa cry. He would hate not being in his child's life, but that would mean Grandpa had an affair on my nana because Mr. Gilbert has to be close to my mother's age and that doesn't make sense.

"I am your father's brother. Half brother," he adds like that makes any difference.

Grandpa nods, as if I need help believing what is coming out of his mouth.

Ash is still standing in the kitchen, a perplexed look tugging his face into a frown. He holds my eyes until I find Mr. Gilbert's eyes again. They're *Green*.

He has the same eyes as me, a shade or two darker. No one in my family has green eyes. I knew I got them from my dad based on a few old photos I found at the bottom of Mom's photo tote. The photos she didn't throw away or cut my dad from like all the others.

"Like, uh, my bio dad?"

A curt nod later my knees are threatening to buckle. Mr. Gilbert's hands twitch from his side like he might grab me, but he doesn't, and I'm glad he doesn't. I don't want him touching me.

It shouldn't be a big deal finding out this is my bio dad's brother. I know nothing about him, so what difference does it make meeting his brother? Except all the difference—this whole time I've had a piece of my dad around and I never knew it.

"My mother married Hunter's dad after my dad died. They had Hunter a year later." Hunter. That's a name I haven't heard in a while too. My dad. It was like a sin saying his name in the house growing up. If it wasn't my mother freaking out hearing it—it was Fred. He hated hearing me ask about my dad. Said he was my dad and there was no reason to bring up that "*piece of shit*," his words, and I remember the first time he said that to me. I was six, maybe seven, and I cried. Jason took me to get ice cream down the road to cheer me up.

"Oookay." I shift and squeeze my body into a self-hug. "Why are you here, though? Why is my grandpa crying?"

His hard exterior breaks. For the first time, he drops his gaze to the ground. "It's a long story, but I'm here tonight because—"

"Payson." Grandpa's cracked voice catches me off guard. He walks to my side and wraps an arm around my back. He squeezes me tightly and his blue eyes fill with tears once again. "Jethro"—Jethro? That must be Mr. Gilbert—"is here—" His voice breaks but I watch him swallow his emotions. He leans in and kisses my forehead and usually that might comfort me, but it does the opposite this time. I wish he would just spit it out.

Mr. Gilbert must grow impatient because his rough voice cuts my grandpa off. "Your mother died this morning, Payson."

Everything moves in slow motion. Me looking at Mr. Gilbert and waiting for him to say he's joking and only finding a blank face in place. Me watching my grandpa breakdown in tears like when we first walked in the room. Finding Ash's stormy eyes and craving the comfort he brings but not even finding comfort in him right now. And me falling to my knees because the weight of the world has finally caught up with me.

25

Payson

"My baby sister." My aunt's cries carry down the hallway, and I nearly drop the razor blade from the sudden noise.

Grandpa made all the phone calls this morning, and I couldn't sit around and listen to him explain over and over that "Anne has passed." Not because it's too hard to hear—I feel nothing about her death—but because hearing the hurt in my grandpa's voice . . . well, it is enough to drag a blade over my arm three times.

Three more cuts to add to the collection. Three more scars that will forever haunt my body.

Kind of like the thought I will never see my mother alive again and how the last time I saw her I basically told her I was too busy for her.

I don't regret it, not really. I *was* too busy for her. I was too busy, like she was too busy to ever listen when I needed her.

My phone goes off with yet another text because word has gotten out now that Grandpa called the prayer service at church, only after calling every family member in his address book.

My heart pings seeing Jason's name on the top of my phone. I'd rather ignore it, but I grab it and hold it to my ear anyway.

"Hey."

I say nothing.

"We are on our way north . . . just making sure you're, uh, hanging in there."

Yep. Totally hanging in there after our mom died yesterday, bro. Totally chill.

"I'm fine."

There's a long silence on the phone. Aunt Vicky cries louder, I cringe.

"When will you be here?"

"Tomorrow or the next day some time."

"Are you staying here?"

Jason lets out a deep sigh into my ear. "No, getting a hotel. Figured Pa's place will be filled for the next few days."

He's right. Which is why I already asked Janelle if I could stay over for a few nights. Ash offered but it was Grandpa's idea to ask Janelle, so I couldn't lie this time because I know he will check in with Janelle's mom. "I'm staying at Janelle's."

"Good."

More silence before he says traffic is getting heavy and he needs to go. I doubt there is even a single car on the road, but I say bye anyway because I have nothing to say to him either. Why's he driving from Texas and not flying? I also don't understand who *we* is, but I don't care either. For all I know, my brother could be married.

It doesn't matter.

Nothing matters.

I toss the blade and wrap my arm before heading from the bathroom.

Aunt Vicky hugs me as soon as she sees me and cries into my shoulder. Grandpa is watching so I hug her back, but I don't cry. I can't fake crying and I don't want to cry, so I just stand there like the heartless *b* I am. Hugging my aunt crying about the death of her sister—my mother—until she lets me go.

I'm off school for the rest of the week but being stuck in the house with a constant string of crying people bringing so much food to Grandpa's—I have no idea who they think will eat it all—is miserable. I tell Grandpa I need a few things from the store, so he kisses my cheek and tells me he loves me and I leave.

I go to the store but end up standing in the aisle staring at something I can't even focus on until a hard hand grabs my arm and forces my attention to them. Jumping, I try to move away but he holds me in place.

Mr. Gilbert frowns down at me, still holding my arm. He's gripping me right over my new cuts, but the pain feels good. "You've avoided my calls."

Huh? "When did you call me?"

He finally drops my arm, a part of me misses the pain when he does. "How many people have been calling you today, Payson?"

"A lot."

He runs a tattooed hand down his face. "Fine. But I need to talk to you. What are you doing staring at cranberry juice? Do you have a UTI or something?"

I scrunch my nose up. "Even if I did, I wouldn't tell you. Uncle or not, that's weird." I also won't tell him why I was staring at cranberry juice because I didn't even realize I was. Or that cranberry juice was my mom's remedy for everything. Upset stomach? Cranberry juice. Headache? You need sugar, drink some cranberry juice. Jason and I used to joke that mom's lips were always purple because she drank so much cranberry juice. It was the shade of her lipstick, but we were kids.

Back when we used to laugh and joke together. Seems like a lifetime ago.

"Payson"—he snaps in my face—"I haven't got all day."

"You seem to have plenty of time to stalk me, corner me in the juice aisle, and harass me."

Mr. Gilbert scoffs. "You are a pain in the ass, just like your mother." We both wince at his harsh words. "I'm sorry. I would just like to talk to you. Last night was a lot to take in for many reasons, and I'm guessing your grandfather is busy with funeral plans and such so I want to make sure you're okay."

He wants to make sure I'm okay? Is he for real? "You have never said more than a word to me before last night, and when you do, you drop the ball that you are my piece of shit dad's brother and that my mom died all in the same breath. Now you are asking if *I'm* okay?" His harsh face contorts like he's constipated or something. "You haven't cared the last seventeen years, lets go back to that because news flash *Uncle Jet*, I'm fine. In my mind, my mother died a long time ago. Guess the world finally caught up."

I leave him in the juice aisle without a glance back and an even heavier weight in my chest than when I walked into the store. Damn him for pulling the truth out of me; since it's out, maybe now I can take a breath.

I'm not sad about my mother dying. In my mind I didn't even have a mother and now I really don't.

The best part is, I never have to be disappointed by her again.

26

Ash

"You think Payson will be okay?" Luca asks as we head into the gym for the last game before districts. A game I really wish we had Payson playing in, but we had Aubrey practice Libero all week so hopefully she can fill the spot. Or mostly, anyway. I texted Payson asking if she wanted a ride if she was coming and if she wasn't that was okay too. I wouldn't even ask any other player if they planned on coming to a game the day after they lost their mum, or any family member, but it's Payson we are talking about. If I know her, she will throw herself into the game as a distraction.

Things were complicated with her mum, and I don't know how to tread this situation. Comfort her and promise everything will be okay or . . . I don't know. That's why I've texted her the last few days and haven't dropped by. I'm sure she has a lot of family around and if she wanted me there, she would ask. I'm cursing the fact our relationship is private right now.

I run a hand through my hair. "I don't know," I tell him honestly. "But I'm here no matter what."

Luca claps my shoulder and with a serious look he says, "Anything you need, brother. You know I am here too, yes?"

I nod. "Of course. She is staying with Janelle so maybe she can fill us in on how Payson is doing."

I hate having to learn how my girlfriend is from other people but she hasn't returned any of my texts and since she wasn't home when I dropped a dish off at her granddad's, it's all I can do. He mentioned the funeral being Sunday and I will at least see her then. I can't hold her during it like I wish I could, but I can stand by her side. She will know I am always there for her no matter what.

"You want to know my main worry?"

Luca stops outside the gym doors and turns to me.

"She will push this down and when her granddad passes . . ." I had to tell Luca, after finding out about her mum, that was the only thing on my mind. What will come of Payson after losing her mum and her granddad?

"She will go off the deep end."

I nod solemnly. The thought of losing my Payson just when I finally got her is excruciating. And I mean lose her physically and mentally. With Payson Murphy, you never know her next move when her emotions are in charge.

"Well"—Luca squeezes my shoulder—"you'll be there to pull her back when the waves get too big."

Yeah, but what if I'm not enough?

I shake my head because it's not something I need to worry about right now. Granddad is okay and so far Payson seems . . .

Fine.

Inside the gym a few of our players are scrimmaging, including Payson.

"Mine!" she shouts as she sprints toward Aubrey's spike. She bumps it perfectly to Shannon and Monica kills it. Payson cheers and slaps Emika's and Monica's butts. Just like always.

Luca and I look at each other. Monica tosses a ball to Payson and she throws it in the air and serves it normally. No jump serves, thankfully. I'm not sure that's wise on her knee, even with the brace. The new brace, by the looks of it. It's blue like she wanted, to match the uniforms.

"She's here," I mutter.

"In uniform," Luca adds.

Yeah, *in uniform.*

"Payson!" I shout.

All of the girls stop except Payson. She stays in form with her knees bent and arms out in front of her. Perfect form, but that's not what is important right now.

I call for her again. She's obviously annoyed as she jogs toward the office seeing where I'm heading.

She closes the door behind her and turns with not a single ounce of what happened last night on her perfect face. Besides the purple bags under her eyes, which she has often, to be fair, you would never know last night she found out her mum died.

"I got my brace today." She kicks her leg out and shows off the blue and black brace hugging her knee. "It feels great. The doctor said I was good to play as long as I wear this."

My head is spinning listening to her. She should be crying, and I should be comforting her, yet here she stands, looking more ready to play than ever before.

I shouldn't let it surprise me because this is Payson. She doesn't do what you'd expect her to. Ever.

"Do you have a doctor's note stating everything you just told me?"

Her green eyes are so forlorn from real life I have to look away because it feels like I'm talking to a shell of the girl I love.

"Yep, on your desk."

Walking to my desk, I find the note she mentioned. It states exactly as she said and that they want to see her after the season is over to do another MRI to be sure everything is still in tact and the brace did it's job.

It's there in black and white, and yet I can't believe she's here, in uniform, ready to play the day after she finds out her mum died.

I pull out my desk drawer and her file, taking my time to place it inside, then return it to the folder. Once the drawer is locked, I toss the key into my pocket and fold my hands over my desk. "Payson, we should talk about—"

"Can I go practice? I feel a bit out of it after those few days off and this is a big game."

"Jailbird." I try again, gentler this time.

Her body jerks with a wince but she forces the weakest smile. Payson struts across my office, I turn to meet her when she stops next to my chair. My hands go to her hips, needing to touch her, make sure she's real because it's very possible this is a dream. Payson seems . . . happy.

Her smile grows. "I'm okay, baby. Promise."

Looking at her, you wouldn't think she was lying. Maybe she's not and she really feels okay but I see and hear the void inside her. "If you're not, you know I am here to listen, to hold. To love."

When she kisses my forehead, I grab her face and move my lips against hers.

"I know."

I slip my tongue between her lips, not battling like usual, loving the connection. She's the first to pull away, she pets my face and stands.

"Are you sure you can dive and stuff?"

"Yes, I've been here all day practicing. The brace gives me the security I need."

"Good. If it's too much—"

"Tell you. I know, but I'm fine—really."

I am the one to grab her face and drag it back to mine. "It's okay not to be."

"I know, but I am."

I don't want to believe her. It seems like a bad idea—but she seems so sure. I'm teetering on the edge, and she must see it. She moves closer, stepping between my legs and tickling the hair on the back of my neck. "I need this, Ash. Volleyball is my lifeline. Please let me play." For the first time since I walked in tonight, her eyes fill with unshed tears.

"Okay, babygirl. But go stretch. You are going to be sore after tonight and we don't need you actually tearing your ACL."

27

Payson

"CAN YOU BELIEVE THAT save?" I bounce excitedly in Ash's front seat. "Mr. Charles said it was one of the best he's ever seen in high school. Even for Senior Varsity." That had to be the best compliment I've ever received. Even if it was from the rep at Ohio State. A college I will never attend. Because it's Ohio.

"I have no doubts. It was a fantastic save." Ash brings my knuckles to his lips and kisses.

"You guys are seriously gross. You know that, right?"

I ignore Parker because even he can't annoy me tonight. I just played my best game to date and got recognized by another scout. I feel amazing. Everything besides my knee. I'm still wearing my brace but I'm worried how much it will hurt when I take it off. I can already tell it's more swollen than usual.

"Parker," Ash scolds, sounding so much like a dad my stomach twists in a weird way. I'm so attracted to his bossy side but there's also a part of me that wishes he would parent me. My grandpa is amazing but sometimes I wish I had an iron fist guiding me.

I grab his hand and return it back to my bare thigh. "It's fine."

Ash huffs, and for the first time ever, he turns the radio on. "Mr. Bright-side" blasts through the speakers, and he doesn't bother turning the radio down because he knows this is my favorite song.

"I need to run to the petrol station," he announces. I'm not sure Luca and Parker can hear him over the music since I barely could and I'm right next to him, but I settle in and enjoy my good mood and good music.

Luca and Ash run into the store and I'm thankful the music is still loud enough it won't be awkward when Parker and I don't speak. That is until he leans into the front seat, turns the music down, and says, "I'm sorry about your mamma." There are times when his accent is hard to understand, this isn't one of those moments, but I wish it was. Unlike Luca, Parker hasn't been to America, maybe once when he was younger, Ash said, but he's lived in Italy his whole life. He speaks fluent English, but his accent is thicker than Luca's.

I keep my eyes trained out the window. "Thank you."

There's a beat of silence, then he adds, "I don't remember my mamma. Not really. So I can't imagine what it feels like to lose a parent at seventeen."

No, he probably can't. The thing is, I didn't lose a parent at seventeen. I lost a parent at four and not too much longer after that when my mother chose her scummy husband over her kids. Maybe it's different now that she's not walking around and breathing Earth's air, but it doesn't feel different.

"It's probably harder when you consider your mom, a mom," I deadpan. Maybe it's harsh. He's just being nice but it's the truth. I have to lie so much for Ash and me, I don't want to lie about this too.

He mutters something in Italian, and I sigh. Great, now I made it awkward.

I glance back and see Parker looking out the side window from the middle of the back seat with a frustrated look on his face.

"I'm sorry. My family relationships are . . ." *Not relationships at all.* Complicated? Disastrous? "Complex. I don't mean to sound heartless. I'm really not." At least I don't mean to be.

Parker purses his full lips. "I know you are not heartless. You show my Papà plenty of love. *Sei perso.*"

It's awkward for a different reason now but there is no time to remedy it since Ash and Luca just walked out the gas station doors.

"I'm sorry if it's weird. But can we try and get along? It really upsets your dad when we fight. He hasn't said anything, but I can tell."

Parker watches his dad who is looking right at us with such loving eyes. "Sì. Mi spiace. I am sorry."

"Me too."

"Who is ready to party?" Luca cheers as he throws a few bottles, a box of beer, and a . . . box of wine onto the seat between him and Parker.

I spare a glance at Ash. His lips tilt in a half smile as he shakes his head. "I have a feeling you are going to see a very drunk Luca tonight."

Luca rushes forward and wraps an arm around my shoulders. He leans in and presses a sloppy kiss to my cheek and one to Ash's, which he promptly wipes off. "No, no, coniglietta. You are going to see *both* your loving coaches very drunk."

"Does that mean I get to drink?" I ask. I'm joking I have no interest in drinking. But Ash shoots a look at Luca who grins back at him.

"As much fun as that would be to see"—Ash's eyes darken—"you are not yet of legal age."

"You either," Luca says. I look back as he grabs a bottle from Parker's hand.

Parker complains to Luca in Italian to which both Luca and Ash reply—also in Italian.

"You are no longer in Italy, nipote."

Ash pulls behind one of the many cars in Janelle's driveway. I can't believe how many cars are here. Janelle's parents don't throw parties a lot, but when they do, they go all out. Janelle had texted me when Lauren decided she was going to throw a party, but I was busy in the gym all day, so I didn't hear about it until Janelle found me serving.

Luca pulls open my door and offers me a hand, I take it, and lucky I do because when I step, my knee buckles under me and Luca's the only reason I don't fall.

"You need an ice bath." Ash frowns, stopping by my side and replacing Luca's hand with his.

I pull him closer to my body and Luca heads inside with Parker.

Ash tilts my head back so I am looking at him and leans in. The air is cold, creating a fog as our breaths mix before he presses his warm lips into mine. "We could head back to my place. It will be empty for a while."

I consider taking him up on that but we've been locked away behind doors for a while. It'll be nice to hang out with my team. Even though we can't do this inside, or even touch, it'll be good for Ash to relax and let loose a little. I feel like he doesn't do that often.

"I can just take a cool shower here. Jay has her own en suite."

"I said bath, babygirl. Your knee needs to soak for at least fifteen minutes, a shower will not do that."

"I'm sure Lauren has ice."

Ash drops his forehead to mine and sighs. "Why are you so difficult?"

If only I knew the answer to that.

I drag Ash by the hand toward the large colonial-style brick house until there's a chance someone could see us, then I drop his hand and shove mine into my sweatshirt because it's freezing outside.

"Celebration" by Kool & The Gang plays from the overhead sound system they have throughout the house, and I crack a smile. Glancing over my shoulder to Ash, he lifts his stare from my ass and grins.

"Brette has the best taste in music!" I shout over the noise.

Ash breaks into a huge smile. We continue through the crowd of people, definitely not just the team and our parents like Janelle said Lauren was inviting. It's not overly crowded that we are bumping into people or anything, but I know a few are from Brette's work and others are neighbors. Mika's dads are sitting on a couch chatting with someone I don't know. Aubrey's mom is on the other side of them.

We break into the kitchen and the noise dramatically decreases, meaning they must have the kitchen speaker turned down. "Wick's really know how to throw a party," Ash tells me.

"Considering it's a Thursday." I snort and head for the freezer across the huge kitchen.

The door from the garage swings open to my right. Brette and Luca walk in, each carrying several cans and bottles of beer, laughing at something in such a guy way I nearly roll my eyes.

After checking the freezer, I come up empty-handed on ice. I grab out one of the fudgsicles that Lauren buys for me and let the door close behind me.

"Hey big guy where is all your ice?"

Brette whips around hearing me and obviously not seeing me before now. His big brown eyes soften immediately. "You need a bag for your knee?" He drops a look at my leg and his eyes grow. "I'll take that as a yes."

I laugh and wobble over to the island. Luca has since emptied his arms of the beer into the buckets I hadn't seen before.

Ash moves closer, looks at my fudgsicle and lifts a challenging eyebrow.

"I just won the first round of districts, *Coach*. Don't be annoying about your diet thing. No one follows it, anyway."

He rolls his eyes and throws the liquid in the glass Luca handed him down his throat before slamming it on the counter. "I was just going to tell you to eat real food before junk."

I take a dramatic suck off my popsicle, loving how his eyes brighten and how he cringes when I aggressively bite the tip off. "I'm good."

"Here you go, sweetheart." Brette passes me a bag, not noticing or caring that my coach is staring at me with the heat of a million suns. "Lauren ordered food. Should be here anytime," he tells us.

"Sweet," I say.

The kitchen door opens along with Lauren and Janelle, with a pizza boy trailing behind them.

A very familiar pizza boy.

Hero.

He is carrying at least twenty pizzas and hasn't yet noticed me, but Janelle has definitely noticed who it is, and her eyes are nearly popping from her excited face. Somehow, I have no clue how, her hair is curled, her makeup is light but done and she's wearing a short skirt and floral top. She doesn't look like we played a hard game less than an hour ago. Me, on the other hand, my hair is in a sweaty ponytail and I'm still wearing my uniform, with an added sweatshirt on top.

"Right here, dear." Lauren pats the counter next to the drinks, right in front of me. Hero places all the pizzas down and that's when his brown eyes find mine.

I swallow. I'm not sure why but it feels weird. Like I've been caught doing something I shouldn't, having Ash to my side and Hero in front, both watching me.

"What do I owe you?" Lauren asks, unaware of the tension.

Ash steps closer to my side—all but wrapping an arm around my waist. It doesn't go by Hero, but his face stays blank as he rattles off the total. Lauren says something about needing to find her checkbook and wanders off. That's when Collins, Alyssa, and Parker walk into the kitchen.

I narrow my eyes at Collins. This is the first time I've seen him since Janelle told me about his cheating. I could beat the shit out of him. Like he knows what I'm thinking when he sees me, he looks away.

Parker wanders forward and opens the top pizza, stealing a slice. Everyone else is standing around awkwardly staring at each other. Ash moves closer to my side, pressing against me, and his arm hangs loosely behind my back. He tugs on the end of my ponytail, jerking my head back.

"Pay, want to ice your knee in my room? You can put it up," Janelle asks loudly, for everyone to hear and maybe cut the tension. I'm not sure but it's appreciated.

Stepping forward, Hero is forced to step back since Ash has left no room for me to move to the side. I sneak around him, still feeling like everyone is watching me as I fill my bag with ice.

Hero stands by my side. I glance up at him quickly and offer a weird smile. "Hi."

I don't hear his reply if he did, but Janelle is tugging me from the room as soon as my bag is full anyway.

She doesn't stop until she is slamming her door behind her. Mika and Monica saw us, and Janelle pulled them along too. Now the four of us sit in her room while I ice my knee. Janelle is filling them in on the "tea" as she called it but there is no tea. So we bumped into Hero? What does that matter? Everything Monica and Janelle said about him wanting me or whatever makes no difference to me. *I* don't want *him*. I have Ash. It felt a little weird but not because I'm into Hero. It's cool he has a job, though.

"You should have seen our coach," Janelle says.

I groan and throw myself back on her bed, covering my eyes with my arms. "He looked pissed, didn't he?"

"Yes." At least two of them answer.

"I didn't even see him but I *know* he was pissed," Monica says.

I groan again. I cannot afford him to be mad. I don't want another punishment right now. My ass still hurts, and last night I had a dream about him fucking Maggie in the rain. No thank you.

"Collins is here too," Janelle says bitterly. "It's Thursday. What the hell is he doing here on a random Thursday in October?"

"I think they have a fall break or something," Mika tells her.

"How convenient," Janelle grumbles. The bed bounces when, who I assume is Janelle, falls onto it next to me. I don't open my eyes to check. "Why the fuck was Alyssa hanging around him?"

"They're 'friends.'" I lift two fingers on each hand to make quotation marks.

"Friends my ass," Janelle growls. "If I hear they fucked, I'm going to rip her pretty extensions out."

Yeah, welcome to the club.

"I'll give you a turn." She nudges my arm.

"Thanks," I grumble.

"Has he told you what happened between them anyway?" Monica asks.

"No, and I haven't asked. We agreed eventually but it's been so hectic and of course my . . ." I furrow my eyebrow. Was I just about to talk about my mother's death so casually? I know what I said to Mr. Gilbert—*Uncle Jet*, what a joke—but it's not the best thing to talk about her death so casually with everyone else. Especially Janelle, who I know is bursting at the seams to talk about my mother's death. I just don't want to. "Ya know. That's not been on my mind."

"Really sorry about your mom, Pay. I know we already said that but . . . I don't know. Just feels like we need to say it again," Monica chimes softly.

"Yeah, sorry Payson," Mika adds in her sweet voice.

Janelle grabs the hand to my side. I stare up at the Usher poster above this side of the bed, her side, and sigh. "Thank you."

"Remember when Ash Pearson was up there and now he's downstairs waiting to get you alone," Janelle says so casually I can't help but laugh.

"Yeah. Your mom saw a magazine with an exclusive from him. His picture was half the size of Usher's and yet we still hung it even though it was almost impossible to see."

Monica lies on the other side of Janelle and Mika lies to my right. We all shift closer to the middle giving everyone enough room.

"Can you believe it's already districts?" I ask.

"No," they reply at the same time.

"How are you liking volleyball, Mika?" Janelle asks.

I roll my head to look at Mika. Her profile has to be the best I've ever seen. Mika is probably one of the cutest girls I know, and I say cute because there is no other word for her pert nose, freckled cheeks, and kind eyes.

"I love it. Of course, Alyssa makes it hard sometimes but I'm so glad you talked me into it, Payson."

I smile at her. "Me too."

"Lucky for you guys you'll get a break without her," Janelle says, probably annoyed it was never her that got a break.

I purse my lips, looking back at Usher. "It will be nice, but I've only ever played with you guys. I don't know anyone on the JV team. What if I hate them all?"

"That would totally suck." Janelle snorts.

"You will," Monica deadpans. "But you'll have Mika and Aubrey with you."

"What if I don't make the team," Mika asks.

"You will," I assure her.

Janelle replies, "Yeah and if not, Payson can just change Coach's mind by blowing him in the office."

We all laugh until our stomachs hurt. Then I smile more because this feels good. I haven't been to a real sleepover since . . . before I stabbed someone at the last one. Obviously besides my nights with Janelle.

"Remember when boys were simple crushes," Janelle mutters.

After a long pause we all sigh.

"Now we have to pretend not to date because Payson's boyfriend is a crazy controlling—"

Someone knocks on Janelle's door, interrupting me from having to reply, not that I know what I would say anyway, she's right.

One by one we lift our heads to look at the large wooden door.

"Who is it?" Janelle yells.

"Coach," Ash barks from the other side.

Mika stiffens next to me, obviously nervous. It makes me want to smile. I forget how intimidating Ash can be when you're not fucking him.

"We're naked!" Monica shouts.

"Then get dressed," he says.

"Just come in!" I tell him because the last thing I want is his loud voice drawing more people up here. It's been nice with just the four of us.

Ash turns the knob so slowly and opens the door just enough to speak through a mouth-size gap. "Is everyone clothed?"

"Everyone but Payson. She's naked." Janelle grins.

The door opens the rest of the way and Ash steps in, frowning.

"You realize the party downstairs is to celebrate our win, yes?" He crosses his large arms.

The four of us trade faces and nod. "Yep."

"How is your knee?" He trails in, looking down at my leg and the ice I had forgotten about on it.

"Fine. Numb." I shrug.

"It's been fifteen minutes."

That's it? After lying in bed, I'm not in a party mood, not that I was before but I'm so comfortable now. "Will five more minutes hurt it?"

His jaw clenches as if he doesn't like the sound of that, Monica must notice because she's the first to stand. "I think I hear someone calling us." She nudges Janelle dramatically, not trying to be subtle at all.

Ash moves so Mika can slip from the bed, but I stay in place, ice still on my knee.

Janelle squeezes my hand, rolls over, and presses a fat kiss to my lips. Then she grins up at Ash sweetly. "Just kissing my girlfriend goodbye."

He turns to stone and shoots her a deadly look. "Not funny."

The rest of us laugh, his reaction makes it even funnier than it was. They are still laughing as they head for the door. "Oh, Coach?" I say.

"What?"

"Monica has a boyfriend."

He glances over his shoulder to her and sighs. "Whatever, just get out."

"Thanks, Pay!" Monica shouts as she sprints from the room. Most likely going to find Patrick.

"No fucking on my bed!" Janelle shouts next before the door slams closed.

Ash stares after the door for a few beats before swinging his head my way. With heated eyes he stares over my body.

I settle into the bed more. "I'm staying up here."

He grabs the ice from my knee and sets it and the towel wrapped around it on Janelle's floor. Then he kicks off his shoes and crawls in next to me, wasting no time before he's crawling up my body and wrapping my good leg around his back. "You want to explain who that *boy* was downstairs?"

The way he emphasizes boy is comical because it's like he's saying it as an insult. "No."

He rears back. "Excuse me?"

"No, because there's nothing to tell. He was at the pizza place with some friends when we were the other night." I shrug. "That's all." I don't know if that's technically lying, but I'm becoming a good one so might as well use it. It's not like I'm lying about anything big. I bought him food? That's pretty innocent, especially considering he looked like he needed it. Ash would have done the same thing.

"He looked at you like—"

I cut him off with a kiss, holding his face close to mine. "I can't control how people look at me. Only how I look at them. Did I look at him in any way?" I'm confident asking that because I know I didn't; I don't have eyes for Hero. Only the two-hundred-and-something-pound man lying on top of me right now.

"Like you two knew each other," he argues.

I roll my eyes. "Fine. When we were out, he looked hungry so I bought him a meal on my way out. I gave it to him, his friends ditched him, so I offered him a ride with us because it was cold, and you saw how small he is. He said no, and I left. That was all."

His voice turns to gravel. "So you lied to me."

I frown now. "No? When?"

"You said you saw him. Not that you chatted."

"Ashley"—I grab his hard face and force him to look at me—"stop."

I can tell he wants to say more but something is holding him back. I don't care what it is, I'll take it because arguing about Hero is pointless. We aren't even friends.

Who knew someone else washing your hair could feel so good? Ash stands in front of me, his long fingers sunk deep into my hair, massaging my scalp with some of Janelle's soap. I love Janelle's large shower. It's so big and has so many spa settings. Ash commented about it being good after a long practice and I agreed. We are only using two of the showerheads, never mind the other spa settings it has.

The best part is the bench so I can sit down. Not because I'm sore, I actually feel good, but when I am sitting, my face is eye level with Ash's dick. His *hard* dick. Neither of us has attempted anything sexual since getting in the shower but he says he can't help but get hard when I'm naked. It's nice being together and not jumping each other's bones. I wouldn't say no to sex in the shower, but I'm enjoying my head massage.

"This feels so good," I groan.

His chuckle is soft and comforting. "I would wash your hair everyday if I could, babygirl."

"Can that be a part of our wedding vows?" That's the first time I've talked about us getting married, and Ash must realize too because his hands freeze. I lift my chin and look at him with heavy eyes. "What?"

"You've thought about marrying me, yes?"

The hope in his eyes is enough to make me want to ask Grandpa to marry us tonight. "I've thought about marrying Ash Pearson since I was eight."

He tilts his head and continues washing my hair. "So should we head to the courthouse now, or tomorrow?"

Surprisingly my heart isn't beating overly hard like it usually does when we talk about marriage—because it's absurd, not because I don't want it—but I'm just sedated enough to not freak out. "I want a spring wedding," I mutter. "In England."

I've never once thought about my wedding. I've thought about getting married but never what I want in a wedding. I'm not sure why that came out, but I don't hate the idea.

"My mum will be thrilled to hear that."

I let my eyes fall closed and I lean forward, resting my head on his hip and attempting to ignore his gigantic cock just to my left.

Ash strokes a hand over my head and back now that the soap is all gone and I'm showered.

"I'm so sorry about your mum, Jailbird." I stiffen in his arms. I hadn't been thinking about her but of course he would. We are talking about my wedding day. A wedding day that won't have my mom. I said I never envisioned my wedding but like most little girls, I always assumed my mom would be there. For the first time since finding out about her death, a ping of sadness weighs on my heart. Like Ash knows that, he flips the water and grabs a large towel to wrap around me. While he dries, I stay seated on the bench, enjoying the heat from the towel.

"Come here, babygirl." Ash carries me into Janelle's room, his towel wrapped around his lap as he pulls me down to straddle him. I burrow into his chest and he rocks me. He moves back and forth and I can't help but feel five again. It's so nice. Weird, considering he's my boyfriend and right now he feels like a lot more than that, despite his dick struggling under me.

"I know it's not easy—your feelings for your mum—and I'm sure you are going to go through so many different stages. But I want you to know I'll be here for all of them. Even when you want to push me away, I will be here."

"I don't want to push you away."

"I know. But if you do, it's okay. I'm not going anywhere."

He has no clue what that means to me. I don't want to push him away; I said volleyball was my lifeline today, but I think it might be Ash. Only he brings me the sense of calm I've never felt before.

Safe, he makes me feel safe. Grandpa's house has a peacefulness about it. Janelle and even Ronni allow me to relax to a point, but Ashley Pearson knows me inside and out. He's seen my worse—my arms—and my best—volleyball. I know as long as he's around, I'm safe.

I'm loved.

Ash rocks me in that chair for a long time. So long I nearly fall asleep until his deep voice startles me. "Payson,"

"Hmm?"

His heart is rhythmically beating against my cheek and most of the reason I'm close to falling asleep. It's so soothing. Now it roars quicker.

"Marry me."

I don't freak when he says it this time, I don't even open my eyes and my lips stretch into a weak smile. "I just said I would."

"No, now. Marry me now."

He shutters when I press a kiss to his neck. He didn't use soap in the shower, so he still smells like Ash.

"I said I wanted a spring wedding."

His arms tighten around my body and he kisses the top of my head forcefully. "Fine. But it will happen this spring, Payson. I will not wait a year."

Sure, sure. Whatever makes the big guy happy.

28

Payson

WHEN WE EVENTUALLY EMERGE downstairs, the party is still going. I'm not exactly in party gear but after the hard-core cuddle session there was no way I was attempting to get ready. I could barely stay awake to get dressed, but Ash refused to let me stay upstairs and sleep so I'm here and wearing a pair of Janelle's old basketball shorts and my volleyball sweatshirt. Ash even helped me braid my hair, said his mom taught him so he could braid his daughter's hair someday. I thought that was cute, a little weird, considering he was braiding my hair—not his daughter—but it was still nice, and he did a good job. I ignore the ping in my heart about him having a daughter one day.

As we hit the steps, I spy Lauren heading our way and quickly drop Ash's hand. I can tell by her surprised eyes that it's too late. *Frick frick frick.*

"Where did you two disappear to?" she asks, an accusation heavy on her tone.

I glance back and cringe seeing Ash's hair isn't dry either. It doesn't take a brainiac to know we obviously showered together and Lauren's mom is close.

"Uh . . ." *Shit. What do I say?* We haven't been caught many times—somehow, but when we are usually Ash covers but he seems as lost as me. Unlike me, he's not panicking though. Simply staring at me, waiting for me to come up with something. "Coach was just, uh, checking on my leg. Janelle had told him I was in pain so he helped me do a few . . . exercises to stretch it out."

Lauren narrows her beautiful eyes. "In the shower?"

Kill me now. "No," I blurt, obviously guilty. "I mean, I showered because I didn't after the game. We just bumped into each other in the hall after."

Lauren purses her lips and nods her head once. "Mhm."

Ash stiffens behind me.

"Nelly was asking for you," Lauren tells me. "Might want to find her."

I force a weird laugh but nod my head. "Totally. On my way now."

Janelle and the rest of the team sit haphazardly on the couch in their second family room, away from the noise of the party supposedly meant for us but has quickly turned into adults gone wild. Ash was called away on my way here, and I didn't look back to see who called him because after the interrogation on the stairs from Lauren, I think it's best if we aren't seen together for a while. And it was a man's voice.

"You better not have had sex on my bed," Janelle mumbles as soon as my ass hits the white couch.

"I didn't. We didn't have sex at all." Disappointment contorts her face. "Not even in the shower?" She lifts one of my braids as if I need to be reminded it's wet.

I slap it away. "No, but your mom saw us holding hands with wet hair."

"And?"

"And? Are you crazy? She definitely knew something was up. Coaches and players don't hold hands. Besides, you miss where I said *our* hair was wet?"

I let Janelle have her moment squealing and such before I have to bring her back down to earth and help her realize her mom knows and she didn't exactly look happy. She wasn't mad, I've seen Lauren mad before—never at me, but I've seen it.

"Did she look mad?"

"She looked indifferent."

Janelle clicks her tongue and falls into the back mostly lying down now. "Then you're fine. She gave me and Collins that look for years."

That actually makes me feel better because I know she's never confronted Janelle for their relationship. She waited until Janelle told her, and hopefully she will do the same for me. That day might never come and that's totally fine with me. I don't want Ash and me to be a secret forever but I'm also not making a huge announcement when we're not. One day people will just see us in public as a couple, word will get out and save me from having to tell anyone face-to-face.

I fall back next to Janelle. "Is it weird him being here?" I lower my voice even more because Collins, Alyssa, and another couple sit across the room talking.

Janelle sighs deeply. "No. Well, yes, it's weird but not in the way I expected."

"What do you mean?"

"I expected to be more upset. Like seeing his face would make me want to cry." A look of puzzlement comes over her pretty face. "That's not how I feel, though. Of course I don't like seeing them hanging out because I hate her; I'm not sure I want to see him with anyone, but whatever, it's going to happen one day, right?"

Had you told me Janelle and I would be having this conversation a month ago, I would have laughed in your face. This is coming from a girl who ate nothing but strawberry ice cream in bed for days, jumping between crying and screaming at various couples on TV because "they were lying" about this and that. I mean HGTV couples as well as fictional and trashy TV too. I was just as upset without the theatrics. Janelle was going through it for the both of us, but I'm happy now, so who's saying she can't be?

The difference is, I'm happy because I'm in love. *Oh, shit*. Did I just think that? Am I in love? I've loved Ash Pearson for a long time but am I in love with him? I shake my head because now is not the time to contemplate that mess.

I roll my head to look at Janelle and she does the same. "I think I'm in love."

Her eyes blow wide and a big smile is quick to follow. "No shit." She snorts.

"What's no shit?" Someone falls onto the couch next to me, then another someone. Monica and Patrick. I greet him and he smiles back.

"Payson's in looooove," Janelle singsongs. Louder than she should. The rest of the room glances our way. Mika wanders over and falls onto the floor in front of us, crossing her legs and smiling so sweetly. "I thought we knew this."

The rest of us fall into easy laughter as everyone else goes back to their own conversations. "Apparently not all of us." Monica nudges me.

"Payson and Pear-pie sitting in a tree K-I-S-S-I-N-G," Janelle sings loudly.

I throw a hand to my mouth, muting the surprised gasp. "No! I forgot about that nickname."

Monica is slapping Patrick and me because she's laughing too hard. Janelle and I have tears in our eyes and even Mika is holding her stomach while she laughs.

"I don't get it," Patrick says.

Everyone else is laughing too hard to explain but I do my best between laughs to explain how when we were in middle school, we used to come up with food-related names for our crushes. Collins was Cocoa Puffs. Ronni's crush, Troy, was Twizzlers and Ash was Pear-pie because his last name has pear in it. Monica had a crush on a guy named Logan and his was Lunch Meat. When I remind her of that, she's starts slapping again. We are nearly hyperventilating when someone else joins the group. *She's* not laughing.

"Will you guys shut up? We are in here to get away from the noise."

My and Mika's laughter dies right away but Monica and Janelle are still chuckling, and that seems to piss Alyssa off even more.

"You mean you're not in there looking for husbands to seduce?" Janelle blurts. I shove her, not wanting to start anything tonight.

"We're just laughing, A. Calm down." Monica is the most reasonable and the closest with Alyssa but even that doesn't change Alyssa's overly exasperated expression. Nothing does until Janelle makes a comment about her agreeing not to be a bitch anymore. Then her anger shifts to an ugly smirk and my stomach falls because who knows what will come out of Alyssa's mouth.

She glances back to the group she left behind now staring our way. Collins is on his knees like he's ready to run over here if necessary. The pit in my stomach grows.

He meets my eyes but quickly looks away like he did earlier in the kitchen.

"I just made it possible for you to come to Week of Pink. I can tell Coach never mind."

Her eyebrows that give away her natural hair color even though she's tried to convince us the blonde is "definitely natural," dip. To my surprise, she shrugs me off. Meaning, I'm obviously not the focus of her anger right now—Janelle is.

It doesn't make sense for Janelle to be, what the hell has Janelle done to her besides that stupid—but funny comment?

Janelle crosses her arms over her chest. "What Alyssa? You obviously have something you want to say, so say it. I'm trying to have a good night."

Alyssa runs her tongue over her teeth and once again looks back at Collins. He moves to his feet.

"Don't," he warns.

I shoot a look to Janelle.

"You know we used to be friends," Alyssa pouts, and for once I can't tell if it's real or not. "You, me, and Ronni."

Hearing Ronni's name causes an unwanted ping in my stomach. Must be the same for Janelle because she shifts, bumping shoulders with me on accident.

"When was that?" Janelle snorts.

Alyssa rolls her eyes. "Not you, you"—she angles her body my way—"Payson."

"When?" I was *never* friends with Alyssa, sure she was around—sometimes, but we weren't close.

"When we were little. We were always at Ronni's house."

I used to get so annoyed whenever Alyssa would crash my playtime with Ronni. Because she wasn't our friend, not mine anyway. I never understood why Ronni hung around her but she always said, "she's nice." I don't know if we know different Alyssa's but the one in front of me right not claiming to be friends has never been described as *nice* in my book.

"We were friends until you came to town," she snarls, focusing back on Janelle. "You came to town with your long blonde hair and stole my friends right out from under me, all because Payson liked you better than me. Ronni was quick to follow behind and soon it wasn't Alyssa, Ronni, and Payson it was Janelle, Ronni, and Payson—the infamous trio."

It's obvious Janelle has no idea what she's talking about. Hell, I don't even know because it was never like that with Alyssa. "I was never friends with you. You were friends with Ronni, and I was friends with Ronni. That was it." Hurt is quickly washed from Alyssa's face. "I'm sorry if that hurts you, but it's true. You and your sister were awful to me from the very beginning. Why on earth did you ever think we were friends?"

"It doesn't matter," she snaps. "The point is you stole my friends and so many other things over the years, so I stole your boyfriend."

The room falls eerily silent. Everything besides Collins's quick footsteps. He stops next to Alyssa.

It takes longer for Janelle to pick up on what Alyssa is hinting at, no doubt her mind trying to protect her from what is right in front of her. When it does, her eyes fill with tears, and for once I wish I could pass my emotionlessness onto her, because I hate the fucking smirk Alyssa is wearing, knowing those tears are caused by her.

"You—" Janelle croaks. "Y-you fucked my boyfriend because . . . you think I stole your friends when I was *nine*?"

"You did." Alyssa blows a harsh breath. "Look how close you two are. If Ronni was here, she would be right by your side completely immune to me."

If only we were all immune to her.

Janelle pushes to her feet, ignoring Alyssa on her way from the room. Collins runs after her. I will check on her but right now, I need to deal with Alyssa.

"You are pathetic," I mutter.

Alyssa scoffs. "Me?"

"Yeah." It's not me that says that. Monica, who usually stays neutral in these moments, furrows her black eyebrows. "What the hell, Alyssa? You fucked Collins? You know they have been a couple forever."

"I wasn't the only one there, Mon."

"No shit." I scoff. "But you knew they were dating. I'm not blaming you anymore than Collins, he has a nut punch coming, but why? Really because you think she stole your friends?"

"She did," Alyssa bites out. "She showed up and all of a sudden Ronni was too busy to hang out with me anymore."

I'd be lying if I said there wasn't a small part of me that feels bad for Alyssa. It's obvious she believes Janelle stole her friends from her, but that's not an excuse. Over the years, Alyssa has been awful to all three of us—Ron, Jay, and me—and we've all kind of brushed her off because it never meant much. Sleeping with Collins? I'm not just brushing that off and neither will Ronni.

"You think Janelle replaced you, but you couldn't be more wrong because it was never you. Ronni might have been friends with you, but I never once considered us the same." I stand, needing to go check on Janelle, but cross my arms and stand in front of Alyssa first. "Sleeping with Collins was low, even for you."

I turn, heading for the door.

"Ronni was too good for you. That's why she left. Her manager thought you were a bad influence."

Pathetic.

"He's probably right." I shrug.

"Don't you think Ash will come to the same conclusion? That he's too good for you? He could do better. You and I both know it."

I glance back, eyeing her and doing my best to pretend that didn't feel like a punch to the gut. "You think I don't know that?" She says nothing and I laugh humorlessly. "He's Ash fucking Pearson, of course he can do better than me. I guess I'm just lucky enough that he doesn't want to."

Her face contorts with anger. "He's going to leave you just like everyone else."

Fucking hell, she's really digging it in deep tonight. Still, I crack a half smile because my mom just died and there's not much she can say that will bother me more than not being upset by my own mother's death.

"You know what happened after your little phone call the other day?" I make my way toward her. The room has cleared out beside Monica, Patrick, and Mika so I have no issues saying what I'm about to. "After your pathetic little phone call of you begging him to pick you instead of me, which by the way, how did that go?"

Her mouth snaps shut after falling open.

"Oh, right. He said it was *never you* and it was *always me*." I wave my hand in the air. "Anyway . . ." I drop my head and bat my eyelashes to her. "We fucked and it was mind-blowing, as always, but that's not the part I want to tell you about."

Alyssa's tears feel like fucking heaven right now. Knowing I made her cry after she made my best friend cry is priceless. "He asked me to marry him."

"He did?" Monica gasps.

I snap my eyes to her and smile for real. "Mhm. He did."

"Are you getting married?" Mika hiccups and looks up to me with excited eyes.

I capture my lips between my teeth but regard a silent Alyssa again. Tears still fall from her eyes. "Eventually."

"So, while you're lying in bed with whatever guy you convince to fuck you tonight, just remember that Ronni didn't choose you, Collins didn't even choose you, and neither did Ash."

"You fucking bitch," she hisses.

"Maybe. But only because I'm sick and tired of you hurting the people closest to me. It'll never be you, Alyssa. Get over it."

I back away and say my goodbyes to my friends before walking from the room. I truly hope one day Alyssa can find someone that chooses her, but that will only happen if she stops going for people that are already spoken for.

Janelle's bedroom door is shut and I'm pretty sure I know who is inside, and instead of interrupting whatever kind of conversation Collins and Janelle are having, I head back downstairs, hoping to find Ash. We need distance but I'm over the drama and just want my boyfriend. Or maybe I want to make sure Alyssa didn't move onto him; in the mood she's in, I know that won't be the last I deal with her tonight.

I pass Parker on the stairs with an awkward smile and hurry down.

When I find Ash, I'm surprised to see him and Luca attempting to do a keg stand in the middle of the living room. I cross my arms and prop myself in the doorway, watching them struggle and the crowd of adults cheering them on. I smile, it's not big but it's there. It's comical how different this room is from the one I came from. It's almost backward but I'm not surprised, because drama tends to follow me.

Which is why I'm not even surprised when a dark figure steps to my side. It doesn't stop me from jumping at his voice, though.

Jethro peers down at me, confused by my reaction, probably. "Hi."

"Hey."

The crowd erupts in loud cheer, and we look up to Luca upside down and Ash holding onto him for dear life with a goofy smile.

"Idiots," Jethro mutters.

"Just because people can let loose every now and then, doesn't mean they are idiots. Just because you don't even smile—"

I think he attempts a smile and I pause, because it's foreign and weird and looks like a creepy face filter and not natural at all. "Okay, stick with not smiling."

"Fine. Can we talk now?"

"You want to talk about my dead mom at a party? Why are you even here, anyway?"

Something like impatience passes through his eyes but he just sighs. "If you come talk to me, I will explain why I'm always around."

I do want to know but also don't want to be alone with him. I don't trust people, especially men who I know could easily take advantage of me if they wanted to. He might be my uncle by blood but I wasn't raised around him, and the man I was raised around made me promise him my virginity, so you can understand why I might not be trusting.

Curiosity gets the best of me, though, and it helps I don't get overly bad vibes from him, so I agree and he leads me out the front door and across the large deck to the porch swing. He doesn't sit but I do, and I pull out a blanket from the little basket, shaking it off in case a bug claimed it as it's home. Once I know it's clear, I lay it over my lap. It's not the slightest bit warm because it's been outside, but it should be soon.

Jethro stays standing.

"What do you want to know about my mother?"

"Nothing. I know everything about your mother, Payson." He must see the questions on my face because he continues with his explanation, "You know I'm a lawyer but you aren't aware what else I do. Which is private investigation. I started about seventeen years ago. When you were born."

There's that pit again. "That's creepy. Are you like . . . stalking me? It that why you're here?" Alarms blare inside of me.

"No. I was investigating your mother and before you ask why, because I see you wanting to, just shut up and listen. And I'm here because I'm still a very big part of this team, even without Olivia in town."

I huff but don't say a word.

"Good. About twenty-seven years ago, when I was in college—"

"How old are you?"

His jaw ticks because I've not shut up like he told me. I don't care, I don't have to listen to him, uncle or not. "I'll be fifty soon."

"When?"

"October twenty-sixth."

"How old is my dad?"

"Forty-five. He will be forty-six in a few months and our baby sister, Jennifer, is thirty-nine. Okay? You filled in now?"

"Oh my gosh, I totally forgot Aunt Jenny is my dad's sister. So that means she's your sister too?"

"Half sister, yes. She was born when I was eleven."

"She never mentioned you."

"We weren't close."

Accepting that answer for now, I lean back and gesture for him to continue. Sighing, he walks over and sits next to me. The swing creaks under his weight, and I wonder if it will break. Lauren would be so upset.

"As I was saying, twenty-seven years ago I met this girl at a, uh, strip club." My eyebrows furrow but he doesn't give me the chance to interrupt. "Things happened and well, we started dating. We dated for about two years, then she fell pregnant and everything else fell around it. I was twenty-five at that time and had no interest in having children. I loved my girlfriend but did not want a child. I asked her to abort but because of her strong religious background, she refused, so I broke up with her."

"You really are an asshole."

"Yes, I am." At least he's not trying to deny it. "She went through with the pregnancy, and I was not there for her once. No appointments, no late-night runs to the store for cravings. Nothing. I was out banging other girls while my ex-girlfriend was miserable for nine months growing our son."

"You have a son?"

Jethro's gaze fills with something but I can't place my finger on what. But he nods. "I do. I missed the birth and didn't even meet my son until he was eight months old because I was so mad at my girlfriend for going through with it. Of course, at that point, she hated me but there was still love in her eyes, and when I walked back into the picture, I took advantage of that. We fell back into bed together, but I didn't stop fucking other girls. In her eyes, we were a happy family. I let her believe that for a long time, years even, until I met Sarah."

"Sarah? Olivia's mom?" I have heard the name in passing.

He dips his chin. "Yes. Olivia's mom. The moment she started interning at my work, I stopped sleeping with my girlfriend altogether, stopped coming home on time, started staying late at the office. It's no surprise Sarah caught feelings; I didn't give her much of a choice. I enjoyed Sarah's attention more than my girlfriend's but there was a part of me that loved my girlfriend—in a way. Not like I loved Sarah, plus we had a son.

"I couldn't just stop being a dad. I could break up with my girlfriend but couldn't break up with my son, and at that point, I didn't want to. I fell in love with being a dad. I loved my son despite not wanting him in the first place. So, I broke up with my girlfriend in hopes we could co-parent. Unfortunately, she was over my bullshit, and when I told her there was someone else, she took my son from me, moved back to her hometown and that was it."

"You didn't go after them?" I'm growing to hate him more and more by the moment.

"Of course I did. I was a dick but not heartless." He scoffs. "I drove all the way to her hometown; I had never been there, but she'd mentioned the town a time or two. Mentioned her dad being a pastor and whatever church it was, so when I got to Bayshore, I slept outside the church for the night. It was Saturday so I knew there would be church Sunday. I was awoken by the pastor and he invited me in, thinking I was just a sinner looking to be led down the way of God. I was a sinner, but that wasn't what I was looking for. I interrupted him in the middle of his preaching to ask where I could find his daughter.

"He never told me, in fact, he continued with his preaching like I hadn't interrupted him at all, and I walked out. I asked a few places in town where I might be able to find her, but I must have come across as a psycho because no one told me. No one besides a little old lady I met at the flower shop."

I have such fond memories at the flower shop. I guess my nana used to work there for a long time, but that was before I was born. Anytime she needed flowers, she would take me with, and they would spend no less than an hour catching up. To make up for making me listen to them, Nana and the owner would take me to the back and let me make any kind of bouquet I wanted to bring home to my mom. Speaking of my mom, I wish Jethro would get to the part where my mom and his stalking comes in because I really don't care that he was a terrible boyfriend or father. I feel sorry for his son, but not him.

"She said, 'I could tell you where she is but what are you going to bring to her life? Good or bad?'"

I didn't know how to answer because I knew it wasn't all good, but I was focused on getting to my son. So I lied and said good. She saw through me and gave me the address of the church and said I could find what I needed, not wanted, *needed* there. I was so mad at everyone in this fucking town I drove home. Over the next few weeks, I went crazy because I missed my son. Oddly enough, I missed my girlfriend too. I didn't like not knowing where they were or what they were up to. I imagined him crying for me and me not being there. It sucked. Also, I convinced Sarah to move to Bayshore. Sarah was an angel and agreed even though I knew she didn't want to. We were moved and settled into a shitty apartment two weeks later, and a week after that, I bumped into my ex and my son at the park. There was only one back in the day, so I'd go every weekend afternoon at night, waiting."

"Oh my God, you really were a stalker."

He rolls his eyes but shrugs. "I was, yes, I suppose, but we call that private investigating now. If you had a child on this earth, wouldn't you do everything you could to see them?"

"*Most* people would." I roll my eyes digging at his brother.

He sighs. "Yes, *most* people would."

There's a few beats of awkward silence before I encourage him to continue so I don't have to feel awkward anymore. This story is rather entertaining because he's coming across as a huge prick and he doesn't even sound sorry.

"We argued, and she told me she moved so I couldn't hurt her anymore. She didn't want her son growing up around someone like me, someone so selfish." I mean, fair. At least this little boy seems to have a good mom in his life.

"She was right, I was selfish. I took advantage of her love for years. I took advantage of everything about her for years and I made a promise to only be there for our son. I wouldn't hurt her anymore. Unfortunately, at that point, my son was five and didn't want anything to do with me. I was a stranger and he saw how his mom cried anytime I was around and that was enough for him to forget about the years we spent bonding. I don't blame him, in fact, I never respected anyone more than that five-year-old. He saw through my bs even before I did.

"So, I stopped trying. I promised I would be around whenever he wanted but I wouldn't force a relationship. I had begged my ex to give me their number and she reluctantly agreed. I called weekly but neither of them wanted to talk to me. I sent letters. I sent her money when I started making some. I did everything I could—from a distance. A year later, Sarah and I married, and I invited him to be in the wedding. He didn't even come. A couple years after that, we still hadn't fallen pregnant. I would see my ex and my son in town periodically, and anytime I did, I hated the feeling of jealousy. Then Sarah fell pregnant and everything was perfect, I had a new family so I didn't need my old one."

"You aren't making me like you any more than I already do. In fact, I already wasn't your biggest fan and you are making me hate you. You know who you sound like? My bio dad. Your brother. Does shitty dads just run in the family or something?"

"I don't remember my dad much, but Hunter's dad is okay. Treats my mom good and that's all I can ask."

His mom. I didn't even think about the fact I have another set of grandparents. Fred's parents died before he got with my mom, so I've always just had my grandpa and nana. "Where do your parents live?"

"Florida."

So nowhere close. Not that I would go see them tomorrow but if they were in the state, at least there was a chance I could meet them one day. The odds of me going to Florida are slim.

"They would love to meet you one day, Payson. If and when you're ready." I take comfort in his words but don't say anything more on the subject. I don't know if I'll ever want to meet them.

"So why are you telling me how shitty of a person you are?"

"Don't cuss. But I'm telling you because my ex is your mother."

Jethro never once builds up to a drop, he just randomly pushes you off a cliff just when you think he won't.

"My mom . . . is your . . . *ex*."

"That's what I said."

"So that means . . ." I swallow hard, hoping whatever is swimming around in my stomach doesn't decide to come up. "Jason is your son."

He nods once. "He is."

What the hell is going on? "Your brother is my dad and you are the dad to my brother? My brother is also my cousin."

"Half cousin, half brother."

Oh my word. "W-well. Well, what the fuck?"

"Payson, language," he scolds.

I jump off the swing and pace the floor in front of it, shaking my head because what the hell just happened? In the span of ten minutes Jethro Gilbert has uprooted everything I've known. "When does your brother come into the picture? I'm only a year younger than Olivia."

For the first time, an emotion passes over his face and it's not a good one. "My brother was up for a visit. I was at work and he decided to go to the local restaurant. Your mom had just started working and I guess tripped and dumped water down the front of him. When I got home, I found them naked in my spare bed together."

I cringe for many reasons. "TMI, Uncle Jet."

"Excuse me?"

"Too much information."

"Right. Anyway, skip ahead and my brother announces Anne's—your mom"—he says like I don't know my mother's name—"pregnancy.

"It just so happens that I had recently found out Olivia wasn't mine around the same time." He lets me have a moment to gasp, then he continues, more of a growl this time. "She cheated on me and fell pregnant but because I was so happy to finally be getting another family, she didn't have the heart to tell me."

Holy karma.

"So she let me believe Olivia was my daughter until I met her boss for the first time. I know it's hard to believe I hadn't met him, but I was so busy with my work I never paid attention to Sarah's enough to notice how

Olivia who never really looked like me looked exactly like him. There was a huge fight and we never really recovered from it."

"Because she died?" I ask timidly.

His sharp eyes flick away from me for the first time. "Yes, because she died. But, also, because she died in the same car with him."

Oh my God! If this wasn't real life and if he hadn't just dropped a huge bomb on me, I might feel bad. But then I remember all the terrible things he did to my mom. My mom and brother. Brother-cousin or whatever. "That's some rough karma."

Not bothered by my lack of empathy he shrugs. "Yes, it is."

The cold is messing with my knee and causing it to lock up, but I don't want to sit next to him again. So instead, I plop down on the porch and lean against the railings and ignore how freaking cold it is.

"I became obsessed with looking out for your mom. I never liked my half brother, and I hated him more knowing he was living in a house with my ex. My son. He was living the life I should have been. Then he wasn't. I got a call from my mom days after he left here, left you, saying he just couldn't do it anymore. He wasn't cut out to be a dad. Which obviously we both know."

"No, he wasn't."

"Exactly, so when he left, I kicked it up. Started sitting outside the house."

"You're a total freak!"

"I'm a dad, Payson. A dad who wasn't getting the chance to see his son. You'll understand when you become a mother."

"If," I mutter.

"What?"

Frick. This isn't a conversation I have ever talked out loud about. I certainly don't want to do it with my uncle. Although, maybe it could be payback for everything he said about my mother. "I don't know if I'll be able to have kids."

"Why not?"

"I've only had like three periods."

He lifts an eyebrow in question. "Ever?"

"Mhm, yep." This conversation isn't as awkward as I imagined it would be. It's almost easy to picture him as an uncle, or a dad. A good one.

"You need to be seen about that."

I wave him off. "I will worry about it when it becomes an issue. It's not one right now." I can sense he's going to argue so I say, "Why did you pull me into the freezing cold to discuss how you fucked over my entire family."

"I'm not going to tell you again, watch your mouth, kid. I pulled you out here to ask if you know of anyone in your mother's life that could be capable of murder."

"M-murder?"

Jethro dips his chin. "Your mother was found—" He pauses and for the first time tonight, I think I recognize hesitation in his face. "She was found with a slit throat. Your mother was killed, Payson."

I hadn't asked how my mom died. I'm not sure but it never occurred to me to ask. She was dead and that was that. But it wasn't. She didn't die—she was *killed*. I think he is talking but I can't hear past the noise in my head. No—not noise. Voices.

I lie on my stomach on my bed, flipping through my econ homework. Mom went to bed about an hour ago, and I know he will walk into my room soon but I really need to get this work done. The lack of sleep is affecting my schoolwork, and Amanda warned me that if I fail another test, I won't be able to play. The work isn't too hard for me, it's concentrating on the work. Anytime I try, my head takes me somewhere else. Somewhere darker where I don't want to be. Then I'm down and out the rest of class, trying to recover by the next one.

I wish it would end. I wish I could move away and never look back. I hate it at home. I stay with Janelle or Ronni a lot but I still have to go home sometimes.

Like clockwork, my door clicks open. I didn't lock it; it doesn't stop him. I've tried.

"You're meant to be sleeping." His voice is like nails on a chalkboard. I blame it on smoking for years but maybe it's the drinking. Maybe it's karma, because he's the worst freaking human to ever exist.

"I have homework."

My door clicks shut and I go numb. His footsteps used to be so soft I could hardly hear them, but now they are heavy because he doesn't care if my mom hears him in here. She won't do anything. She never does. My bed dips under his heavy weight. I'm already as far over as the wall will let me but I wish it was farther.

When his hand brushes down my head and back, I shutter. The noise he lets out makes me think he likes it and I wish I hadn't done that.

"You doing well in school?"

I don't answer.

"You get good grades, babe?"

When his hand skims over my butt, the page in front of me turns blurry but I will not cry. I'll wait until my hot shower after he leaves, but the urge is there.

He wraps a fist around my hair and yanks my head back. I whimper at the pain. Wide, soulless eyes bore into mine. "I asked you a fucking question."

"Y-yes, I'm getting good grades."

He yanks on my hair one more time before letting it go, and I fall face-first into my pillow. Do. Not. Cry.

"One day, it'll just be you and me, babe."

Over my dead body.

His hands rake up and down my bare legs. I want to kick him so bad, but I'm always scared he will do something worse than just touch me if I fight back. I can stand in the shower for hours and wash his touches off, mostly. I'll never be able to erase the trace of him if he . . . enters me. The thought alone sends a sob up my throat but I don't let it out.

Fred lies next to me, rubbing his crotch on my hip. He's hard, like always. Lunch churns in my stomach. A single tear falls into the safety of my pillow. No matter how much I try and block out his voice, I can't. It's always there.

"Your mom will be gone." My heart hammers against my ribs. He must hear it because a hand slips under me and he drags it over my breasts, setting just over my heart. He stays there a minute before moving up and encasing my throat with his rough hand. "I'll slit her from ear to ear. Watch the blood drain, then we can be together."

He's never talked about harming my mom before. I like that even less than the other disgusting stuff he has told me. My arms are weak but I bring them under me and push onto my knees to peer down at him. "Why would you say that?"

He traces a finger down my chin, over the middle of my chest, and down my stomach. And he doesn't stop until his finger is resting over my most-private spot. He's never touched me here before. My body is revolting, begging me to move but I can't. Begging me to scream, but I know there's no use.

"We can't be together as long as she's alive, Payson."

"We're not going to be together if she's not," I snap. I never fight back; I stopped doing that a while ago because he gets rough when I do, and the bruises are hard to hide. At least when he is touching me like this, no one else can see the traces.

Anger takes over his smug face. He snaps an arm out and grips my throat. He holds me as he stands, cutting off my air with each passing second. "You're my property, Payson. I pay for everything you have. You owe me and what I want is your tight little virgin pussy on your eighteenth birthday. If you're smart, you will save it for me. If not . . ." He sucks on his teeth and gives me a nasty smirk. "You'll end up just like your mom."

29

Payson

"Why did you stop watching us?"

There's a beat of silence and then he says, "Your mom started dating someone knew. Someone with a good reputation. She seemed happy and I assumed things were fine. Olivia started acting up as well and I needed to be home with her."

"She always did ruin my life." It's not a fair comment, but really if she hadn't been being a brat, maybe he would have still watched the house and saw what was happening behind those "happy doors." "Sometimes people with the best reputations do the worst things behind closed doors."

"What did Fred do to you, Payson?"

I turn my head and force a sarcastic smile. "What he didn't do to *me*, he did to *your* son."

So many emotions pass through his bitter stare. I thought whenever I saw him, he was angry, but seeing how angry he is now, I know that was just his face. If looks could kill, I would drop dead. Then my mind wanders with the thoughts of him actually killing someone. It wouldn't surprise me.

"What the fuck does that mean?"

"It means Fred used to use Jason as a punching bag. That's why he left as soon as he graduated."

"He fucking did what to my son?"

"And when Jason was gone . . . who was left?"

Uncle Jet pushes to his feet and I fall back to lean against the glass shower door. He brought us into the hall bathroom upstairs because I mentioned I was going to throw up. "He fucking hit you?"

"I wish." Looking back, I was so worried about having to cover marks on my body, but I would gladly have accepted that over the marks that aren't seen and can never be forgotten. Physical pain eventually heals but the wounds caused to your mind never leave. You might get to a point they don't haunt you daily but then something will trigger them and before you know it, you are sitting on a bathroom floor telling your uncle about how your stepdad molested you. All while your breath smells like vomit.

"Payson, I swear to fucking G—"

The door behind Uncle Jet flies open and Ash stands in the doorway breathing hard and . . . wobbling on his feet.

"Sssomeone tttooold me youuu werrrre crrrying."

Great, he's drunk.

Jet looks between the two of us, he narrows his eyes more and more with each glance. "Why the fuck do you care if she's crying?"

I swallow and regret it as vomit burns my throat. With shaky arms and legs, I stand, grab a spare toothbrush from the cabinet next to the shower, and head for the sink while the two big oofs stare at each other. Ash is swaying and his eyes aren't focused but you can tell he's trying to look mad. He looks anything but.

"I'm her coach. I care about my players."

"That better be all it is, Pearson. If Payson tells me you touch her like that POS, I'll kill you with my bare hands."

Ash slaps a hand to the doorway, trying to gain his balance. He eyes me in the mirror as I brush my tongue, ignoring Jet and his threat completely. "You told him about Fred?"

I cringe and spit. "He killed my mom."

"We think," Jet adds.

I roll my eyes and toss my toothbrush in the trash next to the sink before turning and leaning against it. "No, we know. He told me he would one day. I didn't believe him because he said a lot of things..." Guilt hits me like a fucking truck. Jet and Ash move closer to me, one scowling at the other. Ash rubs the back of my head and Jet places a firm hand on my shoulder.

"I really need you to come in and make a statement against him."

The thought of making everything public has me eyeing the toilet all over again. "I don't want anyone knowing what he did to me."

"Jailbird..." Ash mutters softly.

"People knowing or not knowing won't change what happened to you. But it might keep it from happening to someone else. I'm sorry it happened to you, and trust me, he will pay for it but we need to make a case, and I can't do that without you."

I look up to Ash's dilated stormy eyes, even through the alcohol I can tell he agrees with him. I look to my uncle. He glares at Ash, then meets my eyes.

"Fine. But only because he killed my mother while I still hated her."

He dips his chin. "I know you are gone next week, but the sooner we can get you in, the better. Can we meet tomorrow? The station will be dead. I will meet you there. One p.m. work?"

I roll my lips between my teeth and nod. "Sure. One p.m."

Seemingly happy I agreed, he lifts his hand and drags it down his face. "Okay, I have some work to do. But I will see you tomorrow."

There's a second I wonder if he will hug me. Then he does. It's a weird and awkward side hug but he's out the door before either of us can comment on it.

Ash closes the door behind him, then he pins me against the sink and drops his head onto my shoulder. "I'm sorry, babygirl."

"It's okay," I tell him because there's nothing else to say. It's not okay, we both know it's not. Fred killed my mom.

He killed her like he said he would. *"Then we can be together."* I suck in a sharp breath. Ash pulls away, frowns, and grabs my face. His limbs are still heavy, and I know he's way too drunk to deal with this right now.

"Fred told me he would kill my mom one day . . ." I swallow to calm my breathing. "He also told me when he did, we could be together."

Ash sucks in his own breath. He clamps his hands on my shoulder and squeezes. "He won't come near you. I can promise you that. I might be drunk right now but alcohol, drugs, none of it could keep me from protecting you."

I step into his arms, ignoring the smell of a distillery on his neck, and wrap my arms around his waist. "I'm scared," I admit. I wish I wasn't but for so long I believed he couldn't hurt me. He wouldn't. I was too out of reach but knowing what he did to my mom . . . it doesn't seem so impossible anymore.

Ash kisses the top of my head. I sink further into his arms, loving how good they feel wrapped around me. "No one will hurt a single hair on your head as long as I'm around, babygirl. I promise. Stay the night with me. Stay every night with me."

"You know I'm staying at Janelle's. Her mom is already suspicious of us; if I don't come down for breakfast tomorrow morning, she will know what's up."

"Say you're staying with Parker."

Ew. "No."

He groans. "Fine, but I want your location. At all times."

That'll make me feel safer, so I agree. Neither of us have our phones on us but we agree to set it up before we separate.

Ash sends me to find Luca and Parker while he takes a piss, stating that he is ready to go. Finding Luca is easy. All I had to do was listen for his obnoxious voice. I found him chatting away with a group of parents who seem just as liquored as him and Ash. Ash seems a little better now, like seeing me cry sobered him some, but I have no doubts his head will hurt in the morning.

I drag Luca with me so I don't lose him while looking for Parker. Janelle bounces over and hooks her arm around my free one. "What are we doing?"

"Looking for Parker," I tell her. She's barefaced and blotchy instead of a full face of makeup like she was wearing the last time I saw her. She holds my stare but shakes her head, telling me not right now. Then she pauses, probably seeing my blotchiness too. I splashed my face several times with cold water, but I can still feel how swollen my eyes are. I shake my head too. She hooks our pinkies and we each kiss our hands as a promise to spill later.

"Enjoying the party, Coach?"

"Sì, molto!"

Janelle lifts an eyebrow and I shrug. "Yes, something."

"It has been a long time since I was this drunk."

Janelle and I laugh.

We search the whole downstairs for Parker but come up empty-handed. I send Luca and Janelle to the garage, and I head for the steps. Ash stumbles out of the bathroom as I hit the top step.

"Find him?"

"No, geeze you've been in there a while."

"I think I might have passed out for a short period of time."

I snort and he walks toward me. "You look so beautiful." Ash wraps his arms around me and smiles.

"You just saw me throw up."

"It's not the first time."

True. I shake my head and wrap my arms around his waist. "I'm in gym shorts and my eyes feel swollen, are they?"

"Yes. You're still beautiful though."

He's so ridiculous. His big hand spans my neck and he drops his lips to mine. I should be weary of people since anyone that comes up the stairs will see us but I need his kiss. I need to know that he is as much mine as I am his.

Ash holds my lips to his with a firm hand while the other kneads at my ass under my shorts. I maul him as much as he will let me, which is a lot because he's as lost in this as I am. I think I get drunk from the liquor on his tongue, but I suck harder.

"Fuck, baby, it's been so long since we kissed."

I smile against his lips. It hasn't been long, but I love that he feels that way.

He hooks his arm under my ass and lifts me; it's so hot knowing he can hold me with one arm. I wrap my legs around his midsection. He backs us to a wall, I'm not sure who humped first but it's paused when someone clears their throat behind him.

I pull off Ash to look but he doesn't let his mouth leave my body and moves to suck on my neck instead.

I'm so beyond thankful to see it's Luca and Janelle and not Jethro or Brette. Someone who wouldn't be smiling like these two at seeing Ash bruise my throat.

"Ash," I breathe.

He tongues at my throat. "Tell them to go away," he growls.

340

"It is you who summoned us," Luca states.

Ash's breath is hot as he groans. He kisses my tender neck where I no doubt have a new bruise I'll need to cover. "I need sleep if I'm going to function at all tomorrow."

"When did you get so old?" Luca teases.

"I thought I was going to see my niece or nephew be conceived in my hallway," Janelle says.

I nearly choke to death on nothing but air.

"Not for lack of trying." Ash winks.

Janelle's eyes pop open wide. "You're trying for a baby?" She looks to me for the answer but Ash cuts me off. I attempt to scramble from his arms, but he keeps a tight arm around my waist.

"We're not, not trying." He shrugs.

I gape at him. "No! Oh my—no!" I gasp. Looking at Janelle instead of the big drunk idiot to my right, I shake my head. "No, we are *not* trying for a baby. My word, Jay, I'm a junior in high school."

"No judgment here." She holds up two hands. "I will say it might be best to wait till you're at least not living with your grandpa, that might kill him."

I wasn't even thinking about that. Even Ash cringes at that. "I do not wear condoms and she is not on birth control. If it happens, we will deal with it."

He is trying to kill me and my best friend. I knew how casual he was about this from the first time we had sex. He doesn't know I have issues with my period, which I'm pretty sure is what you need to get pregnant and that's the only reason I'm not freaking out about my boyfriend trying to get me pregnant while I'm still in high school.

"'My Volleyball Coach is Trying to Impregnant Me.' You know if I ever decide to write a biography about you, I'm using that as my title to entice readers."

Luca chuckles. "Do you write?"

"No, but I might start if these two keep being so crazy." She throws a thumb our way.

I drop my head to my hands and sigh. "Can we find Parker? I'm ready for you two to go home."

The three of them join in laughing at my misery and mocking it. I drag Ash over to a spare room to start looking. He's not in the first room or the bathroom next to it. He's obviously not in the bathroom Ash was just in. The four of us head to the second spare. Janelle reaches for the handle but stops when a girlish moan comes from the other side.

We each shoot a look at the other. Then I turn and look to Ash and scowl. I shove him over so he's not in the doorway.

She pushes the door open and my mouth falls seeing a naked Alyssa on top of a naked Parker. Riding him.

The room was dark before we opened the door so they both look our way. Parker freezes but Alyssa continues rocking her hips, smirking in our direction.

I'm so distracted from what is happening in front of me I don't see or hear my best friend crying until the door slams and Luca pulls her into his arms. Janelle cries into his chest and I blink at them. I'm not exactly happy seeing what I just saw but I'm surprised to see Janelle crying.

"Jay?" I ask softly, placing a hand on her arm. She pulls away from him and throws herself into my arms. "I hate boys. I hate them all." She cries into my shoulder. "I hate her, Pay. Fuck, I hate her so much."

I hug my best friend but eye Luca curiously. For the first time ever, he looks pissed. Ash walks around and he looks just as pissed.

"I hate her too," I agree with Janelle. "But why are you crying?"

She wipes her face on my shoulder, pulls away, and wipes her face with the back of her arm next. "Parker and I were hooking up. Since the night of the movies."

My mouth drops. Ash flattens his lips. Obviously already aware of this confession. Her lips tremble and I pull her back in for a hug because, truthfully, I don't know what to say. I guess that makes sense why she stayed at Ash's that night and insisted I sleep in Ash's room and not with her. I assumed it was for me, but it was probably for Parker who was across the hall. "I don't know why he would d-do this."

I do. "Jay, it's probably my fault. I pissed her off by telling her Ash asked me to marry him."

Ash's eyebrows shoot up his forehead; Luca is next and is quick to look at his best friend. They mutter back in forth in Italian which is wildly annoying and makes me want to learn Italian quickly.

Janelle squeezes me tighter. "I expect to hear about that and a good excuse why you didn't tell your best friend. But right now, I want to take a lesson from the Payson handbook and stab the two people in that room."

She pulls away and scowls at Ash. "I'm not sorry." She looks back to me and frowns. "When you are Parker's mom can you ground him, like, for life."

Oh my God.

"Never say that again," I complain.

Ash storms over and throws the door open, ignoring Janelle's comment in his angered stupor. Thankfully, they were smart enough to stop fucking and Parker is even mostly dressed. Not Alyssa, she's taking her sweet time making sure everyone can see her tits on display.

Ash pays no attention, instead grabbing his son by the shirt and tugging him into the hallway. He slams the door behind him.

Janelle and I watch Luca and Ash rip into him in mixes of English and Italian on both sides.

"I need to learn Italian," Jay mutters.

I nod, agreeing.

"She cheated first!" Parker shouts, cutting both Ash and Luca off.

The three turn our way.

"This true?" Luca asks.

Janelle's satisfaction morphs into anger. "Absolutely not. I'm not a cheater."

"I heard you," Parker growls. "In your room with that boy."

It's like a movie watching these two go at each other. Even Ash and Luca have stepped away so they could go toe to toe.

"Who were you in your room with, Jay?"

She thinks for a minute shaking her head until it hits her, then she clenches her fists. "Are you talking about Collins?"

Oh no.

"Sì. Collins. Your ex. You were in your room with the door closed."

Then something happens that I did not expect. Janelle . . . laughs. Not a full-on belly laugh but a sarcastic chuckle. "He was trying to win me back after he cheated on me. With the same girl, no less." She laughs again. "You're all the same." His eyes flick to Ash. "All of you."

Ouch.

For the first time ever, Parker is silent. The regret is obvious on his face but he's still trying to battle that he's in the right in his head.

"Did you see them doing anything romantic?" Ash asks his son.

Parker clenches his jaw and like a bad dog lowers his eyes to the ground. "No, Papà."

"No, he didn't because while Collins was begging and crying for me to take him back, I was telling him I found someone else. Someone that *wouldn't* cheat on me." She drops her eyes to the ground, her humorless smile fading.

Ash mutters something in Italian, based on Parker's slow nod, I assume it was a *we will talk when we get home* type of thing. "Time to go," he snaps.

"Need a driver," Parker mumbles.

Luca curses, then him and Ash look at us.

I roll my eyes, not even needing to hear the question. "Fine."

"Janelle, I know you don't want to be around him, but I do not want Payson out alone. Would you mind coming for the ride?"

"Whatever."

The door behind us opens and I swear things move in slow motion. Janelle spins first but I'm right after her. "How could you!" Janelle shouts.

Alyssa leans against the door frame, smirking. Ash, knowing me, wraps his arms around mine. Caging me in. I notice Luca move closer to Janelle, looking to be ready to do the same if necessary.

"Heyy, guys," she draws out.

"Go home, Alyssa," Luca demands.

Her smirk tightens. "Gladly. I got what I came for, anyway." She brushes by us. I urge forward but Ash holds me back, muttering sweet things in my ear in a way to calm me down. It doesn't work. Seeing Janelle crying, again, because of her, again, has my blood boiling.

Ash tightens his grip. He must feel my bones vibrating.

Alyssa purses her lips. "How long did it take our coach to get you to open your pretentious legs, Pay-pay? Three days? A week? You want to claim to be so high and mighty, but you are no different than me. We both fucked our coach."

"Go home, Alyssa," Ash demands bitterly.

"No different?" I snort, not letting her comment bother me this time. "I've fucked *one* guy, one. And that guy belongs to me. I don't need to fuck other girls' boyfriends because I'm so fucking pathetic and unhappy with my life."

"You know, Pay." She purses her lips and saunters toward me. "Girl to girl, Daddy is good. Real good." I will kill her. "But the son—" She bites her lip and rolls her eyes back. "Mind-blowing. Right, Janelle?"

My chest caves as if she just hit me where it hurts. Because she did. Saying she fucked Ash is one thing, talking about how good he is? No. Then throwing it in Janelle's face she fucked Parker too. Hell no.

"I want her off my team," I snarl.

"Done," Ash growls.

"No, off. Not on the bench. I want her gone. I don't want to see her anymore."

Alyssa's smile falls for the first time since walking from that room. "You can't kick me off because I slept with someone's boyfriend." She crosses her arms.

"I have a hundred reasons why I can kick you off, and I will."

Her eyes blaze with hatred. "I'll tell everyone you two fuck."

Ash's chest rumbles against my back like a wild animal. "Do it."

"My dad will be hearing about this."

"Can't wait," Ash grits.

The car ride to Ash's is probably the most awkward car ride I've ever been on. Janelle is in the front, crying silently. Parker is in the middle back and every so often I see him texting, and a second later, Janelle's phone will light up, she looks, then ignores it.

Anytime I glance at Luca, I swear he is getting angrier instead of less so. I wonder what is up with that but its probably just him being disappointed in his nephew. I know I'm disappointed in his nephew. Parker and I haven't really gotten along this whole time but this is probably the worst thing he could have done. Hurt my best friend. I'll have his balls for this. Just like I'll have Collins's when I get the chance.

"Daddy is good." Fucking bitch. I know she only called him that to fuck with me. She doesn't know we've used that name in the bedroom. I think.

Did they do the same? I cringe at the thought.

Ash leans forward and his arms snake around my shoulders. "You're letting your mind take you places it doesn't need to go, Jailbird. Come back to me," he whispers for only me to hear.

"It's hard," I admit.

His arms tighten and he moves around the seat and presses a deep kiss to my cheek. "You and me, babygirl."

I suck in a deep breath and let it out. We pull up outside Ash's, and I leave the car running since Janelle isn't coming in, but Ash is nearly forcing me out of the car.

"I'm not leaving her waiting," I tell him as he drags me up the front stairs.

Instead of heading to his room, he pulls me into the living room, pushes me down on the couch, and falls on top of me. "I love you, Payson. *You* are my babygirl."

"Did she ever call you daddy?" I'm not sure where Luca and Parker are but I don't care right now. I have to know.

Ash drops his lips to my ear. "I'm only *your* daddy, babygirl." He kisses the shell of my ear, and dammit if it doesn't make my pussy ache. "I've never used that title before you. Promise."

He pulls back so I can look deep in his eyes. I sigh and pull his lips back to mine. "I'm going to cauterize your son."

"Not if Luca does first."

I laugh and press a kiss to his lips.

Luca nudges us to move over, and Ash sits up, pulling me onto his lap. I spot Parker across the room, avoiding eye contact with anyone. Probably because his uncle and dad are glaring at him. I'd hate to be him tonight. Maybe tomorrow since both men are drunk tonight.

I glance at Ash and he sighs. "Let's not keep Janelle waiting."

"Good night, Luca," I say on my way out. I meet Parker's sorry expression across the room and flatten my lips but say nothing.

"It's cold, shut the door," Janelle complains when Ash pulls it open because he keeps me pressed to his body instead of letting me sit and close the door.

He grins against my lips. "I love you. Text me when you get to Janelle's."

"You have my location now," I remind him in case he forgot.

"Still, text me."

I promise and he kisses me another time before I fall into the seat. He waves until we are out of sight and then I sigh and glance at my best friend. She's not crying anymore, but the remnants that she was are still there and a reminder of what a fucking shitty night this has been.

"I am never going to a party again," I tell her.

"Agreed."

30

Ash

"WHAT ARE YOU DOING here?"

"Lovely to see you too, Jason." I sidestep him in the small trailer. The narrow space causes our shoulders to brush.

He spins and grips my arm in a threatening way. "You don't think my family is going through enough without you perving after my baby sister?" His voice is low but I look around for anyone that might overhear anyway. Everyone else seems to be in the living room so I think we are safe.

"Your sister loves me."

"She's seventeen. She doesn't know what she loves," he bites back.

I planned to come here, check in with Paul, and grab Payson before we head to the station to meet Jethro. She didn't ask me to come but she will need someone, and I want to be that someone. I didn't expect to see Jason but his mum's funeral is Sunday so I shouldn't be surprised. Or surprised that he hates me. Any good older brother would. Unfortunately for him, his hatred isn't sending me anywhere.

"Do not underestimate her because of her age. Payson is smart and perfectly capable of choosing who to spend her time with. Lucky for me, that person is me."

His hand tightens. He growls under his breath, "you're grooming her."

Jason says these things as if I am not aware. I am fully aware of the dynamics between Payson and me. She wanted on my team; she would have done anything. She was in love with a version of me she made up in her head when she was young. To Jason, and probably to most, I took advantage of all that. What they don't know is I planned to make Payson Murphy mine before I knew any of it.

"Well, good afternoon, Coach," a raspy masculine voice rings from behind me.

Jason scowls and drops his hand, and I turn to greet Paul. He looks worse than the last time I saw him, and I'm not sure if it's his cancer or the fact his daughter was murdered by her husband. I'm not even sure he knows that part yet. Payson seemed so sure and based on what she's told me about Fred and what he promised her, I believe she's probably right. If she is, then Payson needs someone watching her, and Paul needs to be aware.

I will discuss that with her today.

"Afternoon, Paul. How are you today?"

He offers me a sincere look but doesn't answer. "What brings you by?"

I hold up the pie in my hands. "This, it's store bought, but you don't want me baking." I chuckle. He smiles and grabs the apple pie from my hands.

Americans seem obsessed with sweet pies, and apple pie is actually very good. I follow him down the hall, and Jason follows behind me mumbling something about kiss-ass. He's not wrong, but it's not a crime to want Payson's granddad to like me. I plan on marrying her one day—hopefully soon, she will be more inclined to accept, knowing her granddad likes me. "Also to pick up Payson."

Paul scans the kitchen for a spot to place the pie and really, there's not one. There is various food containers scattered about the little counter space and table. He stacks it on top of a larger container. I glance around the small room but don't see anyone else. I'm not sure where Payson could be, bathroom or her room, I suppose. I checked her location and it said she was home. "Ah, yes."

"I'm going with Payson," Jason says.

He's like an annoying housefly that won't stop buzzing in your ear. "It's a good thing my truck can seat three, then, yes?"

"Amanda is here too." *Buzz buzz.*

I had forgotten they were together and that she would most likely be here. I can feel Paul watching our one-sided, hostile conversation and it stops me from tossing Jason around like a doll. "Payson still has my car, it can fit five. Will you be joining as well?"

Paul shakes his head. "I need to run to the church"—he flips his wrist—"actually now. Would you mind telling Payson where I've gone, I forgot to tell her when she got home this morning."

"Of course," "Yeah," Jason and I reply simultaneously.

My smile is tight but Paul doesn't seem to notice as he scurries around the trailer grabbing what he needs for whatever he is doing. "Make yourself at home and please eat some food." He pauses. "Actually bring your son and friend and come over for dinner. The good Lord knows we have enough. You'll get to meet the rest of the family."

Meeting the rest of the people that Payson grew up around? "Sounds brilliant. Thank you, sir."

Paul leaves and Jason plops down in his chair and changes the channel to an action film. After hearing the voices, I know it's John Wick and upon a quick glance at the screen I can tell it's the first one. After making a plate of food, I take a seat at the small couch and set my plate on the wooden coffee table in front of me.

"Brilliant movie."

"Do you always have to talk like that?"

"I'm English," I deadpan. "Would you rather I say, sick movie, bro." I've perfected the American accent in my years living here. At least in my opinion.

He rolls his eyes like the child he is.

"You better get used to me being around. I'm not going anywhere."

Jason clenches his narrow jaw. "You should be going to jail for fucking a minor."

Payson doesn't cuss on her granddad's property. Not even in her head. Jason obviously does not respect him in the same way.

"It's not illegal in Michigan for me and Payson to be together. The only reason we're not official is because I'm her coach."

"Then you should lose your job."

"And leave Payson without a coach? Ruin her junior year season like she hasn't been through enough?" He's bloody pissing me off. "You don't think your sister has been through enough? I'm not hurting her." Not in a way she doesn't like. "I love her, and I take care of her. Better than anyone ever has. But you don't care about your sister's happiness, so I'm not surprised."

My fork scratches against the plate but it's a better sound than his constant fucking buzzing.

"You're wrong, you know," Jason says sometime later, his tone heavy. He doesn't look my way, but I can tell he's not watching the movie anymore either. "I love my sister. We don't see eye to eye on some things." He shoots a look at me, making sure I know he means me, but I don't care. I don't need him to approve. "But she's my sister. I only ever wanted what was best for her."

"Then why did you leave her with that . . . monster?" If I wasn't in Paul's house, I would have said way worse.

"I never thought about what he might do to her. I thought the looks were just to piss me off. Fred is a dick, but I didn't really believe he is a perv. I thought that if I left, he would stop. He would leave her alone because I wouldn't be there to give him the reaction he wanted. I thought *I* was his issue."

"Well, he didn't." I shove my half-empty plate away, not hungry anymore.

"I know," he growls. "You'll never understand the guilt that eats at me daily knowing what I left her to. Why do you think it's so hard being around her? I've been in town for two days and saw her for the first time today despite Amanda's begging."

His guilt doesn't take away from Payson's trauma. As much as I would love to hate Jason, I'm certainly not his biggest fan, but I don't hate him because at the end of the day it's not his fault. Asking him to feel guilty about saving himself is selfish. So is leaving her behind but he was young. Scared. I'm sure there were moments he wondered how far Fred would take it. If he would go too far and Jason wouldn't see the next day. That's a lot for a kid to deal with. I'll never forgive him for leaving her to face Fred on her own but the common denominator in all this—Fred. If I ever see that bastard again, I'll rip his bloody head off.

"It is a shi-crappy situation all around for everyone involved and now someone is dead because of it." God, how I'm thankful it's not Payson. I wouldn't survive on this planet without her.

She is slowly breaking down. More and more, day by day, she is losing a sliver of her spark. She was already struggling before we met but I helped put those broken pieces back together and it worked, for a while. Until life set off bomb after bomb. I worry daily about her and her mental health.

When it's just us, I can hold her together physically and mentally but when we are apart, the darkness that stays at bay when I'm around crowds her and drags her back into the thick of it. I'm hopeful one day there won't be dark, or at least less that she won't have to use all her energy fighting it off.

"Payson told me she thinks Fred did it," Jason says.

"Do you agree?"

He flattens his lips and nods once. "Do you know what it's like to hate someone that's dead?"

He doesn't wait for me to answer.

"It sucks. I hate my mom, so much. She watched Fred beat the shit out of me for years. Allowed him to do unthinkable things to her daughter in the safety of our fucking room. What kind of mother allows her children to go through that shit?" His cold eyes blaze with hatred. "I'm an alcoholic and Payson is addicted to hurting herself." He laughs with no humor. "And it's all that bitch's fault."

Again, I stay quiet. I can't argue. I have the best mum probably in the world, so I can't fathom even something similar to that.

"She got what was coming for her." He falls into the back of the chair and from out of no where, he pulls out a silver flask and pulls a long drink, staring right at me. "As long as he stays the fuck away from Pay and me, he can get away scot-free. I don't care anymore."

"How long have you been an alcoholic?"

He twists the lid back onto the flask and tucks it back wherever he keeps it. "I drank heavily for years. Only since getting out of the Army did it become a problem. Amanda is trying to help me but can't help people who don't want to be helped, right?"

I wonder if Payson is close to reaching the same I-don't-give-a-shit attitude that her brother has. Maybe volleyball is the only thing keeping her from diving off that edge. We only have weeks left. I really hope that's not the case. "I hope you want to be helped soon. No one deserves to be in a relationship with a good-for-nothing drunk."

Jason scowls but the sound of the spring door distracts him.

"Ash?" Payson calls. She walks into the room and sighs when she sees me. I do the same seeing her.

Payson is beautiful beyond words. My heart skips a beat whenever her green eyes lock with mine, but lately it's not just love I see in her eyes anymore. It's need, *obsession*. Like she relies on me to breathe. And I fucking love it.

"Hey, Jailbird. Where have you been? I checked your location before coming over and it said here."

Jason scoffs.

Payson ignores him and stops in front of me. I grab her hands and she smiles. "Amanda needed to get a dress for tomorrow. She picked me and Janelle up this morning to go shopping and I left my phone here to charge. I meant to text you, I'm sorry."

"How is Janelle doing?"

Payson's smile falls and she shrugs. "She says she is swearing off guys."

"That might not be a bad idea."

Amanda's shoes click against the vinyl flooring announcing her entrance. She smiles seeing me. "Well, hey, Coach." She gives Payson a knowing look.

"Coach Dillon."

She walks over and falls onto the lap of her boyfriend and kisses his cheek. To my surprise, Jason leans into the kiss like he actually enjoys it. I kind of thought he was too stubborn, selfish and the relationship would be one-sided. It's nice to see he at least finds comfort in her.

Payson strokes down my beard, hooks my chin, and turns my face back to her with a pout.

I take in her outfit, seeing she's not in sweatpants and an oversized sweatshirt like usual. Her dark jeans are stuck to her body like glue and her top is cropped, long sleeve, and the perfect shade of brown to complement her hair and the little flecks in her eyes. Her hair is down with big curls. She's even wearing a subtle amount of makeup. She looks remarkably older like this. Much older than she did in her uniform last night. I love Payson for who she is and at every stage and every look but when she looks older, it's easier. My morals don't fight me so hard when she looks not so illegal.

"Where did you go looking like this?" I lift an eyebrow. Her thigh flexes as I drag my fingers up and hook my hands around her thighs to pull her closer. I press a kiss to the small bit of skin showing above her pants. Her smell is so overpowering I have a hard time pulling away, especially hearing how fast her heart is beating, matching mine.

"Knock that shit off," Jason snaps. Amanda scolds him but Payson takes over.

"Don't use that language in Grandpa's house."

"Shit. Asshole. Bitch. Fuck. What's going to happen?"

I stand and tug her into my body, glaring at Jason as my hand drifts down and rests over her belly in a dominant way. Proving that she is mine. "You'll watch your mouth if you know what's good for you. Which, judging by the flask you're hiding from your girlfriend. You don't."

Amanda whips her head to Jason. "You're drinking? You promised you wouldn't drink during this trip."

Payson glances at me in question.

"Your brother is a drunk. Alcoholic, even."

"Of course he is." She snorts. Payson grabs my hand, pulling me toward the back of the trailer.

"You're so fucking pathetic. You think he actually loves you? Like he's not just going to trade you in for a younger model as soon as you're legal and the thrill is gone?" I stop, shove my hand into his chest, and crouch so I'm in his face. I can smell the alcohol on his breath. I'm not sure how Amanda didn't.

"You question my love for Payson again and what Fred did to you will look like child's play." Shit, I will have to apologize to Payson for that one. He tries to grab the flask from me when I snatch it from him, but I'm bigger, stronger, and he's drunk.

I dump the alcohol down the sink and toss the flask on the way to the back, with Payson leading the way.

Amanda is scolding Jason, but I ignore it, close the bedroom door, and crowd my girl, and not just because this room feels even smaller than the last time. "I missed you."

"We saw each other, like, less than twelve hours ago." She giggles when I lick under her ear.

"I don't like the makeup. I can't taste you with it on."

She giggles again. "You're in luck because I hate wearing it."

Payson's giggle might be my favorite sound in the world. I drop onto her bed, the springs groan under my weight, and she complains I'm going to break it as if that would be a bad thing. I could buy her a new bed, then.

I glance at my watch and frown at seeing we have to leave soon. Instead of bending her over for a quickie, I tug her between my legs and grip her hips. Her small fingers sink into the back of my hair.

"Twelve hours is too long to go without you. Your voice, your smile, your giggles, and your touch. Your smell. It's too damn long, Jailbird."

"Don't make me scold you like I did my brother."

"Scold me like that and the next thing filling your mouth will be my cock."

Even her gasps are cute. "Ashley!"

Payson's door rattles with a hard knock. It doesn't take a brainiac to know who is on the other side. "Time to go," he huffs.

Payson drops her head to the top of mine. "I don't want to go." Her voice is soft.

"I'll be with you the whole time, babygirl."

"Promise?"

"Always. You and me, remember?"

Her chest hums happily with my confession. "Okay." She kisses my forehead like I usually do to her. "Let's go, and after, you can do what you threatened me with."

I bloody love this girl.

Watching Payson converse with her family, knowing she is full of my cum, is a type of erotic fantasy I didn't think about until right now. She is helping her Aunt Vicky lay out the food, nothing sexual, but I'm fucking aching for her again.

After the meeting with Jethro, we dropped Amanda and Jason off, then I took her back to my place for an hour. In that time, I fucked her mouth and her pussy until I came, twice. I can't even remember how many times she came, but it was exactly what we needed after that meeting. I knew it would be hard but fuck, *fuck,* it was hard. Payson did her best not to cry but eventually she broke down. Jason even cried but he pretended he wasn't. Amanda was crying, the only two who weren't were Jethro and me. Seeing Payson so upset gutted me, but not being able to hold her the same way Amanda was holding Jason, was worse.

I made up for it after. I pinned her between my mattress and my chest the entire hour and made love to her. Slow and deep, and her pretty pussy took it all.

"You keep looking at my niece like that and I will gouge your eyes out," Jethro threatens under his breath.

I pry my eyes from Payson to make him happy and scowl. "So, you're Jason's dad?"

He flattens his lips. "Yes."

We are sharing the small sofa in the living room. Mostly everyone else is in the kitchen area chatting but our sizes make it difficult to be around. I felt like I was taking up the entire kitchen, and I'm guessing Jethro felt the same way. Or maybe he's just uncomfortable. That's a big possibility since Jason doesn't seem to be any bigger of a fan of his dad than he was of his mom. Maybe worse. When he saw who was interviewing them, he almost turned around.

But Jethro has been in a bad mood—even more than normal—since seeing me. He commented about how I must be trying out for best coach award. We both know it's more than that but I'm not admitting shit to him. The guy is an asshole. Probably why it wasn't a big surprise when the bomb dropped about him being Jason's dad. Of course Jason knew, Payson even seemed to know but it didn't make the moment any less awkward.

"Great kid," I comment. It's obviously sarcastic and he glares in my direction.

"He wasn't raised by me."

Jason is trying his best not to look at us but every now and again I catch him looking. When Payson invited Jethro for dinner tonight, I figured he would say no. The thing about Payson Murphy—she's impossible to say no to.

"I met your daughter who was."

"She's not my blood."

I lift my glass and take a drink from the apple juice Payson brought me. Like I said, Americans and apples, they love them. Parker and Luca are playing a game of chess on the floor near the window, less than five feet away. Parker didn't want to come but he's grounded so I didn't give him the choice. He didn't want to come because Janelle is here and he feels like shit, which he should. A little guilt is good for him. Maybe make him learn you don't do shit like he did. Of all the girls he could have fucked last night he chose fucking Alyssa Burton. Christ, that girl is like mold on my life. Just when you rid one part of it, it pops up elsewhere.

"Yeah, well that one is my blood, and he made a big mistake last night." Jethro eyes Parker, then me. "Cheated on his not-girlfriend."

"Happens to the best of us."

No, it does not. Not me. I might have been a fuck up before Payson, and that one stupid mistake in the beginning, but I'll never cheat. Why cheat when everything I love is already mine? Throw away the future I want for one shag? No.

"Anyway, the point is. Kids have to make their own mistakes, but it's your job as a dad to let them know when they make those mistakes." *Like I'm in the position to be giving parenting advice.*

"After you all left, I looked into alcoholics anonymous near him. Already slipped the paperwork to Amanda. I know he won't listen to me—he shouldn't—I was never there, but I'm hoping he will listen to her."

Jason pulls Amanda into his side and places a kiss on her cheek. It's subtle and he lets go right after but you can feel the love anyway. "If he loves her, he will."

"Sometimes love isn't enough." Jethro frowns. Or maybe it's just his face at this point; he's always in a bad mood. I used to be too until I met her.

Feeling her gaze, I lift my eyes and she's staring at me with a small smile on her face. People move around her but don't pull my attention from her. She changed after the meeting into blue yoga pants—she called them—and a long sleeved white school shirt. And finished by pulling her hair up and removing the makeup, not that there was much left after our afternoon fucking. She's never looked prettier than she does right now. Not even the bad fluorescent lighting above her can pull from it.

"Sometimes it is."

31

Payson

SITTING AT A FUNERAL for someone you have no emotional feelings for is weird. That funeral being for your mom when you should be crying like everyone else is even weirder. I think most people are lost in their own grief to realize I'm not. Jason is across the church with the rest of the pallbearers but he's not crying either. He doesn't even look to be aware of where we are.

Grandpa is holding my hand because he couldn't find it in him to do the funeral. It would be too difficult—he said. I wish I could take his grief away; I should be the one grieving my mom. He shouldn't have to grieve a child. I can't help but wonder how much this is weighing on him. He looks more run down than usual. His black suit is crisp and perfect but his cheeks are sunk in. His blue eyes have lost their brightness, and I haven't heard him laugh since the night I found out my mom was killed. Uncle Gary helped him shave and I know he appreciated that.

I stare at the collage of photos in front of me instead of at the cream casket. So many photos filled with smiles and fake happiness. Grandpa made sure there were no photos of Fred, which confused my aunt, but she didn't argue. I'm not sure if Grandpa will ever tell anyone what actually happened. Or if they will catch him and will find out on the news. Uncle

Jet seemed so sure they could catch him but Fred snuck around behind everyone's back for years. I think it might be more difficult than they think.

At least no one misses him. Not one person has commented on his absence. I hope he realizes how guilty that makes him look. Not showing up to your wife's funeral? Huge red flag. But it's not my problem. My problem will come when he comes looking for me. Because he will. I don't know when, but I know he will and this time, it won't be me I stab.

32

Ash

I'M SO FUCKING TIRED of not being able to comfort my girl when she needs it. I'm bloody over having to hide what we have because she's my fucking player. Sitting in the back of that funeral watching everyone but her cry, broke a piece of my sanity. She didn't cry but she was the most fucked-up one in that room.

The wake after the funeral was no better. Hug after hug, person after person "comforting" her and not knowing they are pushing her deeper into numbness. Making her wonder why she's so fucked up and can't grieve like she's meant to. Payson thinks something is wrong with her, but it's not her with the issue. It's everyone around her not knowing how to deal with her mental state. They don't see the little girl inside Payson who has no issues expressing her feelings. They don't see the reason she is the way she is today is because she got so used to those feelings being ignored. Time after time she cried herself to sleep with no one around to hold her. She clung to a fucking poster for bloody sake.

The good part about that is it was my poster and I'm right here with open arms ready to pull Payson back toward the light whenever she sinks too deeply.

Most people have scattered, besides close family. I'm not close family but I will be one day. Janelle is still here too, though. Her and Payson sit at a table on their own. I wander over with my hands in my pockets. Some of Payson's family members are watching me. As they did last night when me, Luca, and Parker were over for dinner. They were all nice enough, but I'm sure they are wondering why I'm hanging around so much.

Thankfully the attention was taken off me when Payson's Aunt Jenny and Uncle Dean showed up. They stole the attention with their loud mouths and her half blue half black hair. Again, nice enough people and maybe my favorites, because if it wasn't for them taking Payson to my game all those years ago, she never would have developed the crush, Amanda would have never reached out, and I wouldn't be here today. Plus, Payson was doing her best to pretend that Parker was the one she was into. I couldn't even get jealous because it was so awkward to watch.

"Can you believe she didn't even call?" Janelle asks Payson.

Payson's answer is a slight lift of her narrow shoulders. "She knew how things were with my mom and me. Probably didn't want to deal with the awkwardness."

Who are they talking about?

"Ronni." Ah, one of Payson's closest friends that apparently, I will meet this upcoming week. I had high hopes when I figured she was like Janelle but the more I hear about her, the more I think she might not be. "Is not like you, Payson. She can deal with the awkwardness." Then she adds, "No offense or anything."

There's a slight flick of Payson's lips. "None taken."

"Ladies." I pull out a chair and sit down across from Payson.

"Coach," Janelle greets.

Payson lets out a deep breath and forces a small smile. "Hey, baby. Sorry I didn't find you sooner."

"Don't apologize. I found you now."

"You two are enough to make me want to become a nun."

"You would never last as a nun," Payson throws back, and the girls laugh. Now it's my turn to let out a breath because seeing them laugh is a much needed breath of fresh air. I don't know how much Janelle liked Parker or anything but she seems to be doing okay. Unless she's better at hiding her feelings than Payson.

Someone falls into the chair next to me and from the harsh smell of liquor, I know it's Jason. I have no clue how he carried the casket. I'm guessing Payson's uncles and other men from the church carried most of that weight. "If you want anything from Anne's place you better go get it today."

"What, why?" She scrunches her eyebrows. "Grandpa said we had the week."

"You won't be here, babygirl."

"Oh my fuck, you even call her babygirl. You're fucking nasty."

"Jason," Payson and I hiss.

He attempts to roll his eyes. "Whatever. I don't want anything so if you do, take your boyfriend."

If we weren't in a church, I'd kick the chair out from under him. I don't care what he is going through, I'm fucking sick of the way he talks to my girl.

Payson is chewing on her lips and pulling at the skin on her thumb. I rest my hand over hers. "Is there stuff you need?"

"A few things. Do you mind? I don't really want to go alone."

Hell would need to have frozen over and that still wouldn't be enough for me to send her into that house alone. Fred would have to be completely idiotic to go back to his house in town when the police are looking for him, but I've never met the man and I think it's safe to say he is completely idiotic. I wasn't joking with Payson when I said he would never touch a single hair on her head. If I ever see his face, he will wish I hadn't. "You and me. Whenever you're ready."

"Now. I'm ready to get out of here."

33

Payson

"So, this is the room you used to masturbate to my face in?"

"It wasn't your face I was thinking about."

I'm thankful he agreed to come with me. I was feeling a panic attack coming on just being on the property. We went in the back door so I just had to pass the living room. Not go in it. I don't want to see if there's blood on the floor. My blood.

My room looks the same as the way I left it. Bright yellow walls and beige carpets. My bed still has my same sunrise bed spread with yellow, orange, and magenta at the bottom. It's not even made. There are books from the library on my dresser. The drawers aren't all closed, and my clothes poke out. Everything looks exactly as I left it and it's eerie to see. It doesn't smell like me, though, stale from having been unused for months.

I turn to Ash expecting him to be taking in more of my room but his eyes are on me. The lust I've been watching in Ash the last couple days bubbles to the surface, he lunges at me, and I let him catch me. His body comes down hard against mine on the bed but his lips are on me before I can focus on his weight. I wrap my legs around his waist and he rips at my dress. Our clothes are discarded in minutes and he falls back on top of me.

"I'm sorry if you want it slow, baby but I'm dying for you hard right now." His breath is hot on my neck.

I lift my hips to grind my center against his dick. "Hard. Always hard."

He eats at my lips while lining his dick up with my opening. I'm not soaked but wet enough his head can slip in. "Fuck. I can barely get it in. Relax, Jailbird."

"You didn't even warm me up, what do you expect? I just walk around soaking wet all day. Primed and ready for you whenever you feel like mounting me?"

"Yes."

He sits up giving me the best view of his body and just like he wanted I dampen between the thighs. "Walk around shirtless and I just might."

His pecs start moving at opposite time and he grins. "I have a way I can make you wetter. Get to your knees."

Ash grips his dick and waits for me to listen. I'm not sure I'll ever get used to the way he looks jacking off. It's so hot. The way he chokes up on it. The way his arm flexes and his chest pops. The small muscle in his jaw constantly working. I lick my lips and bite down on the bottom one. "I'm wet now."

His heated eyes drop to my pussy as I expose myself to him. He tongues the corner of his mouth. "I see that." I shift when a single digit touches my stomach and travels south. My hands fist the blanket and he groans when he reaches my wetness. "It's been a while since I've tasted this pussy, hasn't it, baby?"

"Yes, Daddy." My voice is breathless.

"How is your knee feeling?"

Huh. Now that he asks, I haven't thought about my knee. "My mind has been busy, and I haven't noticed it. So it must be better."

Ash narrows his gaze, looking at my bent leg, but he shakes it away and lowers himself on top of me. "Being in your childhood room makes this game fucking dirty. You know that?"

I wasn't thinking about it . . . but he's right. A new pool of heat settles between my legs. His thigh is pressed against it so he must feel how ready I am for him. "I used to dream about you in this bed."

"Baby, stop."

"I used to imagine what it would feel like to touch you." I skate my hands up his sides, feeling every ripple of muscle. "It was so innocent, my thoughts for you." Ash's chest heaves against mine until he's pushing so hard into me my boobs ache. So I push back, wanting the pain. "Until they weren't. I was . . . thirteen, I think, the first time I touched myself to a picture of you. That was the only time I did until this summer, because I felt so ashamed."

"Did it feel good?" His voice is husky and hits my ear at just the right spot for goosebumps to erupt over my entire body.

"Yes." I rock my hips into his thigh, needing some friction on my clit. "You gave me my first orgasm."

Ash sucks my ear lobe into his mouth and bites hard. "And I'll be the one to give you your last too."

My body shivers against his and his chest rumbles.

"I'm going to fuck you so hard your pussy will mold to my dick and you'll never be able to take a dick that isn't mine."

Ash bites my neck before sitting up, and without another word, he shoves two fingers in my pussy. I gasp at the sudden pressure but swallow it when he drops his mouth on my clit. Ash's eyes roll back when he tastes me, and my chest blooms.

He laps at my clit for so long I'm shaking and nearly begging him to fuck me. When he pushes back onto his knees, I'm hopeful that's exactly what he's doing but then he moves the side of me and keeps his fingers knuckle deep in my pussy.

I squirm and he flattens his other hand on my lower stomach.

"Ash, I have to pee, let me up."

He doesn't. His fingers curl inside me, hitting a certain spot that makes the tingles and almost uncomfortable feeling down there heighten. "Bloody fucking hell. Look at you. Squirming like I'm going to miss out on your first squirt." He tsks.

I throw my head back when the tingles become too much. He's crushing me into the bed and I can't get up, but that feeling comes and it comes hard. I scream out and Ash groans loudly. "Fuck, keep going, baby." He works me harder.

Tears burn my eyes and I gasp. "Gra-grapefruit! Stop, stop! I have to pee, Ash!"

"Not a fucking chance," he growls.

My body deflates against the mattress and eventually Ash pulls his fingers from me but it's too late. I can feel the soaked sheets, feel it on my pussy and my legs. It even sprayed up his arm and splashed onto my stomach.

I feel like the puddle has swallowed me, or maybe I want it to. I cringe when the warm liquid drips down between my ass cheeks. Embarrassment burns in my throat and behind my eyes. I couldn't cry at my mom's funeral but I can cry when I piss the bed in front of my boyfriend. I told him to stop, I said the word and it's all his fault he didn't. The word that's meant to be a full stop.

Glad to know that doesn't work. *Ash-hole.*

"I told you to stop, Ashley." I hate how my voice shakes.

I hate how he cuddles my side and hugs me to him. The dampness on his thighs and arm, even on his stomach feels like shame. This might be worse than what he did to me in the park, *this* wasn't meant to be punishment. "That was a stupid place to use your word."

Ash-hole.

"Babygirl, open your eyes and look at me."

"I'm so mad at you right now."

"It's not pee, Jailbird. I *wanted* that to happen."

I peel my arm from my eyes so I can turn my head and glare at him. "Why would you want *that* to happen?"

He nuzzles his nose against mine and chuckles. "It's called squirting, babygirl. Fuck, I love how clueless you are. Squirting is quite a common thing in sex. Well, not overly common. I've never had a girl squirt like *that* before."

"It's common? It felt like I pissed the bed."

"Common and so. Fucking. Hot." He kisses my lips between each word.

Who knew. "Are you going to pee on me now? Because Amanda mentioned it one time and it kind of sounded hot."

"You were nearly in tears when you thought you peed but now you want me to pee on you?"

I giggle because it sounds silly when he says it like that. "Yes."

Ash is so warm I don't notice the chill in the air until he pulls away and lifts the blankets for us to crawl under. Being curled in my bed with Ash Pearson is like a dream come true. I snuggle into his chest and breathe in his musky scent. He wraps his arms tightly around me.

"We need to fuck," he mutters lazily.

"Then fuck me."

"Turn around, I want to try something else new."

Eyeing him as I roll the opposite way, wondering what he is going to do. He grips my hips and backs my ass into his pelvis. "I've had to watch your ass from a distance for too long . . . I think it's time I take that virginity too, Princess."

Everything inside me revolts at the idea. "I don't think that's fair, and besides, don't you need lube?"

"You're still soaking wet," he comments, lifting my leg and dragging the head of his dick over my soaked and swollen pussy. "I could probably just slip in."

The head of his dick pushes against my ass and I squeal, "I'm scared."

Ash sucks in a deep breath and blows it across my bare shoulder. "If you don't like it, we can stop."

"You mean it this time?" I turn my head and lift an eyebrow. "I recall using my safe word and you said, 'too fucking bad.'"

"Stop trying to mock my accent, you are terrible at it. I knew I wasn't causing you any real danger."

Sometimes he's too cocky for his own good. "Fine but the moment it leaves my lips, I want you out."

"Brilliant. Roll on to your stomach and spread your legs."

My body shakes when he positions himself behind me. He's straddling my ass and he leans down and kisses the base of my ear. "Relax, babygirl. Daddy won't hurt you."

Ash grips each cheek and pulls them apart. He lets out a soft moan, then he spits on the area. Something touches, smearing it around, and I know it's too big to be his finger. "I should warm you up with my finger. But I don't want to." The head of his enormous cock feels even bigger when it's pushed inside my ass.

I scream to the pillow at the intrusion. It's so much worse than my vaginal virginity. So, so much worse. The worst pain I have ever felt. The worst thing I've ever felt in my life. He doesn't move but my body is shaking.

"I think you ripped my hood." Ash hisses.

"I t-think you ripped m-my asshole."

"Yeah, probably," he says without a care. Like he didn't just rip a part of my body with his. Like it's normal.

My pillow dampens with my tears, yet I haven't told him to pull out. It doesn't feel good, so I'm not sure why but I don't want him to pull out.

He spits again, he doesn't need to, I'm still soaking wet.

Then he pushes in even more and I think I pass out. I'm in and out of consciousness until his hips are pressed against my ass. I can't speak. I can't think, I can't even move.

"Do you feel yourself relaxing for me, baby?" He doesn't even sound like Ash right now. My mind is taking me to a place I don't want to go. The pain is causing confusion with reality and what is in my head. Maybe it's the room. I don't know, but all of a sudden, it's not Ash behind me—*assaulting* my ass.

The grunts aren't the ones I love to hear from Ash. His calloused athlete hands aren't the ones gripping my hips, angling me in the way he wants.

I cry, I think. Tell him to stop. Beg him to get off me and remind him I'm not eighteen yet but he doesn't listen.

Maybe it's all in my head.

Or maybe it's not.

Maybe everything has been in my head and the moments with Ash have all been made up. A figment of my imagination to save me from the reality.

I mean, what are the odds Ash Pearson is actually my coach? What are the odds even if he was that he would be in love with me and be the man drilling into my ass?

The girl who gets ass-fucked by her stepdad.

34

Payson

THE SHOWER WATER IS cold because no one has paid the bill. I refuse to open my eyes even though I know it's Ash kneeling in front of me, begging me to open my eyes and look at him. I don't know when he stopped or how we got in the shower. I don't know how long we have been here or if he finished the deed first.

"Babygirl, please," Ash begs, his voice shaky. "I'm, fuck. I-I thought you were moaning. I d-didn't know you were crying. You didn't say the word." His voice cracks, much like my heart hearing it. "You didn't say the word, Jailbird."

I didn't even know who was behind me, how was I meant to remember a word?

"Please look at me. Please, it's me, Ash. Your boyfriend, your coach, your *everything*. Please look at me and tell me how to help you."

My arms are stiff from the cold water, but I lay them across his back and bury my hands in his hair. He sits up and looks up to me with red eyes. I hope that's from the cold and not because he was crying. I won't make it if I think my mind made Ash Pearson cry.

I don't even care about the burn in my ass, I'm just so happy Ash is really sitting in front of me. Unless I've actually lost my mind and am so out of touch with reality, he's real. Everything is real.

"I'm sorry," I tell him before he can say it to me. "I got lost in my head again, that wasn't your fault."

I place a finger over his open lips, silencing him.

"It's not your responsibility to always save me, Ashley."

"I will always save you, Payson Murphy." He pulls me onto his lap and tucks my head into his chest. "We are going to heal your fucked-up mind, babygirl. I don't care if it takes the entirety of our time on earth, we are going to do this together."

How can you save someone from themself?

After seeing pink water run down my body and the way Ash reacted to seeing it, I decided it would be best to leave him to finish his shower alone.

Plus my ass is on fire. I was hoping to find Tylenol in the medicine cabinet but as I pull it open and dig around, it's not Tylenol I find.

Hydrocodone. Rolling the orange bottle, I see that it has my mom's name on it, but I don't know why she would have needed this heavy of a drug. She dealt with headaches, but I don't know what else. Seeing her name sends a weird feeling down my body—an eerie feeling—but it could also be the house. I haven't felt at peace since we walked in.

I head for my room to get what I want and get the hell out of here as fast as I can. I slip into Ash's dress shirt and open my closet first. There's not really much I want, clothes, I guess but I've lived this long without them. I grab them out anyway. I think about throwing them on my bed but the blood stain stops me. I toss them on Jason's bed, then head for my mine and rip the covers off and toss them in the corner.

Everything stops when I open my underwear drawer and only find my boy shorts left. Three pairs of them. I had at least ten thongs and numerous pairs of other underwear in here at one point, and I didn't bring them to Grandpa's; they're just . . . gone. Anger bubbles deep in my stomach, spreading like a forest fire because I know exactly what happened to them, and I hate that I know. I hate that he is always there to be the answer of everything bad in my life.

I grip the dresser and shove it over with every bit of strength I can manage. It's a cheap dresser so it flies into the wall before tumbling to the ground.

"Payson!" Ash's panic is heard from here.

"I'm fine!" I call back. "Dresser fell over but I'm fine."

The shower cuts out and I move onto the boxes at the bottom of my closet.

Two hold clothes I outgrew. I pull out the school and sport related stuff and shove the rest back into the closet.

Ash strides into the room to find me kneeling on the floor in front of a box I think he is really going to enjoy looking at. "Everything okay?"

"Yep, look what I found."

"Your dresser is halfway across the room, Pay." His voice is weary.

"I told you it fell. Now, look." I hold up the old poster of him. He doesn't seem convinced but he tugs up his pants from the floor and sits next to me.

"You really were obsessed, Jailbird." He snatches the photo from my hands. "That is a great photo of me, though."

I nudge him and dig for something else.

We go through the whole box. I think he liked reading the old articles the most. He even spent a while talking about different moments based around the times of the magazines, and it was nice to hear things from his perspective and not just what I read about.

He reaches into the box and pulls out something I never thought I would see again. "I thought you didn't—"

I grab it from him and jump to my feet. "I didn't. How did this . . ." This doesn't make sense. Fred stole this from me. Said he got tired of seeing me in another man's clothing. I pull it to my face and suck in a deep breath. It doesn't smell how it used to, more like laundry soap but it doesn't matter because I thought for sure I would never see it again. "I can't believe it," I mutter mostly to myself.

Ash wraps his arms around my waist. "I'm glad you found it, baby." He kisses the side of my head and nuzzles into my neck. "Should we see if it still fits?"

Ash struggles—a lot—to get the white jersey on, but eventually it's covering his upper body . . . mostly. It's a tank top style but his arms are way bigger than they used to be. I told him if he rips it, I'll never forgive him so he was careful putting it on but now that it's on, he can't lower his arms. The hem doesn't even reach his belly button, and I can't help but laugh. It looks like a toddler's shirt on him. I laugh harder. Like doubled over and holding my stomach from laughing so hard.

I think it's these moments—seeing Ash squeeze into the jersey of his that I treasured for years before knowing him—that confuses my head with reality. It doesn't feel real.

"Just help me get it off before I rip through it like the Hulk."

I'm still giggling when I tug it over his head. But at least it smells more like him again. "I used to sleep in this every night."

"Well, now you can again."

Yes, I can. I'm still confused how it ended up back in the box but I'm not going to question it. I'm just happy it did.

Ash is making trips to his car with my stuff while I make the last few rounds around my room. I take a quick look under Jason's bed in case there is something he might want.

My eyes catch on something silver. Squinting, I reach farther, wrapping my hands around the cold metal; I know exactly what it is. I stare at the pocketknife in my hand. I flip it over because there is no possible way this can be the same knife. But it is. It has Jason's initials. My heart speeds up as I push my sleeves and look down at my bare arms and the fresh cuts from earlier this week. It's been a long time since I've cut with this knife specifically, but I remember how dull it was. How it left jagged cuts and not clean ones like the sharp razor blades I use now. I want to smile realizing how far I've come. I don't shake when I cut, my breathing doesn't alter. I feel nothing.

"What is that?" I jump at the booming of Ash's voice behind me. I know it's too late to hide the knife or my cuts when I look up and see his tight jaw. He bends down and grabs the knife from me. "What the fuck are you doing, Payson?"

"Those cuts aren't new. I just found the knife and was . . ."

"What? Reminiscing?"

I roll my lips into my mouth because that's exactly what I was doing. I will not tell him that, though. *Look how much better I am at cutting myself now! Aren't you proud of me, baby?* Yeah. No, that conversation would not go over well with Ash.

"Fuck. *Fuck*, Payson. Just . . . Fuck." Ash grips his hair. I scramble to my feet and throw my arms around his large, warm body.

"I'm sorry. I-I know I'm fucked up."

His chest caves with a deep sign. He turns in my arms and hugs me back. "You are. But we are going to heal together. Okay?"

Together. *Together . . .*

I roll my lips between my teeth and nod.

"What are you thinking, Jailbird?"

"Nothing. Never mind." *What the hell am I thinking?*

"Talk to me. What is going on in your pretty mind?"

He might not think it's so pretty after this. I suck in a breath and let it out. "I want you to cut me."

35

Ash

I'M STARING AT PAYSON'S naked body lying on her bed, holding a knife and knowing what she wants me to do but not knowing if I can do it.

Bruise her ass? Sure. Choke her? Yes. Gag her, tie her up, and use nipple clamps? All bloody day. But cutting into her perfect, soft skin so it leaves a scar? I don't know.

We are teetering on a balance beam; one side is a rock and the other a hard place. I've been telling myself I'm helping Payson, but I worry she might have dragged me into the dark instead of me lifting her to the light.

The knife lays heavy in my hand. Flipping it so Jason's initials are up, I roll my eyes because he fucking pissed me off again today. He keeps pissing me off and I won't hesitate to punch him again.

Payson's body should have art made after it. She's not built like a teenager, she's built like a woman. Heavy breasts that don't sit overly high on her frame, a good handful when I cup them. Her stomach is flat but soft, and when she sits there are the cutest rolls. Her hips round into the most beautiful set of thick thighs I've ever laid my eyes on. She's simply beautiful and strong. Relaxed she looks so soft and her skin is like a light melted caramel. Seeing her move and work her muscles at practice is equally mesmerizing. Luca has to pull me from my head too many times when I'm lost watching her body work.

I lower my hand and press the very tip of the blade between her breasts. Her nipples stiffen but not from the frigid air this time. "Are you sure about this?"

"Yes. If you are cutting me, I won't need to."

What a blatant lack of logic we have between us. I don't want Payson cutting herself, and I don't want to do it either but if the knife is in my hands at least I can control it.

"And if I cut too deep?" My heart deflates at the thought alone.

"You won't. I trust you."

I've waited months for Payson's trust. All of it, and now is when she gives it to me? "Where?"

"Anywhere you want. Preferably somewhere people can't see in regular clothes."

I hesitate for so long, deciding where to do this. She captures my hand and presses just enough the blade digs into her arm. My eyes fly to hers, watching the way her eyes flutter and her tense body relaxes in a way I've never seen before. Is this how she looks every time she cuts or is this because of me?

Payson's blood is as equally beautiful as the little whimpers she lets out every time I dig the blade into her skin. Three new cuts. Two on her arm to match the others there and a small one on her outer hip.

The blade glides over her skin like butter as I drag it along her body—not cutting until I spot the scar on her ribs. It's not overly large but a deeper pink than the other scars on her body. The scar caused by this knife in my hand. I don't particularly enjoy knowing this is the knife Payson was using to cut herself at such a young age, but she seems to find something romantic about it.

I angle the knife so the blade lines up where she stabbed herself.

"Does it hurt?"

Payson has been so calm this entire time. Breathing steady, eyes heavy, and the faintness of a smile on her lips. I have been tense as fuck. I've never cut someone. Never really hurt anyone besides a few punches here and there. But here I am, kneeling over the love of my life, dragging a blade up and down her; slicing into that same body that I love so much. I should worry how I went from throwing my desk across the room at the mere thought of her cutting herself, to being the one who cuts her, but Payson makes any logic I have disappear. Especially when she is looking at me like this. We've hit a new level in our relationship and I'm not sure it's a good thing.

"Not even a little."

It should hurt. Her blood isn't pooling, not even a steady stream. I'm not cutting deep enough for that, but it should hurt.

I hate that it doesn't hurt her. Not because I want to hurt her, but because if it did, she would ask me to stop. I ripped her ass already, made her bleed from *sex,* and now from a knife less than an hour later.

Payson has infected me and I can't stop myself from sinking the knife into her stomach, deeper than I have yet, deep enough to leave a vivid, permanent scar.

Her hips buck and she gasps as I make the last slash of the first letter. The next letter goes through her healed scar, and she cries out but still doesn't push me away. She grips the sheets, and her breaths fall short.

I'm breathing enough oxygen for both of us. In and out, my chest heaves. I clench my jaw, finishing the s. "One more, babygirl. Can you handle it?"

I stab the tip in next to the bloody s before she answers. The blood from the first two layers is thick and running down her stomach, pooling on the bare bed beneath her.

I sit back on my feet and drop the knife to the floor. Then I smile. A real, probably feral smile like you would see from the big bad wolf but fuck, if I don't love her new scars. They are art.

They are us.

"W-what did y-you write?" Payson's voice cracks and shakes.

"Why don't you go look and find out?"

She slips from the bed with shaky legs, I follow after her to the bathroom since there is no mirror in her room. She stares at the word on her stomach in awe. I've never seen her look so excited, and my chest greedily sucks in a breath at the sight. *I* did that. *I* made her happy on the day of her mum's funeral. My pride outweighs my disgust with myself—at least for now. Especially when she turns and leaps into my arms, wrapping her arms around my neck and legs around my waist.

"I love it." She bounces eagerly, dragging her pussy along my dick, stiffening it. It never went fully soft because she was naked but I lost myself in the cutting. Now I'm not lost, and am aching to slip into her pussy.

"I love you," I growl, shoving my pants down as she clings to my body. Payson grins, waiting for me. I worried anal might have scarred her more than I thought but she's soaked and I'm able to slip right in her pussy without a problem.

I push her against the wall, slapping a kiss to her lips before dropping my head to hers. "You're mine forever, babygirl. No going back now."

"I always was."

Pink balloons. Pink streamers. Pink jerseys and balls. Pink everywhere. Everything you could imagine that could be turned pink in a gym, it's here.

The name *Week of Pink* should have given it away, but I truly wasn't aware how much pink there would be. The hosting school even made sure our rooms were decked out in the theme with pink towels and snacks. The water I grab from the fridge even has a pink wrapper.

I take a swig before passing it to Payson.

She rolls over so she doesn't have to sit up fully and sips the water at an awkward angle. I chuckle and take it from her, returning the lid before slipping into bed behind her. Pulling her against me, I make sure to not grab her stomach with the healing scar. We put a bandage on this morning, but I wanted to see it when I fucked her, so I ripped it off halfway through our last sex session.

Even in my euphoric state, I looked for any sign of infection but there is none. I made sure we cleaned it last night before patching it and we cleaned it again this morning on the plane. We will have to put a new one on after the shower which we desperately need. Not because today was a hard day, it was mostly introductions. The girls played a few lighthearted games with another team but that was all. Tomorrow the real fun begins which is why I dragged Payson back to my room as soon as I could, because I know we might not get the opportunity the next few days. I'm predicting she will be pretty tired.

"You went deeper today," she mutters.

I blink my eyes open seeing the dried blood on her arms. She asked me for another cutting session, and she's right, I did go deeper. I spent most the night and entirety of the plane ride researching blood and knife play. I'm no professional but I felt more confident today, which would explain her noticing they are deeper.

"Do they hurt?"

"No."

Well, that's good. I guess.

"We need to shower before dinner."

Payson sighs and rolls over so she is facing me. She pets my beard, then knifes her slender fingers into my hair. "I'd rather stay here and ride your dick for another hour."

"I require some cooldown time." I usher at my flaccid dick laying across my hip. Mostly flaccid.

She kisses my lips before rolling off the bed onto her feet. "Fine. But only because my pussy is still sore from the last time."

Yeah it is.

"Isn't it so peaceful without Alyssa?" Janelle nearly cheers. Dinner is being served at the hotel in a banquet room. Probably the only place that could fit so many people.

Janelle is right, though. We've only been in California for half a day but it's been half a day of no drama. Sure, more of the day was spent between Payson's thighs, but still.

"Yes," Payson chimes. She leans back in her chair next to me, and I take in the entirety of her outfit. The hosting school forwarded everyone a dress code for dinner tonight. Men in slacks and dress shirts and girls in dresses. She's beyond uncomfortable, considering she didn't bring a dress and had to borrow from Janelle. She swears it's two sizes too small, but I see nothing wrong with the way her breasts spill from the sweetheart neckline of the short maroon dress. It's tight in all the right places and she looks stunning. Of course Payson threw a short black jacket, that she also borrowed, over it but it doesn't even come close to zipping, and I couldn't be more thankful. There's nothing wrong with what she is wearing besides the fact other people are getting to see just how perfect of a body she hides behind her usual attire of jumpers and sweatpants.

Our waiters seem to be in seventh heaven waiting on a banquet room of nearly sixty girls. Doesn't help my annoyance that most of them don't look a day older than the girls.

It's a buffet-style setup so we don't need them for much, yet they always seem to be around.

Monica bounces at the end of the table with a plate in her hand. "You guys see the chocolate fountain yet?"

I narrow my eyes.

Payson and Janelle swap faces like they are five-year-olds that—well, that heard about a chocolate fountain.

Janelle jumps up and Payson is right behind her. My hand that was stroking her thigh falls. I grab her arm instead. "Have you all forgotten the rules I passed out at the beginning of the season?"

Monica takes her seat next to Payson. "Come on, Coach, we're on vacation."

"Yeah, besides, you really think we listen the rest of the time anyway?" Janelle snorts an ugly sound.

My frown deepens. "I expect you respect your coach, yes."

Payson giggles. "We respect you. But your rules suck. You already got rid of the boyfriend one." Her eyes twinkle knowing I never enforced that between us. "Drop the rabbit food one for the week, please?" She bites that bottom lip that I love.

I pull her down so only she will hear what I have to say. "Eat your chocolate, babygirl. But when we are done here, I'm getting my dessert back at the hotel room. Do you understand?"

"Yes, Daddy." Her whisper shoots straight to my dick. I let go of her arm and drop it to my lap. She giggles again, then her and Janelle are gone, basically running toward the dessert table.

"You ever heard of the word subtle?" Monica asks, stuffing a chocolate marshmallow into her mouth at the same time.

"Yes, not a fan."

Her dark lips pull into a smile. "You know like, all our families are here?"

I am aware. That's why I sat us at the table farthest from them. The teams are all sat in the middle with the families and the rest of the coaches surrounding the outside of the room. "Yes."

Monica shrugs. "Okay. As long as you know."

I steal a look at Janelle and Payson standing at the table, no doubt grabbing enough food to make them sick. I meant my warning. I've not properly licked Payson's pussy in far too long and I'm starved. So if she makes herself sick, then it will be a very miserable night for her. I know this will be one of the few nights we might get alone. Ronni is coming tomorrow and plans on staying in the hotel room with Janelle and Payson. I know she hasn't seen her friend in a while so I will give them their time together.

"Can I ask you a question?"

Monica pauses with a pineapple halfway to her mouth. I let her chew and swallow. "What's up?"

"What do you think of Payson's friend, Ronni? I've not met her and am curious."

Her eyes shrink with suspicion. "You could just ask Payson. They have known each other the longest of all of us. Well, besides Alyssa. Think they might be tied."

"Payson doesn't ever seem to want to discuss the third to their trio." I've not let it bother me much since I have more on my mind, but with her coming around tomorrow, it has me on edge. I know models and what their life is like. I don't want Payson exposed to that. We are trying to heal from so many other things without the influence of a drugged-out model with an eating disorder.

"This isn't because you heard she's a model, right? Like you're not going to up and leave Payson for her best friend? Ronni might be a model, but Payson has curves any of us sticks would kill for."

Payson has curves *any* female would kill for. "Most certainly not. I am only interested in Payson."

"Okay, but if you're lying, Janelle will kill you." Yeah, I do not doubt that. "But Ronni is . . . cool. She's different than those two, though." She nods her head in the direction I know Payson and Janelle are.

"How?"

"Janelle and Payson are like platonic soulmates." I do not enjoy my woman being placed in a soulmate category with anyone but me, but I cannot argue with her claim. "They move in sync. They can read each other's minds with a single look, like a full-on conversation with a few eyebrow twitches." I have seen this firsthand; it's jarring.

"Ronni is not the same?"

She shrugs. "I never thought so. I felt like they were friends because they grew up being friends, not because they wanted to be. Don't say I said this but it always felt like Ronni had a secret she was hiding."

I thank Monica and allow her to finish her food and conversation with Emika so I can think. I was hoping Monica would ease my mind, but she did the opposite. A secret. I'm not sure what kind of secret a teenage girl can hold. What am I thinking? Of course I am. I'm dating Payson Murphy. The girl who holds too many secrets.

Janelle is like the sunshine for Payson's dark life. By the sounds of it, Ronni might be more like a freak snowstorm in March.

The next time I look at Payson, it's not just Janelle by her side. It's the waiters. I clamp my hand onto the side of the table. Janelle is all boyish smiles and keeps touching her fluffy hair, obviously flirting. Payson is hardly paying them attention, but it does nothing to calm the anger growing inside me. Especially when Payson turns her back to them and one guy nudges the other with wide eyes.

That's *my* ass on *my* girl, and I'll be dammed if I allow anyone else to gawk at it. I push from my chair.

My anger only grows with each step until I'm ready to rip someone's head off.

I pass the coaches' table, and a long slim hand snaps out and grabs me by the tie, halting my steps.

My chest rumbles with a growl but it falls short when I meet the blue eyes of my ex—Valerie.

Fuck.

36

Payson

THE MORE I'M AROUND guys my age, the more I know why I like older men. Boys are annoying. Sure, Ash is annoying sometimes too but at least he's ridiculously hot and can grow a beard. The two guys who haven't left Janelle or me alone since we started picking at the dessert table are the anti-Ash. Blond fluffy hair, bare faces, pale despite being in California, and skinny. Like if I sat on their lap, I would crush them and I'm not even that big of a girl.

Janelle seems entertained and I'm genuinely worried about her choice in guys. I know she's still upset about Parker, but come on. She can do better than these two. I'm not judging a book by it's cover either. It has nothing to do with their bare faces, and more so the fact I've caught both looking at my chest and ass and the same for Janelle. They haven't held one full conversation because they can't stop drooling. Maybe it's meant to be flattering but it's pissing me off.

"There's going to be a pool party here at the hotel, after close," one guy says, I didn't pay close enough attention to catch names.

"Yeah, it's totally chill," the other adds.

"Sounds fun," Janelle tells them. I shoot her a look but I know she's ignoring me.

"Sweet. Pool at ten," the first guys says.

They warn us they need to get back to work, thank God, and they scurry off.

"Coach will kill you if you go."

Janelle pops a chocolate strawberry into her mouth. "That's why he won't know."

"He's doing room checks, you know?"

Janelle finishes chewing. "Yeah. But we also know he has something kinky planned for you after seeing you in that dress all night. So you'll keep him busy for a few hours so I can check out the party, see if there is anyone hotter than dumb and dumber, and I'll be back in our room by midnight, with or without a guy. Hopefully with." She pumps her eyebrow happily.

"You know we spent all afternoon doing kinky stuff. I told you he's big, I don't think my vagina can handle much more today. We have a long day tomorrow."

She puffs out her bottom lip in the most pathetic way. "Please, your best friend is horny."

"Can't you just masturbate or something?"

She scoffs like that's the worst thing I've ever said to her. "You get hot-as-sin sex all the flippin' time and you expect me to masturbate. Selfish!"

Groaning, I reach for another pineapple and run it under the chocolate. "You're so dramatic. You were having sex for years before me."

"It's not the same. You didn't know what you were missing and unless you're willing to share our coach . . ." I glare at her. "Exactly. Please. Just till twelve."

I don't even know why I'm disagreeing as if Ash is going to let me out of his room before then.

Seeing my defeat on my face, she throws her arms around me and wiggles us back and forth. "I love you. I love you. I love you."

"Yeah, yeah. I love you too."

Janelle halts her wiggles. "Did you just say *you love me too?*"

Huh. I hadn't even thought about saying it. I didn't freak out and overthink it. It just fell out of my mouth without a thought. Like normal people. "I guess I did."

Her eyes fill with big fat tears and she hugs me even tighter than before. "Oh my gosh! You love me!" We are a good distance from the crowd but the team closest to us is eyeing us like we're freaks. Or she's a freak and I'm a bystander hugging a freak.

"Okay, okay don't make me take it back."

Janelle slaps a sloppy kiss to my cheek, no doubt leaving behind a bright red stain. "Wait—" She pauses again and crosses her arms. "I'm the first person you've said that to, right? Not Ash?"

"You are the first."

She squeals again. This time grabbing my hands and turning us in a circle while jumping. I make her stop because my boobs are close to knocking me out, she stops and smiles. "I can't wait to rub it in his smug—" Her smile falls as she glances over my shoulder. "Payson don't turn around."

As if anyone has ever listened when someone has said that. I turn and it takes only a quick glance to see what caused her smile to fall so dramatically.

Ash stands closer to us than before, next to the coaches' table, in front of him is one of the other coaches. I think she's the hosting coach. Coach . . . Buckingham, I think. I didn't work with her much since she's coaching the hitters. She's tall, blonde, and like every single other female that comes into the view of Ash Pearson, beautiful. I hate her already. I hate her more seeing her claws wrapped around my boyfriend's necktie. She strokes a hand down his tie, then perches it over his shoulder. The shoulder my legs were on a couple hours ago.

"How do you figure they know each other?" Janelle asks.

I suck in a sharp breath when she turns and throws his arm over her shoulder. She flashes a big smile and a flicker goes off. "I'll give you one fucking guess," I growl. It's so obvious there is a sexual history, one she seems to not have left in the past. I'm learning any girl that knows Ash has some kind of sexual history with him. *Okay, this might be where younger guys are better. Less time to fuck everything that walks.*

"Oh, her?" Parker steps to my opposite side, holding a bottle he's too young to have.

"You know her?" The pit grows even more.

"Not really. I spent one week here like years ago. She was around." He shrugs.

Ash finally steps away from the woman, but he doesn't look my way. I know by his stiff body he can feel the weight of my stare. Like I could feel his when those guys were around.

"So, who is she?" Janelle asks.

I notice Parker flinch a small amount hearing her voice. Then he sighs. "His ex-wife."

I don't know whose mouth falls open faster. Mine or Janelle's. Parker saunters off but Janelle and I stand there gaping at my boyfriend slipping into a booth next to his ex-*wife*.

Three steps forward, three *hundred* steps back.

"You know he's going to kill you when he finds you?" Janelle tells me like it's not something I already know.

"Better him than me." Then I cringe because I'm aware how that came out.

Janelle is frowning but she waves me away. "At least you'll look hot when he does."

I turn toward the mirror. For the last half hour, Janelle has been attempting to tame my hair. The California heat is not doing it any favors. It's not even humid, just the heat in general, I guess. We decided on two boxer braids but it took her extra long because how frizzy it is. Janelle tried to get me to wear one of her swimsuits but dropped it when I gave her a look and she remembered the scars on my arm. What she doesn't know about is Ash's name under my left boob, which has me feeling extra stupid right now.

Ex-wife.

"No, stop that. I see where you are heading. We are going to go to a pool party and enjoy our time as best friends. Okay? No cheating-boy drama or ex-wife drama." Ugh. "Just Pay, Jay, and hella fucking party food."

That actually sounds amazing. "Thought you were looking for a lay."

"That was before you found out your boyfriend has an ex-wife. Now tonight is about distracting you. But not with boys. I saw how you were looking at those two earlier. You couldn't be less interested."

"Can you blame me?"

Janelle shrugs and fiddles with her minimal makeup in the mirror. "They weren't bad, P. Your vision is just warped by our coach. You never stood a chance at having a normal life when Ash Pearson walked in."

Tell me about it.

"So, how is your knee, anyway? You didn't seem bothered by it today?"

"Yeah, no, it's good. My brace helps a lot."

"I can't even tell you how happy I am Alyssa isn't here."

I shoot a look her way as we step onto the elevator. She presses the ground floor. "I mean, you probably know but shit am I glad."

I think everyone is. Even Shannon, Alyssa's closest friend on the team, seemed more relaxed today. I think that says a lot. We will definitely miss her skills but we will make do. I will pull double the work if I have to. Anything to prove that we don't actually need her.

We reach the pool doors and already can hear the girlish screams and the music. I can't believe a ritzy ditzy hotel like this would allow this. It's very obvious it's being ignored. When we passed the front desk, the guy just smiled at us and you could hear the noise from there.

Eases the bit of anxiety I had about coming. I don't want to get in trouble. Legal trouble, I'll get in team trouble all day long because *he's* in trouble too. I thought we were past the secrets. Apparently not. I'm not sure what kind of excuse he will have this time but I'm tired of hearing them. I know that much.

"Hey"—Janelle grips my hand in hers—"you okay? We can totally just go watch a movie in bed and curse out the main love interest."

I smile and grab her hand back. "No, I'm fine. Is that what you want to do?"

We exchange looks and I know that's exactly what she wants to do and it's what I want too but, for whatever reason, we throw open the door and step in. The pool room is the biggest I've ever seen but having all five teams, plus more I don't recognize, in here, makes it feel small. The pool is also the biggest I've seen. Like Olympic size, if I had to guess.

"Holy cannoli."

"Yeah . . ." I sigh.

We stand awkwardly, holding hands for what feels like a long time before someone walks up to us. Unfortunately it's not who either of us wanted.

"Hey, guys." Alyssa's voice is sickly sweet and her smile is even worse.

Janelle ignores her and after following her line of sight, I see why, Parker sits against the wall across the room holding a bottle, again, staring at her.

She turns her head and we both sigh because there goes our drama-free night.

37

Ash

"POSE FOR A PHOTO. We need some for the newsletter." Some guy instructs; I want to deny him because I can feel Payson's eyes on me, but it's snapped before I can even get the words out.

I'm about to turn when Coach Fulton barks out for me to sit down and catch up. I reluctantly agree since I sat at the table with my team earlier and not them. I know a few of them, but to my dismay there's not a seat open anywhere else besides next to Valerie.

Payson will lose her fucking mind over this and there's nothing I can do about it because if I chase after the player I sat with all night, someone will be suspicious. Monica was right, we need to be more careful, at least while we are here. A lot of important people in the volleyball world are here, and keeping Payson's image spotless is my main focus. I can use this time to promote my girl. Not that she needs it, I know she will prove herself over the next four days but a little inside help might be nice too. Unfortunately, after some chatting, it seems everything is going through Valerie.

"Yeah, my dad retired and basically left everything to me," Valerie tells me with a big smile.

I try to offer one back to be nice, but I don't think it works because she loses hers pretty quickly.

"You okay? You've been pretty distracted the entire time we've been chatting."

Most of the table has cleared out. Even my best fucking friend left after I saw one of the other coaches making fuck-me eyes at him. He better have gone to her room because as soon as I'm done here, I will have my tongue so deep in Payson's pussy she won't remember anything from tonight. I'll tell her who Valerie is as soon as she asks, but I know shes not going to be happy. We've been so good lately; I don't want the set back.

There is only three of us left, and I haven't been able to get in a single fucking word between these two. It's obvious there is something going on between Coach Fulton and Valerie but it's not obvious enough to make it seem like they are together. Since it cleared out, I move to the opposite side to put some space between Valerie and me. Fulton seemed to relax after that. If only he knew I had my mind on another pussy, maybe he wouldn't be so uptight.

"Sorry. Yes, I need to speak with one of my players. She has a hurt knee and I want to be sure she is icing it before tomorrow." Easy enough lie and not completely wrong.

"Ah, yes. Payson Murphy. Your Libero," Coach Fulton says. I smile, happy he already knows who I'm talking about. That means he must have gotten my tapes. Coach Fulton is the Colorado State coach for the men's team, he's not here with his team but he's here as a scout. We go way back since he's been in the industry for years. He was the one who bitched at me about throwing my jersey away at the game Payson was at. Said I needed to stop wasting my team's money. He was more upset than my coach. I think I could easily get Payson an in because over the years, we grew friendly, but I know she doesn't need me. I want her skill to get her there because I know it can. She played so well the other night, even with her knee.

"Yes. We had an accident with another player. But she's fine. No tears, just strained and will be fine as long as she ices."

Coach Fulton belly laughs. "Taking after her coach, hey? You all healed up from the last one?"

"Getting there. My body doesn't bounce back as easily as it once did," I joke.

He laughs again.

"Sucks getting old, doesn't it?" Valerie adds.

I spend the next twenty minutes chatting about Payson in the most casual way I can. I mention Janelle and Monica as well. I know Monica plans on going to college for basketball like her parents, but I really think she could have a future in volleyball. She's a fantastic Middle. Probably even better than Valerie. And Janelle has exceeded any expectations I had for her being an All-Around. By the end, I'm giving Fulton the rest of our schedule. I nearly jump to my feet after that because it's been hours, and I need to find Payson. Now. I can only imagine what she's got herself into.

I hit the main lobby, heading for the stairs because it'll be faster than the elevator, but someone shouts my name. I want to ignore her because I can only imagine what she wants now.

"I'm in a bit of a rush."

"I just have one thing to say."

I sigh and spin. She walks toward me until she is stopped far too close for comfort. I prepare myself to deny her approach but it never comes. Instead, she crosses her arms over her chest. Now that I'm really looking, she doesn't look like she's trying to seduce me, she looks annoyed.

That's not much better in my opinion.

"You seem very interested in Payson Murphy's future."

"Are you not interested in your players' futures?" I challenge.

"Of course, I am. I'm interested in a *coach* way. I want to see them thrive in whatever it is they do because I've been coaching most of my girls for years. You seem to be interested on a deeper level. You've not known this girl more than what, a couple months? You cannot compare our situations."

I run a hand through my hair.

"Your hair has gotten long and your beard is thicker than I've ever seen it. In fact, I don't think I've ever seen you with a beard."

We dated for a few months; I could have had a beard and she wouldn't have known because she paid no attention. I didn't, I only have it now because Payson likes it. I think she likes my hair too because she always plays with it when we are together. I can't be bothered to take the time to shave or get a hair appointment, Payson requires my undivided attention right now.

"Just get on with it, Val." I don't remember her being this annoying back in the day.

"Are you having an intimate relationship with one of your players, Ashley?"

"No." The lie is like acid on my tongue. "How dare you accuse me of that."

She purses her lips. "You haven't looked at my body once."

"And that automatically means I'm fucking a player?"

She rears back at my harsh word. I couldn't care less. She's pissed me off. Not because the accusation—she's right, obviously, why would I look at her body when I have Payson's waiting for me . . . somewhere? I'm pissed because of that. I have no clue where she is. Her location isn't precise enough, so it says the hotel. That narrows nothing down for me.

"You're not my type anymore. Simple as that."

Hurt passes through her eyes. There is the Valerie I knew. She was insecure but not in a way like Payson. She craved validation from everyone. Payson craves it from just me. Valerie is the ex I told Payson I invited someone over to fuck in front of her. We broke up shortly after. It was never a great relationship, but her dad was the head of everything and she was around a lot. It was easy. I used to only go for easy. One dramatic to the next. I love Payson, but it's not easy with her. Not yet anyway, one day it will be.

"I hope you're telling me the truth, Ashley. I won't think twice before reporting you for misuse of power."

I clench my jaw until my molars cry out. "Noted. Now, if you'll excuse me."

I don't wait for her reply as I fly up the steps. She's not in my room like I wanted her to be. I knew there was a fat chance but I was still hopeful. I knocked on her and Janelle's room for a long time, but no one answered. I was about to break the door down when a groggy Parker strolled out from his room. His room is a suite with ours but since Luca and I will need to be up early and he doesn't, we let him have his own room so he could sleep in and head to the gym once he's up.

"Papà," he groans.

"You better just be tired, Parker."

He waves a lazy hand my way. "If you are looking for Payson, she's down at the pool."

"Why?"

"There's a party going on." He wanders back into his room, and I turn back for the stairs. Mad or not, she should not be at a party. None of my girls should be. They are in for a rough two weeks when we get back to Michigan. We are in crunch time for our season and I'm not letting us fail this close to the finish line.

I throw the door to the pool room open, looking for my girls. There are gasps and "oh, shits" from random kids who think I'm here to bust them. I couldn't give two shits less about them. My team, however, I definitely care about.

It takes me longer than it should to find my team but they are all huddled up in the back corner and not scattered around dancing. My heart swells for a moment before I see a little brunette staring up to me, a passive look on her face. She can pretend to not care all she wants. I saw the look earlier when she saw Valerie's hands on me.

"Ladies." My voice booms and the ones who didn't see me approach, jump.

"We're just talking." Emika is the one who blurts it out.

"You shouldn't be down here."

"We're not the only ones doing things we shouldn't."

I cross my arms over my chest and level my stare. "Everyone to their rooms. Now. And meet me in the lobby at six a.m."

"But it doesn't start till eight," one of them whines.

I glare at all of them, and they scurry by. Everyone but Payson and Janelle. The two biggest pains in my arse. "You two as well."

"Tell us about your ex-wife first, then we will go," Janelle bites out.

My what? "Excuse me?"

Payson is on the verge of tears. It takes everything inside me not to lean down and pull her into me. "Parker told us. Please, *please*, Ash, don't do this again."

Do what again? Parker told them Valerie is my ex-wife? He's obviously upset about something still and I'll need to check on that. "I have never been married, Payson, you know this."

"I don't know anything about you." Her eyes fall. She hugs her knees and my heart aches. She trusts me, but not completely. If she did, she would never second-guess me.

"You know everything, babygirl, look at me."

"Coach." Janelle twists her lips, looking like she's about to cry too.

I crouch down to be closer. "Ladies." I soften my voice. Both lift their watery gazes. Everything Monica said earlier hits me right now. I knew she was right but seeing how upset Janelle is for Payson is both heart warming and infuriating because what they are upset about. "I have never been married. I'm guessing Parker said that knowing it would upset you."

There's a few beats where the only noise is whatever is happening in the background.

"Upset with who? Saying that upsets Payson. Why would he be upset with Payson?"

If only I knew. "I'm not sure, but I'll figure it out." Payson still isn't looking at me. I can see the battle in her head whether she should believe me or not. Knowing her, it won't end in my favor. I'm not having this week ruined because an unimportant ex and a lie. "Jailbird." I reach to hook her chin with two fingers but stop because of the conversation I just had with Valerie. I won't ruin Payson's chance at the future she wants. It doesn't mean I will like it. I curl my fist and stand. "We can't talk here but I will tell you everything if you just come with me. I promise on my life, it is not what you are thinking."

Janelle grabs her best friend's hand. I shouldn't be irritated that Payson will look at her and not me, but I am. They stare at each other for a long time before Payson's shoulders deflate.

I give them space to stand as much as I wish I could pull her into my aching arms now, I can't. We walk silently for the elevator.

The doors open and much to my dismay, Valerie steps out. Her eyes narrow in on my hand on Payson's shoulder, then she sees the one on Janelle's the same way. "Ash."

"We are heading up."

Payson's shoulders tense. I squeeze, reassuring her as best as I can.

She steps to the side, and I have to force the girls to walk past her. I worry about one of them throwing fists, but they don't. "You must be Payson," Valerie says with fake sweetness. "And . . . Monica?"

"Janelle," I correct.

"Ah, yes. Your coach has said quite a lot about you. Both of you."

"He's a great coach," Janelle says with a fake smile. Payson says nothing. I'm not sure she's even paying attention. Her rapid pulse is beating against my finger.

"And what do you think, Payson? Is Coach Pearson a good coach?"

Seconds pass of Payson just staring at her. A sheen of sweat actually coats my forehead waiting for her.

"Yes." One simple word but it says a million. *Come on, Jailbird.*

Sensing Payson's apprehension, Valerie tilts her head in question. "I'm not going to lie, that surprises me. He wasn't very assertive like a coach needs to be. Well, besides in the bedroom." Her laugh is easy and my hands burn to wrap it around her skinny throat and choke her just to stop it. No one else laughs. The elevator falls dead silent, besides the heavy beating of Payson's heart, but I think I'm the only one that can hear it.

Janelle's mouth gapes and she looks from Valerie, to me, to Payson while she waits for someone to speak.

To my surprise, it's Payson. I open my mouth to bitch her out because I know why she did that. She's testing Payson's jealousy.

"It is highly inappropriate to discuss our coach's sexual appetite, don't you think, Coach *Fuckingham*."

"It's Buckingham!" Valerie gasps.

Payson slaps a hand to her mouth in an overdramatic way. "Oh, good. I thought Fuckingham was a terrible last name. By the way, he is plenty assertive in all places."

She leans forward and presses the door close button. Valerie glares at us until the doors close and I blow out a breath and pull Payson against my chest. I kiss her cheek. "You should not have said that, Jailbird."

"She was annoying." Janelle speaks instead of Payson. "And not to mention what she was wearing; talk about inappropriate."

"Was it?"

Janelle shoots her stare my way and even Payson cranes her neck to look at me. "You're joking, right? It was totally see-through. You could see her nipples through the lace."

I shrug. "I didn't notice."

Payson scoffs. "As if."

I drop my hand from her shoulders to circle around her waist and drop my mouth to her ear. "I was too busy trying not to get a boner with your ass just inches from my dick, Princess."

"She sure had no issues checking you out. And throwing that comment about the bedroom. So low class. I actually liked her today, not now." Janelle crosses her arms and leans against the wall.

"She was trying to get a rise from Payson."

Payson tilts her head. "Why me?"

The doors beep and I let my arms fall from her, she frowns. After seeing the hallway is empty, I take a deep breath. "She called me out on fucking a player. You specifically because I'm 'too invested in your future.' And is trying to prove her assumption is more than an assumption."

Payson pauses halfway to her room. "What? Why? Did you talk about me or something?"

"Of course I did. I will talk to anyone who listens about you." Janelle keeps walking and makes a little awe noise from up the hall. "The reason I was absent all night is because I was forced to endure hours of stuffy coaches discussing mundane things just so I could spend thirty minutes talking about you."

"I don't understand."

"One of the coaches at that table was Colorado State's coach—"

"Ash—"

"I told him about you being interested, and guess what? He's interested back. He's not the women's' team coach but he watched the highlight reels I sent and was impressed with you and mentioned about passing them on."

Her walls crumble and the faintest of smile lifts the corners of her lips. "Really?"

"Really."

We stop off at my room but there's an athletic sock on the door handle. Fucking Luca. "Who does he have in there?" Payson giggles.

"One of the coaches. I think Florida's coach."

She nods. "Yeah, she was pretty. Big tits."

I chuckle under my breath. "You think Janelle would mind if we crashed in your room for a while? He won't keep her overnight and we can come back."

"I think Janelle will want us to stay." Payson grabs my hands and walks backward to her room across the hall. "She wanted to find a guy to hook up with at the party but when Parker mentioned you having an ex-wife," she growls the last bit, "it kind of ruined those plans."

I cup her face and back her into the door, so we are out of sight from any camera's. "Did you really believe I had a whole ex-wife you didn't know about?"

"You had a whole son, Ash. Yeah, I did."

Fair. Unfortunately. "Well, no. Parker couldn't be more wrong. I've never even come close to marriage. Especially with Valerie. We dated on and off for a few months." I shrug. "She is the ex I told you I fucked another girl in front of."

Payson gasps. "She certainly didn't mention that part of your relationship."

I grab the card from her hands and unlock the door before backing her inside. "No, she didn't."

"What didn't Fuckingham mention?" Janelle pokes her head out from the bathroom.

Payson walks right by her, pulls her pants down, and sits down on the toilet. A second later, her pee hits the water. I lift an eyebrow, glancing between the two girls but they just laugh. "Ash fucked another girl in front of her when they were dating."

Janelle's mouth drops open. "You whore!"

"She had gotten another guy's number at the bar." I turn for the beds, bored of this conversation. "Which one?"

"Guess!" Payson yells back. "You guess wrong and no pussy."

She's not stopping me from getting to her pussy tonight, I don't care which bed is hers or not, but it's a cute thought. After some careful consideration, I choose the bed next to the window and kick off my shoes, lose the tie, drop my pants, and quickly slip under the covers. Then I unbutton my shirt and toss that next to my pants in the chair. I should have asked if Janelle was okay with me being partially naked but I'll be in bed the whole time I'm here and she's seen me shirtless so it shouldn't be an issue.

"Well, alright but I call little spoon," Janelle says.

Payson quickly rounds the corner and shoves her friend's shoulder.

"Good job, baby." She grins.

She runs and bounces on the bed next to me, attacking my face with numerous kisses. "You might get lucky tonight, after all."

I was getting lucky whether she thinks that or not.

"Nooo, I want you to stay up and watch movies with me." Janelle whines from her bed.

"You have practice at eight," I deadpan.

Janelle sighs overdramatically. "Thanks, Dad. I'm aware."

Payson giggles and flips so she is sitting between my legs, facing the TV Janelle is now scrolling through.

I've never witnessed two people decide what to watch as fast as these two. Luca and I will spend forty minutes sometimes debating what to watch, but not these two. As soon as *Bring It On: All or Nothing* pops onto the screen, they squealed, then again when they saw it was just starting.

The movie isn't my cup of tea and halfway through, I'm bored. And horny. Payson wiggles anytime music plays and that creates friction on my dick. I know she must be able to feel my raging boner but she's too preoccupied with the movie.

Not for long.

I drag my hand from her stomach, down her short torso, and easily slip under her tiny sleep shorts, pleased to find her bare. She angles her head to look back at me. I love the way her eyes flutter when my finger parts her and connects with her clit. I thought she was too focused on the movie to notice anything else, but I'm pleased to find her soaked and her clit swollen and needy.

She chomps down on her lip, and I slip a finger inside her greedy cunt and drop my mouth to hers. Her lips part for me, allowing me to slip my tongue inside and tease her with my piercing like I know she loves.

I know where she would like it teasing her more. I pull off and glance over to Janelle's bed. My grin grows finding her facing away from us, meaning she's sleeping. Payson follows my eyes and I hear her swallow. "We can't."

I've never let her tell me no before, and I'm not going to now. "Tell me you don't want my tongue buried deep in your pussy," I whisper directly into her ear and love the shutter I receive back.

"I-in the same r-room?"

I slip another finger inside and she greedily accepts it, rocking her hips. The cutest little moan slips from her lips before biting down on her lip, stopping any more from coming out.

That's all the answer I need. I move her to the side so I'm able to lie on my back, then I grab her hips.

"What are you doing?" she hisses.

Her shorts easily slip over her beautiful thighs, she's hesitant to pull them off, shooting looks toward her best friend. Once her bottom half is bare, I tug on her shirt. She shakes her head.

"Off."

"No."

I cock an eyebrow. "Do not tell me no."

"I'm not going to be completely naked, Ashley! What if she wakes up?"

Payson has the silliest reasonings, but I don't feel like arguing with her right now. I want my tongue in her cunt and I want it now. I'm so lucky I can overpower her so easily. Even when she fights me, like right now. I pin her down and rip the shirt over her head, leaving her completely bare to the dark room. It takes everything inside me not to dive into her and get lost because her legs are wide open as she gapes at me, but I want her to ride my face. She's not done it yet and it's something everyone should experience. I know she will love it.

Once again, I pick her up, ignore her many curses, and set her down over my face.

She hovers over my mouth, trying to shield her tits in her small hands and failing, while shooting panicked looks between Janelle and me.

The smell of Payson's need is mouthwatering. I know she will enjoy this, she just needs to get over the fact someone else is in the room. Janelle is sleeping and as long as Payson can keep it down, she will stay that way and it'll be just like when we are alone.

It's nearly comical to see Payson so worried. Luca wouldn't blink twice if roles were reversed and he was lying in Janelle's bed while Payson was sucking me off. That probably comes from being roommates for years. Not like we had our own space, so we had to get real comfortable with each other very quickly. That's how threesomes came about between us. When one couldn't be bothered to pick up a girl, we would share—with the girl's permission—and we never once got turned down.

I grip Payson's hips and force her full weight onto my open mouth. She gasps and her eyes blow wide but the moment my piercing presses against her clit, her head drops forward and she whimpers.

There's my girl.

Sex with Payson in any form is the best I've ever had. Could be the love we share but I think it's a mix of that and the experience she lacks. Something I didn't notice until being with Payson is that sex with other girls was superficial. They were so worried about how they looked, sounded, or whatever. Too worried about impressing me because who I was or how I looked, they never let themselves go in the way Payson does, and I chalk that up to me being her first experience in everything. She allows herself to feel anything I throw at her. When we fuck, Payson is not lost in her head worried about doing it right, or looking perfect from every angle as she does—which she does. She's only worried about how it feels. Seeing her eyes roll back and the expanding of her chest, the deep moans she lets out when something just feels that good. She filters nothing and it cranks me to the fucking max. I hope she never changes.

Even now, she is doing her best not to moan but she's tugging on my hair, not worried about hurting me and only worried about grinding her pussy into my mouth.

I squeeze her breasts in my hands and her mouth drops open. Her head falls back on a whimper. Her nipples tighten under my palms, and I tweak each one.

I know when she's close, her pussy tightens around my tongue and she dampens tenfold, I lap it all up. Drinking from Payson's cunt like it's the bloody fountain of youth.

I stab the ball of my piercing into her throbbing clit and she falls apart. She slaps the wall, stopping it from being her forehead as she bucks forward. No doubt her lip will bleed with how hard she is biting it.

And this, this is what sex with Payson is all about. The dance between pleasure and pain. In Payson's world, you can't have one without the other.

She's altered my needs and wants as well. I'd be lying if I didn't like looking up and seeing the scars I left behind. Particularly the A, s, and h under her left breast.

I lap at her sensitive cunt until she falls to the side onto her back, then tug her into my arms and place a kiss onto her forehead with a smile on my lips. "How was it?"

"I love your beard," she mutters lazily. "I want to do that every day."

She curls into my body under the covers and I chuckle. "Gladly."

38

Payson

"WELCOME TO WEEK OF PINK!" Coach Buckingham shouts into the microphone from the middle of the gym. Everyone on the bleachers erupts in claps and cheers, including my team. The loudest of them all has to be Janelle and Monica, and somehow, I got stuck between both. She rattles on about what Week of Pink means and what we will do for the next four days. "Last year we exceeded our goal of five hundred thousand by bringing in just over one million dollars. This year—" She pauses as the crowd cheers again. "This year we have set a goal of one million from the start. So, let's not disappoint." There is again more cheering and then it's time to announce the teams. It goes by alphabetical school names. Usually, we are first but there is a new team here from Abraham High School. Apparently, they are from New Jersey.

"Our next team has been attending for some years now. Coach Dillon first reached out with her interest a few years back and they haven't let us down since." What a nice sentiment coming from such a bitch. "Unfortunately, Coach Dillon isn't coaching the team anymore, but, they do have two new coaches who I go *way* back with." I hate her. I swear she meets my eyes from here with a bitchy smile on her face. "Please welcome Coach Ash Pearson and Coach Luca Beruiti." She even says Luca's name right. *No one* says his name right.

Ash grabs the mic from her, and after a ridiculous amount of clapping, he starts his introduction. "Let's start with our captains. Monica Maddox and Payson Murphy."

Monica pulls me after her down the bleacher steps. I'm more sore today than I was yesterday, so she's quicker than I am, but she waits at the bottom. "Payson wanted to be like her coach and is nursing an injured knee so please be patient with her." He flashes his leg with the knee brace and the room falls into quiet laughter. I scowl as we walk to the floor and stop in front of them, turning to face the audience.

There are so many people here. I knew there was but it's so different being in front of them. This is the biggest gym I have ever been in, and it's over halfway full. Not just from teams but families and I'm sure random people from here. It's only eight a.m. and the scrimmage doesn't start till two. That's when the gym will be packed.

Ash announces the rest of the team until all seven of us are standing side by side. Then each coach does the exact same.

By the end, I'm antsy to start and stop standing here like a zoo animal. Unfortunately, Valerie apparently has a "special surprise," so it means more waiting. "What do you think it is?" Monica asks me.

"I have no clue."

The doors far across the gym open and a huge group of . . . guys trail in.

I did notice the lack of boy teams this year, but I assumed none signed up. I guess they did. I don't understand this weird entrance, though. They're just male volleyball players yet everyone is acting like they are royalty.

"The hosts of this year's Week of Pink are so excited to introduce the top three male teams from last season. The first team here"—she gestures to the guys walking behind us—"Traveled all the way from Greece and took second place against the next team who joined us from Russia."

Wow, Greece and Russia and the next team is from Brazil, they came in third. Amazing. I guess that is worth a dramatic entrance. I didn't keep up on last season or anything but I skimmed an article about how good Russia was doing.

I glance behind me expecting to see Ash but come face-to-chest with the guys from the Russian team. The couple behind me grin and one wiggles his fingers at me. The other one lets his eyes drift down my body before zeroing on my ass. His blond eyebrows inch up his forehead.

Huffing, I turn back to the front but it doesn't make the feeling of a bunch of guys checking me out go away. It's flattering, I guess, but I don't enjoy the attention.

"Oh my God. They are so hot." Janelle sits on the floor next to me while I adjust my brace. My knee is giving me more problems. All morning it's been a constant ache in the back of my mind.

"I like their accents."

"Which ones?"

I grin at my best friend. "All of them."

She laughs along and teases me about my obsession with accents. It's not an obsession, I just enjoy a good accent.

"Did you guys hear?" Mika falls next to Janelle. "Tomorrow there is going to be some kind of mixer for the players. It's going to be in the same room as dinner yesterday and we are meant to dress up and *mingle*."

"That sounds terrible."

Mika rolls her lips between her teeth and shifts. "Mhm. The thing is . . . It's just for the players because . . . the coaches are having their own mixer in the penthouse apartment."

My stomach free falls straight to my ass. "You're joking."

"I figured you didn't know. I'm sorry. I wanted to tell you before it was announced."

Groaning, I rub my palms into my eyes. I didn't tell Mika everything but her and Monica overheard us talking about Valerie and wanted to know what we were talking about, so I filled them in with the basics. She is Ash's ex and thinks we are fucking.

"Jay, you better find someone to fuck, to at least make the night worth it for one of us."

"One? Pshh. I want at least one of each, then I can decide who gets doubles."

At least Janelle will make what sounds like the worst night, interesting. Plus Ronni might come. That will definitely be interesting.

"Have you heard about tomorrow?"

I'm in line for lunch when Ash walks up to me and mutters those words.

"Yep," I say keeping my head forward. "Should be miserable."

He grumbles, "I am not happy with the thought of you being in a room full of boys."

I snort at the image of just that; me in a room filled with nothing but guys, and Ash on the outside ripping his hair out.

"I'm not laughing." He drops his voice to a whisper and hisses, "*baby-girl.*"

"You think I am?" I shoot a look over my shoulder at him. "You're going to be in a hotel room—*with your ex.* Probably other stupidly pretty women too."

His head falls forward and he pinches the bridge of his nose. His brown hair is on the messy side, and I can tell he's been running his hands through it repeatedly—probably from stress. I've noticed he does that a lot now that his hair is longer. "I cannot wait until you are legal, Payson. None of this pretending, lying, and sneaking bullshit. You can come to parties with me, and I with you, where no one can do anything about it."

"Me too," I tell him softly. "I really don't want to go."

He reaches around me and grabs two plates and does the same for cutlery before passing me one set and the other to Parker behind him who looks dead to the world with his hood low on his forehead. I'm not even sure his eyes are open but he's walking.

"What if we don't?"

My heart skips at the thought alone. "Ashley Pearson, are you suggesting we play hooky?"

His eyebrows sink and confusion fills his face. "Hooky?"

After I explain, his smile is wide. "Skiving—that's exactly what I'm suggesting and instead of the parties, I take you out."

"Like a date?"

"Your first ever."

And suddenly I'm not, not looking forward to tomorrow anymore.

"Where is she?"

After another sweep of the studio, I shrug. "This is where she told us to come, right?"

Janelle scoffs. "She didn't tell us anything. Whoever kidnapped our best friend did."

"Now imagine if that were true and you just joked about it."

She shrugs. "I'm not joking. If her mom didn't periodically post something about Ronni, I would have called out the SWAT team already."

I actually don't doubt that.

We've been standing in this small photo studio for ten minutes waiting for Ronni to show her face so we can get back to the hotel. Since Janelle has to be primed and ready for the party tomorrow and I want to be for my first date, we agreed on having a spa night in our hotel room. Ash wasn't happy about not having me for the night, but Luca promised he would keep him busy—without strippers or exes.

I've gotten several texts and I've been keeping him informed with us just standing here.

I don't know how much time passes, a long enough time of Janelle and me waiting around that we play "I" spy. Surprisingly there is a lot to spy in this white box.

It's Janelle's turn and she takes her time looking around the room, then she goes rigid and a huge smile spreads across her face. "I spy with my little eye—our best friend."

I whip around. Ronni is crying and a choked sob comes from Janelle before the three of us are running full speed at each other, not caring when we collide and fall to the ground in a three-way hug.

"I can't believe you guys are here," Ronni cries into Janelle's shoulder while choking me with her thin arm.

We hug for a long time before pulling away. Then we just stare at each other, smiling, because the truth is, I can't believe it either. It's been so long since we have been a trio and now here we are. We get three whole days with Ronni, besides volleyball, because she flies out to Milan on Friday and her manager is giving her a break until then.

"So, are you like free to go?" Janelle asks.

I pick up how Ronni winces with that question. It's not that obvious, and if I wasn't staring at her so intently, or hadn't known her my whole life, I might not have seen it.

"Yeah, let me just . . ." She looks around. "Oh, there he is. Hang on."

She pushes to her feet, then strides across the room, looking more graceful than I've ever seen.

"She looks so different," Janelle mutters while Ronni interacts with some guy. I'm guessing her manager. The manager that apparently doesn't think I'm a good influence on Ronni.

Ronni does look different. Her chestnut brown hair is still pin straight but it's longer now, mid-back, or so. It's only been three months since I saw her but it feels like a lifetime. Her manager seems to remind her of something because he's pointing at his watch. Ronni nods as she glances back at us and offers a weak smile before her manager hooks her chin and drags her attention back to him. Then he scowls at us.

"Did you—"

"Mhm." Janelle frowns. "Does Ronni look . . . too thin?"

Ronni has always been the smallest of the three of us and that's saying something because Janelle is thin too, but this Ronni is like all skin and bones. It's very noticeable in her white tank top and blue jeans. "Yes."

My mouth falls open when the manager leans in and kisses her on the lips. Janelle grabs my hand, and her eyes widen as well. The guy pulls away and glowers at us before turning in the opposite direction and walking away without even saying hello. You'd think the man managing Ronni would want to come say hi to her best friends. He's been working with her for six months or so but we've never met. Maybe what Alyssa said is true. Not to mention, they just kissed.

Ronni doesn't turn to us right away, staring after him, but when she does, she's in a completely different mood than before. She doesn't run to us, she's smiling but it's forced.

"Guess both my friends have daddy issues."

This doesn't feel the same as me and Ash. Maybe because it's my relationship, but that guy seems . . . off. The way he forced her face to his, and the kiss didn't look loving either. I don't walk away from a kiss from Ash frowning, that's for sure. Plus his looks, because looks aren't everything but he has to be midforties and he's bald. Not ugly by any means but . . . I'm not getting a great feeling. Him being her manager and apparent boyfriend is . . . weird. Maybe I'm out of place thinking that because of who my boyfriend is, but high school volleyball is different than a real-life career.

Hopefully we can get Ronni away from here and get to the bottom of the weird texts and letters, because I have a feeling there is more to this social media break.

"You guys ready?"

Janelle and I swap looks, wondering if we should ignore the fact she kissed her manager or not.

"Uh, yeah." Janelle shrugs awkwardly. "Let's go."

"Oh my God. I haven't had *In and Out* in forever." Ronni groans, taking a bite of her grilled chicken. Not a grilled chicken sandwich, just the chicken. Her exact order was grilled chicken with two tomatoes on the side. When Janelle mentioned it, she shrugged and said that's what she likes from there.

I rip into my burger and shoot a look at Janelle.

"Tell us about Cali, Ron. What's it like living here? Being a big-time model?"

"It's great." There's not even one hint of excitement in her voice.

"Can we get something more than it's great?" I laugh, it's awkward. "It's been months since we've really talked. We don't know anything that's happening with you."

A look of sorrow passes through her hazel eyes, but it's gone before I can focus on it. "Yeah. I'm sorry about that. Moving here has been . . . a change. A big one and it was hard to get settled."

"Was?" Janelle hints.

Ronni shrugs. "I'm getting used to it—slowly, but I am. I got my own apartment because my mom and her boyfriend never stop fucking."

"Why the hell are we here if you have a whole apartment?" Janelle looks around the hotel room.

Ronni rolls her lips between her teeth. "Well, it's kind of . . . mine and my boyfriend's."

As long as I have known Veronica Quints, never in my life would I have been able to tell you she would live with her boyfriend at eighteen. Her *older* boyfriend at that. Ronni is the most independent person I know. She's huge on doing things for herself and not the type to just fall into a relationship without thinking about it. She doesn't believe in soulmates, and she definitely isn't the kind of girl that moves in with her boyfriend at eighteen. None of this is making sense.

"You mean your manager?" Janelle asks, narrowing her eyes as she does.

Ronni laughs, and like the room right now, it's awkward. Suffocatingly awkward. It only gets more awkward as she tells us this bullshit story how they just fell in love after she turned eighteen. Late nights, weekends away, it got to them. They are still new—and yet they live together—but she couldn't be happier.

I'm calling bullshit on everything. That was the most scripted story I've ever heard. I'm tempted to call her out on it, but we just got back to the hotel. We need to at least finish our food before we call bullshit on life choices.

As the evening goes on, Ronni loosens up and conversation flows easier. It's like old times. Janelle painting all our nails and Ronni helping us pick out outfits, I just sit back and let them do whatever they want.

That's why when I open the door after hearing a knock and Ash stands on the other side, laughing, I try and close it on him. The size difference has him pushing it open and walking in anyway. I don't want him seeing the mess we made or us in face masks.

"Oh. My. God. It's really him. Ash Pearson is really your coach!"

I cringe at how excited she sounds about it. "The one and only," I groan.

Ash places his hands on his hips while taking in the state of the room. Clothes, food wrappers, and other various items used for nails are scattered about. "Are you ladies having fun?"

"Don't we always?" Janelle pumps her eyebrows twice, cracking her face mask as she does.

He rolls his eyes to me. My nails are wet, or I would take my hair down from the towel. Just glad I was smart enough to get dressed after my shower, before we started on makeovers.

Ash's eyes blaze seeing my Winnie the Pooh sleep clothes.

"Since you already know who he is, allow me introduce *him* to *you*. Coach, this is Ronni Quints. The trio to our duo that you've heard us discuss a time or two."

Ash takes Ronni's slim hand in his. He shakes it a few times before letting it fall. I watch to see if his eyes linger on her because all men linger on Ronni. All men but Ash apparently. He looks away from her at the most appropriate time and finds me again. A real-life model is standing in front of him and he couldn't care less.

"Well, I am just doing my rounds before bed. I will let you get back to it, but girls, don't forget the day starts at eight a.m. No later. If you are late, you will be running double once we are back in Michigan."

Everyone exchanges goodbyes after that threat. I don't think he would actually make us run double—especially with my knee, but I'm not willing to risk it. I follow him to the door and as soon as we are out of sight, he spins, pins me against the wall, and kisses the life out of me. When he pulls away, I'm breathing hard and laughing because some of my face mask rubbed on him during our kiss.

"I'll see you tomorrow, babygirl. Be good, okay?"

I think I mumble a few words but I'm still recovering from the kiss and not able to focus. He pecks me again before leaving, and now I know there is definitely something weird between Ronni and her *boyfriend* because the last thing I'm doing right now is frowning.

By morning, I think we got maybe three hours of sleep and that includes waking up ten minutes before we need to meet the team in the lobby. Ash scolds us for almost being late but there is a softness in his face, so I know he isn't really mad.

We told Ronni to stay back and sleep, just come to the gym when she got up, but she insisted on spending the maximum amount of time with us. The entire team greeted her with open arms and for a minute, it was like old times. Over the course of the night there were a few moments that felt weird, like Ronni wasn't our oldest friend but someone we just met. Those moments were few and far between, though. We have filled her in on the Alyssa incident. The part where she tripped me on purpose and landed me in a brace, not the Ash stuff. I'm not sure why but none of that came up. Janelle gave me a look a few times like she was expecting me to bring it up, but I didn't. We had enough to talk about without mentioning our relationship statuses. Besides, I figured we might get on the conversation of her boyfriend, and I don't know how to tread that conversation when I don't think it's a good one.

I jog over to Ronni and my water during our morning break. "You miss it, yet?"

Ronni passes me my water and I chug it. "Some parts, yes, but I was never as good as you. It's not as fun when you're not as good, P."

I drop my water to the ground near her feet and frown. "Yes you were."

"No, she wasn't." Janelle drops into the seat next to her and laughs breathlessly. Ronni laughs with her. "See?"

"Well, whatever. I think you're both full of shit."

Ronni smirks to Janelle. "The gym is empty during lunch?"

I tell her it is, already knowing what she's getting at, and I can't agree fast enough. I haven't got to play with Ronni in a long time, but I know she's not shit.

39

Ash

"WHERE IS YOUR GIRL?" Luca stops next to me in front of the cafeteria and looks over the large crowd the same way I am.

"That's what I was just wondering."

After more looking and finding all of my girls besides two, I relax. If Janelle is gone too, it's likely they are causing chaos somewhere with Ronni and not what I was thinking.

It hasn't left my mind that Fred is somewhere out there. Just because we are in California, doesn't mean all the issues from home leave us behind, as much as I wish they would. This is a volleyball convention where every single player is wearing pink shirts and black shorts. There are numerous brunettes and while none are Payson, I do lose sight of her periodically. It would be the perfect place for him to get his claws on her.

"I'm going to go check the gym."

We head that way without grabbing the attention of Valerie or any of the other coaches. She's been breathing down my neck. Even when she's not nearby, I can feel her watching me, waiting for me to slip up and do something un-coachlike to Payson so she can report me. I don't know why it's so important she catches me doing something I shouldn't. It's not like she wants me back, she is with Fulton. I have no fucking clue, but it's annoying as shit. If I can get three minutes where I don't have to try so hard not to be into Payson the way I am, I will jump at it.

"What do you think is happening with Parker?" I ask since it's a few minutes walk.

Luca sighs. "I am not sure. He really liked Janelle and he thought she hurt him but ended up hurting her instead. I think the guilt is eating at him."

I tried to talk to him yesterday, but he didn't say much. A lot of shrugs and head nodding. I told him I was always here to talk to and wouldn't judge him. Luca and I were hard on him right after but after some thinking, I remember what it was like to be his age. Those emotions are big and mistakes can be made. It's not fair to make him feel even more guilty than he already does. I really wish the girl wasn't Alyssa, though.

I can't believe she's here. She hasn't been around our team, but she is sticking by Valerie's side, which is even more unsettling than her being here. She's not bothered us and hopefully it stays that way.

"He needs to let it go. He is hurting himself and innocent people around him." Like Payson. He gave me no reason why he told her Valerie was my ex-wife, just that he did. I scolded him but didn't want to ruin the good night we were having just being guys.

"I agree, fratello. I will talk with him more tonight when you are on your date. Might be able to get more from him."

Hopefully. Whatever the issue is, I will fix it. I don't want my son upset.

"Any idea what you will do for your date?"

That lessens the weight of everything else. I smirk to my best friend. "A few."

This is Payson's first date. I want it to be memorable, and I also want to take advantage of the fact no one will know us and we can kiss in public. Sure, she looks young, but I'm confident no one will ask for her ID. She deserves a stress-free night for maybe the first time ever, and I can't wait to give it to her.

"Any idea what your excuses are going to be? If Valerie finds out you're both missing, she will probably call all reinforcements to find you."

"Let her look. She won't find us."

We find the three girls exactly where I thought we might. Janelle tosses the ball up for Payson who drops her weight and bumps it exactly how she should. Pride blooms low in my chest, knowing she has only improved since I started coaching her. It's good to know I'm able to teach her more than how to ride my face. It's a perfect bump to set. Ronni is ready but her hands are all unbalanced and she looks uncomfortable—awkward even. Probably why the set is barely high enough for Janelle to hit and not even in the right place.

Luca rolls his head my way. "That is the infamous Ronni, I take it?"

"Yes. She sucks at setting."

Luca chuckles. "Yes, she does." He slaps my back and we trek forward.

"Oh my word." Payson gasps after Janelle's spike hits the ground. "You really do suck, Ron."

Janelle barks out a loud laugh and Ronni is quick to join. "I told you!"

"How did we ever go anywhere with you as our Setter?" The wonder in Payson's voice causes Luca and I to chuckle. I have to say, I'm very curious about that as well.

But Ronni just shrugs. "I guess it helps when you have the best Libero ever."

Luca chokes on his spit and the three girls whip around to face us. Payson's eyes light up immediately.

"I wouldn't say the best ever. I am the one who has been to the Olympics, remember?"

"I thought I was the one who got us there?"

Luca waves me away; he stops next to Payson and throws an arm over her shoulder. I lift a brow. "Everyone knows the Libero is the best player on the team. We just allow the Setters to believe it is them. Right, Pay?"

Payson nibbles on her lip, then nods. "Sorry, ba—Coach." I love how her cheeks bloom a deep pink with the slip up. I got the feeling last night she did not fill her friend in on the relationship. I'm not sure why, but I guess she still hasn't. That's disappointing, as I was hoping to pull her away for a quickie. "He's right."

I cross my arms over my chest, challenging her. Lust burns deep in her bright green eyes, threatening to stiffen my dick.

"I have an idea!" Janelle cheers, far too excited about whatever is on her mind. "Us against you two. That will prove who is better, Payson or Coach Luca."

Luca grins to me, then down to Payson. "What do you think, conigliet-ta?"

"I think it's unfair." She moves so she's not under his arm anymore and she smiles. "You guys are so old. Out of practice."

Oh, I'll show her just how *in* practice we are.

Luca and I agree to let Ronni stay on their team even though that gives them an extra person, because honestly, I'm not sure how much she will help them. No offense to Ronni, I'm sure she's great at modeling but volleyball isn't her calling. I'm not even sure if she had stayed in Michigan and tried out for my team, she would have made it. In fact, I'm positive she wouldn't have.

I've played volleyball for over half my life. I've been to the Olympics and played against the best players in the world; so, tell me why two—and a half girls are kicking our ass right now?

Sweat flows from every pore on my body. We've had to stop and towel the floor more than once because Luca is the same. That can be the only explanation as to why Luca misses Janelle's spike and they get the winning point. We only played to ten and the game maybe lasted fifteen minutes, but it felt like a lifetime.

Luca falls to his back onto the floor. I bend at the waist, wondering if I'm going to throw up.

The girls cheer and celebrate, rubbing it in our face but neither of us care since we are trying not to die. I work out every single day, yet I'm sweating and breathing like I haven't touched a gym in ten years. I don't do cardio much outside fucking Payson, but still. Playing with two people differs from playing with six. Especially when Luca can't hit a ball to save his bloody life. His bumps were perfect, my sets were more than perfect, but when it came to any spiking, he failed miserably. He hit the net more times than I could count, and the girls just continued playing even when he did because it was happening every time.

"Hey, Pay. You know what this means?"

"What's that, Jay?"

I lift my head just enough to glare at the girls. They don't care and their shit-eating grins stretch even more. "That we are better than the Olympians."

"Huh." Payson taps her chin obnoxiously. "How about that?"

"Shut up." My voice is breathless.

But they don't. The three of them hook arms and jump around singing, "We're better than the Olympians" repeatedly.

"I want a rematch." I stretch to my full height, ignoring how my newly worked muscles ache already. "But I want Payson on my team this time."

After some back-and-forth with Janelle she reluctantly agrees. Ronni sits this game out with little argument from her friends. I look over my shoulder, watching Payson adjust her blue brace and can't help but smile. She has two good friends on her side. I'm glad for that.

Watching Payson play volleyball is mesmerizing; playing next to her is a completely different kind of experience. I prefer watching because I don't need to remove my eyes from her once, but celebrating a good play is nice too. I haven't gone as far as slapping her ass—as much as I want to—her smile and high-tens will do, for now.

"Luca, you suck," Janelle groans.

I walk over and pull Payson into my arms. She's stiff but I hold her anyway. A normal hug. A hug anyone would give anyone. It's not sexual, besides my dick stiffening because her fucking breasts are pushing into my stomach.

She pushes away first, avoids my eyes and ducks under the net to get her water. I watch after her, confusion, disappointment, and frustration all weighing on me. We won and she hardly seems excited.

I'm not used to Payson pushing me away. She's never tried to hide us before, it's only her friend. If they are really friends, why would she feel the need to hide us?

"Don't feel bad," Janelle whispers. She stops in front of me and keeps her voice low. "Things are a little weird between us right now."

Payson laughs at something Luca says and he shakes Ronni's hand, greeting her.

"Weird how?"

Janelle purses her lips. "Long story, ask Payson, but I will say when Payson and you first met, I kept making jokes about you two. Which they all ended up being right, by the way—anyway, it was obvious Ronni was so not about it. Which doesn't make sense since she has her own old man." She cringes. "Older man, I mean."

"She is dating an older man?"

"Yeah, her manager. Guess I'm the only one who missed the memo and went younger . . . How is he?"

He? I'm guessing she means Parker. I drop my eyes to her because it's odd she would ask how he is doing, considering he's the one who slept with someone else when they were meant to be exclusive. "He's quiet."

"I really liked him, you know? I would never have cheated."

My throat tightens, "I know."

"I had been in a relationship with Collins for years. Before our parents married, so it wasn't as weird as you think. Or maybe it is, I don't know, but I didn't care either way; I loved him, really loved him and was okay with everyone finding out we were together. He wasn't. I watched so many girls flirt with him, but it was okay because he would crawl into my bed at the end of the night." Her voice breaks but those tears flooding her lower eyelashes don't fall. "Anyway, I was really sad over the breakup. Sadder than I thought I could be. Payson was always the sad one. She holds her sadness so well that sometimes you forget she even has it." My brow knits.

She's right, I blamed her friends and family for not noticing, but she hides it well. I'm still not sure how I picked up on it before we even met, but I could feel it.

"Obviously I didn't even know him for long but instantly I felt a connection. It's like he was a breath of fresh air in a stuffy room. It seems stupid because we weren't even dating but I can't forgive him. Maybe it's because I threw myself into whatever we were as a distraction or maybe it's because I went years of being second option, I won't do that anymore. Both guys I ever felt feelings for cheated on me with fucking Alyssa Burton. What's that say about me?"

Two tears streak down her cheeks but she quickly wipes them away and they are replaced with a subtle blush. "Payson was right, you're easy to talk to." She thinks I'm easy to talk to? I can feel her watching us, so I meet her eyes and she tilts her head in question. "Sorry, I know he's your son and you and Alyssa have . . . history or whatever so maybe it's awkward, but you've probably learned I have no filter by now."

"Alyssa is completely irrelevant. Those boys doing what they did have nothing to do with you and everything to do with their self-respect." I run a hand down my face. I need to talk with my son before I go out tonight. "My relationship with Parker doesn't stop what he did from hurting you. I love my son but you are my player and I care for you as well, Janelle. Your feelings are valid. Besides, you are Payson's best friend and I'd like to think that friendship extends to me to a point."

Janelle lifts her head and smiles at her best friend who is still watching us intently. "Yeah, it extends—" She pauses, then adds, "As long as you treat her as good as she deserves."

"Always. But I am sorry for the hurt Parker has caused. I would like to blame his age, but that would probably be inappropriate."

Janelle's shoulder shakes with a halfhearted laugh. "Yeah, a bit hypocritical."

"I do know he feels bad."

She lets out a deep breath. "Wish he would have thought about that before."

"Me too."

After a long day at the gym and a long talk with my son, I am looking forward to a night to myself. I feel better about things with Parker. He talked about how bad he feels, and he doesn't even know why he did it. He cried and confessed how much he cares for Janelle and wants her back. I didn't know how to tell him she isn't going to forgive him, at least not anytime soon, so I told him he needs to start with an apology. I warned him she might not forgive him and he needs to accept that too. He messed up and has to deal with the consequences from it. It ended with us hugging and him saying he loves me, and for the first time, I feel like a real dad.

I pull my phone from my pocket and shoot a text off to my dad. It's late over there since it's nearly eight p.m. here, but he will get it in the morning.

Me: Thanks for being the best role model growing up. Love you.

Parker wanders into my and Luca's room, he stops and holds his arms out. "Well?"

"Like father, like son." I mock his pose because we are essentially wearing the same outfit. Black trousers, black shirt. I have my sleeves rolled and first two buttons undone just enough to show some chest hair I know Payson loves. I help him roll his sleeves, telling him how it looks better and women love men's forearms.

Luca, on the other hand, wears only sweats and is lying on the bed, hand deep in a bag of crisps. "It's terrifying how similar he looks to you at that age, fratello."

"Just means he will stay good looking as he ages."

Luca grins and stuffs his mouth with more crisps.

"Why are you not getting ready?" Parker falls onto the bed next to him and grabs a handful as well.

"The adult party isn't until nine. I need twenty minutes to shower, twenty minutes for my hair, and five to dress; plus, you don't want to be on time. I don't plan on stepping out of this room until ten p.m."

Someone knocks on our door and immediately my heart beats harder in my chest knowing who is waiting on the other side. The girls had gone shopping for dresses for tonight and Janelle had promised she would make sure Payson got something I would enjoy, and I told her make sure it's easily removable because I missed out on touching her all day in the way I want. She will be lucky if we make it outside the hotel room.

Bloody fucking hell. Yeah, she will be very lucky if we make it outside this bedroom. Payson stands in front of me with big eyes, a bright smile, looking so beautiful it fucking hurts. Then I take in her outfit and the pain drops to my dick as it struggles to grow against my two pairs of compression shorts and the zipper of my pants. I do not want my boner to ruin our night. However, if I am forced to stare at the curve of Payson's mostly exposed tits all night, it's inevitable.

Her dress is a short, long sleeve wrap-style with a deep v neck that's making it impossible to look away. I've seen her breasts naked, in a sports bras, in a sexy as fuck dress at the fashion show but never have I seen her wear anything that accentuates her breasts in the way this dress does. It's classy but her body is making it look anything but. Her nails are freshly painted light pink, probably from her night with her friends, and she uses two fingers to tip my chin so our eyes meet again. Her makeup is done similar to the fashion show night, dark eyes but her lips are bright red. My heartbeat drops to my cock, imagining them wrapped around it.

"Bloody hell, Jailbird."

She smiles even more and flicks her fluffy ponytail over her shoulder. "Bloody hell yourself."

I wrap my hand around her back but pull away when her dress stabs at my flesh. Not painful, just irritating. Especially because I'm used to the softness of her skin.

"And that is why we went with that one." Janelle strides into the room, not bothering to wait for an invite. She spins and pins me with a hard look. "This is my best friend's first date. You're not going to ruin it by never making it out of here, or worse, pulling her into the bathroom of wherever you are taking her and ruining all my hard work."

"Remember the friendship agreement from earlier? I'm calling it off," I growl.

Janelle grins, unbothered. "No takesies backsies."

Payson giggles and walks the rest of the way in the room as well. I let the door shut, then pull her back into my body, ignoring the irritating material.

"You ladies look divine," Luca says, with a mouthful of food.

"You don't, why are you not dressed?" Janelle says.

"He's planning on being fashionably late," Parker tells her. There's a few second stare between them before their eyes wander over the others' body. Payson cranes her neck to look at me with a look that says *are you seeing this*? I dip my chin once.

Janelle breaks the spell first by spinning and sitting on the edge of my bed. She grabs the remote and changes Luca's channel. "Great, me too; it's embarrassing to be on time."

"Well, we have reservations, and unlike you all, I do not find being on time embarrassing." I step away from Payson long enough to grab my wallet and the keys to the car I rented.

I stop and kiss Parker's forehead, cupping the back of his neck, I give him a stern look. "No drinking tonight."

"I'm not."

I kiss his forehead again and straighten, eyeing my girl like a hungry lion, she shifts under my stare.

"Ready?" My voice is husky.

She chews on her bottom lip but nods. "Yep."

"You two aren't going to make it an hour," Janelle complains.

I prowl toward Payson, hoping she's right.

40

Ash

Janelle was right. As soon as Payson closed the car door behind her, I was on her. Didn't help I was in the back seat waiting for her when she climbed into the back not knowing I was already there. We laughed at the fact we had the same idea, but it quickly died when I cupped her heavy breast. Unfortunately, they are taped in some way, so I wasn't able to play with them as much as I would have liked but I still got her off twice and me once. I'm feeling better, but I know it won't be long before my balls grow heavy for her again.

I'm driving to dinner while Payson fixes her makeup and hair. I did my best not to mess it up, we didn't even kiss a lot. I had to turn her reverse cowgirl to stop from mauling her lips.

"It's a good thing we didn't walk down together because I ended up bumping into Valerie," she tells me.

I suggested we head to the car separately for that exact reason. Luca made up the excuse I was ill and that's why I wouldn't be there. Janelle and Payson have some kind of excuse too, but I don't know what it is.

"What did she say?"

Payson flicks the mirror closed looking just as perfect as she did before we went at it like wild animals.

"She said, 'well don't you look *nice*,'" she mocks Valerie in a weird voice.

I bite the corner of my cheek to stop from laughing. "What a vile woman."

"I know!" Payson gasps. Then a laugh tumbles from my mouth and she squints. "You're being sarcastic, aren't you?"

"Baby, it sounds like she complimented you." She attempts to pull her hand from my grip, but I don't let her.

"It's not what she said, it's how she said it, Ashley. Like *don't you look nice—for a slut.*"

Knowing it's best to agree, I kiss her knuckles. "Well, we do not have to worry or think about anything but us tonight."

She sinks into the seat and sighs. "I can't wait."

Me either, babygirl.

Payson must look older than twenty-one because when I ordered us champagne, I wondered if they would bring two glasses, and they did. She was offended but I assured her it was the makeup.

"I've never been somewhere so fancy." She hasn't stopped looking around the interior of the Italian restaurant in wonder since we walked in. I haven't been able to look away from her.

"My mum came to visit me several years ago and she was craving Italian food. I looked up the best Italian restaurant west of the Mississippi and Giulio's was the one that came up. The next day, we got on a plane and were here by dinner that night."

"You traveled from school to California for your mom to eat some pasta?" Her eyes round more with each word.

"I did. It's a short flight."

"Yeah, but . . . wow. You must really love your mom." I follow her rough swallow with my eyes.

"I love my mum very much."

"You also must be rich-rich." Her smile is real and teasing.

I laugh under my breath. "I am smart with my money, yes."

"Are you going to make me sign a prenup when we marry?"

I bloody love hearing her speak of marrying me. It's good to know she's slowly becoming more comfortable with the conversation. "No."

"But I have nothing."

"You are—" I drop my voice even though I know no one is around us. "Seventeen. I wouldn't expect you to have anything. I'm not marrying you because you have money. I am marrying you for love, Payson. What's mine will be yours."

I've learned so many new things about Payson tonight. If there were any doubts we had nothing in common outside volleyball and enjoying sex together, they are gone. It's not often we just get to sit down and talk. Her dress is just as much of a distraction as earlier, and she keeps giggling whenever I ask her to repeat what she said because she knows I'm distracted too, but chatting is nice. Usually, our time is limited so we rush to get our clothes off and jump into bed.

"So where was Ronni when you and Janelle showed up to the room?"

The smile Payson has been wearing most the night slips into a conflictive frown. "She peaced before we even made it to the mall because Monica made a comment about us, not knowing Ronni wasn't fully aware."

My spine steels. "You had a falling out over *me*?"

"Over us," she clarifies. "Ronni thinks it's weird. How it's weirder than her and her manager—I don't know, but yeah. Then Janelle stepped in and stood up for you—us, and that upset her more because she was the only one seeing the issue. We tried to tell her you weren't grooming me or anything like that, but she didn't want to hear it. She said she will be at the gym tomorrow; she just needed the night to think. It was . . . unexpected, I guess. Or maybe it wasn't. I don't really know Ronni anymore. That much is obvious."

We're seated in a circle booth, so I move to her side and pull her against my body. She burrows her head into my chest. "We have been lucky thus far, as far as people supporting us. Unfortunately, Ronni is just the start of the hate we will receive when we go public. I don't know why people can't mind their business."

I kiss the top of her head and breathe deeply. Her vanilla scent is strong from her shower, and it's comforting. "Me either."

"I think it's more upsetting because she is one of my best friends. Like, friends are meant to support you, no matter what."

She's right. Unless it is dangerous to your health—which I'm not—your friends should support you. I figured Ronni would have seen how much I care based on how many times I asked about Payson's knee today. She hasn't had any problems with pain—so she says, but the swelling is still there after a day in the gym.

Our food comes but I stay on the same side as Payson. She asks how my family is doing and I fill her in on what is happening lately. My parents are renovating their kitchen after years of my mum complaining they need to. My brother is still a tit but climbing his way up the company he works for.

"What about your sister?"

Speaking of people who do not approve of us. "My sister is fine, she's a stay-at-home mum and her life is pretty much the same thing over and over. We don't talk all that often on the phone; I catch most updates through my parents."

Payson eyes her plate of pasta. She let me order for her, and the moan she lets out after her first bite, I'd say I did a good job.

"Who all will be here for Thanksgiving?"

"Supposedly everyone. My sister has only visited a few times over the years I've lived here because flying her whole family is expensive, but she says she's coming, and they all have their flights booked. They are flying into Chicago. They will swing by and pick up my nan, then head to my place in a rental."

She nods. "And they all want to meet me?" Her eyes sparkle against the chandelier light above us. I cup her cheek and stroke my thumb over the roundness.

"My family is very excited to meet the girl who stole my heart."

Her cheeks warm under my hand with a blush. "I'm nervous."

I ask her to tell me why and she fills me in. Something along the lines of she wants them to like her and it's a big deal being introduced to parents, and she doesn't know how to act. Basically, very naïve worries. It makes me smile.

"Jailbird—" I run my finger over her full lips. "Your worries are irrelevant. My parents already like you and their opinion is the only one that matters and even that only goes so far because *I love you*. And—" I lean in and steal a kiss. "You just need to be you. They will be happy with that."

She sighs. "Okay."

"Okay."

Payson's eyes fall, tracking the movement of my tongue while I drag it across my bottom lip. Hungry eyes meet mine.

I move to the curve of the booth and pat my lap, then she is quick to scurry on, straddling me. I can feel just how hot she is between her thighs. Hot and damp from our time in the car, ready to take me again.

"Kiss me," I demand.

She seals her lips to mine, threading her fingers into my hair at the same time, not caring about the gel I put in it. I work against her mouth, not rushing this moment, just enjoying the kissing. Fully aware my lips will be painted red too. My hands rest firmly on her back, not moving because the rough material of the dress is pulling me out of it. Dammit, Janelle. I give up and drop them to her bare thighs. She shivers under my touch.

"Daddy."

I stifle a groan.

I don't even have to tell her to grind against me, she's already doing it. No doubt soaking my pants with the mixture of our cum through her tiny black panties. "Take it out." She pants.

My breathing trips. "What?"

She meets my eyes. "I want to have sex. Here."

How can someone refuse that offer when she looks so bloody good? You can't. We are away from prying eyes, secluded on our own so unless someone purposefully comes to our table, we should be able to do this without drawing attention. If anything it will look like we are kissing deeply, a little humping maybe but there's no law about public kissing.

"Pull my dick out and shove it into your tight cunt. You're still wet for Daddy, right, baby?"

She whimpers but works at my belt with impatience. I lost one pair of compression shorts after our quickie in the car. It was too annoying trying to deal with both. She slips my pants and shorts down just enough my dick springs free. A quick glance around and she's grinning at me like a feral cat while she positions herself over my dick.

"This is so exciting."

She's so fucking cute. I reach my hand between us and push her soaking wet panties aside. "Guide me in, babygirl."

Her hand wraps around the base and my head falls back onto the booth. I wonder if her touch will ever not feel so fucking good. I keep my eyes partially open, just enough to watch her struggle to fit me inside. My foreskin has been through hell lately, trying to fit into her tight little body, but he forgives me every time her walls flutter around him. With her pussy still full of my cum, we have no issues making it fit, and we breathe out once her hips are flush with mine and I'm completely seated inside, like we've been waiting all dinner for this moment.

"You feel even bigger in this position."

"You take me so beautifully." She grips the collar of my shirt and pulls until the buttons pop open. Her hands drift up and down my exposed body as if she can't decide where she wants to feel first; I hiss when she hits the spot under my left pec, but she doesn't notice. She's needy, too lost in the moment.

"You've been squirming all dinner, were you waiting for this moment?"

The sexiest little blush creeps up her cheeks. It's barely noticeable under her makeup. "Yes."

"Then roll your hips, Jailbird. Show me how badly you wanted Daddy."

Payson doesn't get to ride me often. I like having control all the time and do whatever I want to her body when I want it, but watching her slide up and down my dick with her head thrown back at whatever pace she wants, might just make me let her on my lap more often. She moans and I pull her lips to mine, warning her to be quiet, not to draw attention.

Her face pinches and she gasps. "I'm coming." Her voice is breathless.

I grip her thighs as she rides out her orgasm. Cursing and whispering my name, along with Daddy in the mix. She looks bloody breathtaking and judging by the other set of eyes watching her come on my dick, I'm not the only one who thinks so.

Our waiter stands less than five feet away enjoying the view as she comes, and I want to kill him for it. Her dress and the table hide him from seeing anything I would actually need to pluck his eyes out for, but it's no secret what is happening. Payson's head is thrown back and even though she's biting her lip, her moans are hardly muffled.

Her thrusts slow as she comes down from the high and she gives me a sleepy smile. She must feel the waiter watching because she turns her head and freezes. Small goosebumps coat her skin. The guy is maybe twenty-two, blond hair, blue eyes and looks like a golden retriever. I'd bet money he's never been fucked in a restaurant or maybe fucked at all.

I wrap a hand around Payson's slim neck and pull her to my lips. "If you don't keep going, I'll take your ass right here for everyone to hear your screams." She shutters at my threat, but moves her hips, different than before she knew she was being watched. Slow and unsteady. I smooth the hand not around her throat up her thigh and press my thumb against her swollen clit, loving the gasp she lets out when I do. "Show him what he's missing. Show him the pleasure only *I* can bring you."

She meets my eyes, unsure excitement resting in the depths.

I let go of her neck but keep my thumb on her clit, lazily circling. My eyes flick to the guy. He's dropping the check holder in front of his crotch. Payson leans forward and presses a kiss to my neck as a growl rumbles out. "Only you, Daddy."

"You've made him hard," I growl.

Payson turns her head to eye the guy and her pussy clenches. His mouth falls open seeing her face for the first time. "Put the check down," I snap.

It takes a second but he jolts from his stupor and his face turns crimson. "Y-yes, sir."

"I don't think you need a tip, do you?" Payson's thrusts skip and I snap my eyes to her and demand she keeps going.

"No, sir," the guy mutters, obviously embarrassed.

The need to come tingles deep in my lower back. I grab Payson's hips and lift her off me. Both of them gape at me, waiting to see what I will do. I turn her and she scurries to get onto all fours. Her back arches and I lift her dress just enough to slip myself into her. The guy licks his lips at seeing my dick for a second before I slip into Payson's cunt. I figured he was watching her . . . but now I'm not sure. Maybe both. It's been a long time since I've been watched while I fuck. There was a short time I went through an exhibitionist stage where I would purposely make sure someone was in the room while I fucked the nameless girl.

Those moments feel nothing like this. I absolutely hate the fact someone else is getting to see Payson in her most intimate state, but I can't stop thrusting into her. He can see nothing more than he could before because my hand is holding her dress to her ass so it doesn't ride up, and her tits are pressed into the booth. She keeps her eyes on me and I keep mine on her. The boy still doesn't leave. Payson flicks a look his way, periodically checking to see if he left, I assume. The next time, I reach forward and wrap my hand around her pony, then pull her up against my body. I ignore how fucking annoying the dress is on my chest and hold her tight. "Keep your eyes on the man nine inches deep in your pussy."

She licks her lips. "Yes, Daddy."

The guy's eyes bounce from Payson's tits to where he knows we are meeting but can't see. His hand has since dropped to his dick but he's not doing anything besides cupping it. If he knows what's good for him, he won't.

"Touch your pussy, babygirl. I want you to come again."

She hesitates so I tug on her hair.

It doesn't take her more than five minutes before she's screaming and I have to throw a hand over her mouth to muffle it. I bite down on her shoulder to muffle my moans as I come deep in her pussy. She flutters around me, milking every last bit before melting in my arms.

I reach into my pocket, pull out my wallet, and toss it to the table with a thud. "Black card."

Payson holds my hand tightly on our way to the car and turns to me once we step into the warm evening air. "You tipped him."

I keep my eyes forward but dip my chin. "What we did was illegal. I figure a tip might help keep his mouth shut." Not that I think he is on his way to the police as we speak, but a few grand should be enough of an incentive.

Her giggle is a nice sound compared to the raging inside my body.

41

Payson

ASH HAS BEEN QUIET ever since we got into the rental car after dinner. I'm not sure where we are going next, or if that ruined the night and he is taking us back to the hotel. Guilt lays heavy in my stomach. I'm not sure if I did anything wrong but I can't help but feel I did. I didn't tell the guy to come over, I didn't even know he showed up until Ash was growling and not in the way he normally does when we have sex.

A minute turns into thirty minutes of complete silence. We've not gone farther than a few miles because the traffic here is crazy. Unfortunately it gives me more time to think. By the time he parks the car, my breathing is elevated and my vision is blurred with unshed tears.

Ash lets out a heavy sigh and that breaks the dam because he sounds disapointed. A sob breaks through my lips. He pushes from the car right after and I sob harder. I hate myself so much for what just happened. I hate how I liked someone watching us. It was exciting claiming Ash in front of someone else. We never get to touch in public and I liked it, a lot.

My door flies open and a feral Ash stares down at me. I cry more. My seatbelt is undone and I'm being pulled from the car into his strong grip before I can even breathe. I jump and he wraps my legs around his body and holds me there, rocking us back and forth until I've calmed down and my sobs are only broken breaths.

"You want to tell me why you are crying?"

His accent doesn't affect me as much as it used to but there are moments, like this, when his voice is so low, so husky that it's thicker and tickles my ear perfectly. I don't lift my head from his shoulder. "You're mad at me."

Ash sighs again and kisses the top of my head. "Oh, my beautiful, *naïve* little girl. I am not mad at you."

His smile grows when he sees my face. My makeup must look so bad now. "You're not?"

"I'm not mad at all. I'm ... confused. Just thinking through things in my head."

"Like what?"

He twists his lips but doesn't answer. "Let's go for a walk."

My ears pick up the waves crashing to the shore before my eyes adjust to the dark night. The ocean. I scramble from his arms and run to the edge of the parking lot in front of the car. I can't see much but I can hear it. "I've never been to the ocean."

Ash steps by my side with his hands shoved deep into his pockets. "I know." He takes a step, turns, and reaches a hand toward me. "Let's go see the ocean, Jailbird."

It's close to forty feet from the car to reach the edge of the water and I don't stop bouncing the entire way. Ash is laughing at me, but I don't stop. I'm too excited. I love water, all forms of it. Going to the Great Lakes is one of my favorite things to do, but seeing the ocean is so cool. Even when it is almost pitch black. The air smells exactly how I imagined it would, and the sound is exactly like you hear on those peaceful noise machines but better because it's right in front of me and not through a speaker. My bed mate had one in juvie, and she used to listen to it all night long.

Ash sits down in the sand and pulls me between his legs. I lean back into his hard chest and watch and listen to the white caps on the waves for a long time. It's chilly but Ash is so warm it balances it out. I bury my toes in the sand, since we left our shoes at the car, and smile. "This is the best first date."

"I'm glad."

"I'm not sure how you are ever going to beat this one," I tease. "We have a lot of dates in our future, and you've set the bar pretty high, Mr. Pearson."

His chest shakes with a deep laugh. "That's a good problem to have, I'd say."

I rest my head against his shoulder and anxious bubbles boil in my stomach. "You gonna tell me why you were upset?"

Ash pulls away and grabs my hips, turning me to face him instead. I lay my legs over his and wrap my arms around his neck to play with his hair. "You could almost put this in a pony," I acknowledge.

"You like my hair long."

I meet his stormy eyes. "I do, how can you tell?"

A *duh* look crosses his face. "I know you, Payson. I know everything about you. When you like something your eyes light up and your face relaxes. When you are not a fan of something, your nose scrunches and your eyebrows pinch together." My hand falls from his hair to his rough beard. "You also enjoy my beard."

"I do."

The peaceful look on his face tightens. "I am obsessed—with you, Payson."

My heart skips a beat. "Okay." *Okay? That's how you reply to that?*

"I've known for a little while but tonight proved that. With that guy—"

"Ash—" He places a finger over my lips.

"Let me finish." I roll my lips into my mouth so he knows I'm not speaking anymore. "Good girl." My pussy is sore but those words will always affect me. "Letting him watch us—watch *you*, made me want to kill him. I used to enjoy that—being watched." My face sinks into a frown and he smirks. "I cannot help I have a past, Jailbird. Anyway, I've never felt this way. This . . . *need* to make sure everyone around us knows who you belong to. I'm past obsession and it is full-on possession now." He breathes out and brushes a hand through his long hair.

"I'm possessive of you, Payson. You are on my mind night and day. When I go without touching you, I get tense and no amount of working out or stretching helps. When I go without seeing you . . ." He drops his hands to my hips and squeezes, hard. "I'm the biggest asshole around."

"Aren't you that already?" I tease to lighten the mood, but he doesn't smile. He pushes me on to my back and crawls over me, holding his weight with his arms. The sand is cold from the night air and no doubt getting buried in my hair.

"You've not seen anything compared to that. You will never see me at my worst because it's impossible to be at my worst when you are around. You are the light of my day, babygirl."

I shutter beneath him, could be from the cool sand but I think it's him. "You are my light too."

Ash moves up my body to where I have to bend my neck to see his face. He tells me to undo his shirt completely, so I do. Then we just stare at each other. Confusion etches onto my face but still, he says nothing. I look to his chest since it's in my face but see nothing unusual. I love his chest, the hair, he knows this but—

I freeze as I catch sight of dark black ink right underneath his left pec that definitely wasn't there the last time I saw it. I run a light finger over the wound, he hisses but I don't stop. He got my *name* tattooed on his body.

My name. Tattooed. On his body. *Forever.*

Ash whispers and cuts through the blood rushing through my ears. "I worry that together we may burn too brightly."

I push open my dress to show off my healing scar. I run a hand over each, and eventually a huge smile splits my face. "Never."

What's the perfect end to a perfect date? Well, the frozen yogurt I begged Ash to stop at on the way back to the hotel, but that and a hot bath with the hottest man in the world. I'm so glad him and Luca got a fancy suite to make this possible. Everyone is still at their respective parties, so we have plenty of time to enjoy the solitude of the bath.

When we crawl into bed, I'm too jittery, too excited to sleep, but I'm too tired for more sex. Besides, my pussy aches from the two rounds this evening. But I need something.

Ash didn't seem too happy when I asked for a few cuts, but eventually he slipped off the bed and grabbed a blade from the box he packed. When we're done, I have a few cuts on my arms and another *A* carved into the outside of my hip. He wraps everything so I don't bleed on the bed, then I'm able to happily drift to sleep with him nearly crushing my body.

"I'm going to work out, babygirl." Ash kisses my cheek. "Stay in bed and I'll wake you up with my tongue buried deep in your pussy."

Even in my sleepless state I open my legs and beg him without words to do just that but when I wake, my pussy is not being licked and Ash is still not in bed. I groan not feeling the weight of him on me and throw the covers off. I have a small headache as I stand to my feet. The room is dark, and I stumble my way to the bathroom to pee. I'm washing my hands when I hear the hotel door unlock.

"I woke up with no tongue in my pussy. How are you going to make it—" My feet and words halt seeing Luca instead of Ash stepping into the dark room.

He closes the door, then flicks a gaze over my naked body before turning and heading for his bed. I tiptoe quickly behind him over to Ash's suitcase and pull out the first t-shirt I find. I tug it over my head, then spin to Luca collapsed on the bed with an arm over his eyes.

"I have seen hundreds of naked women, Payson. That being said, I would not tell Ashley that I saw *you* naked or that you asked me to lick your pussy."

"Why are you just now getting home at"—I flick my eyes to the clock—"six a.m.?"

He drops his arm and turns his head to look at me. "I may have made a semi-large mistake last night."

I open my mouth to ask but he cuts me off.

"And that is my shirt. If Ashley sees you—" The door unlocks and Luca groans and curses in Italian.

Ash storms in, glaring at anything that comes into his eyesight. "I told you to stay in—" He squints at my shirt, then stomps across the room. He grips the bottom of the shirt I'm wearing and rips it off my head.

I gasp and throw my arms across my body, but he picks me up and tosses me onto his bed. He pulls off his shirt in one fluid motion and pounces. His lips are hard against mine and I let him take whatever he needs, but he seems to have forgotten his best friend is in the bed right next to us, watching curiously as Ash bites his way down my body. I hiss as he nips at his name. "Mine," he growls.

"Y-yours."

"I see you in another man's clothes again and you won't be able to sit for two fucking weeks. Don't try me, Payson."

I shoot a helpless stare to Luca but he is too busy watching his best friend assault and, no doubt, make me bleed with his teeth.

"You okay, fratello? What happened?"

Ash drags his teeth the entire length of my stomach. A gasp-scream erupts from my me, and he spanks my pussy.

"I went to check on Parker before coming in here. Found him in bed with a girl," he growls and bites the inside of my thigh. I look down, watching my blood pour from the new wound between my thighs. He sucks in a deep breath, his nose skimming my clit when he does. "After some interrogation he admitted to fucking her." Well, I'm not exactly happy about that and I hope Janelle kept up with her plans to fuck one—or three guys, I don't understand why Ash is so mad. "Without a condom."

Oh, that's why.

Luca cusses. "Do you want me to talk with him?"

"No." Ash pushes to his knees. He tugs on his shorts, then he is walking up my body until he is sitting on my chest, his dick in my face. He strokes it with a tight fist, his jaw is set even tighter. Maybe he was right last night when he said I haven't seen him at his worst. I don't know if this is it, but he looks so scary. Also, so ridiculously hot. I rub my thighs, craving any friction, and since my arms are pinned to my body, that's the best I can do.

"No," he says again. I tilt my head because there is something running through his mind, but I can't tell what.

Not until he says, "I want you to get over here and eat my girl's pussy while I fuck her face."

That definitely is *not* what I thought he was going to say.

42

Ash

I DON'T LET PAYSON say a word before I'm shoving my dick down her throat. I'm fucking pissed. Pissed at my son for being so irresponsible and pissed at myself for transferring that anger to what I'm about to do to Payson's throat.

"Uh, I do not think that is a good idea, fratello."

Payson gags and I shove deeper, scowling at her. I pull out enough to let her have a short breath, then push farther. "I don't care," I growl.

"Ashley."

Reluctantly, I force my head Luca's way. He sits on the edge of the bed, watching my dick disappear down Payson's throat. He swallows. Luca doesn't claim to be gay, or even bi, but he loves a good dick, and I have a great one. Luca is okay with whatever can get him off. He doesn't care what's in their pants. He will happily fall into bed with anyone who interests him. I do not swing that way so the closest we've ever gotten is fucking the same girl. But I know my best friend enough to know he wants this. Anyone on this bloody earth would kill to eat Payson's pussy, and here I am offering it on a fucking silver platter. Our talk last night had me up late thinking. Different scenarios when Payson is around another guy that's not me. It didn't matter if they were sixty yards apart or grinding on each other, I wanted to kill every single one.

I want to test how mad this actually makes me. Luca is my best friend—the likeliness of me killing him is low. If I can watch Payson come on his tongue, maybe, just maybe I can get through today without being thrown in prison.

"I bumped into Valerie in the gym." Pain shoots up from my dick and I whip my head to Payson who just bit me. I rip out of her mouth and grip her throat, still not allowing any air to pass to her lungs. "She mentioned how last night went so well, she wants to continue the *mixing* today. Since Payson missed out." I squeeze harder, probably leaving behind a nasty bruise.

Luca says a string of curses in Italian. I turn to look at him. "I need to know if I can handle it. There's no better test than this."

Luca flicks a worried look to Payson, and I let go. She gasps for air and glares at me. "You asshole." Her voice is even raspier than normal. I smile but it doesn't meet my eyes.

"I think you mean Ash-hole."

I glance to my best friend, still sitting on the edge of his bed struggling to decide what is right or not. His dick is hard and pressing against his slacks, but I know he worries what will happen after.

"We go back to normal," I answer his unsaid worries. "Just a one-time thing. Just to push me as far as I can go without breaking."

"Payson?" Luca asks.

She looks from him to me with so much care in her eyes, subtly shaking her head. "I'm don't. . ."

I cup her swollen face from the breath play. "If I get upset, it will only be at myself."

"I don't know how to keep feelings separate, Ash. I'm scared I'll . . ."

She's worried she will catch feelings. I didn't think about that part. I've had sex too many times to remember that it's not emotionless for everyone. Well, it was emotionless before Payson. Now she makes me feel everything.

"Remember what I said in the kitchen, coniglietta? About riding a bike?" Luca stands. My shoulders tense as he moves closer. Payson also tenses under me.

"Y-Yeah, but I'm not you." Her voice wobbles.

Luca drags a single finger down her thigh. I snap my hand out and grip his wrist.

"You are in love with Ashley. Any sexual experience outside of that will feel like nothing. You might enjoy it physically, but it is empty, otherwise. You will not catch feelings for me when I make you come. Understand?"

Her eyes flutter as he slips a single finger between her legs. I'm still holding his other wrist; I'm tempted to break it. So instead of breaking his arms, I turn my head and focus on Payson. Her eyes are still closed and her jaw is clamped tight, but her thighs are opening.

"Open," I demand with a growl.

Her jaw shakes as she opens. I force my dick through her lips, stretching her as wide as they will go. I settle in her throat and don't move. Not until I feel the bed sink with a new weight. Everything in my body fights with me to turn around and rip him off my girl's pussy by his hair. This is the most fucked-up thing I've put myself through, but Valerie knows Payson was with me, and if I know her, she will punish me today in the only way she can think of. The G-rated version of what I did to her. Payson is going to fuck other guys. Not really, but in my mind that will be what is happening.

And Parker, why he has a random brunette in his bed instead of Janelle? Who knows. I thought after the looks last night they would have been back on, or at least in a place where I wouldn't find out my son fucked a random girl without a condom. That is the shove I needed to push me over the edge.

I fuck Payson's face until she's purple again. I can hear how wet she is, knowing that wetness is going in someone else's mouth sends a new shot of anger through my body. I grip her hair, forcing her to look at me. "You like him eating your pussy? Blink twice if yes."

Blink . . .

Blink.

I grip harder. "Better than me?"

Her eyes soften and she shakes her head no as much as she is able. It does nothing to help me relax.

"We will see about that." Luca's laugh pushes me over the edge. I brutally fuck Payson's face until she's turning blue. Her moans, screams, everything she might want to let out is stuck in her throat as I'm coming down it.

"Do not swallow," I demand breathlessly. Fat tears fall from her eyes but she nods. When I pull out and move off her, she scrambles to her knees, doing her best to keep her mouth closed and my cum inside but failing as she coughs it onto the bed and down the front of her. I wouldn't be surprised if she threw up, but thankfully, she does not.

Payson's cries are heaven and hell to my ears. I want to push and pull her away. I don't know if she came, and I'm guessing she might not even know. That was a lot. I almost feel bad she has to go play volleyball all day when I just abused her throat. Almost. That asshole I mentioned last night that she has yet to see? She just saw him. It's not fair I took my frustrations out on her, but she's the best way for me to let them all out.

She lifts her head after a while and looks to me like she's waiting for something. I open my arms and she crawls on shaky limbs into my lap. She kisses my chest, my neck, my ear. "I only want you to touch me ever again."

I chuckle darkly. Luca smirks having heard her too. "It was good, no?"

Payson shoots a murderous glare at him. "Are you trying to die?"

I pat her back in a comforting way. "It is okay. You can say it was good, babygirl."

A few beats pass before she mutters, "It was *okay*."

Luca barks out a loud laugh. "I made her come in five minutes, fratello. Do not let her lie to you."

"Is this true?"

Payson shivers in my arms and it's answer enough. "I like your tongue piercing, though."

"I know you do." My eyes fall to her bare breasts. I forgot she was naked. When I look at Luca, his eyes dart to mine, from her body. My hand flexes and Payson whimpers.

"Lick my cum off her."

I slip Payson between my legs. She angles her body to Luca but keeps her eyes on me. I watch him drag a tongue over her sternum, collarbone, then down to a drop of cum sliding down her nipple.

His eyes close, making out with her nipple and she shifts. He pulls off, moves toward her mouth asking my permission with his eyes since his mouth is full of my cum.

My jaw steels and my hands tighten on Payson's soft waist. "Open up, baby. Lick *Daddy's* cum off his tongue."

He's watching me when he leans forward. He purses his lips and drops my cum into her waiting mouth. "Don't swallow," he tells her.

Luca presses his lips to hers, then his tongue slips in. His hand moves to his dick but he's not stroking, just holding it. Payson kisses him but never removes her hands from mine, not because I'm holding her there either. Then she turns to me. She drops a mixture of my cum and their spits into my mouth. She greedily kisses me, crawling on my lap and tugging my hair.

She swallows, then drops her forehead to mine. "You and me."

A deep breath rushes to my lungs and I hug her tightly. "Me and you, babygirl. Always."

"Forever."

43

Payson

IF I NEEDED PAIN medication ever in my life, it's right now. I look like I was gang banged for hours. But nope. Just an angry Ash. I have no clue how I will hide the red handprint on my throat, or the bite mark he left on the inside of my thigh. Everything else is covered by my long sleeve shirt but spandex shorts don't hide much. They hardly hide my ass.

I stare at the white pill in my hand, debating like I've done all week. I know I shouldn't be taking these; they aren't prescribed to me, but they really do help with my leg. I pop one in the morning and basically, I'm pain free the rest of the day. Of course by night time, I can hardly walk but I don't walk much anyway. When Ash isn't fucking me, he is carrying me around, or we are lying in bed. Last night, the champagne helped ease the pain, because before that it was insufferable. Thankfully it mostly goes away when he is balls deep inside me and replaced with Ash's version of pain. I prefer his kind.

The pill goes down like a bolder but once it's down, I close the bottle and shove it into the bottom of my bag, and the reminder of how wrong it is, is gone. I jump when Janelle bangs on the door.

"Well, good morning, sleepyhead."

She groans and shushes me before hurrying by and dropping onto the toilet to pee. "Too loud. Way too happy too."

"You weren't meant to drink last night, remember?"

"He told Parker not to drink, not me. I'm not his daughter, or his girlfriend." She flashes a sloppy smile my way with her eyes still closed.

"I think it was implied."

She pushes me from the bathroom, saying something like I'm making her lose her buzz. The shower flicks on and I settle onto my bed. The good thing about Janelle being hungover is it should take her longer to see how rough I look.

My lips are still swollen from making out; Making out with two guys back-to-back, or whatever you would call what we did. I'm still not sure how Ash will react when what happened hits him. He shooed me to the shower right after, then basically shoved me from his room, saying he needed a shower without my body as a distraction today. I tried pouting, but it got me nowhere. I guess Luca was right about one thing, it wasn't awkward between us after. Almost like it didn't even happen. Once I was dressed and his boner went away—everything was normal. I hope it stays that way. I like Luca, he's hot, but not like that. I'd never want anything to come between me and Ash. Besides, it would be really awkward if something did and I had to change Ash's name on my body to Luca. That's actually a funny thought; I'll need to tell Ash that. I'm sure he will appreciate it.

Someone knocks on the door, and I force my heavy body to roll off the bed and answer it.

Seeing Ronni on the other side has our argument, or whatever it was, rushing back. She said a few hurtful things about me, and I'm not quite over them. She can say I'm young as many times as she wants but it's lost on broken ears. I might be young but I know what it feels like to not be loved, to be taken advantage of and be sought after in a truly unwanted way. Ash makes me feel none of those things. Yes, he's older and holds a position of authority, but never once has he used that to get something from me. Yes, I liked him when I was younger but that has nothing to do with now. He loves me and he only wants what's best for me—I just wish she could see that. Ronni has known me long enough to know when I'm truly happy, and right now, I am. Sure there are some deeper things I need to deal with—eventually, but Ash makes me happy; he protects me from my head.

"Hi."

"Hello."

The bathroom door opens behind me, and Janelle's groan can probably be heard clear down the hall. "I'm hungover—none of this awkwardness, I physically can't handle it today."

I step aside and Ronni strides in. "Good thing you have a whole day of volleyball to play."

I smile, head for my bed, and fall back on it. "It's only a half day, thank God. I'm exhausted."

"Well get over it because Dad is taking us to axe throwing after."

Shit. I forgot Janelle's dad comes up today. I don't think I mentioned that to Ash. I know I definitely didn't mention the crush I had on him at one point. It was nowhere near my crush for Ash; I just found him attractive so there is no reason to mention it, but after whatever Valerie has planned today, he might be extra . . . sensitive, seeing me hang out with another guy, even if it is Janelle's *married* dad.

"I can't believe this is already our last day together," Ronni says softly.

My stomach twists with the thought. Having Ronni here has been nice. Also has opened my eyes to the fact I don't think Ronni and I were as close as I thought. Or maybe this small bit of tension between us is new. It's hard to remember.

"Well"—I sit up—"let's make the most out of it."

Valerie wasn't kidding when she mentioned mixing, but I figured I'd at least have one other female on my team. Instead, I'm in a sausage fest. The only good thing about this is I feel like I'm getting in the best workout. Their hits are harder, quicker, and I'm having to dig constantly but I've only let three balls total get by me and even the guys seem impressed. That means a lot coming from the number two team.

They set the Outside Hitter up and I get into position. The Middle Blocker fakes but it's so obvious how the outside is positioned that it will be his hit. Being the Outside on the number one team is not surprising because his hits leave my arms burning for legit minutes. I'm waiting for the hit so when he tips it, I jump up and bound over for the save. It's coming down fast and I'm the closest but I'm not as quick as I once was. I dive for it, flattening my hand and praying for the best. Must have someone on my side because the ball smacks right onto my hand and bounces up. I roll out of the way to let the guys save it, and they do. The Setter is right next to me setting the ball so perfectly for the Back Hitter. The ball smacks the floor on the opposite side.

Next thing I know, I'm being lifted from the ground and sitting on top of two guys' shoulders. Pride blooms in my stomach. They congratulate me, and I them. I look around the gym at the other teams for a set of gray eyes but come up empty-handed. He was just here watching the entire thing.

The guys set me down and more crowd around, throwing their arms around my shoulders, and shake me. They say things in their native language or in broken English that I'm not able to understand but their smiles are big, and that makes me feel good.

"Good games, American," someone with a thick Russian accent says.

"You're not so bad yourself," I say to the Libero of the other team. "Not as good as me," I joke.

He rolls his light eyes playfully.

"Maybe if we had Payson on our team, we would be number one." The guy with the best English on my team wraps an arm around my shoulders and grins.

"Do not give her so much credit." The Outside Hitter from the Russian team saunters our way. "I bet she is crying on the inside from some of my hits."

"I think she is tougher than she looks, Igor."

"I am," I agree, the guy wrapped around my shoulders tightens his grip. "See?"

Igor steps forward and grabs my wrist. My heart picks up speed even more than it already was from the game. "Let us see the damage I have caused."

I attempt to rip his hand off but he has my spandex sleeve pushed up before I get the chance. The guys around me go quiet as they all take in the bloodiness hiding under my shirt. I knew cuts had broken open, but I didn't imagine it would look like someone took an axe to my arms. I didn't even feel it. I still don't and I'm staring at several open cuts. My arms are red and angry, which makes it look even worse.

His blue eyes shoot up to mine and he drops my arm. I quickly tug my sleeve back down and fold my arms over my stomach.

"I am so sorry," Igor mutters, he steps backward like I'm diseased.

Some other guys step away and more when Igor looks at his hand that was holding my wrist and it's tinted red. I quickly pull my arms from my body and cringe when I see the blood on my pink shirt.

"Here." Another Russian player rips his shirt over his head and passes it to me. I don't want to wear his shirt, it's obvious Ash left because he didn't like what he was seeing, so seeing me in another guy's shirt might push him over the edge, if he's not already. But I can't walk around with blood on mine. "Thank you."

The guys turn their backs and create a dressing room around me. I quickly rip my shirts off and replace them with his. It's way too big but I just need to get a spare shirt. They are selling them in the lobby, I just need to get someone to buy one for me while I clean my arms. I wrap my soiled clothes around my arms, shielding them from people seeing. I don't know how much attention we drew but the less, the better.

Luca stops me on my hurry to the front to buy a shirt. He eyes the scene at hand and the shirtless guy behind me before narrowing his eyes.

"Luca," I beg, pulling my arms away just enough to show him the problem.

More curses in Italian before he's dragging me under his arm and out the doors.

"I thought you stopped cutting." His voice is low.

I tilt my head to look up at him. "Ash didn't tell you?"

"Tell me what?"

I swallow and lower my voice even more. "*I* don't cut anymore . . . he, uh, he does it for me."

Luca pauses. "*He* cuts you?" He follows with a string of Italian I don't even attempt to understand.

I leave him behind and hurry for the lobby. The sooner I can get a new shirt, the sooner I can get out of this sweaty one before Ash can see me, hopefully.

Someone catches me by the elbow. "I will get you a new shirt. Go clean up and just toss the others."

"What about a long sleeve? I can't walk around like this."

Luca runs a hand down his face. "I will bandage what I can but you are going to have to, Payson."

It's been years since I've walked around in short sleeves. Even bandages won't hide all of them. But he's right. I have no other choice.

My head is foggy as I round the corner for the bathrooms, that's the only explanation as to why Ash is with his back to me and a blonde ponytail in front of him. My heart stops altogether. He couldn't be that upset I was playing with guys. There's no way he would cheat on me, especially not wit—

"This is the last warning I will give, Alyssa. Go. Away."

Alyssa. Of course, it's Alyssa. It's *always* fucking Alyssa.

"Remember how much fun we had?"

Ash's shoulders tense and he clenches his fist. "No. I don't. If you don't recall, I was drunk."

"Well, I wasn't, and we did. You loved the way I fucked you." Her pale hand wraps around his elbow but it doesn't stay there long. Ash grabs it before I get the chance, but I'm shoving her away from him before he can do anything else. She slams into the wall.

"Payson," Ash says with a passive tone, but I ignore him.

"Why are you even here?"

She adjusts her boobs and that's when I see what she's wearing. She's not dressed to play, she's wearing the same pink shirt as the rest of us but her neckline is cut and the bottom is cut making it a crop top that shows off her expensive breasts.

"My daddy happened to have some work to do here and let me tag along. Fun fact! I went to a volleyball convention this summer, you know, when you were under house arrest? Yeah, well I went and guess who was the head coach?"

I don't even have to guess to know because my luck is just that amazing. "Valerie."

"Yep," she cheers. "And when I told her how my coach was favoring another girl because they were *sleeping* together"—my stomach drops—"she told me to come, and she would talk to some scouts in my favor."

"You told on us? Are you five?"

She steps closer and because of her height she towers over me, but I don't let it bother me. "I didn't say who. Just that Ash was fucking one of the girls." She regards Ash still standing behind me, silent. "He told all on his own by kissing your ass like he *always* does."

"He doesn't just kiss it," I mutter.

"You're disgusting." She scoffs.

"Yeah? Disgusting like fucking two different boyfriends of the same person?"

"I'm slutty. Not disgusting."

There's something to be said about her being self-aware. Doesn't make me hate her any less. "Why can you not just let him go? How many times does he have to say he's not interested in you? You fucked a couple times, and? We tripled that by now."

"Did he get you pregnant?"

I freeze.

"Then make you abort it because he didn't want the responsibility?"

Maybe if I wasn't high on painkillers that weren't mine or there wasn't blood dripping down my arm, I might have a bigger reaction. Or maybe not.

"The difference is—" I step toward her, not caring that she's crying. *Cry harder, bitch.* "If Ash gets me pregnant, he won't make me terminate it because he actually *wants* to have a baby with *me*." I turn and stride into the bathroom without listening to whatever reply she might come back with.

My arms are mostly clean when Ash opens the door.

"Are you alone?"

I nod and he walks the rest of the way in and locks the door behind him. I should mention this is the main bathroom besides the locker rooms, but I don't. I watch the last of the pink water turn clear.

"We need to talk about what she said."

"No we don't."

"Pay." Ash grabs my chin on my way to the paper towels. He watches me with caution. "Yes we do. I want to explain what she meant—"

"Ash." I sigh. "I fully understand what she said, but I am in no mood to discuss it. If you can't see I'm dealing with a bit of my own thing right now."

"You need to know I wasn't hiding that from you. I truly forgot, and before you ask how does someone forget about something like that, she did it without me. Then she told me after, and if you're wondering if I was upset, no. I was only upset that it was necessary in the first place, but I never told her to do that because I didn't even know she was pregnant. That is what she was talking about the day you caught me throwing her out of my office."

I can't even comprehend what he said. I cup his face and offer my most reassuring smile. "Everything is fine. We can talk when we get home, but I promise, Ash, we are good."

I let go of him and he lets go of me so I'm able to dry my hands. He's holding the shirt I need and passes it to me. "A guy gave me his shirt because mine was covered in blood." His jaw ticks but he doesn't say anything, just nods.

I switch shirts and Ash pulls the guy's from me, claiming he will return it to it's owner. Guilt rests deep in his stormy eyes but I ignore it.

"We should not cut anymore during the season."

"Okay."

He sighs and pinches the bridge of his nose. "We will discuss things—"

"Okay." I roll my eyes before Ash and I freeze with my snapping. "Okay. . ." I try again, less aggressive this time. "Sorry, I, I just don't want to deal with this right now, okay?"

"Okay."

I can't leave him looking a mixture of upset and angry, so I press my front into his and hook the back of his neck. "I'm sorry."

"It is fine."

"Luca offered to bandage me."

He scoffs. "I will do it. Meet me at our benches."

I can't stop the giggle from tumbling from my lips. Ash scowls more. "How are you feeling with Luca right now?"

The muscle in his jaw pops. "I want to rip his tongue out his mouth and shove it down his throat."

"Oh . . . so no round two?"

"You'll be after him, little girl. Now go, before I send you out there with a bruised arse as well."

I laugh and kiss his cheek. "Yes, Daddy."

"Oh. My. God."

I shove a finger into Janelle's lips. We are out to dinner, but we had to pee and what happened this morning just spilled from my lips out of nowhere. I shouldn't have taken that second pill, but my knee, and arms, everything—was throbbing before I did. Now I can't even remember which is my hurt knee.

"You can't tell, um . . ."

"Ronni?" Janelle asks with a laugh.

"Yeah, no, she will not get it."

"No, shit, I don't even get it, P." She turns to look in the mirror. I back out of the way of the other mirror. I don't want to see myself right now. "I mean, *I get it*. But I don't *get it*, ya know? Ash is . . . next-level obsessed with you. It doesn't make sense for him to let Luca do that."

You're telling me. "I know."

"So"—she spins and crosses her arms over her chest—"did the happy couple just become a throuple?"

A rushed laugh spills from my lips. "Ash would kill you for even saying that."

She grins, knowing I'm right. "I'm just saying, being fucked by both of them—" She bites her lip. "Yum."

"Stop. Besides, you're the only one fucking Luca." Apparently Luca's "large mistake" from this morning was spending the night with Janelle. Is it weird he fucked my best friend then ate my pussy? Probably. And if people find out our coaches are going around and fucking their players, there would be a huge controversy.

"Yeah, but I don't want a relationship with him." I don't get why not. Luca is lovely, good with his tongue too, but you won't catch me saying that out loud. I didn't lie when I said I like Ash better, but Luca is not lacking skills. "I like Parker, remember?"

No, actually I didn't remember that. "Ohh, so you fucked his *uncle* because you like *him* so much. Right, that makes sense."

She shoves me. "He fucked Alyssa! And whoever that slut was in his bed." I don't know if I should have told her that, but she was saying he disappeared from the party, and it kind of just came out. "Besides, Luca and myself were drunk. Everyone knows sex doesn't count when you're drunk."

I don't think that's accurate and if that was the case, then neither would Parker's cheating . . . but I'm not going to be the one to mention that. "Yeah. Tell that to Alyssa."

"She giving you problems? I thought it was weird she let us have a few days of her being around with no bitchiness."

I thought we were lucking out, apparently not. I fill Janelle in on everything Alyssa said and what happened after with Ash in the bathroom.

"Oh my God."

"Yeah, I know."

"She's fucking crazy. I doubt the baby was even Ash's."

I wince at the mention but quickly recover. "Guess we will never know."

"Ash definitely had a type before you: blonde and bitchy." *Yeah, no kidding.* "At least you didn't walk in on them fucking in the hallway or something."

I shoot a look to her. "Why the hell would you say that?"

She shrugs casually. Then she grabs my shoulders after seeing my reaction. "Sorry, I must still be drunk from last night."

"I think we are both a little fucked."

She tilts her head and asks what I mean. Then panic should come, but it doesn't so I shrug. "I just mean showing my arms today was weird, that's all." I hadn't told Janelle about the blood; I don't want her to know about the cutting, so when she asked what happened, I told her I spilled some Gatorade on it and had to change and the bandages were to protect my bare arms from the balls. She believed me, because, why wouldn't she? We're best friends and best friends don't lie to each other.

"Anyway, you know what all this means, don't you?"

She drops her head to her hands and groans. "Don't you dare say it, Payson Murphy."

"We both fucked our coaches." My smile couldn't be any bigger than it is right now. "We're sluts!"

"Yeah, all I need to do is get my pussy eaten by Coach Pearson and we are twins."

Ash's mouth goes nowhere near any pussy but mine, I don't feel like testing how mad I would get because I already know how mad I would be. I'd be murderous.

Dinner with Mr. Johnston is nice, even Ronni seems to loosen up. She's been weird all day, but I've been too preoccupied to focus on it or ask about it.

Janelle's dad has gotten even hotter. He's completely gray now but his hair is thick, cut to a military high-and-tight but he has a thick mustache, and it does something to my stomach. He just looks so *daddy*. Janelle didn't appreciate me telling her that when we were walking back from the bathroom, and she didn't appreciate the look I gave her after he said he was recently single again. I'm kidding, but it was funny seeing her genuine worry.

Somehow me being with Ash has made Janelle think I'm a dad fucker now but when Mike asks if we want to get frozen yogurt, I'm that much closer to being one.

"Payson, how is having your childhood crush as your coach? Is it weird?"

We're sat at the frozen yogurt place and I'm halfway to my mouth with a bite when Mike drops that bomb of a question. I shoot a look to his daughter in hopes she will save me, but I'm almost positive Janelle was stealing sips of her dad's whiskey because instead of helping, she does the exact opposite and shoves me under a bus going sixty down the road.

"It's definitely not weird." She giggles. "In fact, she's not the only one with a crush now."

All I can do is blink at my best friend because, *what the hell is she doing?* I hid it from her mom, and I would rather tell Lauren than her dad.

Mikes gray eyebrows furrow. "Excuse me?"

I lick my lips and drop my spoon back into my bowl. No way I will be able to eat now. "Oh, uh, a few of the other girls on the team think he's hot. You know, n-normal teenage girl stuff."

Mike studies me for a long time, so long I start to sweat. A sheen of sweat coats my skin with his narrowed gaze on me. He drags his tongue along his bottom lip, debating whatever is going through his head and if he should say it out loud. When he's about to say something else, I blurt the first thing I can think of to get him off my back.

"Janelle was dating his son." *How's that bus feel, Janelle?*

Mikes eyes pop open and he turns to his daughter. "You're dating someone?" I know Mike is strict about his daughter dating. Which it really doesn't matter since she lives with her mom, but he's had strong feelings for years regarding this conversation, and it's never been an issue because her relationship was always kept under wraps.

Janelle stutters over words before saying, "Ronni is dating her totally weirdo manager who is like sixty."

Oh no.

Ronni's face flames an angry red. "He's forty-nine and he's not weird." She doesn't even sound convincing and I'm high on pain medication.

"You're high on pain medication?" Mike growls.

Oh my word. I slam my hand over my mouth.

"Uh, I, uh. I was, uh prescribed some for my knee." Lies. Everything I say anymore is a lie.

"I didn't know that," Janelle says.

"I don't share all my medical stuff with you." I'm laughing but it falls on dead ears. The next ten minutes are spent in silence. I don't think anyone finished their yogurt, we more or less just kept pushing it around in our bowls before Mike said it was time to go.

The three of us walk out with our heads hung low like a dog that's been scolded. I've never felt this way before. Like I upset a parent. I'm not close with Mike, and I was literally making a joke about fucking him an hour ago, but he is giving off so much dad energy, I want to run away with my tail between my legs.

The car ride to the hotel isn't any better either. Especially when he talks to all of us about our confessions. One at a time he runs through all of us. Janelle was a simple—no more dating and she didn't argue or tell him they weren't dating anymore because he's a cheating bastard and she fucked his uncle less than twenty-four hours ago.

He tells Ronni she is eighteen, so can make her own decisions but he would advise against her dating her manager as mixing business and pleasure does not end well. Then he meets my eyes in the mirror until I turn my attention outside. "I'm going to hope there isn't anything more going on as far as your coach goes, Payson. You are only seventeen." I wish the car would swallow me whole. "As far as the pain medication. You need to be careful with them and tell the people around you when you are taking them in case you start acting out of sorts. You're taking the prescribed amount, right?"

I nod. *Yep, taking the amount the doctor prescribed to my mom.* Plus an extra one, but that was just today. Only because I wanted to have fun tonight. And I did, until Janelle had to go and blow it.

"Alright, get out of my car. Go straight to your room and think about your decisions, girls, because even though you are young, they do, in fact, still matter."

44

Payson

THE THREE OF US lie on Janelle's bed, saying nothing and staring at the ceiling. We've been this way for an hour, since Mike dropped us off.

"I hate living in California," Ronni says out of nowhere. "I hate being away from you guys and I really hate what we have become since I moved. It's like we're not a trio anymore. There's you two and then there is me."

"We miss you, Ron. But you cut us out, remember?" Janelle says.

"I know." Ronni's voice is small. "There's just been . . . a lot going on."

"Like what?" I ask.

She doesn't answer right away and when she does, it's too vague to even be considered an answer.

"Come on. Don't lie to us," I urge.

I drop my head to the side to look at Ronni. She looks back at me, offering the slightest wince. "I'm just struggling at fitting into this life. It's harder than it was before. I miss when it wasn't my whole life, you know?"

No, I don't know. I love that volleyball is my whole life, and I'm worried what might come over me when the season is over.

"Why don't you go back to what you were doing and come home?" I offer.

She blows out a breath, fluffing her bangs and turns her head to look back to the ceiling, so I do the same. "I'm in a contract for the next three years at least. Then I will decide what I want to do."

"Do you know what you want to do when you're done modeling?" Janelle asks.

"Not a clue. I love the industry, the fashion, the makeup. Maybe something in that. Maybe even a photographer. Jump behind the camera instead of in front."

I can't imagine Ronni being behind the camera. She's always been the center-of-attention type. It was always helpful for me because she kept me out of it.

"My dad wants me to move in with him when the volleyball season is over."

I sit up so I can see Janelle over Ronni. "What?"

She avoids my eyes but nods. "I'm considering it."

"Why? What's here?"

"My dad," she says softly, her voice thick with emotion. "I miss him, Pay. I didn't realize how much until we were playing in the gym together during a break. And tonight. He's right, the decisions we make now affect us, and I've been living like they don't. I fucked the uncle of the guy I like, for fuck's sake."

"You what?!" Ronni gasps. I cringe and Janelle is right behind me.

"We were drunk."

I fall back onto the bed with a thud. "I've had sexual encounters with both my volleyball coaches."

Ronni chews on her lips then blurts, "Sometimes I fuck the photographers for benefits."

"I think I fell in love with a sixteen-year-old the day I met him," Janelle spits out next. Then their heads turn my way, waiting for me to word vomit something that will make them feel better, no doubt. So I do.

"My mom died and I'm not sad."

Ronni grabs my hand and Janelle grabs hers. We lie there for a long time, once again in silence, probably thinking about everything we admitted.

Morning comes and I wake in the arms of Ronni and Janelle. They put me in the middle after a while last night, and somehow, we all fell asleep cuddling. I almost slept as good as I do with Ash. Almost. Ronni and Janelle don't weigh as much as him, even combined, but they also don't sweat as much either.

I thought I was the first up, although I have no idea how because the curtains were left open and the sun is shining into the room, but when I shift, Ronni moves her arms and we both slip from the bed. I replace my body with a pillow for Janelle to hug.

We don't have to be at the gym until three for the last games of the week, but Ronni has to catch a flight at ten, so she will have to leave soon.

I head to the bathroom to get ready, and she follows after to pee while I shower.

"I'm sorry I didn't text you about your mom, P. I . . . I didn't know what to say, honestly."

"I know. It didn't bother me."

She pushes the curtain back and sits on the edge of the tub, no doubt getting wet from the spray. "I've been a really bad friend. I know, but I'm going to be better. I don't think I'll be able to text every day but every few? And maybe we can go back to weekly phone calls. I usually don't work much on Sundays."

"I'd like that." I smile over my shoulder at her. "But I've been a bad friend our entire relationship, so no need to apologize there."

I turn, not thinking about it and jump when Ronni gasps.

Seeing what she's looking at I throw a hand to my forehead. *Dumbass!*

"He . . . *carved* his name in you." The judgment is thick in her voice.

"It's not a big deal. He got my name tattooed on him too."

Her wild eyes fly to mine. "Not a big deal? Oh my God, Payson, that's a huge deal. A tattoo can be covered. You can never get rid of *that*." She points to my stomach.

"That's the point," I mutter. I step closer to her so her finger pokes into the scarred flesh. "I can never get rid of him, Ron. I know you don't like it, but he's it for me." Her face scrunches and she traces each letter with her finger. "He's always been it for me, you know this."

"That's the problem, Pay."

She reaches the end of the *h*, then her hands drift to my arm, she angles it her way too. A deeper frown than what was there tugs at her perfect face. "You're still cutting."

I hope Janelle is still sleeping. When she doesn't barge into the room seconds later, I know she must be, but I drop my voice just in case. "It's different now."

"What does that mean?"

That it's not me cutting. "I don't know, but I'm getting better. The last one was from a few weeks ago. They just broke open yesterday from the Russian Hitter."

She does not believe me, but she drops my arm and sighs. "I'm in no position to judge you but I can't help but look at you like a little sister, Pay. I want what's best for you." She pushes down her sleep shorts, pulls her tank over her head and steps into the shower with me. "If you think Ash Pearson is the best for you . . ." She twists her lips, obviously not thinking the same as what she is saying. "Then I'll do my best to support that."

"Did you move because your manager thought I was a bad influence?"

Ronni pauses under the shower stream, her eyes are closed not to get soap in them but her eyebrows furrow with disbelief. "What?"

"Alyssa said—"

"That's absurd, Pay. No, she was just trying to hurt you. I moved because there was an opening in the agency he had been trying to get me in for a while. I meant to tell you the night of the sleepover but..."

"Right." I should have known Alyssa is full of shit. I doubt Ronni has even texted her once since she moved.

I finish my shower and leave Ronni to finish alone. I'm glad I at least got closure on why she moved.

I dress and am braiding my hair when Janelle walks into the room, yawning.

She eyes us and scoffs. "I missed the community shower?" I chuckle at her honest disappointment. "Your braids look like shit."

"Rude."

The curtain opens and Ronni eyes my handiwork. "She's right. Sit down and I will fix them."

Fine, but only because my arms are cramping. It doesn't actually matter how my hair looks. Janelle showers while Ronni fixes my hair. We are reliving old memories when Ronni blurts another confession out.

"I think I'm bi."

Janelle rips the shower curtain open, then turns it off. She meets my eyes in the mirror and I meet hers. Then we laugh.

"Yeah, no shit." She snorts.

Ronni scowls at us and shoves me off the toilet now that my hair is done.

"I didn't even know until this year, there's no way you knew."

"Ron—" I giggle. "We've known."

"How?" she demands, crossing her arms.

"Maybe we didn't *know* but that's the least surprising thing that's been said the last three days."

I nod, agreeing with Janelle. "Not to mention you were staring at my tits the entire time we were in the shower."

"Hey, now. That's not fair. You have fantastic tits," Janelle chimes. "I'm straight and still admire them when I can."

Ronni grins. "You should totally look into nipple piercings."

They go on a rampage about how *it's not a want but a need* and I leave the room. The last thing I need right now are nipple piercings. Maybe when I'm done playing volleyball, as I don't want to worry about them while I'm playing. Plus, I'm seventeen and would need a parent to come with me, and since my mom is dead and I'd rather die than ask my grandpa, it's a hard pass.

Ash

I knock on Payson's door, hoping the girls are awake. She hasn't texted me since last night when she got back from dinner with Janelle's dad, and I'm itching to get my hands on her. I know Ronni isn't cool with our relationship, Payson's words, but I need my girl. I was up most of the night double checking Luca was still in his bed and not in hers finishing the job from yesterday morning. That's got to be one of the biggest mistakes I have ever made, letting Luca lick Payson's pussy, and it will never happen again.

It's not Payson who opens the door, it's Janelle. I wonder how she feels about Luca fucking her, then eating Payson out in the same night. Luca said what they did was casual, but you never know if she will feel the same. She grins seeing me but it slips a little when she actually looks at me. "You okay, Coach? You look busted."

"Where is Payson?"

"Pay!" she calls, not taking her eyes off me. "Let me see the tattoo."

Tattoo? Oh, my newest one. Word spreads fast amongst girls, I see, because someone else, I'm guessing Ronni, shouts about wanting to see it too. Janelle pulls me into the room. Monica and Emika are here as well, but I scan the room looking for the one I'm actually here for. She is propped on her bed, grinning at me like I hung the stars. I take a deep breath. Another thing about girls is their perfumes, they don't always mix. It smells good in the room but like a perfume tester store. Besides that subtle smell of vanilla and rainwater. I suck in a deep breath and head her way.

I jump over her body and lie next to her, pulling her into my chest. Throw an arm behind my head and the other I wrap around her waist.

She smiles up to me and I smile down to her. "Hi."

"Hi."

Janelle kneels on the foot of the bed with her phone in front of her face. Snapping several photos of us. Then she promises to send them to Payson.

"Okaaaay, now show us the tattoo," Monica singsongs.

Payson giggles and beckons me so she can whisper, "Ronni saw mine, but I didn't show anyone else. She spilled the beans about your tattoo."

Ahh.

Payson pulls me to my knees and lifts my shirt enough to show my latest tattoo. The girls ooo and ahh until I've had enough of their attention and drop back onto the bed.

"When are you getting yours, Pay?" Monica grins.

Payson flushes a deep pink. And Ronni hits me with a knowing look, not exactly a happy one either. "Maybe when I can legally get a tattoo," she teases.

The girls fall into an easy conversation about tattoos they like or don't like, and I press my lips to the base of Payson's ear. "How was your night?"

She chews on her lips, pondering my question for a while. "Good. Surprising, informative, but good." She drops her voice and crawls farther up my body. "I missed you, though."

"You have no idea how good that feels to hear because I have been miserable."

I tilt my head back when she nuzzles her nose into my neck. She kisses me and licks before pulling away and glancing back at her friends. I don't know if they are watching, they are talking so maybe not, but it's not like I care. I've missed her too much to care. Which is why I grab her hips and roll us and position myself between her legs. My stomach is on her panties so it's not overly inappropriate.

Who am I kidding? Everything Payson and I do is inappropriate. I'm her coach for bloody sake.

Something I seem to forget often.

45

Payson

I STARE INTO MY best friend's eyes, still in my groggy state from the nap we took after seeing Ronni off at the airport. Apparently she woke up before me, and during my sleep, I must have removed my sweatshirt. I don't remember doing it but when Janelle woke up, she got a clear look at my newest cuts. "Jay—"

"You're fucking cutting *again*?" She doesn't waste another second before storming out of our room and into the hallway.

"Janelle!" I run after her. She bangs on Ash's door and my stomach twists.

"Don't even try and stop me. I warned you the last time and I shouldn't have even waited then. I'm not making the same mistake now. Ash! Open up!"

"He did it!" I slap a hand to my mouth after the words slip out.

Janelle's fist freezes right before she's about to slam it into the door again. "He *what*?"

I swallow thickly because I'm not awake enough for this conversation but also, I don't know what to say. Janelle won't understand my need to cut and Ash's need to keep me from cutting. I'm thinking blood play isn't in Janelle's wheelhouse.

The door opens.

Janelle sweeps her gaze to a shirtless and sleepy Ash. He rubs his tired eyes and freezes when he sees Janelle.

His arm falls. "Janelle?" He flicks his confused eyes to me, then back to her when I don't answer. My stomach fills with a million nails for dragging him into this. I could have simply said I did it. I continued to cut even when I said I wouldn't. Ash would have pretended to be mad and that would have been it.

"Payson cuts herself," she blurts.

Ash blinks. Then blinks again. By the third blink he's finally waking up enough to realize what is happening. He looks at my exposed arms and cringes.

"Oh my God . . . she was right . . . y-you cut her."

That little muscle in his jaw flexes under his beard. "I—" He falls silent, because if there is one thing about Ash Pearson—he never lies.

Janelle steps back like you do when a stranger gets too close. She looks back and forth between us, her eyebrows sinking more each time. "You sick fucking bastard."

"Janelle!" I gasp, subconsciously moving in front of Ash. He is quick to place a hand on my shoulder.

Seeing my best friend looking at Ash like . . . like he says everyone else will, hits harder than I thought.

"I stood up for you, *multiple times.*"

"I am forever grateful for you, Janelle." Ash places his hand over his heart.

"Just shut up. I wasn't done," she snaps. "People say terrible things about you—both of you." Her gaze turns sad. "You know how hard it is to hear terrible things about my best friend constantly? But I let them talk because at least I know the truth. How *happy* you guys are. I'd always think—*at least I know she's cared for.*" She laughs without humor and the sharp pain in my leg intensifies.

The hand on my shoulder tenses and even I shrink because she's right. She's supported us from day one. Even before day one when she was chatting me up to Ash before we even met. She's never once made me feel bad about dating our coach. I've never felt judged by Janelle before right now.

"I fucking told Payson to forgive you, for *everything* you've put her through . . . and you fucking *cut* her?"

"It's call blo—"

"Seriously? You think I give a shit what you call your kinky games? Because I don't. You cut her, Ash. You fucking make her *bleed*. You've added to the hideous scars on her arms and I'm meant to understand?"

I rear back into Ash's chest. "Hideous." My voice breaks.

Ash wraps a strong arm around my middle and tugs me flush. "They're not hideous."

Tears well in her eyes followed by a look of regret. "That's not what I meant, Pay. You know I don't think that." There's nothing to say because I do know, it doesn't mean it doesn't still hurt.

"After everything with F-Fred." She hiccups.

"Do not compare me to that monster. Everything I have done to Payson's body is consensual and wanted."

"How do you not see the issue here, Ash?! Come on, you *cut* her. You pick up a knife—" She slaps a hand over her face and cries, not able to even finish the sentence.

Emotion burns the back of my eyes and I reach out for her but she's quick to move back before I can. "And you cut her." Her breath shakes. "I thought she was safe with you. All this time I've spent worrying about Payson and her mental health, I thought you were helping because I thought she was getting better." She drops her eyes from Ash to me. "I thought you were getting better."

"I am."

"No, you're not! You've only moved onto the next bad thing for you. Him. Somehow, you've convinced him that this 'helps' you. It doesn't."

"Jay, you don't understand. I can't breathe without these cuts." I push my arms forward, but she refuses to look. "These save me *daily* from making worse decisions. Do you know what it's like to walk around with the thoughts I have in my head? The ones that remind me the guy who promised me he would rape me on my eighteenth birthday is out there, free, after murdering my mom. You have any clue what it's like to carry the weight knowing he is most likely coming for me next?"

I'm shaking from head to toe as the truth pours from me. "I'm scared," I admit. "I'm scared all the time, this—" I look down at my hideous arms, she was right about that. Not only from the cuts now but the large bruises from yesterday. "This helps me."

"Payson," she whimpers and my nonexistent heart cracks down the middle. "Please, I couldn't handle it when you were cutting yourself but now you're letting someone else do it . . . you *need* help."

"I'm fine."

Her lip disappears in her mouth before she turns her head, refusing to look at us anymore. "I can't watch this."

"What do you mean?"

"I don't know. All I know is I need time." She blows out a deep breath. "I'm going to take my dad up on that offer."

"Jay . . ."

She winces as if I physically hit her when we couldn't be farther apart than what we are right now. It feels like there is an ocean between us. I've never felt so disconnected from my best friend. She looks at us one last time and the only thing keeping me from falling to my knees is Ash's arms around me. He knows how much this is killing me and he's there to hold me. Like he always is. Why can't she see how much he loves and cares for me? So he's given me a few cuts? I survived, didn't I? I'm fine, this is the reason I'm fine and she refuses to see that.

"*I* love you, Payson." She emphasizes I as if saying he doesn't. "But as long as you are putting yourself in harm's way . . ."

"I'm not," I beg. "Jay, I'm really fi—"

"I swear to God if you say fine." Anger crosses her tear-filled eyes.

"I am!" I shout. "I am fine. I wasn't fine before him, but he makes me feel better."

She only shakes her head like a disappointed mom. "You are so far gone to see, Pay. You too." She regards Ash and he stiffens. "One day you both will finally open your eyes and see what you are doing is destroying *both* of you. Ash is destroying you physically and one day your body will give up. You—" I try and cut her off but she doesn't let me. "You are destroying him mentally. You have him so brainwashed that he actually believes the bullshit you just told me about needing it. You only need those cuts because you are too weak to face reality."

"Low fucking blow, Janelle," I hiss as tears stream from my eyes.

"If no one else in your life will be honest with you, then I will. But what I won't do is stick around to watch your downfall." Her breath shakes. "I'm going to pack and call my dad. I will stay there tonight so our room will be open."

"Jay, please."

"You gotta let me go, Pay. You are killing me. This"—she gestures between us—"our friendship it's too much for me right now."

I've always thought I was too much. But I tried so hard not to be. I tried to be a good friend, I think. As much as I knew how, but I failed.

"Are you sure about this?" Ash stares down at my naked body on his bed with a new blade in his hand.

I pinch my eyes so I don't have to see the battle in his eyes that wasn't there before Janelle said anything. "Yes, either you do it, or I will."

A second later, the cool tip of the blade is digging into my arm. He doesn't stop with a single line. Looking down, I see what he's carving this time and the tears pour more than before.

"Beautiful." He sits back and eyes his work. I drop my head back to the bed and let out the kind of breath that comes only after cutting. Janelle doesn't understand. Ash doesn't do this to hurt me. He's not brainwashed. He does it because it *helps*, and he sees how much I really do need it. Ash is the only one who sees the real me. Maybe I'm a little too reliant on him—but it's still new. Eventually we will calm down and won't need all the dramatics in our relationship, but that's not today.

Ash said I am his light but he is mine. My life is so dark without him, and only he can make it light again.

"I love you."

His eyes flare hearing those words from me for the first time. He falls on my body and kisses me so intensely. I smile and he kisses me harder, pouring the love that only we understand between us.

"I love you more, Jailbird. Always."

"Forever."

The thing about lights? They eventually burn out.

"Are you in pain?" Ash's voice is soft, not to alert anyone else.

I snap a quick look to Janelle, then look forward to the large crowd when I see her smiling at something Erica said. "Nope."

"Not even your arm?" His voice drops even further.

"No. I'm fin—feel great. Never better."

I think I hear him sigh but Valerie begins her introductions and cuts him off. After introductions, there is a ball auction, then it's time for the games. We play third and last, so we have a while before our games. I excuse myself to the lobby because I didn't get a chance to look at everything, but also to avoid the heavy stare coming from Janelle. I don't know how to deal with that right now. Maybe I'm meant to apologize, but I can hardly see straight, let alone apologize for . . . whatever it is I'm meant to apologize for. I'm wondering if I should have taken two pills at the same time.

Maybe I need to eat something. I walk over to the concession, stumbling—I think. Or the room is spinning.

A rough hand grips my arm and drags me the opposite way of the food. I try and fight, I think, but I'm pulled into a room instead. The person pulling me lets go and the rush has my head spinning. I sit, or fall maybe, to the ground.

"Are you drunk?"

I try my hardest to force my eyes open but the room stays dark. I should be panicked being in a random room with someone I don't recognize the voice of—but I'm not.

"Payson."

The way he says my name . . . it's so familiar. Then it hits me through the fog. "Igor?"

"How fucked up are you?"

"I've been taking pain meds for my knee. I think I'm having a reaction."

I'm assuming the hiss of noise is some curse in Russian. He lifts me again and drags me somewhere that smells like a bathroom.

"Throw up."

It is a bathroom. "I can't just throw up on command."

"You do it. Or I will."

"How—" Two long, I assume fingers, invade my mouth. He jabs and jabs until my stomach is turning, then he shoves my face into the toilet, and I throw up. Then I throw up again without his help because my body hates me. I fall to my back and try to not think about how gross this floor probably is. "Are we in the men's room?"

"I am male."

I'm definitely lying in dried piss. The squeak of what I assume is the door because I still can't open my eyes catches my ears, but I still don't move. When it happens again, there are more footsteps.

"Fuck, Payson. What have you done?"

I don't know who that is but he's Russian too. I'm tugged off the ground and it swirls my stomach and head, again. They set me on the sinks, and someone keeps their arms on my shoulders so I don't fall forward. Someone with really cold hands removes my brace. I open my mouth to argue but aggressive Russian cuts me off.

I'm finally able to open my eyes just in time to see someone from the Russian team shove a needle in my knee. One of the two guys holding me grabs both my wrists and the other throws a hand over my mouth muting my scream.

The guy giving me the shot scowls at me and mutters something I don't understand.

"It will help with pain and not make you high," Igor tells me.

"Is it safe?" The guy holding my mouth drops his hand and washes them.

"Da. Most of us on the team get shots a few times a season."

There's a quick but aggressive conversation between the shot guy before I realize he's not being aggressive, that's just the way their language sounds. He must not speak English.

Igor nods at whatever he said before relaying that this isn't a cure all and I still need to wear my brace, but it should help. And to stop taking the drugs.

"Yeah, okay."

The guy at my knee grabs my wrist and shoves my sleeve up. *What is with these guys doing this?* He eyes my arm, then looks to Igor who is looking at the newly carved word. Ash wrapped it to stop the blood from transferring onto my jersey, but the stupid guy pushed that up too.

"Me and my boyfriend are into . . ." I can't finish that sentence.

Igor nods and mutters something in Russian to the guy. He flattens his lips and goes back to taking my pulse. I'm so glad I will never see these guys again.

"Zdes."

I grab the toothbrush and travel size toothpaste from the shot guy and the other two help me off the counter. "There wouldn't happen to be any food in that bag, would there?" I ask, after brushing my teeth. Half joking.

"No, but you should eat. It will help absorb some of the drugs."

After a quick glance in the mirror to make sure I look fine. Igor tugs on my arm. "You look fine, let us get you out of the men's bathroom."

It was the guys' time to warm up, so they left me to get my own food. Which is fine. I'm actually feeling better, and I don't want Ash asking questions because there's not really a good excuse why I was in the men's bathroom with three guys. If Ash finds out about the pills, he will lose his mind.

Igor was right, the food helped make me feel even better. I almost feel normal now. After a walk around the lobby, I find myself eyeing a table with homemade jewelry. I originally stopped because I saw some earrings I thought my mom would like. Then I remembered she is dead so it doesn't matter what earrings she would like. I pick up one of the other pieces—a bracelet this time. Orange and gold beads with black thread. I'm not sure why but it makes me think of Ash, so I buy it. The lady was so happy with the sale, it made me smile.

She passes me the bracelet in a bag and a small card.

Once I walk away, I pull the card out and read what it says.

It is said whoever wears this bracelet will have luck on their side.

The lucky numbers are 4,4,4,3,0

"What is that?"

I jump hearing the rumble of Ash's voice in my ear. Spinning, I grin up to him. "For you, actually." I push the bracelet in his direction.

He grabs it and holds it up, then lifts an eyebrow. "You bought me a bracelet," he deadpans.

"Just put it on." I giggle. "I think it will look good against your skin."

"It is funny you got this for me because . . ." He reaches into his pocket and pulls out a small bag that looks the same as the one I just bought.

"You're kidding."

He smiles a heartbreaking smile and tips the bag upside down in his hand. He holds a blue and green beaded bracelet toward me. The thread is white, and it really is so pretty. "Made me think of you. I was going to wait to give it to you on the plane."

I wish I could kiss him right now. "I love it."

"And I love you."

My heart thunders and my cheeks blush. I can tell he is waiting to hear it back, but the words are caught in my throat. So, instead, I take a step back toward the gym. "Want to go watch?"

I've disappointed him, but he pushes it down and nods. "Sure, lets go."

46

Ash

THE GYM ERUPTS IN the loudest cheering yet, or maybe I'm bias because it's my team they are cheering for. They deserve it. My girls kicked fucking ass. This game might not count toward our season, but I couldn't be prouder.

Maybe when we win states, but for now, this is the proudest I've been all season.

It's been the longest week and they have had really no breaks. I know they are tired, but they still pulled through and we won. Now if we can just do that for the next couple weeks.

So many people congratulate me and the girls, I'm lost in a sea of people, pink confetti, and pink balloons.

Valerie is announcing how much we raised, I listen to hear million, then I stop. I'm not sure how many millions but we raised a million. That feels fucking good.

I high-five each of my girls besides two. Janelle because she ignored me and walked away to greet her dad, who was not shy about his glaring either. And Payson. Because she's too busy being passed around like a rag doll by the mens' teams.

If I could punch every single one of the scrawny guys for hugging my girl, I would. Eventually, after way, way too long, they stop passing her, but she's stuck under some tosser's arm like they are old friends.

Unable to help myself, I tread forward and wrap a hand around Payson's front, spanning almost the width of her flat stomach. There are enough people around I don't worry who might see besides the ones I want to.

Their smiles and laughter stop right away as they watch me place my claim where my claim is due. Payson shoots a worried look at me, then to her new *friends*. She struggles to step away, but I don't let her.

"You are Ash Pearson, right?" one of the guys says after a long and awkward minute. Awkward for them, not me.

"Yes."

He rambles something to the guy next to him, and he snaps his fingers like whatever they talked about connected the dots. The guy who didn't ask rushes forward and grabs my hand, shaking it.

I narrow my eyes to him, then look back to his friends. "We are all huge fans, but he is our Setter. Big, big fan."

"Big, big fan," the guy still shaking my hand repeats in broken English.

"Thank you. I appreciate that."

After a short but nice conversation, most of the guys disperse and I move my hand to Payson's shoulder without their cover from the audience. A few guys hang back, the ones who don't seem as excited to see me.

"May I speak with you, Payson?" the blond guy in front asks, pinning me with a hard stare.

Payson squeaks under the pressure of my hand on her shoulder.

"I don't think that is necessary," I answer for her and that seems to piss him off even more, so he squares his shoulders and crosses his arms over his narrow chest. There was a time I looked like him, body type, I mean. Now

I'm at least twice as wide and could crush him like a bug. He keeps trying to get my girl away from me and I just might put that theory to the test.

He spits something in Russian at me, then says, "I think it is since you have your hand pressing into her shoulder so hard she is wincing."

I drop my eyes to Payson and lessen my grip. I hadn't realized.

"Igor," Payson mutters softly. "I'm fine."

How many times must I hear her say those words? *I'm fine.* According to who, because apparently not according to her best friend and now this guy. She's not fine to me either, but they're acting as if I am the one making her not okay.

He stares hard at her for quite a few seconds, then a defeated sigh leaves his lips. "If you need to talk, find me on Instagram. It's just my name."

Payson's eyes widen. "Oh, uh, yeah, okay."

He walks away but not before shooting me another glare. I'm too busy trying not to throttle him to care about a stupid look. "If you—"

"I'm not going to. Come on." She hurries from my grip but stops when she's a few feet away and nods to me to follow.

Several coaches stop Payson on our way to wherever she is heading, the last ones being Coach Fulton and Valerie.

"I am quite impressed with your performance this week, Payson."

Payson grins. "Thank you so much, Coach Fulton. I love this sport."

"That's very obvious in how you play. Even with a bum knee, you were the best Libero I saw here."

Payson lets out a silent gasp. My eyebrows inch up my forehead because that's a huge compliment. He's right, but sometimes I wonder if I'm bias. Glad to know I'm not. "Wow, I don't know what to say to that."

"Say you'll come see my school." He thrusts a hand forward, holding numerous pamphlets with the school's mascot on the top.

Payson is too distracted looking at the papers in her hands to say anything back. I know how she must feel knowing her dream school is interested. I am surprised to hear how much emotion is in her voice when she finally replies.

"I'm speechless. I'd love to."

"I'm not the women's team coach but I am in close contact with that coach. Unfortunately, he couldn't make it, but I've sent him videos. He's definitely interested."

He. If she goes to Colorado, she will have another male coach. I can't keep her from that dream, but I can't sit back and watch her be coached by a man that isn't me. At this point, I'm not sure I would want anyone but me to be her coach. Male or female. It's not like I don't have the experience. We haven't talked about what happens when she goes to college. I can't just get hired anywhere. I'm sure after state I will have more opportunities, but what if none are where she wants to go? And what about Parker? I can't tote him around the country when he is just getting settled here. I know he wants to go to school for football, American Soccer, and he will need to be settled in a school for that opportunity. Payson going away to college hasn't been something I've thought about, but it should be. I can't let her go.

"Coach?"

Her sweet voice pulls me back to the present. Fulton and Valerie are nowhere in sight, in fact, the gym is slowly emptying. There is a huge party in the banquet room from the first night where everyone is invited but that's not for another hour.

I know what I want to spend that hour doing.

Judging by Payson's glazed over eyes, I'd say she is thinking the same thing.

The music is too loud, room is too crowded and the air smells like a mixture of cheap cologne and perfume. By the time Payson and I made it down here, shots were already being thrown back by the coaches and the teams were crowding the dancefloor, and it hasn't stopped since.

Payson stands off to the side with Monica chatting. It's weird not seeing Janelle by her side. Or Janelle here at all. There are a lot of blondes so it's possible I'm missing her but I'm sure I'm not. I'm hopeful they can make up. I know nothing about what she mentioned with her dad, but a friendship with Payson and Janelle doesn't come along often. It would be a shame to see it fail.

Speaking of friendships.

"Fratello." Luca holds up his glass and I cheers it, then we throw the contents inside back. "Great games, yes?"

"Very," I agree. "We had several scouts sniffing around our girls."

"I am not surprised. I see all these girls going far."

Me too. "How do you think we will manage for state? Did you watch Frankenmuth's videos I sent you?"

"Si, yes. They are good."

"We are better."

Luca slaps my shoulder. "Also, yes. But we have a long couple weeks ahead of us."

Yes, we do.

"So, relax and enjoy the party, Ashley. Come Monday we will be in, uh, what do they say? Bootcamp?"

I chuckle into my glass. "Something like that."

The next morning, everyone is extra quiet. I'm fairly sure half my team is still sleeping after the late night and early morning, but we have all seven girls. I take my seat and wait for Parker and Payson to follow behind.

"Sorry," Payson mutters after she bumps into Janelle. She ignores her and Payson slumps into her seat next to me.

It's breaking my heart seeing her so upset. I cup her hand and place her bracelet inside. Her smile is small until she slips it on and holds our arms together, comparing our two bracelets. "I love it."

"I love you."

She blushes and bites her lip. My eyes fall to her lips, wishing I could capture them and hating that I can't.

She settles in next to me and pulls out her phone. She offers me an earbud and when I say no, she offers it to Parker. They were watching *Forrest Gump*, but within the last thirty minutes of me working on my computer, they have fallen asleep. Her head on his shoulder and his head on top of hers. Half of me is jealous because that could never be us. The other half has my lips tilting because it's nice to see them getting along.

Eventually I settle back into my chair, with a hand on her thigh, and I drift to sleep because Luca was right. The next few weeks will be bootcamp. Hell, if you will, but we have to win. We have all worked too hard not to.

47

Payson

Winning the last game of Week of Pink and bringing home the pink trophy might have been the highlight of my junior season. That was before we won states. States. I can't believe it. *States*. I'm so proud of my team. Ever since we got back from Week of Pink, we have worked our asses off for this title, and we got it. This has been the longest volleyball season of my life, but at least it has paid off. My knee might be fucked and I might have a serious pill addiction now, but we did it.

I'm excited, obviously, but the pills keep me from registering the emotions. I meant to stop once we were back from Week of Pink, but practices only got harder. My knee was throbbing by the second practice even though Igor said the shot should last the rest of the season. Luca and Ash picked up on my limping, and I couldn't risk them pulling me. I haven't taken two pills at a time again, but I am up to one a day. I'm almost out and I guess that's good. It doesn't feel good, though.

"Murphy!" someone from my teams shouts and waves me over for the group photo. Ash looks worried but I ignore him and jog over to join my team.

My cheeks ache by the time they are done taking our photos. I'm adjusting my brace when a familiar set of court shoes stop in front of me. I'm nervous as I stand and meet the blue eyes of my best friend. It's been weird the last two weeks not talking to her outside of volleyball-related things we couldn't avoid at practice. We kept up being pepper partners, but we didn't talk like we normally do. I've been eating lunch at school, Ash's idea to eat as a team so we could bond, but Janelle never spoke a word to me.

"Congratulations," I spit out. "Great way to end your final season."

She flattens her lips and nods. I know that look, she's about to cry.

"Jay—"

But she cuts me off and shakes her head. "I fly out to California with Dad tomorrow. I won't be back."

Tomorrow. I knew what she said about going, but we've been so busy, I've not even been able to keep my eyes open after our late practices to remember that my best friend is moving across the fucking country.

I lick my dry lips, but my mouth is dry too so it doesn't help at all. "Already? We just won states. I . . . we haven't even made up."

She chokes on a sob and says, "There is no making up, Payson."

My throat thickens.

"There's no making up because we didn't fall out. I still love you, Pay. You're still my best friend. I just need to do what is best for me. Okay?"

No, no this is so far from *okay*.

"It feels like forever I've been worrying about other people, you know? Worrying about Collins and his feelings. Worrying about Ronni being alone. Worrying about you." Her eyes turn sad. "I love worrying about you, and I will forever, but this is a great opportunity for me, you know? I'm sorry for what happened between us at Week of Pink, not for what I said, I think what you two are doing is so stupid and—" She snaps her mouth shut.

Hurt rips through me. "We haven't," I whisper, "done that, recently." We've hardly even touched besides a few sneaky kisses here and there.

"Good." Janelle threads her fingers with mine. "I don't hate Ash, and I don't hate you. I'm just really mad at both of you, but you were right about one thing." I tilt my head. "I don't understand. I can't begin to understand why you think you need something like that, but you are my bestest friend ever, and I don't want to leave the state with our friendship as a question mark."

"Me either." I roll my lips between my teeth.

"I know your grandpa and Jason are down here, but you think they'd be cool if I stole you for the night? I want one last night with my best friend before the real world whisks me away."

I know my grandpa will be fine with that. The trip down wore him out, even if it was only a few hours; he napped most of the afternoon we arrived, and I'm sure after the long day at the gym, he will be ready for bed too. "Jason has Amanda and I'll be surprised if my grandpa isn't asleep in the bleachers," I joke.

Janelle laughs and it sends the biggest shot of serotonin throughout my body. I can't stop her from going, as much as I want to, I know this is what she needs, and what kind of friend would I be if I tried to stop her from following her gut?

"You look like you did not get any sleep," Ash comments.

I take another drink of the coffee Mike has bought me and Janelle. "I didn't."

He squeezes my shoulder, then drops his hand from me when Mike and Janelle walk up to us.

Janelle hasn't stopped crying all morning and I've been crying off and on. I'm so tired, I'm not sure I could cry anymore even if I wanted to. I'm ignoring the other feeling in my body, the feeling like I'm missing something because I haven't swallowed a pill today.

She throws herself at me and someone is smart enough to grab my coffee before she tackles me to the ground. I breathe in the feminine scent of my best friend and pray it stays in my nose until the next time I see her. We will plan something for spring break since her and Ronni will already be in California. I'm pretending I will not be jealous they will be together. Knowing Janelle will be busy with her new advanced schooling and Ronni is busy with modeling, plus they live three hours apart, calms the jealousy. Not that I don't want them hanging out, I don't want either of them lonely. I will just miss out on what feels like a lot. That feeling Ronni had of being the outsider? I'm already feeling that, and Janelle hasn't even left yet.

I squeeze her as tight as she's squeezing me, and those tears I didn't think would come, burn my sore eyes. "I love you, Jay."

Her cries grow even louder. "I l-love y-you, Pay." She pulls back and cups my face. "Don't do anything I wouldn't."

"Right back at you." I choke on a laugh.

Then she kisses me. Right on the lips in front of our friends and family.

We stand and she turns to face Ash and giggles. "Coach." She sticks a hand out between them. He rolls his eyes and shoves her hand away, pulling her into his strong grip. He whispers something that I can't hear. But when they pull away, she regards me and nods. "I trust you. Don't make me regret saying that."

"Never."

Luca pulls her in next and despite what happened between them that one night, their hug isn't the least bit sexual. I'll never understand, but more power to them. Janelle goes down the line hugging everyone that's here. Which is everyone because no way the team would miss out on sending Janelle off. Even Grandpa is here and ready to say a prayer for Janelle and her dad's travel.

"You take care, Payson," Mike says as he hugs me tightly. "You make smart decisions. Do you understand me?'

"Yes, sir."

"Good girl." He pulls away and squeezes my shoulders.

Janelle and Parker are off to the side, awkwardly swaying and neither of them making eye contact. Then she wraps her arms around him and hugs him just as she has everyone else.

Mike turns at the same time, his eyebrows knitting in the middle of his forehead.

"Good luck." I grin.

He grumbles something before walking over there as they pull apart. Parker's eyes widen and I can't help but giggle. Mike shakes his hand before regarding his daughter.

You can see how happy he is to have his daughter moving with him. I think it was a long time coming. Lauren hasn't stopped crying, but I know she and Brette will go visit often.

Janelle makes her way back in front of me. Our eyes are glassy and at the same time, a tear tracks down both our cheeks. I brush hers away and she brushes mine. "You better answer all my texts and calls."

"Of course."

"I'm serious," she pouts. "None of that reply-days-later stuff."

"I'll be waiting by my phone."

We cling onto each other until Mike says it's time to go.

Janelle disappears up the stairs and at the very last second, she bends down and shouts, "I love you!"

"We love you!" The rest of us call and I don't even care that the rest of the airport looks pissed hearing us yell at nine a.m.

Grandpa wanders over to me and cups my face. "Are you going to be okay?"

Why does someone asking if you are okay make you breakdown? More so when it's your grandpa.

He hugs me while I cry and strokes my back in the most comforting way. "It's okay to not be okay, Ray-Ray. You'll see her soon."

"I know." But soon isn't everyday like I'm used to.

A: I miss you.

Me: Imiss you more.

A: Stay with me tonight.

Me: You know Ican't.

A: I hate Janelle for moving.

Me: I'm telling her you said that.

A: That's fine.

Me: I'll see you soon, okay?

A: No. That's not okay.

Me: Want me to send another photo?

A: . . . I'll never say no to that, but you shouldn't. It's not safe.

Me: I'll figure something out. But I have to go to class. I'll call you later!

One thing I didn't consider with Janelle not being around anymore is not having an alibi when I want to stay at Ash's. It's been two weeks since we have done anything, and the only time we have seen each other is at church. Yeah, I don't know how I convinced Ash Pearson to come to church, but he does. He figured that was the only way he could be around me, and after Grandpa invited him over after that first service and we spent the afternoon together, he kept coming back. It's only been three Sundays since states, but those three Sundays are the only thing getting me through.

I miss Janelle, a lot. Clay and I sit at a quiet table at lunch time, and while I like Clay, he's not Janelle. Janelle calls me every day during her free period because my free period is the same time as hers. Besides that, we also talk every night for at least an hour but it's not the same.

"Payson, it's quarter to," Mrs. Jennings announces.

I have a checkup today on my knee, and I have a weird feeling it will not go as well as I want.

You'd think since they make a whole schedule, there would be no waiting, but apparently that's not how it works because I've been sitting in the small room for twenty-five minutes. When the door finally opens, I let out a breath just to suck it back in when it's not the doctor that walks in. It's Ash.

"What are you doing here?" I jump from the bed and land on wobbly legs, his arms are around me before I have the chance to fall.

"Fuck, it feels bloody good to touch you."

"It feels good having you touch me, but what are you doing here?"

"I knew about your appointment; I want to be here." He pulls away and studies my face as if it's been years since he's seen it. I do the same to him. His hair has gotten even longer. Nearly to his cheekbones now. His beard is long and if he wasn't in jeans and a semi-nice-looking jacket, I would say he was the hottest homeless man I have ever seen.

"Ash." I lift a hand and knife my finger through his beard. Worry lays heavy in my stomach. "Are you okay?"

His stormy eyes darken, and that's when I notice the circles under his eyes too. "I just miss you, Jailbird. That's all."

That doesn't seem like all. "I miss you more." I bury my face back into his chest. "Maybe I can make up some kind of excuse to come over tonight."

He jerks back and a faint of a smile touches his harsh features. "Really?"

I shrug because I don't know what I can say, but if he misses me that much, then yes. I'm feeling . . . numb, Ash is the one struggling, and I need to be there for him like he always is me. "Yeah, I'll figure it out."

He slams his lips against mine and at the same time, we exhale the same breath, because the few kisses we have shared the past few weeks have been rushed and panicked thinking someone will walk in. On my side, anyway; Ash seems to have finally lost the care of anyone catching us, because I'm always the one that has to pull away. I hate having to pull away, but my grandpa would not appreciate us making out every time he turns his back.

Speaking of pulling back, someone knocks on the door, and I pull out of Ash's grip and jump back onto the bed. He scowls at me.

"I'm tired of you pulling away from me." So he has noticed the pattern. "You think I like to?"

"You do it enough," he snaps back.

Dr. Hennigan pokes her head in. "Ready—Oh! Coach Pearson." She pushes the door open and walks the rest of the way inside. "I didn't expect to see you here."

"I want to know about her knee." His jaw says it's more than that and the way he is keeping his eyes locked onto me says it's worlds more. Dr. Hennigan laughs awkwardly and takes her seat in front of the computer.

"Well, I can't say much without another MRI, so I am going to order you one, but it'll probably be after Thanksgiving, unfortunately."

"That's okay," I say. "The season is over, so I'm not doing much besides school."

Dr. Hennigan types on her computer for a while, then she pulls on my knee in a bunch of ways. Ash even growled when she touched me. I had to ask a random question to distract from the brooding man across the room.

I don't know what is happening between us, but it feels different. Like there is a disconnect that there wasn't before. I hate it. I hate seeing him like this and I hate this is all because we are apart when neither of us wants to be.

"Well, it feels looser than before." She sighs.

"Is that good?"

"No," her and Ash both say.

She clears her throat. "I have felt knees where their ACL and MCL are completely torn that feel like yours. But you said you're not having pain?"

"Uh, no. I mean, sometimes. Like when my knee gives out but—"

"Your knee is giving out?" she asks. "In what way?"

I take time explaining everything that has been happening since states while she is taking notes. I can hardly remember the details, I just know that sometimes when I'm walking, or even just standing there doing dishes my knee will give out when I'm not wearing my brace. I didn't think it was that big of a deal, but now I'm thinking it is.

"You should be having pain. I truly am not understanding why you are not . . . but if you say you're not in pain, then I'm going to suggest you just wear your brace as often as you can until the MRI, and we can see what is actually happening in your knee."

Great.

Ash only agreed to give me enough time to go to Grandpa's and tell him whatever excuse I could come up with, but pulling into Grandpa's, I still have no clue what my excuse could be on why I wouldn't be home. I guess this is why people have more than one friend. I could use Mika or Monica, but I'll have to text whoever I choose, and it'll probably be Mika because

Monica's family attends Grandpa's church, and the last thing I need is for him to ask Mrs. Maddox how the sleepover went.

I never came up with an excuse and now I don't need to.

48

Payson

CANCER. MY GRANDPA HAS cancer. Of all the things I thought the doctor was going to say, that wasn't one of them. Not only does he have cancer but it's *really aggressive.* Truthfully, I stopped listening after he said cancer. It doesn't make sense. How does someone like my grandpa who probably hasn't touched a cigarette in sixty years—at least, get lung cancer?

I've been trying to make sense of it and maybe that's the issue. Maybe there is nothing to make sense of because this doesn't make sense. It doesn't make sense to have cancer and it doesn't make sense why all the bad things happen to good people. I know my grandpa would be so disappointed, more than he already is, in me, but I feel like spitting in God's face right now.

Fred beats my brother, sexually abuses me, and kills my mom yet he is somewhere in the world no doubt making another little girl his victim, and my grandpa, who is the best man I know, lies in a hospital bed with a crazy amount of tubes coming from all parts of his body.

Apparently, he had another stroke and that's why I found him unconscious, on the floor of the trailer, when I got home. This one is smaller than the one before, but he hasn't woken up yet. The doctor said he's meant to, but it's been hours and random nurses keep coming in to check on him. They say nothing, but I can tell by their scrunched-up foreheads they expected him to be up. They don't have a good poker face like Grandpa's doctor who could have been telling me the ice cream truck was waiting outside offering free popsicles for how unemotional he was.

"Payson." I cringe hearing my aunt. I know what she is going to tell me. *Go call Jason*, or *why don't you go take a walk*? Something to get me out of this room I have been in since last night. I can't leave him. What if he wakes up and I'm not here? What if he doesn't wake up and these are my last moments with him? I squeeze my eyes shut. I'm not going to think about that. He can't die, he just *can't*. If my grandpa dies, who do I have left? Jason? I nearly laugh. He's not been here for me once. When he was home for Mom's funeral, he couldn't put the bottle down long enough to even talk to me and when he did, it was a snarky remark about Ash. Amanda did her best to smooth things between us, but the damage is already done. It's been too long, there's too much hurt and resentment between us.

Nothing matters because my grandpa is dying. If he doesn't die today, one day he will, and unfortunately, that day might be sooner than I thought. I've noticed things about him over the last couple months—small things, but I never would have guessed cancer was invading his body.

Maybe if I would have been home more. I've been distracted lately, high on pain meds that aren't mine. I should have noticed. My aunt says its not my fault, but it is. It is my fault because I'm too fucking selfish. Too lost in my own head. That's the reason Janelle left and even though we are fine now, she can't take back her words, and I wouldn't want her to because they are right. I am selfish. I only care about the things I deal with in my head and never think about anyone else.

I jump up as my aunt brushes my hair from my face.

Immense guilt is the only thing that pulls me toward the door despite weighing like a million pounds. "I, uh, think I'll go on that walk now."

The hallway doesn't bring me any comfort, so I head for the elevators.

I'm too lost in my head—like usual—I don't realize someone is in there with me and talking until he snaps a finger in front of my face.

"Hero?"

"The one and only. What are you doing here, Streaks?"

I don't know why he calls me that. "My, uh, grandpa."

"Ah. Yeah, cancer's got my mom. Being a real bitch about it too. Third round."

My eyebrows shoot up my forehead. "Third?"

He dips his narrow chin and squints at something on the wall behind me. After a quick look, I realize he's just avoiding my eyes. That's fine, I don't want to see him cry either. If that's what he was going to do, I'm not really sure.

I brush the tears from my eyes and lean against the metal wall. "What kind?"

"Breast. You?"

"Lung . . . I think." That's what the doctor said, right? "That's what it started out as anyway."

He runs a thin hand through his ginger hair. "Sucks."

I don't know why but I laugh. Hero doesn't seem to know why either because his eyebrows pinch together. He stares at me like that for a long time. Basically the whole way to the bottom floor before his smile breaks through. "You're a little fucked, aren't you, Streaks?"

"What gave it away?" I think he was coming up but when I step off, he follows after me. Right outside, not caring that it's storming. Again. It's December in lower Michigan—it's meant to be snowing and yet it hasn't stopped raining.

I love the rain, but Christmas is next month and I'd like snow for that. It's definitely cold out. My school uniform does nothing to keep me warm either. I should have put my blazer back on, but I forgot, or maybe it's not even here with me.

"When did you get here?" he asks.

"Last night. You?"

He pulls something from behind his ear, a cigarette. "I come by daily, right now, anyway. While she's getting her treatments." He pops it between his lips, and I watch in amazement as he lights it.

"You know, I just told you my grandpa has lung cancer and now you are smoking in front of me."

He sucks in a long drag, holds it, then blows it toward the sky. "What does that have to do with me?"

"Well, for one, you're definitely not meant to be smoking here." I point behind him to the sign that specifically says "Tobacco-free Campus." He shrugs after seeing it. "And that's what causes lung cancer."

"Is it?"

"Are you trying to piss me off?"

His annoying smirk says yes. "It's better being pissed off than sad, trust me." I can't imagine Hero sad. "The sky's been crying enough without you adding to it. Weird weather, huh?"

I stare out at the parking lot full of cars as the rain continues to assault them and the ground. "Yeah, but I like the rain."

He moves closer. "Sad people love the rain because they aren't the only thing crying anymore." I peer up at Hero. He shrugs. "Or maybe because we are meant to believe that rain is sad so when we are sad, it makes us feel less alone."

"Are you sad?" My voice is soft because he's right. Maybe I grew up loving the rain because it made me feel less alone.

He drops his eyes, and for a split second, his walls fall and it's like I can see a younger, sadder version of Hero under this version. "Nah." *Liar.* "Used to be, though." He's still sad. He can lie all day long to himself, but I don't believe it. Watching your mom, who he obviously cares a good amount for, go through cancer three times, isn't easy, I imagine.

"I was trying to come up with an excuse to go spend the night at my thirty-three-year-old boyfriend's house when my grandpa had his second stroke of the year."

Hero pauses at my confession. Why did I just tell him that out of nowhere? I don't know but I think it's suffocating me. The guilt. I love Ash and I want to be with him forever, but the lies are suffocating.

My nose burns at the smell of smoke, and blinking, I realize Hero has lit his cigarette again. "Did that drive you to smoke?"

He squints, sucks in a long breath, then blows it straight into the sky. Without missing a beat, he nods. "Yeah, what the fuck kind of confession is that?"

I shrug. I don't even know the answer to that.

"You're what, eighteen?"

"Seventeen."

"My fuck. What the fuck are you doing being involved with a man twice your age?"

That's a can of worms I don't feel like entertaining. Thankfully someone bitching at Hero about his smoking saves me from having to. He puts it out against the wall, then tosses it behind his ear, again.

"If you ever need a breather, my mom will be in here for a while, come find me."

"How do you know I need a breather?"

He cracks a sloppy smile, then brushes the top of my head like I'm some kid. "Takes one to know one—or something like that. See ya, Streaks."

49

Ash

THEY SAY THERE ARE many stages you go through during grief. They also say when you find out someone you love is dying, it is possible to start the stages early.

Payson is going through her denial stage. I watch with the heaviest weight on my chest as she begs her granddad to go through treatment. And the weight increases when he shakes his head no.

He was released from the hospital this morning and neither Payson nor I have left his side since. Vicky seems curious about my presence, but Paul doesn't. I would think maybe he knows but I think if he did, he wouldn't be okay with me being here. He's nonjudgmental but I can't imagine he would enjoy me being in love with his granddaughter.

"There is a cancer treatment center right here in Bayshore. My friend says it's good." Which friend is that? I'm not sure about Ronni but I don't think Janelle has had anyone with cancer. Not that I know her family's medical history, so maybe, but then Payson would have said Janelle not *friend*. "If it's about cost, I'll get a job."

"It's not about cost."

Her shoulders sink. "I-I can switch my school to online. I'll be here to take care of you if the chemo is too much."

"Payson."

"I'm sure someone can step up in church." She rips a hand through her messy hair that's fallen from her bun in the midst of her pacing.

It's physically killing me to watch her breakdown with each suggestion.

"Payson Ray."

"Lots of people survive cancer. Lung cancer too. I looked up the statistics last night and they say fifty-six percent survive if it's still in the lungs a-and if not, then it's like five, but five is not zero, Grandpa."

Paul pushes to his feet. It takes longer than it used to. Payson continues her argument until he cuts her off for the last time. "Payson Ray Murphy."

Paul is thinner than I've ever seen him. He looks weak and frail, and I know if Payson would really look at him, she would know why he insists on not doing treatment. His kind eyes look tired as he glances at me before he focuses on his granddaughter. My throat tightens more, seeing the love pour from him. It's very obvious how much he loves his granddaughter. Especially when he pulls her into his body. He might be smaller than her, but right now, it's so easy to imagine a young Payson—child size—being hugged by her grandpa. All those memories she told me about flash before my eyes.

"It's not zero, Grandpa." Her voice cracks, my heart right along with it.

"I love you, Payson Ray." Paul tightens his grip, and her sobs begin. Everything inside me begs to pull her into my arms but I know she needs this.

After a long while, they pull away. He holds her face between his hands as she sniffles. "I am too old for chemo, sweetheart."

"I asked—"

"I am not doing treatments. My mind was made up when I found out about the disease." His voice is firm for the first time ever—leaving no room for arguments. Probably why Payson pushes to her feet and sprints down the hall and outside.

The trailer falls to a sorrowful silence, besides my heart thundering for me to go after her. Paul stops me before I can.

"I'm eighty-seven years old." He shakes his head and the faintest of smiles ghosts his face. "She's always believed me to be younger. About ten years ago, she wanted roller skates for Christmas, so we got her a pair. When she opened hers, she asked where mine and her nana's were so we could go together." His blue eyes gloss over, but he's still smiling. I want to smile but it's impossible right now knowing my girl is out there crying and probably going through every emotion, alone. Things are hard right now; we're not getting time together and I'm slowly loosing it. Luca is pissed at me, Parker is going through something since Janelle is gone. I'm trying to balance Payson, Parker, and everything else. Things in the universe are off kilt and I can't fucking stand it. "She did not like the answer we gave her that we were too old." He chuckles. "A week later, the three of us were at the roller rink, roller skating. And you know what?"

I swallow, attempting to rid the lump from my throat. It doesn't work and my voice is hoarse. "What?"

"That is one of my most fond memories before my wife's death. Without Payson's pushing, I wouldn't have that."

"She's very good at arguing her side."

He nods. "Yes. But this is one thing I can't cave on. If the cancer wasn't killing me, the chemo would. I would be a shell of the man I am. I do not want to go out like that. I truly believe God has a timing for everything. If he wants me to live for another ten years, he will. Treatment or not."

I'm not sure I believe that, but who am I to argue?

"Should we go check on her?"

Paul leans back in his chair and sighs. "Probably. Payson likes to be alone, but she shouldn't. Not as much as she's used to."

He has no idea. I push to my feet, planning on doing just that but he stops me with a question.

"How are Payson and your son doing?"

I'll never forgive myself for that idiotic lie. "I'm not sure. I would assume fine. I've not heard any different."

"Hmm. It's odd that he's never comes around here."

I pause. My back is still to him, so I know he can't see me racking my brain, but he sounds suspicious enough that it has me wondering if just maybe he can. "I think Parker is just trying to adjust. He means no disrespect, sir." I step back and turn so we are facing each other, him still in his chair. His eyes crinkle and his chin lifts.

"How old did I say I was, Coach?"

"Eighty-seven." My jaw works overtime to stay loose, but it doesn't work. I'm a thirty-three-year-old man. Far too old to have my relationship questioned. Unfortunately, the girl I am in a relationship with—is not.

"Mhm. Correct." He pulls out a handkerchief and coughs into it several times. There are a few small dots of blood when he pulls away, but he wraps it up and we both ignore the elephant in the room. "Meaning I am far too old to be fooled." My stomach tightens. "Also, I have been around long enough to know when two people are in love, and when two people are not."

He holds my eyes for a long time, I don't drop them once so he knows I'm not backing down this time. I didn't want to be the one to tell Paul but I'm drowning, and if he knows, maybe I can finally have my girl back. I can be around without question.

"I think you should sit down, son."

Fuck me. *Forgive me for that, Payson.* "What about Payson?"

"I won't keep you long. In the meantime, maybe you can text your son and see if he can track down his girlfriend?" He lifts an eyebrow and curves his lips into a knowing look.

"What do you mean you can't find her?"

Jethro frowns. "Do they speak a different language in England, or are you just fucking deaf?"

I slam a fist onto the desk. "Tell me where my girl is or so help you God."

He pushes to his feet and gets in my face. "You better rethink the *my girl* thing real quick before I throw you behind bars, Pearson."

My chest rumbles, shooting vibrations of adrenaline throughout my body. "I'm not fucking taking it back. I'm bloody over hiding it. I love Payson, she loves me. I do not care if you are a cop or whatever, you are not keeping me from *my* girl."

His lip twitches and his face burns a bright red. "I could fucking kill you."

"Try it," I growl back.

"Someone want to tell me why I was picked up in a police car? Hello, PTSD, assholes."

I whip around hearing Payson's sweet rasps. Unfortunately for me, that leaves me wide open and Jethro is able to get a hard punch to the side of my face. I drop from the weight of his fist. It's been a long fucking time since I have been in a fight.

Payson gasps and sprints over to me. She argues with her uncle, but I'm just so happy to see her, I don't care. I wrap my arms around her and pull her onto my lap despite her fighting.

"Ash, we are in a police station." Her voice is a low whisper I can barely hear over the throbbing in my bloody ear.

"Good, because I want to report an assault."

Someone scoffs, must be Jethro because he walks in front of us. His jaw ticks but he tosses me a bag of ice that matches the one he's holding to his hand. "Get up. She is correct. At least there is a small amount of brain between the two of you."

Payson crosses her arms over her chest. "I'm not coming with you if you're just going to be rude. I don't need to hear it—"

"Yes, I heard. Sorry, now get up before I have to punch him again."

Payson slips from my lap, and I let her attempt to pull me up but because of my weight, it's just for show. "Try and I'll knock you out, you fucking wanker."

When he rolls his eyes and turns, I highly consider it. That is until a nicer, softer set of hands wrap around mine. I drop my eyes to her; despite everything going on there is still one set of pale green eyes that will always level me.

Payson's face is red and blotchy, and she's wet. Like soaking wet. "Where were you?"

She twists her lips and blinks several times. "The park."

"Why?"

Her eyes fall to her fingers trailing over my chest and across the place she knows her name is, even with me in a shirt. I didn't think twice about getting this tattoo because even without Payson's name physically engraved on my body—she was already there. I don't know where we go from where we currently are, but I know in the end it'll still be us. It will *always* be us.

"That's where everything changed. Something knocked us off center. That's when our relationship shifted into what it is now." Her shoulder digs into my arm when she shrugs, but I don't move it. "I don't know. I just . . . needed time."

The conversation with her granddad went longer than expected. It was not an easy one, but I knew it wouldn't be. It ended okay and that's all I could ask. He's not thrilled with our relationship, but he said he cannot control how others choose to live their lives. He can only pray about it. By the time he was finished, I had fifteen missed calls from Jethro. All with voicemails telling me to "fucking call him back." When I finally did, he told me he couldn't find her and I needed to get to the station immediately. Paul has enough going on that I decided to keep this to myself. Glad I did because Payson seems . . . mostly fine. Surprisingly.

I'm in no state to drive and that's the only reason I agree to ride with Jethro in his fucking limo. Why he's riding around town in a limo, I have no clue and I don't feel like asking. I lean my head back. It took some convincing getting Payson to come, but I wasn't leaving without her. Fucking wanker got me good, and I will return the favor one day. A day when my head doesn't feel like bricklayers are attempting to build the next Great Wall of China in my head.

The conversation with Jethro goes a lot like the one with Paul. If Paul breathed like a bear in the spring, that is. I couldn't care less how upset he is. Payson, on the other hand, has apologized several times. I want to tell her to stop. She owes him nothing. He's only recently come into her life and already he's making her feel like a bad person because of who she is with.

"Stop scolding her like you are her father."

Jethro narrows his eyes at me. "You want a black eye to match that headache you're sitting with?"

"I want you to stop lecturing Payson like you have any authority in her life."

"I'm her uncle."

"For like three seconds!" Payson groans, throwing her hands in the air.

"For seventeen years, little girl. Just because I wasn't around in the way I should have been, doesn't mean I wasn't looking out for you." Payson shifts closer to me. I'm not sure if she means to but she does, and I relish in the fact she needs to touch me for courage. Or maybe to calm her down so she doesn't blow up in the way she wants. Either way, I enjoy wrapping my hand over her thigh.

"How have you looked out for me?" Jethro clenches his jaw at her request. "Because as far as I know, the only thing you have done for me is give up stalking my mom when we needed you most. Run out on my brother and raise one of the worst humans I've ever met. And I've met quite a few."

His spine steels. "Who do you think sent her away?"

"Well, you, obviously but—"

"Me. You know why? Because I couldn't stand looking her in the face anymore. Do you know what it feels like to despise the girl you raised as a daughter?"

My heart beats rhythmically inside my chest. Jethro is completely untamed, and for once, it's nice it's not on me. Payson has since shrunk back into her seat and is picking at the skin on her thumb again. I grab her hands and she shoots me a worried look.

"Jethro," I warn.

"Who do you think pays for your schooling? You know the guilt I have lived with knowing my brother was the one that ran out on you and caused your issues, or some of them?" His face pinches with anger. "Or how about the guilt I deal with every day now knowing I could have stopped everything if I had just *looked*."

Payson is quiet as a mouse to my side for a long time before she drops her head. "I didn't know you were my sponsor."

"Yeah, that's why it's anonymous. I didn't *want* you to know. I never wanted you to know who I was because of this reason. You asking where I've been. I can't apologize for where I've been because I have no excuse other than it was easier to keep the distance. But I am here now, Payson, and I am telling you, you are not going to date your fucking coach under any circumstances."

Bloody fucking hell, he is relentless. "You do not get a say."

"The fuck I don't."

Payson screams, rattling the windows. "Enough! Both of you shut up! I found out my grandpa has cancer and is refusing treatment, and the last thing I want to deal with is two testosterone-filled men arguing over who they think I can, or cannot date."

"There is no argument," he deadpans.

Both Payson and I growl this time. "If her granddad can try and come around to the idea of it. Then so can you."

"What?" Payson gasps. I push back a dark stray hair that's hanging in her face, not caring that her *uncle* is radiating with anger in the seat across from us. "I had a long chat with your granddad about us and how it's us and not you and Parker."

"And?" The little bit of hope in her dilated eyes warms my heart, like maybe my Payson is still somewhere inside this broken shell.

"He's not sold"—the hope in her eyes dims slightly—"but he said he's not judging."

"He won't, but I will."

Payson rolls her eyes to her uncle. "I only care about my grandpa's opinion."

His glare hardens even more and he looks between us with disgust. I know he's giving up his argument, but that doesn't mean he will change his mind. I'm just glad neither of us care.

"I will never support this and when you realize this is wrong"—he shoots a murderous look my way—"I will be here."

Deciding not to argue any more, Payson settles into the limo seat, dropping her head on my arm, and closes her eyes. "Whatever."

Payson drifted asleep in the car, and I carry her into her granddad's much to Jethro's dismay. Her aunt opens the door and her eyes go wide seeing her niece in my arms. It's innocent enough but I don't waste a breath explaining everything. I'm not explaining my relationship to her, or anyone else again. I push open her door and glance behind me, checking to make sure her aunt is gone, so when I lay her in her little bed, I lean down and press my lips to her cheek.

"I love you, babygirl," I whisper. One more kiss and I stand.

A soft hand wraps around two of my fingers and her bright eyes look up to me, darker in the dim of the room but also because they are still dilated. I should keep an eye on that too.

"Go back to sleep."

"I don't want to lose my grandpa, Ash." *Fuck me and my heart.*

I squeeze her fingers, but I catch some movement outside of the room. No doubt her granddad checking in. I lean down and press my mouth to her forehead. "I know, Jailbird. I don't want you to either."

"I can't survive without him on earth, Ash. I'll die."

My stomach drops. I won't even think about that. I told Luca my fear, and it was just like that but I will not let it become reality. I'm not losing Payson. "No, you will not. You will get through it, and I will be here to hold you together so you do. Okay?"

Her bottom lip wobbles. "Promise?"

"Always. You and me, babygirl."

Her throat bobs. I squeeze her hand and she pulls it back under the small blanket that just barely covers all of her and would no way cover me. "Forever."

I drop another kiss, this time to her soft lips. So inviting I'm tempted to test the weight on the cot, but that's not what she needs right now. So I steal another kiss, then stand. "Text me when you wake."

Paul stops me outside Payson's room, eyeing the closed door behind me with a worried glance. "How is she?"

How do I answer that? Payson is not okay, but she hasn't been okay the entire time I've known her. Reading my thoughts, he sighs and taps my arm a few times before lowering his hand. "Thank you for bringing her home."

"Always."

Figuring that's the end of our conversation, I take a step toward the door.

"I hope you will take care of my granddaughter in the way she deserves, Ashley. She's had a rough go and all I want for her is peace and happiness. Safety and consistency too."

Peace. Happiness. Safety. Consistency. I can do that. I haven't been focusing on those things thus far, but from this moment on I will.

Even if it kills me.

50

Payson

CUTTING IS EASIER THAN pills but Ash will be able to tell I'm cutting again if he ever sees my arms. Which at this point, feels like never since he refuses to touch me outside of a deep kiss when he sees me and before he leaves Grandpa's. He can't tell when I'm high. I think. I don't even feel high anymore, it's more like my body is getting used to it. It's been a week since my grandpa came home from the hospital and he's not gotten any better.

Seeing his health decrease daily is the reason for my pill popping. I might worry I have a problem, but I only have a few pills left before I'm out, and it's not like I can go and get more hydrocodone just because I feel like it.

Ash is not only not touching me, but he is smothering me—again—but not in the way I want. It's worse this time, so much worse. I wake up to numerous texts that he sends after we've been talking late in the night, meaning, he's not sleeping. He stops by Grandpa's every day, and while he doesn't touch me, besides the quick peck on the cheek in front of Grandpa whenever he has to leave the room, he hasn't touched me in the way I've craved for too long.

Probably why I eyed my razor blades for a long time this morning before taking my pill.

I'm burning with the need to cut, to breathe in the only way I know how, but I don't want to do it myself. I want Ash to do it. It feels better when he does. The way his eyes glass over and his jaw clamps anytime I make a noise, or he assumes he's cut too deep. It's addicting.

"Payson." I blink, catching Clay's eyes. "You are bleeding."

My eyes drop to my arms but I see nothing. "What do you mean, where?"

"Your cycle, I am assuming by the blood stain on your skirt."

Embarrassment burns up my neck and across my face. Clay doesn't seem bothered by it but I sure am. "Why didn't you tell me before? Like when we were in the lunch line." *Yes, because lashing out at him makes up for the embarrassment, Payson.*

"I did. You did not listen."

I need to get out of my head. I cringe and shoot him an apologetic look. "Right, sorry." I twist my lips, trying to decide what to do. I don't have an extra skirt. I have my gym clothes, but I'll get detention for not being in uniform . . . not like I have a choice. I can't walk around in a bloody skirt all day. I need to figure out how to get to my gym locker from the lunchroom without everyone seeing. I'm guessing plenty have already, but I wasn't aware of it then.

"This is going to be weird but would you mind walking behind me to the gym?"

Without so much as a blink, Clay agrees. Whoever Clay Kjelberg ends up with will easily be the luckiest girl ever. If they have kids, I hope he has a little girl because I know he will be the best dad to her as well.

I sit forward and let Clay finish his lunch. When he's done, he picks up my full tray and frowns. "You did not eat, Payson."

"I'm not exactly hungry anymore, Clay."

"You should be used to periods by now. I have a protein bar in my bag you may have."

Clay follows behind me, but he's so close, he keeps stepping on my sneakers, nearly making me fall over the whole way. Until he does, and I do. He reaches for me but trips and lands on top of me instead. His blue eyes go wide, as do mine. He scurries back to his feet, and I hurry to push my skirt back down.

"Sorry about that." For once, I think he's embarrassed, and that makes my embarrassment from having his groin pressed against mine disappear; I don't want to make it worse on him if he thinks I'm mortified. I am, but I won't let him know.

"You lost your glasses, let me . . ." I trail off, not finding his glasses but instead seeing a deep red stain on the front of his pants. I gasp and my first instinct is to throw my hand over it. This keeps getting worse. He jumps back, looks down, and snaps a look behind him at the noise. Students file into the hallway but I don't move—I *can't* since one of the first students I see is Parker. He doesn't notice us until Clay lunges for me then his dark eyebrows pinch and my stomach free falls. Clay wraps a hand around my middle, and pushes open the gym door getting us out of the sight of prying eyes but I already know how it probably looks to Parker and I'm sure he can't wait to tell his dad.

Clay drops his hand, but I still don't move. My mind runs a million miles an hour. Should I text Ash and explain? What if Parker doesn't tell him, then I just stress Ash out for no reason? He's already on edge. Nothing has ever happened between me and Clay, and Ash already hates him. The fall was innocent, but I know Ash. Maybe I should talk to Parker and explain everything so he knows there is no reason to tell his dad.

"Payson." Clay's voice is straggled. Stepping away from his front I see why.

Clay moves his hand in front of him, covering the red spot and his *bulge*. I quickly advert my eyes as embarrassment burns up my neck, matching the same crimson on his face.

"Sorry." "I am sorry, Payson." We say at the same time.

"Do you have extra pants?"

"Yes."

The loud noise of students walking by fills the dead silence between us. I steal a look to Clay who still hasn't looked away from the wall. He's not wearing his glasses.

"Your glasses fell off." I cringe, remembering they fell off in the hall and are probably stomped on thirty or more times now. "Shit, Clay.

"I can get new ones."

"I'm going to go get changed . . ." I take a step and throw my thumb over my shoulder.

Clay glances down and nods. "Me too."

In the locker room, I drop my forehead to the cool metal lockers and sigh. I never get my period so why am I suddenly? It makes no sense. Good thing the school provides pads and tampons for free because I don't carry them.

Since I don't have extra underwear, I grab a tampon and my spandex from my locker. It's like a massacre, the spot on my skirt is semi-small but the entire crotch of my blue underwear is stained reddish-brown. No wonder I stained Clay's pants in the two seconds he was on top of me.

Eventually I get myself cleaned but it takes forever, and I'm thankful I have a free period next, so I'm not late for any class. I can't remember if I have homework to work on, but I don't care right now anyway.

Clay is waiting for me outside the locker room when I walk out. I was hoping he would just go to class and we could forget anything even happened.

He's wearing a gray school t-shirt and blue gym shorts like me. My shirt is long sleeve and his is short. With him dressed so casual and the lack of glasses, I pause for a second because he looks . . . *hot*. Huh. I've always known Clay was attractive but something about the way he is leaning against the wall with his arms crossed and his dark blond hair flopping over his forehead instead of gelled back like normal, definitely not bad to look at.

Ash would kill me for my thoughts. I shake my head and continue toward him.

"Did you find your glasses?"

"Yes." He flicks a look to me before holding out his large hand, inside is a pair—of crushed glasses.

"Oh, shit. Sorry, Clay."

He shrugs and stuffs them into his pocket. "I already called my mom. I was due for a new pair anyway."

He kicks off and falls into step by my side. "Ready to get detention, Payson?"

I push open the door, looking at him. "It's possible Principal Erikson might not even see us. We only have two hours left of—"

"And what is the reason you two are not in uniform and sneaking from the gym, alone?" The deep baritone of Principal Erikson's voice booms behind us. My shoulders jump to my ears, even Clay cringes. It's slight but still there.

His footsteps are equally intimidating as he stomps forward and around us. His piercing brown eyes bore into me, then Clay. "Well?"

I open my mouth, close it, and look at Clay for help.

"Payson is on her cycle and bled through her skirt. It got on me and neither of us have extra uniforms."

I elbow him and he shoots me a scowl. Clay has never heard of a lie, ever. I should not have trusted him to say something. I would have said anything other than that. The last thing I want is Principal Erikson's eyes drop to my shorts but to my surprise, he doesn't cringe like you would expect. At least what I would expect. Collins was always so grossed out by periods. Figures.

Principal Erikson has like six daughters or something crazy like that with the youngest being a year younger than me, so he is probably used to it. But still, I don't want him knowing when I'm on mine.

"I see. Well, then, because this is the first time I've ever had to speak to either of you, I will let you off with a warning. But bring in spare uniforms to keep in your locker. Understood?"

"Yes, sir."

He stomps down the hall the rest of the way and Clay flashes me a lopsided grin. "Your cycle saved us from detention, Payson."

"Yay. I wonder what else it will save us from."

"Pregnancy," he deadpans.

Something inside me twists up at the mention of pregnancy. I am in no way, shape, or form ready for a child. I know that for sure. Ash might be with his several comments about it, but this is when our ages come into play. If he wants to be with me like he says, he will just have to be patient.

I sigh and catch up with Clay to head for the library. "True. Wouldn't want that."

"No. Definitely not while you are taking drugs."

I stumble over my feet and gasp. "W-what?"

We're in the library now so he drops his voice, but continues the walk to the tables in the far back. "Your eyes are dilated. You are drinking more water than normal, which might not be an issue if I couldn't tell you were doing it because your mouth is dry and not because you were thirsty. You've also not had a real conversation with me since you got back from California. Not to mention your knee is twice the size of your other and yet you have not complained about the pain once. So, Payson." He flicks a look to me. Not a judgmental one, more or less curious. "What is it you are taking?"

"I don't know what you're talking about." The lie sounds pathetic, even to me.

He spins and pins me with a hard stare. "What did we talk about you being a shit liar, Payson?"

He cussed. Clay Kjelberg *never* cusses. "You swore."

He pushes a hand through his hair and sighs. "I did. Janelle is not here to put you in your place and apparently no one else knows the signs—but I do, and I know when someone is taking medication they should not be. Unless your doctor prescribed it for your knee, which if they did, then you should not be driving because they would have warned you that driving while on . . . Morphine? Fentanyl?"

"Hydrocodone," I mutter and drop my eyes so I don't have to see the disappointment I hear in his voice.

"Ah, yes. Well, you should know misuse of that particular drug can cause many issues. Including death."

There is a long pause filled with so much tension. This isn't a feeling I've felt with Clay before. He's not one to bullshit, obviously, but usually he says what he wants and the conversation is over.

"Unless you already know that."

I lift my gaze and he releases a breath. He shakes his head slightly. "You are really disappointing me, Payson."

Tears threaten to burn my eyes. I should have taken two pills today because it feels like I didn't even take one this morning right now. "My grandpa has cancer."

He says nothing, just continues staring at me with an expressionless face and those bright blue eyes.

"My relationship is fine, kind of, but also not. Janelle moved—" I hiccup. "My mom is dead." I don't know if that affects me or not. I still haven't decided.

Then he does something I never would have expected from Clay Kjelberg. He hugs me. Both his arms around my shoulders. I'm so shocked, it takes me a second to hug him back around the waist. He smells like clean linen and men's body wash. A pleasant smell.

"You're hugging me."

"I have no advice to give you. Seemed like the better option than just staring at you, Payson."

I crack a smile and squeeze him tight before we pull away. "Thanks."

"I would say anytime but I have had enough of touching for today. So please wait at least a month before you require any kind of physical touch from me again."

"Deal."

51

Ash

"THIS WAS PAYSON'S FAVORITE dessert when her nana was alive. I haven't made it in years, but I think it's important for you to learn so let's test our hand at banana crème pie, shall we?"

Since Payson's grandpa got home from the hospital, and we discussed me and Payson, he has been schooling me in the subject of Payson. He says if he will ever be okay with us, he has to know I will take care of her the way he thinks she should be cared for. I don't think knowing how to make banana crème pie will change how I care for her, but I have been enjoying these afternoons with Paul. I follow the recipes he gives me, and he sits in his chair and tells me various stories. Sometimes he will just play music, and while Christian music isn't my go-to, I have to admit it's calming. Which I need lately because Payson and I haven't had sex since Week of Pink and she doesn't seem in a rush to. I don't blame her, of course but I'm addicted to slipping inside her wet—

"Her nana always made the crust first." Paul's voice cuts through my thoughts like a cold shower.

"I will do the same, then."

I followed Payson's nan's recipe down to the ¼ teaspoon of cornstarch. It's nearly time for school to be done and the pie is in the fridge, ready to surprise Payson. Paul even ordered her favorite pizza. I texted Luca since he was picking Parker up today, telling him to let Parker change, then to come by and eat with us. He's still mad at me, after finding out about my and Payson's new hobby together but Luca doesn't turn down free food so he should still show up.

I'm going to attempt to get Payson to come over this weekend, but I don't know how to address that with her granddad. He's not come around to us being together fully; I doubt asking her to sleep over would go over well but I need Luca and Parker to see we are still good together.

"I'm home!" Payson calls. Her light footfalls barely make any noise across the vinyl flooring as she heads toward us. She smiles when she sees me, and my heart settles. You never know what mood you will get from Payson lately. Tonight seems like a good one.

"How was school?" Paul sets his book down and greets her with a kiss to the cheek before he wanders over to the counter for his water. I offered to grab it, he insisted he got it. Yesterday was a calmer day as he was under the weather, but he is in good spirits today. I know there will be a lot of back-and-forth like that, much like Payson, you're not sure what you're going to get, so it's best to enjoy the good times.

I grab Payson's hand on her way past me. I pull her closer and cup the back of her head. She looks Paul's way with shock, but I know he's not facing us, so I press my lips to her soft ones. She melts into me and pets my beard and lets out the cutest little moan that shoots right to my dick.

The sound of someone clearing their throat has Payson jumping back and her face burning bright red.

Paul settles into his chair with a firm look pointed at me.

"Uh, school was . . . good."

"Why are you not in your uniform?"

She's not. I hadn't noticed. This Payson is the one I'm used to seeing, it didn't even register she wasn't in her sexy little skirt and shirt.

"Uh . . . long story." She shoots a guilty look at me. I narrow my eyes. What on earth could cause her to change her clothes at school, and why would she feel guilty about it? "I need to use the bathroom; I'll be right back."

Much to my luck, Paul gets a phone call and I can slip to the back of the trailer to get to the bottom of whatever has Payson acting off. The bathroom door doesn't have a lock, and I don't bother knocking before I barge inside.

Payson gasps and looks at me with wide eyes. In her hand is a . . . bloody tampon. My brows furrow. "You're on your period?" I hadn't expected her to be pregnant or anything, but I'll always be hopeful. Seeing the bloody tampon fills me with a disappointment I wasn't anticipating, and she must see it on my face.

"Obviously," she snaps. "Now get out."

"I love you and understand your hormones are all over the place"—I close the space between us and drop to my knees in front of her—"it has been too long since I've been buried inside your pussy for you to give me that kind of attitude."

Her throat bobs with a swallow and her eyes fill with need. "Well, I'm on my period so it's going to be even longer, I guess."

Silly, naïve little girl. I skate my hand up her bare thigh. She attempts to close her legs, but I hold them open with my other hand. "Ash," she hisses when I slip my hand between her beautiful tanned thighs.

"If you think your period is going to stop me." I chuckle as I hook two fingers inside her cunt. "You're mistaken, babygirl."

She doesn't allow me more than three pumps before she whines, and not in the way she normally does, this one is out of discomfort and that's the only reason I pull my hand back. She locks into the deep red blood dripping down my hand.

"Wash your hand," she demands.

I would lick it off, but I think she would have a heart attack, so I stand and move to the sink to let her finish cleaning up. She joins me after flushing. I look to her in the mirror but she's avoiding my eyes, her cheeks are bright red, so I know she can feel me watching her.

"Jailbird."

She moves to dry her hands, not realizing I am holding the towel she needs. "Can I have that, please?"

"Sure"—I hold it out but don't let go when she grabs for it—"if you look at me."

Slowly her green irises lift. "What?"

I hate seeing her chin wobble the way it is. I cup the side of her face. "Why did that embarrass you so much?"

"Did you not see how much blood was on your hand?"

"I did."

"I've had to change my tampon four times in the last two hours, Ash. It's like a murder scene and you dug around in it."

She's so fucking cute. "It's just blood, Jailbird."

"Still, I didn't like that."

"Okay, I won't do it again." I curl my hand around her and pull her flush with my body. "But do not tell me I can't touch your body again, or it won't be my fingers that slip into your bloody cunt."

She shivers in my arms and bites down on her lip, and I know she likes my threat. "You can't threaten to rape me in my grandpa's bathroom, Ashley."

I've had enough of her thinking she gets to tell me what I can and cannot do. I've had enough of everyone telling me what I can and cannot do. Mostly cannot. I grip her arms, lifting her onto the sink and pull her close so she can feel my dick through my jeans against her cunt. She whimpers as I lean forward and kiss her soft cheek over to her ear. "I won't just threaten,

Princess. Keep pushing me away, and I'll take your mouth, cunt, and ass right now, and I don't give a fuck who hears."

I kiss down her throat before dropping to my knees. Pulling her clamped thighs apart, I let her think I'm going to eat her pussy, and I would if she would let me but right now, I'm more focused on the lesson I'm trying to teach her than actual pleasure right now.

"Please, don't."

Her telling me to stop shouldn't make me so fucking hard. I lift her shirt until I can see what I'm down here to see. I hold her eyes as I lean forward. I press my lips against the mostly healed scar. "What's this say?"

Her hand sinks into my hair and her head falls back against the medicine cabinet mirror.

But she doesn't answer. I open my mouth and let my teeth scrape over the area. She wiggles with discomfort.

"What's it say, Jailbird?" My voice is like gravel and my balls are heavy with need for my girl.

"It says Ash," she nearly cries.

I smile against her soft stomach. "That's right, Ash. *Me*. Meaning, I can do whatever I want, whenever I want, and wherever I want—to your body. Do you understand me?"

She digs her short nails into my scalp and whispers, "Yes, Daddy. Anything you want."

There's my girl. Reluctantly I move to my feet, I need to stop dropping to my knees because getting up is a bitch. I thread my hands into her frizzy hair and tip her pretty face up to mine. Her chest rises and falls at a rapid speed.

She looks at my lips, then licks hers. "I've missed you."

My eyes fall closed, and I drop my forehead to hers. "Me too, babygirl. Me too."

Payson

I haven't had a nightmare in a long time. That's the only explanation for how badly this one is affecting me. I hug my knees and force my eyes to stay open so I see that I'm in my room at Grandpa's and not in a basement chained to a pole like I was in my dream. I didn't see who put me in the basement, but I know the feeling in my stomach and who comes along with that particular feeling.

Grabbing my phone, I skip over the good night message Ash sent me and press the call button. It rings four times before I hear his sleepy voice.

"Jailbird? Whats wrong?"

"I-I had a bad dream." Saying it out loud makes me feel the most stupid I've ever felt. Then I realize it's the middle of the night and I'm calling my boyfriend because I had a bad dream and I feel even more stupid.

There is ruffling on his side, then he says, "I'll be there in five."

"What? No. No I just wanted to hear your voice. You can't come here; you'll wake my grandpa." It's bad enough my whispers could wake him through the wall, let alone Ash's loud truck.

The ruffling stops and he breathes hard, as if he was rushing. I cringe thinking about him hurrying just for me to tell him no, but he must know he can't actually come here just because I had a bad dream. That's crazy.

"Do you want to talk about it?"

"No, I want to talk about anything else."

"Okay, go ahead. Whatever you want." He sighs like he just sat back down.

I rack my head to think of anything that's not my dream, but I come up empty. "I can't pick something, can you?"

After a minute he speaks. "How about our wedding?"

If I could groan out loud, I would. "Haven't we talked about that enough?"

"That is not possible."

I give in because I want the gross feeling inside my body to go away. We spend the next hour discussing every single thing there is to discuss for a wedding. Dress color, I said different shades of light blue because it'll be spring, he said green, so we agreed on pastel blues and greens. I'll only have Ronni and Janelle on my side, maybe Amanda, so I'm not sure how that will work, but I digress, this is hypothetical anyway. He wants basic black suits for him and the groomsmen, but I think I may have convinced him to do brown or gray. The brown would accent the warmth of his skin, but the gray would compliment his eyes. We couldn't agree on flowers, he wants roses because they are traditional, where I think a bouquet of various flowers is nice, again it's hypothetical, but we agreed on light colors. Another thing we agreed on is an English wedding. I think it would be lovely to marry in London where he is from. Since he has more family that would attend than I do, it seems fair. He tried to tell me he is from a place called Croydon or something and not London but in my head—especially this late, or early—it's London.

After a while, our conversation drifts into casual chatting and it feels good. Like the night we went on a date. It eases my mind enough to make me tired again.

"Goodnight, babygirl. No more bad dreams, but if you have one, you can call me and we can discuss our children's names." He chuckles and the deep vibrations are felt through the phone.

"Okay, deal." I giggle back, still in my sleepy stupor.

"I love you."

I pause for a moment, then whisper, "Me too."

As soon as we hang up, I drop my phone to the floor and turn over to hopefully a dreamless sleep.

52

Payson

"FUCK YOU."

Ash grips my throat and slams me against the wall of his office, knocking the air out of me when he does. "Say it again."

My throat burns trying to speak under his grip but I'm too angry to not try. "Fuck. You."

If I could feel my arms right now, I would slap, punch, or claw him for what he just fucking put me through.

How did we go from talking about our wedding a few nights ago to him ripping my spandex off me while holding me by the throat against his office wall? Well, he found my pills. The empty bottle, and when I told him I flushed them—which I did, after the talk with Clay, he didn't believe me. Then I asked him to cut me, and he said no. Oh, then Parker kindly filled him in on the rumors going around school—*I gave Clay his red wings.*

Everything is happening and my grandpa is doing worse. His health has dramatically dropped in the last week. It's almost Thanksgiving and I'm not even sure I will get that with him.

I might not get Thanksgiving or Christmas. He won't live to see the New Year. I squeeze my eyes closed, enjoying how my vision is blurring and my head is clouding from lack of oxygen. Ash doesn't warm me up before he shoves his cock inside of me. I'm not dry but I've definitely been wetter. He hisses something but I'm lost in the state of euphoria, not listening. Until he moves his hand.

"You are going to stay awake for me to fuck you, then you'll be lucky if I don't choke you until you pass out," he spits.

As if he hasn't tortured me enough with a six-hour long open gym on a Saturday. *Ash-hole.* Just me, too—no one else and he didn't even give my knee a second thought. Not that I feel pain anymore.

I thought the practice was to give us time alone since it's been so long but nope. He was pissed and took it out in the only way he knows how that doesn't involve any of the ways I actually enjoy, like him fucking me so hard, I'm positive my pussy is ripping—like he's doing now after the actual torture so I'm not even able to fully enjoy it.

I don't even know how he found the bottle. I thought I buried it deep enough in the garbage, but apparently not. Grandpa asked him to take it out last night when he left, then I got a text when he got home telling me to be up and ready for an out-of-season practice today. He was fine the entire way to the gym, a little tense but that's normal for Ash right now, but when he walked into the gym he freaking jumped me, barking for me to go run. Then he ran me most of the day.

I know when he comes because he pushes so deep inside me, my cervix cries out and he mutters something about how a *baby would keep other boys away.* He's so unbelievably wrong, a baby wouldn't keep other boys away, I would. *I do.* He doesn't want to hear what actually happened with Clay. He doesn't understand the power he has over me that makes it impossible to want any other guy but him, I guess I don't understand the power I have over him either because he's as lost as I am.

His hair has gotten longer, his beard is untamed. He's not working out regularly and when my aunt offered him extra dessert yesterday—he agreed.

The Ash I know and love is slipping. I don't care how he looks, he's still easily the hottest man ever but he's not caring for himself, and I know that's because I keep him awake every night talking because my dreams. He's not sleeping, he's barely eating, and when he does, it's shit.

When he pulls out of me, I drop to the floor, and he leaves me there, storming from his office and slamming the door behind him. His cum drips out of my pussy onto the floor, but I leave it. Standing, I cringe at the pain in my knee but pull my spandex back up.

We don't talk the entire way to my grandpa's, and when he stops the car, he doesn't follow me inside like he always does. I don't stop and ask either. I don't even watch him drive away.

Ash is broken and it's all my fault.

I knew I would play the next season with almost a completely new team, but I hardly know these girls. Sure, some are familiar because they've been on the team since they started high school, but I never paid attention to the JV team enough to know names. The season hasn't started, but Ash and Coach Maddox are hosting an open gym once a month until spring, then it'll be once a week to give us plenty of time to prepare for next fall. We had a good season this year and he wants to continue that. That was a part of his speech at the beginning of practice. The part I listened to when my body was screaming at me to lie down. Ash hasn't answered my calls the last two nights and I haven't been able to sleep. I'm running on fumes, but he hasn't looked at me once to realize how much I need him.

Another thing I didn't expect about a new team was the immense jealousy I would feel having Ash's attention on girls I wasn't friends with.

Alyssa was bad—but these girls are almost worse. They are wild cards. I don't know if any of them would try anything or not. I don't think he would entertain the idea, but my head likes to remind me who I am and that I'm no different than them.

But I am. I'm way more fucked.

Take the little brunette he is working closely with right now. She's cute, her name is Sadie or something cute. She's seventeen like me, old for a sophomore. Her spandex fit her perfectly, showing off her small but perky ass and her shirt is tight. Not in an obnoxious way, an athletic way proving her narrow waist and probably B-size tits. It's short sleeved because she doesn't have anything to hide. She's been smiling and happy since we got here. Laughing with her friends like she has no issues in the world. I'd bet she even has a dog.

I've always wanted a dog.

She's a Setter like Ash, and when she makes a perfect set, Ash's smile is the biggest I've seen in so long. Both Coach Maddox and Ash congratulate her and the Hitter I didn't see. But Ash lingers on Sadie longer, no doubt complimenting her on form or giving some tips I wouldn't understand as a Libero. Something fucking stupid.

"Pay." I look to my right to see Mika watching me with worried eyes. I glance back to Ash only to have him staring back at me for the first time since I got here. His smile slips right away and my insides crumble. Everything hurts and I want nothing more than to drag a fucking blade across every part of my burning skin, knowing I have no one to blame but myself for the state we are in.

Instead, I force my gaze on Mika, knowing she wants to pepper. Heavy feet carry me over to my spot on the floor. She takes hers across from me, weary to start, but I nod and the game begins.

And the last piece of my soul dies.

53

Payson

ANOTHER SLEEPLESS NIGHT. I think I'm getting used to not sleeping. I stop tossing and turning but it's not the sun that greets me this morning, it's more rain. It stopped raining for a short period and maybe that's why there is an unease in my stomach as I look out the small window at the gloomy gray and knowing skies.

There's a song my aunt sings periodically in church—my favorite song—and I know she only sings it because I love it. As I look across Grandpa's lawn, I can hear that song in my head as clear as if it was coming from inside the trailer.

I angle my ear toward my door. It *is* coming from inside the trailer. I pinch my eyes close and move toward my window, propping it open slightly, just to hear the soft pattering of the rain against the birdhouse outside. Rain used to comfort me, but I have a sinking feeling it's an omen for the worst day of my life.

I don't know how long I stand at the window, or when my brother drags me into the living room, because apparently, *it's my turn*.

My turn to say goodbye to my favorite person, but how do you say goodbye to someone you aren't ready to say goodbye to?

Easy. You don't.

You stand there like a statue, staring into the same blue eyes you grew up looking into as you watch your grandpa take his last breath.

And then your world ends.

Ten Thousand Angels Cried, indeed.

Heavy, but quick footsteps sink into the soggy ground behind me. I don't need to look to know who it is because the overwhelming feeling in my chest expands in a way only he can cause.

He drops to the ground in front of me and swollen red eyes meet mine before dropping, no doubt seeing the blood. *So much blood.*

When I called, I didn't think he would answer, let alone drive over and meet me at the park after how things have been between us as of lately. I didn't tell him where I was so he must have looked at my location. That means I still have a hold on him. I don't know how big or how steady we are but when he's hugging me—I don't care.

"You came."

He drags a heavy hand down my hair, finding my forehead and leaves behind a deep kiss that warms my whole body despite being soaked through from the cold rain.

"Always."

He clamps a hand on each arm, trying to cover the vertical cuts. "Stay with me, babygirl. Okay? Stay with me." Ash promised not to leave me broken, I think it's too late.

I force my heavy eyes open to see him, remembering him.

He's so handsome. Even with the deep worry creasing his eyebrows. It's easy to remember the young version of Ash, the first time I ever laid eyes on him. Even at eight years old, I knew he was special.

"I love you," I mumble with a heavy tongue.

"Keep your eyes open, Payson. Look at me."

"I love you."

"Say it again," he growls, shifting closer and dropping a hard kiss to my lips. "Tell me."

"I love you." It's funny how easy it falls from my mouth now. I held off for so long and looking back, I can't remember why. I have loved Ash Pearson for nine years. I have scarred my body, been through hell and back and yet telling Ash I love him, the one thing I'm sure on in life, is the hard part.

"Again."

I tell him two, or maybe it was three more times before I'm too light-headed to even sit up by myself anymore. Ash moves behind me quickly, not wanting to keep his hands from my arms for long. I lay against his chest, listening to the pounding of his heart.

"Tell me about our wedding." There's a new vulnerability in his voice—something I've not heard from him before. It nicks at something deep inside me, and if I had the energy to cry, I think I would.

"Tell me," he urges, a new panic in his mostly steady voice.

"It'll be springtime."

The rain continues to pour down on us so loud I'm sure it's making it impossible for him to hear me clearly.

"And what day?"

"April fourth."

"Afternoon or evening?"

"Late afternoon because the sunset." I drop my head to his shoulder.

He hums in my ear. "Those photos will look brilliant on our walls."

Yes, they would have.

I choke on a sob, knowing what I know. What he is refusing to accept.

He deserves the wedding we have been talking about and I hope one day he gets it.

Ash tightens his grip but even he can't keep the blood from pouring from my body. "Open your eyes, Jailbird."

But I can't. I can't get my body to do anything anymore. "I'm so tired, Ash."

The rain is like needles on my face, a stark contrast to his warm kisses on my cheek.

"Tell me you love me," he demands in his *coaching voice* that I love so much, but I still don't open my mouth. *I can't.* His heart pounds against the back of my head, making up for the barely noticeable beating in mine. "You and me, babygirl. Remember?"

I love you.

I'm sorry it wasn't enough.

To be continued . . .

Afterword

Thank you for continuing Ash and Payson's story! I hope you don't hate me too much right now. I've said since the beginning that this story is messy, unplanned, and toxic—if this book hasn't proved that I'm not sure what will. There is one more book after this where I promise there will be some kind of happy ending. *Hopefully*.

Also by

Stalk me!

https://linktr.ee/kb.row

Acknowledgments

Listen, I used up all of my emotions writing this story. I'm over writing for the time being so just know I'm thankful for anyone who lays their eyes on this page.

About The Author

I know these are meant to be in third person, but I loathe third person so, here we go. I'm originally from the Mid-west, USA, meaning I put ranch on everything and say "ope" far too often. I grew in a very small town in rural America where I met my loving husband. It was love at first sight... at least for me, eventually he agreed. We've been together ten years with hundreds more to go. We have the most handsome six-year-old lab and an equally handsome and rambunctious toddler. When I'm not writing, you can find me chasing them around trying to control the chaos. Meanwhile, my husband is out turning people on—he's a lineman, get you mind out of the gutter people—making me money to spend on more books I probably won't read for another three years. Peace!

Printed in Great Britain
by Amazon

22315217R00342